PRAY
FOR
DEATH

Available from James Hilton and Titan Books

Search and Destroy
Fight or Die
Pray for Death

PRAY FOR DEATH

A Gunn Brothers Thriller

JAMES HILTON

TITAN BOOKS

Pray for Death
Print edition ISBN: 9781783294909
E-book edition ISBN: 9781783294916

Published by Titan Books
A division of Titan Publishing Group Ltd
144 Southwark Street, London SE1 0UP

First edition: October 2018
10 9 8 7 6 5 4 3 2 1

A CIP catalogue record for this title is available from the British Library.

Printed and bound by CPI Group (UK) Ltd, Croydon, CR0 4YY

This one is for my Wendy, as always

1

She passed him by without so much as a second glance.

Stuck-up bitch.

The corners of Frank Bradshaw's mouth twitched into a smile of cruel anticipation. He had been watching Chrissie Haims for weeks, each day moving closer to this point. It was inevitable. She was his.

He had tried to be nice.

Yet where had that got him?

Nowhere.

She'd flashed him the briefest of smiles two days earlier as he held open the door to Starbucks, her face showing not the faintest glimmer of recognition. She had not even paused for a second in the flow of conversation, cell phone nestled on her shoulder. A slight nod of her head as she hurried past him, leaving the coffee shop with an extra-large skinny latte. She bought the same coffee from the same shop every day on her way to work. Walked the same route. Caught the same bus home. She never noticed him. But he noticed her, oh yes, and then some.

Chrissie Haims was beautiful—her skin the colour of milky coffee, her face a perfect oval, her body toned and tight from the hours of Pilates she taught at the gym. Frank was sure the skintight exercise suits she wore in the classes were for his benefit alone.

She knew exactly what she was doing. Teasing him, taunting him.

Look at what I've got…

You want it, don't you?

Don't you?

"Yes!" Frank's voice was barely above a dry whisper.

She lived in a modest single-storey clapperboard house, just three blocks over from Frank's own Coral Gables home. An easy journey. He had followed her home several times, always just out of the line of her haughty gaze. He'd watched her through the windows as she pottered around her house. The clothes she wore indoors were a stark contrast to her teasing Lycra bodysuits. Big and baggy sweats, shapeless and dull. Further proof to Frank that the revealing gym gear was all for show.

Look at me, I'm perfect. Too good for the likes of you!

Did she even know he existed?

Yes, she knew. She teased him, thrusting and gyrating her ass at him through the plate-glass windows of the gym every day. Frank knew exactly what she was doing. He knew exactly *why* she was doing it.

"You can look but you can't touch." Frank startled himself by voicing his thoughts out loud. A nervous giggle escaped his throat. He pulled his backpack open, slow and smooth. "But today I will touch."

A shape moved past one of the side windows. There she was. Mooching around the apartment. Baggy grey sweats, auburn hair piled high on her head. Thick white face cream slathered over her features like some housewife from a vintage sitcom. *She's in for a real wake-up call.*

Frank approached the front door. Fingers trembling, he pulled out a key. He had followed Chrissie Haims back to her home several times, each time growing bolder, each time getting a little closer. A week earlier he had watched her leave for work, then he'd found the spare key hidden under a stone by the door. It was a simple task to have it copied at the nearby strip mall, returning the original back to its supposed hiding place within the hour.

For a moment, he feared she had discovered his subterfuge and changed the locks. The breath caught in his throat as the key slid home. The door swung open on silent hinges. He moved inside, crouching like a sprinter on the blocks as he listened to the sounds of the house. The floor was cool to his touch through the disposable latex gloves he wore. His tongue flicked across his lips as he inhaled the aromas of the house. Coffee, flowers just a little past their best, a sweet perfume. He had been at the store when she had bought it.

As he moved through the house, staying low, an electric tingle rolled the length of his spine. The sound of the television greeted him as he pushed gently on the kitchen door, a jingle from a commercial.

The syringe that he drew from his bag felt comfortable in his hand. This wasn't the first time he had used it. The generous mix of fentanyl and ketamine would drop her in seconds. She would be out cold until he injected her again with a powerful stimulant. That's when the real fun would begin.

Frank listened. Her bare feet padded on the hardwood floor. She was in the living room.

Swish. Swishhh. The sound of curtains being drawn.

Too late, little piggy, the big bad wolf is already inside.

Frank crept along the hall, his hand brushing the wall with the faintest pressure. The living-room door was open, light from the television flickering an abstract pattern on the wall.

Readying himself for a quick dash into the room, Frank raised the hypodermic. She had her back to him. Tonight, she would pay dearly for her fleeting smiles and cruel teasing. He closed upon Chrissie Haims.

2

A tree branch whipped across the young man's face, drawing blood and sending him stumbling to the ground. He landed in an untidy heap on the hard-packed dirt, losing his remaining shoe as he fell. A shock wave of pain ran up his spine.

The girl running ahead of him turned, a desperate sob catching in her throat. "Dean!"

The young man waved his hand frantically. "Keep going. I'm right behind you."

Fear encompassed every inch of her face. She looked back and forth, searching the trees for the danger that was close behind. The leafy canopy overhead shielded most of the burning sun, but here and there daggers of bright light illuminated the dirt and dead foliage below with an almost theatrical intensity. Vines spread from tree to tree, intersecting at ground level like the veins of a colossal creature. Fiddlewood and mahogany trees stretched impassive, tall and proud like cyclopean gods.

Dean's voice was a dry rasp. "Run!"

He knew Ellen could do it. She regularly ran track and

was part of the school swim team. Despite that, her legs visibly shuddered with each faltering step. Bile rose in the back of his throat.

A chunk of tree bark pinwheeled as a bullet passed close to Ellen's head. She ran.

Dean struggled to his feet and followed her as best he could. His bare legs were caked with dried blood and dirt. He was naked save for a pair of grubby boxer shorts. Two raised welts ran in diagonal lines across his shoulders, forming an oversized X.

Crack, crack, crack.

Another short rattle of bullets cut through the trees to either side of his path. He risked a backward glance. Indistinct shadows flitted from tree to tree, visible for a second, then gone again. Ellen was sprinting, head bent, arms and legs pumping like an automaton. Her ash-blond hair and pale skin gave her an almost ethereal look as she dodged between the trees.

Dean knew he was in no way as fit as he could have been. While the other guys from his school had readied themselves for spring break by hitting the gym, he had laughed it off as pointless vanity. He had been running for less than half a mile and already he had vomited his meagre breakfast. His legs felt like they were slowly turning to stone, his muscles seizing. His chest burned as he sucked in huge gulps of air. The pain in his side was horrendous. He hadn't had a stitch since he was in junior high.

A new ripple of fear coursed through his body. He couldn't see Ellen. Where the hell had she gone? Then a flash of pale skin caught his eye. She was moving at a clip. Had she changed direction?

A man stepped from behind the tree some thirty feet to his left. His face was marked by green and brown camouflage paint; his white hair, spiked into tufts, stood out in contrast. The man raised his crossbow and in one smooth action pulled the trigger.

Dean howled in shock as the bolt lodged deep in his shoulder. He forced himself to continue running despite the agony, but he was stumbling like a drunkard. Blood seeped between his fingers as he cupped his injured shoulder. The flights of the crossbow bolt were the colour of a raven's feather. Behind him he could hear the shooter laughing.

"*Hab dich! Hab dich!* I got you!"

Dean staggered on. The German was one of the worst.

A new voice came to him. It took long seconds to realise it was his own.

"Don't look back. Just keep running. Don't look back. Just keep running."

He repeated the mantra over and over as he lurched spasmodically from tree to tree. Cold sweat beaded over his face, stinging his eyes. Then he was on a path. A narrow path, but one that at least provided a clear line through the trees. "Don't look back. Just keep running. Don't look back. Just keep running."

The new pain struck him like a punch from a karate master. He could not scream. His lungs would not let him. Another bolt must have struck him in his back. The blood bubbled from his mouth as he turned to look at his killer.

The German.

He didn't even know the bastard's name.

The camouflaged killer raised his stubby weapon high in the air and laughed aloud.

Dean fell to his knees. Another five men materialised out of nowhere, like ghosts. A brief exchange of words ended with the German pointing in the direction that Ellen had taken. The other men set off again in rapid pursuit, their camouflage clothing and greasepaint blending with the jungle perfectly. They were lost from sight within a few seconds.

Dean's vision was dimming, dark spots dancing before his eyes. He knew he was dying. Tears ran down his dirt-streaked face.

The German stood over him, crossbow loose in his grasp, laughing softly. He placed a boot on Dean's belly, almost as if he was posing for a picture. Dean struggled to free himself from beneath the man's boot, the last vestiges of his strength almost spent. The German increased the pressure slightly, pinning him down.

A short burst of automatic gunfire echoed through the trees. A woman's choked scream rang out. Then a single shot.

"Ellen..." He couldn't say more. The blood filled his mouth as he died.

3

Chrissie Haims had her back to him. Tonight, she would pay dearly for the weeks of fleeting smiles and her cruel teasing. Frank raised the hypodermic syringe level with his shoulder and stepped into the room. He had done this before… step in close, inject her with the sleepy juice. She would be out for at least an hour. More than enough time to get everything ready.

Frank held his breath as he reached for the back of her neck.

Then she did something that caught him completely off guard. In one smooth motion she pivoted, squatting almost to the floor, and raised both hands. The cylindrical pistol she held spat only once.

Frank staggered back, staring in surprise at the dart protruding from his chest.

Chrissie Haims stood up. *Had she been that tall earlier?*

The drug flooded his system. His own syringe was plucked unceremoniously from his rapidly numbing fingers. Chrissie pulled at her hair. The bushy auburn wig fell to the floor, now resembling roadkill.

"No!" Frank's legs folded beneath him. He stared up at the woman... who wasn't a woman at all! Under that cream mask was a thin, battle-hardened face.

"Hello, Frank!" The voice was cold and laced with a thick Scottish accent. "I bet you're not exactly thrilled to be on the receiving end for a change."

"Who the hell are you?"

"Just think of me as a very concerned citizen." The Scotsman's smile was devoid of humour. "Neighbourhood Watch on steroids, that kind of thing."

Frank tried to pull the dart from his chest, but his hands succeeded only in tracing lazy circles in front of his stomach. They seemed to weigh more than the rest of his body combined.

"But enough about me, Frankie-boy. Let's talk about you. Francis Charles Bradshaw, single, works at Miami Parks and Recreation. Assaulted your first victim aged seventeen."

"I... I was never charged."

"Because the girl was too scared or too ashamed to press charges." The Scotsman began to remove the thick layer of moisturising cream from his face, deception complete. "Attacked another four women in the last five years. You don't get to do that anymore. You're careful, I'll give you that. You've never been arrested. Cautioned only once. What we call a 'sneaky bastard' back home. But not careful enough. All of you sickos are the same; you're so intent on watching your victims you never notice if *you* are being watched."

Frank was no coward. If he could keep this guy talking long enough for the paralytic to wear off, he might have a chance. "I wasn't going to kill her."

"What? Just drug and rape her? That's okay, then, is it?"

"I love her. I wouldn't hurt her."

"Oh, I don't know about that, Frank. Let's take a wee look-see in your goodie bag. Maybe that will shed some light on your noble and purely romantic intentions." The man peered into the backpack. "Duct tape. Condoms. Rope. Hunting knife. And another syringe full of something bad. I know a murder kit when I see one."

"So, what now, big shot? You some Batman wannabe? You gonna kill me in cold blood, or doesn't your code of ethics allow that?" Frank's vision had dimmed at the edges, his voice beginning to slur. Biting the inside of his mouth until he tasted blood, he fought against the effects of the sedative.

"I'm no hero, so you can forget that, and my code of ethics don't extend to streaks of shite like you."

"You're full of crap. If you were gonna kill me, you would have just shot me." Frank's voice was getting louder with each word.

The Scotsman slowly shook his head. "Gunshot wounds leave a mess. Leave evidence. This way's… neater. No one will ever know what became of you, and I don't think you'll be missed by many, either."

Spittle flew as Frank tried to sit up. "Fucking do it, then, if you've got the balls! Or I'm gonna kill y—"

The Scotsman snapped out his right foot in a blur of motion, catching Frank full in the throat. As Frank fell back, choking, the Scotsman looked on with a cold detachment.

Frank's eyes bulged as he strained to take another breath through his crushed windpipe. His heels rapped against the floor in a steady beat as he slowly asphyxiated, choking on his own blood.

4

Danny Gunn sat on the arm of the settee and looked around the room. The house was typical working-class Miami, neat and clean. He liked Coral Gables. The houses here were a mixed bag, some large and luxurious, others small and homely. Chrissie Haims' abode was simple yet stylish. The walls were painted a pale shade of yellow; the furniture was all high quality. No dust bunnies to be found hiding beneath the couch in this house. Danny rubbed the chenille fabric of a throw pillow between his thumb and forefinger as Frank Bradshaw was racked by a final spasm.

A brief childhood memory of making snow angels flitted into Danny's mind, dying at the same time as Frank's final motions. Danny finished removing the cold cream from his face, then picked up his cell phone from the teak table.

Chrissie answered on the second ring. "Danny?"

"Aye, it's me."

"Did he come to the house like you said he would?" Her voice was quiet and conspiratorial, her words laced with a nervous tone.

"He did."

Chrissie made a sharp intake of breath. "What happened? Are you okay?"

"Yeah, I'm fine, Chrissie. Don't worry, he won't bother you anymore."

"I can't believe it. I didn't even realise he was stalking me until I met you at the gym, but once you pointed him out I saw him at least half a dozen times in the next two days."

"Aye, and he was getting closer and closer. He had the shark eyes on. I knew what he was up to, knew what he was building up to. I'm just sad that I was right."

"What did you do to him? Do I need to call the cops?"

"No! No cops. I told you that this was strictly off the books. Guys like him wriggle and squirm their way out of things. They make a deal, inform on someone else, shit like that. Then he would be back out on the streets."

"Did he have a gun?"

"Chrissie, it's best if you don't know the details. Just sleep easy tonight knowing that he'll never bother you again. He's gone from Miami for good."

"But what if he comes back, starts stalking me again?"

"He won't. He's taking a boat across the River Styx as we speak."

"I don't know where that is," replied Chrissie.

The corners of Danny's mouth twitched into the briefest of smiles. "Don't worry about it. Just know he's gone."

"Can I come home now?"

Danny looked down at the vacant gaze of the corpse in front of him, then at the roll of thick plastic sheeting that sat ready behind the couch. "Give me another hour or so. I'll call you again."

"Okay. I don't know how to thank you!"

"Well, I still need more work with those kettle bells."

Danny smiled again as she gave a nervous laugh. He liked her laugh. Liked it a lot.

"I think I can help you with that."

He looked down at the increased definition of his forearm muscles. "Gotta love those kettle bells. I'll give you a call in a wee while, then you can come home."

5

Clay Gunn's closest neighbour lived a little short of three miles away and that suited him just fine. While by no means anti-social, he preferred his privacy on a day-to-day basis. The city of Austin was less than an hour away, an easy drive on a long straight road. More than enough people there if he sought conversation. But his house, standing at the centre of his modest patch of land, was his current destination. *Home.*

Clay guided his bike down the driveway, the light from the twin halogens illuminating his home in a blue-tinged splendour. The Harley-Davidson 1200 Custom was the latest addition to his collection. Another four bikes sat inside, one of his few perceptible indulgences. Clay embraced anything with an engine: bikes, cars, his oversized Winnebago and, more recently, jet-skis and powerboats.

Clay smiled at the sight of home. He had been on the road for over a month. The house was surrounded by an adobe-clad wall, framing the perimeter enough to provide comfortable areas of shade when the Texan sun was proving its most determined. The grounds were pristine and surprisingly green, albeit populated with the hardier plants that favoured the Texan climate. Sebastian Chavez worked tirelessly to keep what he called mini-ZilkerLand in good order. The genuine Zilker Botanical Gardens in the centre of Austin were a thing of true natural beauty, a place he knew Sebastian never tired of visiting.

The Harley announced his approach with the low-pitched rumble from its engine. Shadows from the trees and bushes within the garden danced and lengthened as they were briefly illuminated. Sebastian and Salma Chavez lived in the large house all year round, groundsman and housekeeper. They lived in their own section of the house, into which Clay seldom ventured, though while Clay was away on one of his many extended road trips they had the full run of the place. He hadn't let them know of his return, but he hoped there'd be something on the stove. His mouth watered at the thought of one of Selma's spicy pot stickers and herb-rich mashed potatoes.

The garage interior was pristine. Not so much as an oil spot on the floor. His other motorcycles were parked in a diagonal pattern, each road-ready and perfectly maintained. Two cars sat alongside the bikes. A Nissan Armada SUV used for everyday tasks stood next to a fully restored 1974 Dodge Charger. The SUV looked like an army utility vehicle next to the bright orange muscle car. The garage smelled of wax, the vehicles gleaming. Sebastian had been busy. Clay parked the Harley in its slot and, hefting his travel bag onto his back, went inside.

The familiar coolness was a balm to his sun-kissed skin. The house was quiet. He glanced at his watch, raising his eyebrows. Nearly eight in the evening. Strange there was no pot bubbling in the kitchen. Salma was a creature of habit.

He knocked on the door that separated Salma and Sebastian's quarters from the main house. When the door opened, Sebastian had dark rings below his eyes, which told of more than one sleepless night.

"Hello, Clay. Welcome back." Sebastian's wan smile carried none of its usual enthusiasm. His hair looked unkempt, which was out of character, and even more telling was the thick growth of stubble that darkened his jaw.

Clay frowned. "Everything okay, buddy?"

Sebastian's Adam's apple bobbed before he answered. "No, my friend."

"What's going on? Is Salma okay?"

"It's not Salma. It's Celine."

"Little Celine? What's happened?"

Sebastian rubbed his palms on the front of his plain cotton shirt, as if not sure what else to do with his hands. "You'd better come through. Salma is on the phone to the police in Cancún."

Clay walked behind his friend, a sense of dread growing in his stomach. Although Celine had turned eighteen a few months earlier, she was still a child to him. It seemed only yesterday she had been a kid in elementary school. One day it was braces and pigtails, now she was on her first spring break in Mexico.

Salma slammed the phone back into its cradle. Her cheeks were flushed red, her eyes puffy. The frustration in her voice cut across the room like a knife. She slumped onto the couch, a sob caught in her throat. "They tell me nothing.

'Don't worry. Don't worry.' How can they tell me not to worry? Celine should have been home over a week ago. The police down there are worse than useless." Her voice took on a patronising tone. "'Don't worry. It's not unusual for a young woman to choose to stay a bit longer than planned. Maybe she found a boyfriend.'"

"Have you heard anything from her at all?"

"The last we heard from her was on Monday. They were all going on a trip to see the pyramids."

Clay pulled up a wooden stool and sat down. "We all know Celine would have called if she had met a guy, and would definitely have called if she had decided to stay an extra week." The feeling of dread crept further into Clay's stomach, a sense of dread he kept from his voice. "What about the people she went with? Have they come home?"

"No. She flew down with three others, two girls and a boy from school. None of them have returned. We should never have let her go. I knew something bad was going to happen to her. She's still a little girl, my little girl." Tears rolled unchecked down Salma's face.

Sebastian lowered his head.

"Have the other parents had any word?" asked Clay.

"We didn't even know where two of her friends lived. What kind of parents does that make us? She went all the way to Cancún with those kids and we didn't even know their parents' phone numbers." Sebastian's expression was frozen in misery. "We had to call Marco's parents to find out."

Anger flashed again across Salma's face. "But that's not the worst thing. We couldn't even fly down there to look for her."

"But I can," Clay said. "I'll fly down first thing in the morning. Do you know which hotel she was staying in?"

Salma handed him a sheet of paper, the ink near its edges smudged with thumbprints. The details on the page were written in Celine's handwriting, smooth and uniform. The page contained the name and telephone number of the hotel: the Mayan Fiesta. Below were the names of her travel buddies. Their telephone numbers had been added in blocked numbers that held none of Celine's delicate penmanship.

The telephone numbers of the hotel and the police station had been underscored with an angry hand.

6

Chrissie Haims smiled at Danny, a single bead of sweat tracing a slow path down her face. "Feel's good inside, right?"

"Damn good. But I don't know how long I can last, I haven't done this for quite a while."

Chrissie rolled her hips in slow concentric circles. Danny did his best to match her rhythm. His body shuddered and he let out a sign of resignation. He was done.

"Wimp," teased Chrissie. She held the pose for another ten seconds then slowly stood up straight. She used the motion of a deep lunge to place the kettle bell on the floor.

"Damn, you're good. I've been doing martial arts since I was a kid and I still can't match you."

"Different skill set, that's all. You know I do cardio kickboxing twice a week, but I couldn't step into the ring with a real fighter. I'd get my ass handed to me in a minute."

"That doesn't help my ego. I'm glad my brother isn't around to see this. I'd never live it down."

Chrissie clasped her hands to her chest. "I'm sorry, I didn't know you'd lost a brother."

Danny rolled into a sitting position, laughing. "Oh no, he's not dead. It's worse than that. He's in Texas." Danny crunched out twenty tight sit-ups and thrust his chin at Chrissie as he completed the set. "There!"

"Ah, the natural balance is restored in the macho universe."

"I think so too." Danny winked at his training partner. Chrissie had made good on her promise. She had worked with him relentlessly in the week since he had resolved the problem of her stalker. He had supplied no further details, other than that she had nothing more to worry about. "I feel fitter and stronger than I ever have."

Chrissie punched him lightly on his shoulder. "Don't look so bad now either."

"Does that mean I looked shoddy before?"

"Just take a compliment when it's offered." She moved towards Danny, taking his hand in hers. "Seriously, though, thank you for getting that guy off my back."

Danny brushed an errant strand of hair from her face. The kiss they shared was light, unhurried. The moment was interrupted by the ringtone of Danny's phone. "I need to get this. It's my un-dead Texan sibling."

Chrissie smiled and waved her hand at the phone. She poured them both a glass of organic orange juice. The call lasted less than two minutes.

"You're leaving?"

Danny nodded. "Aye. A friend of the family has gone missing. We need to go and look for her."

Chrissie closed her eyes and exhaled slowly. "When're you leaving?"

"As soon as possible. Can I use your laptop to book a flight?"

A tear blossomed at the corner of Chrissie's eye as she waved him toward her computer. Her shoulders slumped.

"Hey, this isn't goodbye. I'll come back and see you when this is done."

"Yeah?" Her chin dimpled momentarily. "Promise?"

"I promise." Danny again moved that defiant lock of hair. He pulled her close.

7

Cancún International Airport was bustling. Squawking tourists dragged overstuffed cases towards the motor coaches and shuttles ready to spirit them away to one of the countless hotels that dotted the famous beach resort. Clay shifted from foot to foot impatiently, glancing at the arrivals board again—Danny's flight had already landed.

Clay had arrived two hours earlier, and had used the down time to study maps of Cancún, then the wider Yucatán peninsula, on his smartphone. Thousands of square miles of green with very few interconnecting roads. There was a lot of wild ground to get lost in.

A familiar voice sounded from behind him. "Time was I would never have been able to sneak up on you. You're losing your edge, big brother."

Clay shrugged and gave a mock grimace. "I once got bit on my ass by a horse tick. Didn't see that coming either."

"Ah, stop bellyachin'. That's the first time I've ever gotten the drop on you."

"And that's supposed to make me feel better. What's

next? Should I buy a pipe and slippers?"

Danny thumped the side of his fist into the thickness of Clay's chest. "Be quiet, ya big dope. Besides, I don't think they make slippers to fit feet that big."

The Gunn brothers grinned at each other like kids and shared a hug.

"How was Miami?" asked Clay, as he led Danny towards the nearest exit.

"Miami was great. I caught up with my reading and topped up my tan."

"Told you you'd enjoy it. I'll come with you next time. The Cuban sandwiches at Guido's on South Beach are great." Clay smacked his lips. "You hungry?"

"I guess I could eat something. The food on the plane amounted to a mini-pack of pretzels and a munchkin-sized orange juice."

Clay grinned in delight. "There's a Margaritaville over there. I hear they do a decent plate of nachos."

As Clay devoured his nacho platter, Danny opted for the grilled vegetable sandwich. Clay eyed his brother's choice with suspicion. "You still on your health kick?"

"Just trying to keep the cobwebs off."

"Not my idea of fun but I have to admit it seems to be working for you. You look good, little brother."

Danny nodded in agreement. "Feeling good."

Clay scooped up cheese and sour cream with a fan-shaped wedge of nacho chips. "Thanks for coming down at short notice."

"No problemo. Sebastian and Salma must be worried sick."

"They've been turning in circles since she went missing. They couldn't even come down here themselves. If they found Celine, they wouldn't be able to bring her home."

"How's that work?" asked Danny.

"Sebastian and Salma are illegal. They hopped the border twenty-five years ago."

"I didn't realise. So, Celine's legal?"

"Yeah, a born-and-raised American."

"Bad news when a father can't bring his daughter home safe. That must have sat sour with Sebastian."

Clay cleaned his plate. "You got that right. They're both grey with worry. They've been at each other's throats all week."

"Stress'll do that, even to good people." Danny wiped his hands clean with a napkin. "So how much do we know about Celine's movements?"

"She came down here for spring break with three of her friends. They were staying at a place called the Mayan Fiesta. I've booked us in there too."

"Good place to start. What about her friends?"

"Two other young women and one man. They're missing too. Marco Kenner, Gillian Cole and Laura Troutman. They all go to the same school. The last thing Sebastian and Salma heard, they were going out to visit some Mayan ruins—you know, the pyramids and stuff. As far as we can tell, they never came back."

"And what have the local authorities got to say? They been much help?"

"I think they must have read the Idiot's Guide. 'Nothing to worry about, kids do this sort of thing all the time, I'm sure they'll show up when their money runs out.'" Clay clenched his teeth. "Lazy-assed police work if you ask me."

"I hear that. There must be some good cops down here, though, they can't all be polishing seats with their arses."

Clay shrugged, scooping up the last of the sour cream as he answered. "No comment."

"Looks like the party is still a-happening down here." The faces that passed their rental car were young, smiling, carefree. "I was here twenty-odd years ago. Damn, that makes me sound old. Great party town. Looks like it's grown a bit since I was last here."

Clay didn't answer.

"Don't worry. We'll find her," said Danny.

"Yeah, but what kind of state will she be in? Cancún's like most party towns: great on the main strip, but step two streets off it and you can end up deep in Crapsville."

"Yeah, I hear that, big bro. What're the chances of her being shacked up with a college jock? I know she's a bright kid, but she wouldn't be the first to lose her way to the love bug."

"She would have called home. Besides, her three friends haven't come home either. No way they all took the cupid potion."

Danny rubbed his thumb under his nose. "What about another kind of potion?"

"Nah, Celine is part of the school anti-drug programme. She wouldn't touch that shit, no way."

"You sure?"

"I'm very sure."

"Okay. That's the common-sense stuff out of the way. You think they fell foul of one of the gangs down here?"

"I thought that it might be a kidnap job. But there's been no ransom call, no demands."

Danny took a deep breath. "That still leaves a few options."

"Yeah, none of them good."

"Aye, I hear that. Clay, I know Celine's like family to you. This might not have a happy ending."

A low growl rumbled in Clay's chest. "She's the closest thing I've got to a daughter. I'm gonna find her and bring her home."

"I'm with you every step of the way. We might just have to go a bit easier than normal. The outfits down here are the real deal."

"I'll kill every last one of them if they've hurt her."

"That's the thing, Clay, we need to find out who *they* are first."

A group of tourists, dressed in board shorts and baggy T-shirts, jumped as Clay sounded the horn. They scuttled to the side of the road. The closest of them began to flip the bird. Clay glowered back at him. The bird retreated into its nest.

"I forgot what a sunny disposition you have when you're travelling," Danny deadpanned.

"Bunch of assholes. They don't even know how to cross a road properly."

Danny rubbed the back of his hand across his face. "They're just kids on holiday, Clay. They're not the ones we're here to sort out."

Clay grunted in agreement, but gave the young men another sour look in the rear-view mirror before turning his attention back to the road ahead.

"We'll drop our stuff at the hotel and then start asking questions. A quick shit, shower and shave and I'll be ready," said Danny.

"Shit, shower and shave? Who said that, Socrates?"

"Aristotle Onassis."

Danny rolled down the window, enjoying the sensation as the warm air hit his face. His skin was tanned dark from his time in Miami. He lowered his sunglasses as a woman dressed in a bright orange thong bikini strutted past the car. She too was tanned to a golden hue, and had curves in all the right places. She returned Danny's gaze for a moment then looked away, evidently uninterested.

"She loves me, she loves me not," laughed Danny.

"The fact that she's twenty years younger than you might have something to do with it," added Clay.

"I'm hardly an old man."

"You're probably the same age as her father."

Danny gave a wry smirk. "Shut up, Clay. Since when did you become the voice of reason?"

Clay bared his teeth, which elicited another brief chuckle from Danny. He pointed to an ornate road sign. "Heads up, that's us. Mayan Fiesta dead ahead."

The towering building was a shrine to steel and smoked glass, stepped like the famous pyramids that dotted the Yucatán landscape. Manicured palm trees lined the entrance. A circular fountain sprayed water high, each droplet reflecting the sun in an undulating rainbow.

Danny looked around the grounds and gave a brief nod of approval. The sparkling waters of the Caribbean Sea lay to the east while the more sheltered Nichupté Lagoon separated the hotel zone from the mainland proper. Speedboats and catamarans vied for space in the lagoon harbour. The sound of carefree laughter drifted on the air. "Well, this is shiny."

As Clay stopped the vehicle in front of the main lobby area, a uniformed valet opened the driver's door.

"Welcome to the Mayan Fiesta Resort and Spa." The young man flashed a genuine smile, his white teeth contrasting with his mocha skin and coal-black hair. "Do you require any assistance with your luggage?"

Clay towered over him as he got out of the car. "No thanks, we're travelling light."

Danny received a quizzical look from the valet. "Just one bag apiece. I think we'll manage."

"*Sí señors*, I understand. *Travelling light.*" He rolled the words around on his tongue as if trying them for the first time.

"Don't park it too far away, we'll be heading back out in a short while."

He gave Clay a short salute. "I'll keep it close by and ready for you, *señor*."

Clay handed the young man a twenty. "You can stop with the *señor* thing. My name's Clay. This is my brother Danny. I hope dollars are okay?"

The valet glanced between the two brothers and nodded. "My name is Giorgio and US dollars are very okay. If you need anything, anything at all, just give me a call. I know all the best bars, the best beaches."

Danny liked the kid. He was bright and enthusiastic. "I think we might take you up on that."

Giorgio slipped into the driver's seat. "You know where I'll be."

Danny opened the sliding door and stepped out onto the balcony while he waited for Clay to finish showering. Sounds of music and laughter drifted up. Good sounds. *Happy sounds.* The pool deck below was populated by a multitude: holidaymakers lay stretched on sunloungers, while others splashed around in the water. A game of water polo was in full swing. Beyond the pool lay the ocean, the shade of blue a thing of true beauty.

There were two taps on the door. Danny answered promptly. The woman outside was short and wide with distinctive oval eyes. She wore a pale green uniform with the Mayan Fiesta logo embroidered on the upper left breast.

"*Hola, señor.* Is everything satisfactory with your room?"

Glancing at her name badge, Danny answered, "Yeah, everything looks great. Thanks, Geri."

"I'll be looking after your room for your stay. If you need any extra towels or anything like that, just call housekeeping."

Danny thanked her again. Geri turned and moved back to the utility trolley stacked with soaps, towels and toilet rolls.

"Hey, Geri."

She paused. "*Sí, señor?*"

"Did you hear anything about those college kids who went missing last week? Kinda crazy, wouldn't you say?"

Geri looked up and down the hallway before answering. She stepped close to Danny, her lips contorting into an irregular pout. "Those kids are not the first to go missing. Between you and me, they won't be the last."

"Where'd they go?"

"I'm not sure. There are a few rumours going around." She shrugged her rounded shoulders.

"Gangs?"

"Not the kind you mean."

"So not cartels or street hustlers?"

"No, but they both cause a lot of trouble of their own." Geri shook her head and puffed out her cheeks. "But no, this is something… different. But like I say, it's only rumours."

Dropping his voice and adding a little of his Scottish brogue, Danny said, "Well now, you've got me on a hook. What kind of rumours?"

"The hotel doesn't like us talking about it, none of the hotels do. *Bad for business…*"

Danny inched closer. "I guess kids from the States going missing isn't the kind of thing they would put in their brochures."

"You got that right. All of the staff know about the missing kids; we hear the stories. But we have to work here, so…"

"I get it, Geri, but you can tell me. I love a good mystery."

"You wouldn't believe me if I told you."

"Try me."

"Most of the ones that disappear go out into the jungle on day trips and don't come back."

"And what do you think happens to them? Kidnapped?"

Geri crossed herself before she answered. *"El Diablo* takes them."

"The Devil?" Danny raised an eyebrow. "Really? I know I'm a gringo, but I'm not a *stupid* gringo."

Geri gave him the flat-eye. "I know most people do not believe in him but he's very real. He doesn't take many of them but if you think how many people visit Cancún every year, he doesn't have to. If he took one in every ten thousand…"

Danny rubbed his chin. "So, what makes you think this is the work of the Devil rather than the cartels?"

"When the cartels take someone they usually turn up dead in the street as a warning not to cross them. These kids get lost and stay lost—not the cartel's style. They go out on their own into the jungle and are… taken. This has been happening for two or three years now." Geri held up a finger. *"El Diablo."*

"What have the police got to say about it?"

Geri gave a single huff of a laugh that spoke volumes. "Police? Most are fat or lazy or in the pocket of those cartels you just mentioned. Police? Pah!"

Feeling like he was getting nowhere fast, Danny fished his wallet from his pocket. He pulled out twenty bucks. "Thanks for your help, Geri. Would you see if we could get some beers for the room? Modelo, if you have it. No hurry— we'll be out and about for the rest of the day."

"Sí, señor, I'll make sure you get your *cerveza.* I hope you enjoy your stay at the Mayan Fiesta." Geri moved to the next room and gave the door a double tap.

Danny poked his head back into his room. Clay was

inspecting himself in the mirror. He tugged a few strands of dark blond hair down over his forehead. Danny said nothing; he knew Clay was self-conscious about his scars at times.

"You good to go?"

"I am. Who were you sweet-talking? I know we're in Cancún but we're here for Celine."

"I was talking to our maid, Groucho. Just asking a few questions, seeing if she knew anything about anything."

"And did she?"

"Not really."

"Not really or not at all?"

"She knew about kids going missing but swears the Devil is taking them. It'll be the chupacabra next."

"Hmmn," said Clay absently as he adjusted his shirt. "You got any kit with you?"

"All I could bring was a knife in my bag and my shim set. Too risky trying to hide anything more in your luggage these days." Danny tapped his fingers against his narrow webbing belt to show where he kept his compact lockpick set, an item he had used many times.

"I'll have to pick something up while we're out and about. I wish I had my bowie."

"Too big to carry, unless you can get a chest rig to go under your shirt. That's why I like these." Danny used his thumb to open the blade of his Fox ERT. The sturdy tanto blade was less than three inches long, the edge razor-sharp.

Clay took the knife from Danny. The weapon looked like a child's toy in his hand. "I'll find something bigger."

8

The smell of *pancita* filled the room, mingling with the grey streams of cigarette smoke that drifted up from virtually every table. Gavin rubbed the back of his hand across his mouth, the tripe and chilli broth doing a fair job of numbing his lips. A long swallow of the dark Modelo beer helped to cool things down. He stuffed another of the bite-sized *hauraches* into his mouth.

The food was only one of the reasons he liked to visit the rural cantina. The beer was ridiculously cheap. It cost more to buy a crappy Coke than a quality Mexican *cerveza*. The women, if he wanted them, were also very cheap. The half-dozen girls who worked the room had on his previous visits assured him that nothing was off limits, fifty US dollars for an access-all-areas pass. Yet Gavin had no need of such services. Plenty of that to be had back at the compound.

The real reason he felt drawn to the bar was the looks he received from the other patrons. They knew where he was from, knew who his friends were. As he made a circle in the air with one finger he caught the look in the eye of the waitress. *There it was*. That combination of nervousness and fear, and, dare he believe it, respect?

The good-looking waitress brought a second plate of *hauraches* and another Modelo to his table. The smile she gave him showed neat white teeth. As she turned away, Gavin stopped her in her tracks by resting his hand on the flatness of her stomach. The heel of her shoe made a mouse-like squeak on the tiled floor.

"What's your hurry? I might need—" he let the pause drag out, enjoying the young woman's discomfort "—something else."

The energy of the room shifted. Many eyes were upon him.

"I'm very busy. There's only two of us working today."

Gavin dismissed the other waitress without consideration. She was older, short and portly, waddling around the bar on pudgy legs. No, not his idea of fun at all. He increased the pressure of his palm upon her midriff. "But what if I want… something that's not on the menu?"

Her jaw tightened. "We have other girls for that."

Gavin's mocking laugh came as two sharp barks. He pushed her away. "Thank you, Daniela." He laughed again as she heard her name. It was one of the first tricks he had learned from the master. The sharp twitch of the head, the questioning look, the mark wondering how he knew anything about them. *If he knows my name, what else does he know about me?*

Daniela gave him a sideways glance as she moved back to the kitchen. She brushed the front of her shirt where his hand had rested.

Smiling to himself, Gavin finished his food at a leisurely pace. He made a show of standing up, stretching his arms above his head. He stood a foot taller than most in the room. The legs of his chair scraped harshly across the tiles. He dropped the notes from his wallet as if paying his bill was beneath him. There were no comments from the local crowd. The patrons of the cantina seemed more interested in examining the contents of their glasses. He gave another of his canine laughs and strode briskly out through the front doors.

The Dodge pickup was the only vehicle on this side of the parking lot. In comparison to the beat-up trucks that sat in a cluster on the far side of the lot, his vehicle looked like it had just come from the showroom.

The signal lights blinked as he pressed his key fob. He paused, looking back over his shoulder. *Someone there?* He turned slowly, his hand moving towards his belt.

Nothing.

But as he hauled his lanky frame into the Dodge, his world turned to pain. A rapidly moving shadow detached itself from the nearby bushes and closed on him. The shadow held a stubby pistol in its hand. A sharp series of clicks sounded and Gavin slumped to the ground, one foot still inside the truck. *Taser.* His body convulsed as his nervous system was overloaded by the debilitating effect of the stun gun.

He tried to reach for the pistol nestled in the small of his back but his hand trembled and refused to move. Something hard crashed into the side of his head, then darkness claimed him.

Slap!

"Hey..."

Slap!

"Hey. Wake up!"

For a moment, Gavin thought he was dreaming. The sharp edge of the boot pressing into his chest dispelled that illusion in a second. His hands were secured behind his back, his legs taped tightly at the ankles. He lay on a slight incline, his feet lower than his head.

"What the hell is this?"

The voice that answered was as cold as an Arctic wind. "What does it look like?"

Gavin strained at his bonds, bucking from side to side. "You're making a big mistake! Do you know who I am?"

"I know exactly who you are."

"Is this some kinda joke?" He looked around. "Where the hell am I?"

The pressure on his chest increased, making it difficult to breathe. "Well, you're not in Kansas anymore, Toto."

It was a woman's voice. *A fucking woman?*

A strange sensation took up residence in his bowels as he gauged his situation. The figure before him stepped back. She was dressed in a jumpsuit, with an army-style waistcoat buckled over the top. She wore gloves, and her face was covered by a balaclava.

With slow deliberation, she pulled the fabric mesh from her face.

Gavin stared up at her. "Who the hell *are* you?"

Her skin was the colour of black coffee. The right side of her face was smooth and flawless. The left side was an industrial accident. Bands of salmon-pink tissue knotted into a cruel mask. She held up her hand, covering the ruined side of her face.

Gavin stared at her for long seconds. "Shit! I know you. But you can't be you. You died. I watched you die..."

"Correction: you *thought* you watched me die." She dropped her hand. "Now it's my turn."

Gavin rolled onto his side, then managed to sit up. A noose pulled at his neck. Scooting around on his butt, he could see the other end of the rope was tied to the trunk of a wide tree. A length of the same mountaineer's rope traced a path from his ankles to the rear of his truck.

His eyes followed the rope to the truck. The Dodge's engine was running.

He sucked in a great lungful of air. "*Heeeeelp!*"

The woman shook her head slowly. "You can scream like it's an Olympic event. We're five miles into the jungle. Nothing out here to hear you but iguanas and insects."

Gavin pulled desperately against his bonds, the rope biting, rubbing his skin raw. "Wait. I can give you money. I have lots of money."

"Really?" She walked slowly towards the pickup. "How much to get my life back?"

"Wait..."

"How much to get my sister back?"

"Please..."

"How much to give me peace?"

"It wasn't me."

She paused at the open door of the truck. "But you were there. You didn't stop them. You laughed as they played their games, laughed as they did this."

Liquid spilled from his bladder as she tapped her ruined features with a gloved hand.

She leaned into the truck and moments later the Dodge began to roll forward. Slowly at first. The slack in the rope tightened within a couple of fear-filled seconds. Gavin rose from the ground, stretched between the vehicle and the tree. He tensed every muscle in his body in a desperate attempt to free himself. The ropes bit ever deeper into his skin. He tried to call out, to beg for release, but the words were caught fast behind the tightening noose. The skin at his ankles ripped first, then something deeper in the joint gave way with an agonising *pop*. An unbearable pressure invaded his skull, the muscles in his jaws bunching tighter and tighter until one of his molar teeth splintered into jagged shards. Capillaries ruptured in both of his eyes, spreading red tendrils across his fading vision.

The critical structure of his cervical vertebrae held for less than four agony-filled seconds then snapped, severing his spinal cord.

Ghost watched impassively as the truck rolled, driverless, down the hill, dragging Gavin's headless corpse behind. Moments later there was a loud thud. The Dodge had met with a tree somewhere on its path.

Pulling back on her sleeve, she exposed the skin of her left forearm. A series of six straight scars lay there like an oversized barcode. Drawing a compact blade from her belt, she added a seventh. Ignoring the stinging warmth, she turned a half-circle until she found what she was looking for.

Gavin's head had rolled a good fifteen feet down the road. After pulling a heavy-duty refuse sack from her hip pocket, she lifted the grisly trophy by the hair and let it fall into the bag.

9

The girl looked down at her feet as she walked. She could see them moving, knew they were hers, yet could not feel the floor beneath them. Her mouth was hanging open. Stark lights burned above her as she followed with robotic steps the person in front of her. A taste she struggled to identify soured her mouth. Raising her hands to her nose, she inhaled. She smelled like a hospital ward, antiseptic. Had she been in an accident? Was she in a hospital? A burning pain between her legs caused her hand to creep there in turn. *What the hell?*

"Where?"

The person she was following never reacted. A diamond-shaped patch of sweat marked the back of her T-shirt. Another girl. Her shapely hips filled the shorts she wore, long tanned legs, honey-blond hair. A small tattoo was visible between her hair and the collar of her shirt. She stared at the inkwork, then reached out to touch the bold pattern. Dots and dashes. Dots in red ink, dashes in black. Dash, dash, dot. Dash, dot, dash, dot. The pattern held meaning but the significance eluded her.

Something shifted, opening behind her eyes, like curtains in her mind, the sensation alien and nauseating. Then she was aware of the cold tiles beneath her feet. Bare feet. Cold. *Where were her shoes?*

She turned in a half-circle, her hand reaching for the wall for support. The world skewed for a moment, the ceiling becoming the floor.

Strong hands grasped at her shoulders and she was hauled to her feet.

"Keep moving. First door on the left."

She looked up at the owner of the hands that propelled her forward. Tall, muscular, white rock-star hair.

She heard the words again. "First door on the left. Keep moving." The man shoved her again.

"First door on the left." The voice was her own. Disembodied to her ear, but her own.

"Move it."

"Celine?" Something surfaced in her mind like a pocket of air in liquid. She rolled the name around on her tongue. "Celine."

The girl with the tattoo stopped, wobbling on unsteady legs. Her eyes were empty, dark pools of confusion. "Celine?"

The man grabbed both young women by the backs of their necks, fingers digging into flesh. "Keep moving, you two. I haven't got all day. Back in your hole you go."

This room smelled of sweat and perfume and confusion. She had been here before. A simple rectangle, plain white walls, fluorescent lighting, five camp beds arranged on each side, evenly spaced like a barracks. Celine smiled as she was guided to the bed, pushed down to the softness beneath. Home…

"No, not home." This wasn't home. What was this place? Celine looked at the girl she had been following. She knew now that the girl was her friend. What was her name? This was wrong. This wasn't home. What was her friend's name? *Celine? No, I'm Celine.*

Thoughts danced like sparks from a damp campfire. Celine tried to stand.

The same man who had guided her earlier issued a barking command. "Lie down and shut up!"

Celine reclined onto the bed and lapsed into silence. Lie down and shut up. That was what was important.

"Lie down and shut up." Celine's voice was one of acceptance.

"Lie down and shut up," the girl on the next bed echoed, her voice devoid of emotion.

10

"That filled a small gap," said Clay, patting his stomach in satisfaction.

"A small gap? You just ate your weight in chicken tacos and potato salad," said Danny as they waited in the harsh sunlight for Giorgio to bring their rental car.

"And very nice it was too. I'm keen to get going but you never know when you're getting your next proper meal."

"I know what you mean, big brother. This line of work, each meal could be our last."

Clay's rental, a sturdy Jeep Wrangler, arrived quickly. Giorgio grinned as he jumped out, leaving the engine and air-con running. "Nice wheels, man."

Clay nodded in agreement. "It's only a rental but it gets the job done."

"A lot of visitors just rent the cheapest car they can get, which is fine for the main roads around Cancún, but if you venture a bit further out the roads are not so good. I've seen a lot of people get stuck out near the Mayan sites."

Danny agreed. "I went out to Chichen Itza twenty-odd

years ago, and I remember the road wasn't much better than a farm track. More potholes than road."

"The main roads out to Chichen Itza and Tulum are fine now, long and straight, no problems," Giorgio explained, "but when you get out into the jungle to the smaller villages and the sites that haven't been opened yet, that's when the roads become an adventure."

"An adventure, that's one way to put it," said Clay.

Giorgio shrugged, a wry smile creeping across his face. "Mexico is not just a country, it's a state of mind. Every day is an adventure."

"Scotland is much the same," said Danny.

"You're Scottish... that's what your accent is," said Giorgio, snapping his fingers. "I would love to go to Scotland one day. I love watching the movies from there. *Highlander*, *Rob Roy*, *Braveheart*, some of my favourite films. Do they still have the real castles to see?"

"Aye, there's a lot of them still standing. The countryside is beautiful too. If you like the rugged outdoors, you'll like Scotland."

Giorgio clapped his hands together. "I must save my money and go one day."

Clay rested a hand on Giorgio's shoulder. "Hey, I wonder if you could help us out?"

"*Sí*, Mr Clay, anything, ask."

"One of the housekeeping girls was telling Danny about the kids from the States who went missing recently. They were staying here before they disappeared."

Licking his lips before he answered, Giorgio talked in a slightly hushed tone. "They were here. Four of them. Three women and one man. I spoke to them a few times, nice guys, not too loud."

"Did you see anyone suspicious with the kids before they disappeared?"

"No, *señor*, no one like that. They were just kids on vacation." He looked at Clay apologetically. "They rented a vehicle to visit one of the Mayan sites. My friend Miguel spoke to them a lot more than I did. He works at the poolside bar." Giorgio paused, his eyes narrowing slightly. "Why do you ask? Do you know them?"

Clay answered. "One of the girls, Celine, is a close friend. More like family, really."

"I'm sorry to hear that. I don't know which one she was."

"She was the darkest one. Her parents are Mexican. The other two girls are fairer. One blonde and one brunette."

"*Sí, sí,* I remember her now." Giorgio held up his pinky finger. "Very small and slim."

"Yeah, that's her. I always joke that a Texas wind is going to blow her clean off her feet one day." Clay's face hardened as he turned his gaze fully upon the valet. "We're here to find them and take them home. Anything you can find out to help us would be *very much appreciated*."

Giorgio reached inside his uniform jacket and retrieved his cell phone. "I'll call Miguel. He may know something that could help you."

"Did the police speak to him already?"

"I don't think so. They only spoke to the hotel manager and Carolina from personnel." Giorgio wrinkled his nose in obvious disapproval. "Like they would know anything. The manager has his nose so far in the air he only ever sees the ceiling, and Carolina doesn't know half *our* names, so what could she know about a couple of guests?"

"The cops didn't dig any deeper?" asked Danny.

Giorgio's negative answer confirmed what they had guessed already. The police officers who had attended the hotel had paid lip service at best.

"It's ringing," said Giorgio, tapping the phone with his index finger. "*Hola*, Miguel…"

The call was in rapid-fire Spanish and ended quickly. As he slipped his phone back into his pocket, Giorgio told them, "He only knew what they had told him the day before."

"Which was?" asked Clay.

"The group rented a car so they could visit some Mayan sites off the beaten track."

"Did they say which ones they were going to?"

"He said they mentioned a site somewhere just north of Chacchoben. That's a long drive south from here. They could have got lost out there. The roads are… not good."

"What's Chacchoben? A town?" asked Danny.

"No, it's an old Mayan site. But Miguel thinks they were looking for a newer site that one of the girls had read about online."

"Any idea where that might be?" asked Clay.

Giorgio held his palms up in supplication. "I'm sorry, Miguel did not know."

"Hey, we know more than we did five minutes ago. Thank you, Giorgio."

Danny had his phone in his hand. "How do you spell Chacchoben?"

Giorgio spelled it out for him as Danny typed the letters

into the search bar of the phone's browser. Seconds later, Danny tapped one of the results. A map filled the display with a small red pin highlighting the site's location.

Clay nodded at his brother. "That's a good place to start, I suppose."

"Damn right. Chacchoben, here we come."

11

Do they even know the last guy is missing yet?

Probably not, Ghost answered her own question. *Otherwise this dickhead wouldn't be swanning around on his own.*

She had followed him, unseen, to the ramshackle gas station some five miles away from the compound. What was he doing out here? She knew they had a free-standing gasoline tank at the rear of the camp, so he hadn't come for that.

She settled her weight against the gnarled trunk of a tree, relaxing into a half-sitting position, keeping one leg tucked under her, ready to move rapidly should the need arise.

She could see the storekeeper inside, filling a wire stand with oversized bags of potato chips. But where was the guy she had followed? The store looked to be no more than about fifteen feet square. Not many places to hide. He had parked his truck to the side of the two pumps out front.

"But that don't mean you went inside..."

The area surrounding the gas station was devoid of flora, all plant life long since poisoned and trampled into oblivion.

The road she had followed the man in on was barely wide enough for two vehicles, a narrow scar cut through the emerald canopy. To the left of the cinder-block store, a collection of used oil drums was stacked in a haphazard manner like a child's fort.

Uncoiling from her seated position, she flitted from tree to tree, keeping the man's truck in view as much as possible. If he returned to his vehicle she would need to sprint back a hundred yards to her own truck to continue her pursuit.

As she crossed the hard pan of the road she stayed low, and was swallowed by the various shades of green within seconds. Cutting a wide semi-circular path around the gas station, she could see the remnants of a small tractor and trailer behind the arrangement of oil drums. The tyres of the tractor had long since perished and the heavy wheel rims bit deep into the earth. Another assortment of empty crates, the kind that held soda bottles, formed a mini pyramid on the back of the listing trailer. An old soccer ball sat atop the uppermost crate. A dog lay curled in the cavern of shade below the rear of the trailer, its ears twitching against the flies buzzing around its narrow head. A hole marred its left ear. The dog followed her progress but remained in the shade.

A square enclosure built from rusting corrugated tin sheets and timber stood at the rear of the main building. She chose the door that held the legend "Caballeros". She could hear two different voices. Beneath the soft fabric of her mask, her lip curled in resolve. She didn't know who the second man was, but anyone who consorted with her target was likely to be cut from the same cloth.

The two men stared at her with wide eyes as she entered

the restroom, weapon drawn. The one she had followed, with his goatee and pork-pie hat, was just taking a roll of banknotes from the younger man. A bag lay open on top of a stained sink.

The younger man's hand moved towards the pistol on his hip.

"Don't!" ordered Ghost. She angled herself so she had a clear shot at both men.

"Drop the gun. Two fingers! Do it slowly! Kick it over here." Ghost's voice brooked no argument.

He took the pistol from his waistband as ordered, thumb and index finger forming a loop through the trigger guard.

"Now drop it and kick it over."

"Do it," said the other man. Beads of sweat dappled his face, his cheeks flushed red.

The pistol clattered against the grime-encrusted floor tiles.

"Now you!" barked Ghost.

The man she had followed held his hands up in surrender. "I'm not armed."

"Lift your shirt and turn around slowly. Go easy!" she warned, her own weapon never wavering.

The younger one stared at her intently. His voice was full of accusation and contempt. "What's with the mask? What are you, a ninja?"

"Get on the floor with your hands behind your head. And you in the hat, keep turning."

The younger one half-turned and spat on the floor. "You're shaking me down? Do you know who my uncles are? You'll pay for—" Then he launched himself towards her, a wild punch ripping towards her masked face.

Ghost dodged the uppercut, but her weapon discharged high above her head. The suppressor fitted to her Glock 19 took some of the roar from the shot, but in the confines of the bathroom it still sounded like a telephone directory being slammed against a tabletop.

Then he was on her. Clamping tight onto her wrist with both hands, he forced the pistol up and away from his body. Another shot punched a hole through the tin roof. Ghost grunted as she was slammed back against the wall with enough force to send yellow sparks dancing across her vision. The wall buckled behind her, the corrugated metal screeching. He had no real skill but plenty of savage intent. He slammed her gun hand into the wall repeatedly. Behind the two struggling combatants, the man in the outdated hat stared on, motionless.

She knew better than to try to match her attacker in strength. Instead she brought her knee up, aiming for his groin. As he dodged her initial blow by jerking his hips back, she wedged her shin high against his chest. For a moment, their bodies strained against each other, then she brought up her other leg so both her knees were perched high on his muscular chest.

Too late, he realised his mistake as the barrel of the suppressor angled down towards his startled expression.

Blooomph!

The single shot punched a neat hole through his face just below his left eye. As the man dropped dead beneath her, she fell with him. Her head hit the wall as she landed hard on her butt.

The man in the hat, her real target, made a lunge for the door then realised it was stuck. "No, no, no."

The dead man lay in a tangle of limbs, a crimson halo decorating the tiles beneath him. His dead weight wedged against the inward swing of the door. Grasping one of the dead man's arms, the man in the hat tried to pull him clear from the door. "Move, damn it!"

Ghost climbed to her knees and reached for her fallen sidearm.

With a yelp, the man abandoned the idea of trying to move the dead body. He turned, his gaze fixing on the dead man's pistol. His shoulder bounced off the stall door as he lunged for the fallen weapon. Then the porcelain cistern exploded just above his head. He turned onto his side, his hand frozen, dithering a mere six inches from the pistol.

"The next one goes in your head!"

Water began to flow from the ruined toilet, the ballcock bobbing like a feeding bird. Large triangular shards of porcelain lay scattered like toy boats in the spreading water.

"What do you want with me?" asked the man.

Ignoring his question, Ghost took a step closer. Her pistol never wavered from his face. "I guess with that hat, you're a fan of *Breaking Bad*. But how would you like a bad break?"

The pork-pie hat flew from his head as Ghost stamped down with her boot heel. The bones in his left ankle separated with an audible *snap*.

He howled, clutching at his ruined leg. A spray of vomit added to the grime of the bathroom floor. He tried to scoot deeper into the stall but had nowhere to go. She stared on, her brown eyes framed perfectly between the folds of her face mask.

"Why are you doing this?" the injured man demanded between frantic gasps of pain. "Who the hell are you?"

Ghost crouched, her pistol lying across her thigh. She spat her next words as the man stared at the business end of the suppressor, the small but deadly black hole. "I'm the last person you'll ever see."

"Take the bag. There's money and pills in there. Please, take them and go."

Ghost glanced at the bag perched on the sink top. Six bags lay next to a small wad of cash. Each of the bags contained various coloured capsules. She picked up a bag of pinks. "I'm betting these aren't antibiotics in here."

"Take them," cried the man. "Just take them and leave me be."

She threw the pack of pills at the man. She slowly pulled aside the fabric of her mask then turned her face to show the side that remained free of scars. "You still don't recognise me?"

"Please... I don't know who you are."

"That just makes it worse."

"Please. My leg."

"You want something for the pain?" She pointed the pistol at the bag of pinks. "Start eating them. All of them."

"What? No! Wait!"

Ghost put a bullet through his other ankle. "Eat the damn pills or the next one goes in your balls!"

The man with the pork-pie hat managed half of the bag before he began to convulse.

12

They found all the supplies they needed in the first store they visited. As they packed the items into the trunk, Danny busied himself removing any tags or packaging while Clay checked over a couple of climbing ropes. While he didn't foresee scaling any mountains in Mexico, he knew how handy and versatile they could be. A compact mess kit and two lightweight backpacks containing spare clothing and some ready-to-eat meals went in next. Clay groaned at the prospect of consuming vacuum-packed fare.

"Quit your whining, ya big ape. They're better than nothing when you're chin-strapped and starving. There's some proper food in there as well," said Danny. "And I'm sure we've time to pick up some candy bars on the way down."

"Sounds more like it."

"We can get some Cheetos, Ring Dings and chocolate milk."

"I know you're being sarcastic, but none of those items upset me in the least." Clay thumbed his nose.

Danny pointed to the weapon in Clay's hand. "At least you got a Texan-sized knife to play with."

"Damn right." Clay held up the oversized weapon. "I've got one like this back home. Sturdy blades, won't let you down in the field."

Danny held out his hand as Clay passed him the knife. The outer box was eighteen inches long. The picture on the case showed a classic bowie design. The blade was more akin to a machete than a regular knife. Danny discarded the box. The smell from the leather sheath was a welcome aroma. "They didn't have anything bigger?"

"Well, there was a barbarian battle sword, but I thought that might look a little conspicuous."

"Hmmn. What's that?" asked Danny, pointing to a smaller box.

"Backup." Clay showed him the smaller weapon.

Danny again inspected the packaging. "Smith & Wesson tactical, spring-assisted opening. Nice."

"You never know when you're gonna need a toothpick."

"Or to chop a tree down," said Danny, pointing to the bowie.

"Exactly."

"You okay driving for a while? I'll be navigator."

"Sounds like a plan."

Clay opened the packaging on a pair of Motorola two-way radios. The batteries came ready charged. He set the channel to three, then keyed the mike twice on each walkie-talkie. With all the newly procured kit unpacked and secured in the trunk space, both men climbed back into the Jeep. Clay started the engine as Danny brought his phone awake with a tap. The map screen still showed Chacchoben highlighted with a red pin. Danny wedged the phone into a holder on the dashboard. "Just keep heading south until I say otherwise. That should get us to where we need to go."

"Wagons ho!" Clay guided the Jeep into the light traffic.

As the tourist-filled splendour of Cancún faded in the rear-view mirror, a new and raw natural beauty took effect. Thick bushes with spiky leaves replaced the cultivated palm trees and the land lay flat and even in every direction.

Clay slowed the Jeep as they approached a traffic checkpoint. A dozen or so vehicles queued in the two lanes ahead of them. Tail lights blinked on and off as each vehicle was waved through in turn by guards armed with M16s. All the guards, without exception, looked as bored as mall security. Clay nodded as he in turn was waved through the checkpoint with little more than a cursory glance.

A rusting moped sped past, its engine protesting as it struggled under the weight of three riders. The rider alone looked well over two hundred pounds. The other two girls on the back were hardly bikini models either. The bike cut in front of the Jeep, then without signalling veered off onto a side road. A cloud of dust marked their highway exit. None of the riders wore a helmet.

Clay's thoughts turned again to Celine. Where in hell was she? He glanced at an overhead signpost for Playa del Carmen hoping they were heading in the right direction. Clay looked over at Danny. He was sound asleep.

Clay pressed a button on the radio and almost immediately the lively rhythm of a guitar solo filled the vehicle. He looked across at his brother as he began to stir.

"How long was I out?" asked Danny, stretching within the confines of his seat.

Clay glanced at his watch. "Long enough to miss half of Quintana Roo."

"How's the driving?"

Clay shrugged. "Easy going now that we've left the tour buses behind. There were quite a few of the road-blockers back up near Tulum, but after that it's been pretty clear."

Danny woke up his phone. "We're about sixty clicks from Chacchoben."

"I better put my foot down then. Daylight's a-burnin'."

The traffic was sparse as they continued south. Dump trucks and cement wagons seemed to be the vehicles of choice as they reached a collection of streets and ragged-looking cinder-block houses that pretended it was a town called Limones.

"This is where we turn off," said Danny, as he consulted the map on his phone.

They turned onto a dust-encrusted strip of asphalt. The track stretched off into the distance, long and straight. Occasional unfinished buildings, low rectangular frames without roofs or doors, dotted the approach to Chacchoben. The town itself was little more than a dozen or so streets arranged in neat square blocks. Pedestrians strolled along the streets and gave the Jeep and its occupants looks of mild curiosity as they passed. Several children pedalled by on ramshackle bicycles, laughing and chattering as they passed.

"Stop here," said Danny, pointing to a low building. A series of six columns formed a shaded portico. "The shopkeeper might know something about Celine and her friends."

Clay let the Jeep roll to a stop.

"Maybe you should wait out here," said Danny. "Don't want to scare the locals."

"Don't forget your Spanish phrase book," said Clay.

"Hey, my Spanish is better than yours and you live in friggin' Texas!"

Clay rubbed the back of his hand against his chin. "I know, I know. I really should make the effort to learn some more."

"Especially with Salma and Sebastian living with you."

Clay nodded. Danny was right. It had always been easier not to learn. Conversations with the Chavez family fluctuated rhythmically between Spanish and English without a pause; they had only ever spoken to Clay in English.

"I'll go and see if they know anything about missing kids," said Danny.

When Danny returned some fifteen minutes later, Clay was still leaning his bulk against the steering wheel, arms crossed with his chin resting on his forearms. Only his eyes moved as Danny climbed back into the Jeep. Danny dropped a grocery bag behind his seat.

"Anything?" asked Clay. Dark thoughts swirled in his mind.

"Yeah, the folks in the shop were a little cagey at first, but once I convinced them I wasn't a cop they opened up a bit. It turns out there's *two* Chacchobens."

"What do you mean, *two* Chacchobens?" A nerve twitched in Clay's left eye.

"This is the town, and there's also the Mayan ruins of the same name quite a few miles further into the jungle."

"They know anything about the kids? Did they remember

seeing Celine?" asked Clay. The heat in his face was not all due to the Mexican humidity.

"Yes and no."

Clay sat upright in his seat. A single bead of sweat rolled slowly down the side of his jaw. He forced himself to breathe slow and easy.

"Yes, they've heard rumours about people going missing down here and especially closer to the Belize border, but no, they don't remember seeing Celine or her friends. The chances of Celine passing through the first place we try were slim, you know that. What the guy in the store did tell me was that there's a bar between here and the ruins where some of the local desperados hang out. The bar's a good call, I reckon. You fancy getting acquainted with some of the shady locals?"

"Damn right. It stands to reason that the local bad boys would know something about missing kids, even if they're not directly involved."

"Then let's go ask some questions. It's about ten miles on the south road out of town. The guy in the store said we can't miss it, the bar's got a statue of a big red cow outside."

"Did he say which road to take?"

"Aye, back two blocks and turn right. Then it's a single-track road all the way to the bar. The same road goes all the way to the ruins and back to Highway 293."

The engine rumbled as Clay steered the Jeep in a tight arc and sped to the required corner. He slowed to allow another kid on a bicycle to cross the corner, then made the same turn.

A mangy-looking dog with a dime-sized hole in its left ear stood impassively in the middle of the road. The bedraggled canine made no effort to evade the oncoming vehicle. The road was too narrow to drive around the stubborn animal. Clay tooted the Jeep's horn twice. The dog stared back with eyes like marbles but refused to move. Its tail moved in slow motion, tracing a lazy arc in the air.

Danny reached into the bag of assorted of snacks in the rear footwell. He stepped out of the Jeep. "Give me a second."

Danny opened a packet of potato chips and held one towards the immobile mutt. "Come on, boy. You want some? Come on, then." Danny threw the chip towards the dog, who snapped it up before it landed.

Danny held out another. The dog took a single slow forward step, its eyes fixed on the treat. Danny moved back to the roadside and squatted down. The dog hobbled over on tired legs but accepted the remaining chips with apparent gratitude, its tail swishing in a tight motion. Clay watched as Danny ruffled the fur between its ears and the dog rolled over onto its side. A jagged line of scar tissue marked the dog's ribs. The mutt had certainly been through the wars. Danny climbed back into the Jeep.

"You owe me a packet of chips."

"Quit your jiving and let's get driving."

"Wow, poetry. This trip just gets better and better. Quit your jiving... who said that, Keats?"

"Will Smith, I think. Big Willie style an' all that."

Clay pointed below the steering wheel. "I've got your big willie style right here."

"Just get driving or I'll use those nuts of yours like a boxer's speedball."

Clay shook his head in mock hurt but kept his foot on the gas.

13

The statue of the red cow was the only thing about the bar that looked like it had seen a lick of paint in the previous century. The building was a simple single-storey structure; like many others they had passed it was constructed from cinder blocks, with a corrugated tin roof. A wooden stand near the entrance was decorated with remnants of weatherworn bill posters. A screen door obscured the interior.

Two Isuzu pickup trucks sat side by side, one dust-free and in showroom condition while the second looked like it had been rescued from the crusher. To the left of the trucks stood three battered motorbikes.

The brothers exchanged a glance as Clay shut off the engine.

"Is that the same dog that you gave my packet of chips to?"

Danny followed Clay's pointing finger and smiled as he spotted a nearly identical pooch as the one in Chacchoben. Same sad eyes, same mangy fur, same hole in its ear. "Can't be the same dog. Maybe they're cousins."

Danny climbed from the vehicle. He stretched his legs and back then rolled his shoulders, enjoying the sensation in his muscles. "You ready to dance?"

"Shined my shoes especially."

"Alrighty, then. Give me a couple of minutes, then you can come in."

It was something they had done several times in the past. The reaction that they received was always worth the price of admission. Whenever trouble was brewing the would-be antagonists usually felt quite secure when facing only Danny, wrongly assuming his wiry build was of little threat. The looks on their faces when Clay entered the fray were priceless. Danny pressed a button on his cell, and as soon as Clay answered left the call open, so he could hear everything said inside the bar.

Danny entered the building and walked to the bar. He returned the stares he received with a friendly nod. As he perched on a bar stool he took in the details of the room in one practised sweep. One barman, seven patrons: one table of four and another of three, all male. The men looked to range in age from early twenties to mid-forties; all had *the look*.

The bar was little more than a rectangular cinder-block enclosure with a stained wooden floor. A single ceiling fan turned in lazy circles but failed to provide any hint of a breeze. Like everything else in the bar, it was close to giving up the ghost.

Danny held up a finger to the barman. "*Una cerveza, por favor.*"

The barman scrutinised his unexpected customer for a

few seconds then looked to the table of three. Danny watched one of the men tilt his chin in a vaguely dismissive gesture. Only then did the barman reach under the bar and produce a bottle. He removed the cap with a practised flick of the wrist, then he set the stubby bottle of Negra Modelo down in front of Danny.

"*Gracias.*" Danny took a long pull on the brew. As he took a second sip he glanced again at the mirror behind the bar. One of the three men stood up.

The man was dressed in jeans and dirty sneakers with a tight-fitting vest that had maybe been white, once upon a time. He carried no obvious weapons; no knife on his belt, no pistol on his hip or tucked in his waistband. He spoke in heavily accented English. "You're a long way from the *tourista* trail. You lost?"

Danny turned to face the man. "Nah, I'm not lost. I'm looking for a few of my friends, who I think may have come through here."

The man gave a lopsided smile. One of his front teeth was missing. He smelled heavily of cigar smoke and stale sweat. A lock of black hair dangled past his eyes. "What would friends of yours be doing way out here? This is hardly party central."

Danny held his gaze. "Three young women and one man, all college kids from the States."

The man shook his head slowly. "I don't think so."

Danny addressed the barman. "What about you? You remember seeing them? Three girls, one boy. One girl is Mexican descent. The boy looks Italian; the other two girls are white. One blond, one a little darker."

The barman looked to the man at Danny's side but said nothing.

"What's wrong?" asked Danny. "This guy got you on a leash? These kids have disappeared and I need to find them."

The man poked Danny's shoulder with a stiffened finger. "He's never seen them. They were never here. There's nothing here for you."

"How do you know they weren't here? I haven't showed you a picture of them yet." Danny kept his voice to a low and non-aggressive tone.

The barman looked first at Danny then at the man. "Rodrigo?"

Rodrigo shot the barman a brief warning look.

Danny turned to face Rodrigo, the edge of his hand resting lightly on the surface of the bar. "You the man here, Rodrigo?"

"*Sí*, I'm the man. It's time for you to leave."

"Hey, take it easy. I'm willing to pay for information. I don't want any trouble."

The muscles in Rodrigo's face twitched. "You got money? How much?"

"That depends on what you can tell me about my friends. Did they pass through this way or not?"

"Maybe they did. *Tres chicas, un chico*, eh?"

Danny blinked slow and easy, repressing the urge to slam Rodrigo's face into the bar. "They're college kids. I think they were down here looking at the ruins near Chacchoben. You know where they are?"

"Show me your money," said Rodrigo.

Danny reached into his front hip pocket and pulled

out a roll of US twenties. "They're yours if you can tell me something worthwhile."

Rodrigo smiled as he tilted his head to one side. "I have another idea. What if me and my friends tell you nothing, kick your ass, and take your money anyway?"

Danny returned the smile before he spoke again. "That's not going to happen, but I can tell by the look in your eyes that maybe you did see my friends after all. So, we can do this a couple of ways."

"Yeah?" Rodrigo shifted his weight.

"Yeah. Option one, the sensible one: you tell me what you know and I give you this fistful of dollars. Option two, the one I don't recommend: you and your glee club try to roll me for the money and all end up breathing through tubes for two weeks."

Rodrigo flicked his fingers as if strumming an invisible guitar and the six other men stood up in unison. "I like you, you've got *cojones*. But you are one against seven and you are not carrying a *pistola*."

"Let me enlighten you, while you're still able to speak. Three of your seven are looking as nervous as turkeys at Christmas, so you can't rely on them."

The six men shuffled closer.

"Balls but no brains," said Rodrigo. Two of his men laughed at his joke.

"Let me finish option two. You and your boys get to take a trip to the local emergency room but not before I break your wrists and ankles. Believe me when I say that you will tell me what you know about those kids, one way or the other."

Rodrigo faltered. He paused, his eyes flitting between

Danny and the closest of his gang. A switchblade snicked open. Another man brandished a hunting knife with a saw-back blade.

Rodrigo spoke again. "Put the money on the bar and get the hell out of here while you can. You piss me off and we'll skin you alive and bury you out in the big green."

"I hope your boys can use those blades, because I'm going to take them away and stick them in some very sensitive spots." A humourless smile crept across Danny's face. "Just remember I tried to be nice but you wanted to do the tough guy dance."

As the six men moved towards their target, something akin to a force of nature exploded through the door with a roar so bestial it froze the gang in their tracks.

"KILL 'EM ALL!"

14

Carlos Larriva had watched the interchange between the lost gringo and Rodrigo with mild curiosity. He'd felt the tension shift in the room as Rodrigo gave them the signal, his fingers making that familiar strumming action. Carlos had left his knife in the glovebox of his truck, but he'd stood up all the same.

But a bare-chested giant of a man had burst through the flimsy door of the bar, tearing it free from its hinges. The cords on the giant's neck stood out as he roared with berserker fury. *"KILL 'EM ALL!"*

The gringo at the bar kicked out sideways, catching Rodrigo full in the chest. As he landed he curled into a tight ball on the floor, wheezing for breath.

Then the giant was among them.

Diego screamed as the marauder grabbed him by the arm and the testicles. His switchblade clattered to the floor, forgotten like a child's discarded toy, as he was picked up and his body slammed into the wall next to the ruined door. The whole bar shook from the impact.

Carlos watched in disbelief as the gringo at the bar brought his left foot up in a motion so fast it was a blur. The knife that had been in Mateo's hand a second earlier spun end over end and bounced off the wall at the far side of the bar. The gringo's right foot whipped across Mateo's face, spreading his nose into a shape it was never meant to be. Another kick snapped between his legs. Mateo folded at the waist and pitched head first onto the floor.

Three men down in as many seconds.

Santiago, his face red with fury, picked up a chair and swung it at the giant's head. The big man ducked low and rammed a fist hard into Santiago's stomach. The chair catapulted from his grasp as a second punch ripped up from below, catching him under the chin. The sound of breaking teeth was unmistakable. Santiago, who had won many street fights in his time, dropped to the ground as if devoid of life.

Carlos and Jesus were the only two left standing—they made a headlong dash for the bar. There was a small storeroom at the rear of the bar—they might escape that way, if they were lucky.

The big man caught Jesus by the hair and body-slammed him through a table. Jesus lay groaning, his left arm bent at an unnatural angle.

As Carlos vaulted the bar the gringo did the same, blocking his path. The barman skidded backwards on his ass like a crab, yelling that he didn't want any trouble. The gringo silenced him with a short backhand swipe across the jaw.

"I guess you win the prize," said the smaller gringo. "You're the last man standing. Now you get to spend some quality time answering my questions. Now, the answer to my next question better had be '*Sí, señor,*' or you're gonna get it worse than any of these dickwads. *Habla inglés?*"

Carlos nodded vigorously. "*Sí, señor.* I speak very good English."

"That's good. Now we're gonna have a wee chit-chat. Sit your arse down and tell me what you know about the missing kids we're looking for."

Carlos was propelled back to one of the few upright tables. He sat without resistance. A sideways glance at the big man was all it took; his face was deeply scarred and chilled Carlos to the bone. Who the hell were these men? Not tourists, that was for sure.

The smaller man pulled up a chair of his own. He produced a photograph from his pocket, unfolding it carefully. Carlos stared at the picture. It showed a portrait shot of a young woman. She was very pretty and her deep brown eyes carried both intelligence and a curious innocence.

"Have you seen this girl?"

Carlos shook his head. The smaller gringo was difficult to understand, his accent now thick with anger.

"Take another look! She would have been with another two women and a young man."

Carlos glanced around the room at his friends, all lying in various states of desperation. A couple groaned, clutching their faces. Mateo and Diego lay so still he feared them dead. He turned back to the picture. "I have never seen this girl. I would have remembered someone as pretty as her. I'm sorry but I can't help you."

The big man clamped his hand around Carlos's neck, his

fingers digging deep. "Let me break his arm, then we'll find out if he's telling the truth or not."

To Carlos's relief, the smaller of the two held up a single finger. The big man released his grip and shoved him away. The low bestial growl he gave caused Carlos to squirt a little urine into his underwear.

"Okay, so you didn't see her." As the smaller man leaned closer to Carlos he could see a cold ferocity in his eyes. The big guy was a beast, crashing in and tearing up the guys like a wild animal, but the smaller guy was truly unnerving. "You and the rest of the gang… you're the local bad boys, I get that. You must have heard the stories about kids going missing, right?"

"I…"

The big man stepped over to Jesus, who had managed to make it back onto his hands and knees. The punch that the big man dropped onto the back of his head sounded like a pistol shot. Jesus dropped face down, unmoving.

"You were saying," said the smaller man.

Carlos closed his eyes and, after crossing himself, leaned forward, his voice a whisper. "*Sí*, I have heard the stories. People go missing. Not very often. They say the Devil takes them."

"Well we both know that's a pile of shite, so what else have you heard?"

"It's not just kids who are taken."

"No?"

Carlos shook his head. "No. Sometimes older men and women, too. But mainly we hear about the younger ones."

"Go on."

"Someone sets out for school or to go to work but they

never get there. It's the same with the *touristas*, they head out onto the old paths and don't come back."

"Who do you think takes them? And don't give me any bullshit about *el Diablo*."

Carlos held his hands up in supplication. "I don't know. I know that more than one has gone missing near the Mayan site that was found recently."

"That's the one north of Chacchoben?"

Carlos was about to correct his pronunciation but thought better of it. "*Sí*. There is a bar not unlike this one on the roadside near the ruins. The people there may know more; we don't go there much. We don't like each other."

"Show me where it is on my phone."

Carlos pointed to the map display. "I think it is around there."

"Okay. Is this anything to do with cartels?"

Carlos rubbed his face with both hands. Talking about these things could only bring about more bad luck. The Devil, the bad places and now the cartels. All three sent shivers down Carlos's spine. "No, I don't think so. That is not how they work. If you are unlucky enough to be caught by the cartels you would probably end up hanging upside down from a road sign full of holes, or your head would be left out for everyone else to see. No, I do not think that this is cartel business."

The smaller gringo sat back in his seat. "One more thing."

"*Sí*?"

"Your man there." He pointed to the unconscious Rodrigo. "When he wakes up, tell him next time someone asks a polite question, he should bloody well answer it!"

15

Her first attempt to stand up resulted in her landing in an ungainly tangle of limbs. Her knees folded beneath her again as she tried a second attempt to right herself. Groaning, Celine reached out and grasped the end of the camp bed, leaning on it as a geriatric would a walking frame. The curved metal was cool beneath her fingers. A small squeak, like that of a trapped mouse, caused her to start. It was just the bedframe. She stood up. This time her legs held true. The room tilted like a carnival ride as she took several deep breaths, pursing her lips as she exhaled.

How long had she been in the room? Her wristwatch was gone. A quick pat-down of her pockets showed that her cell phone was missing as well. There was no clock visible in the dormitory-style room. The plain white walls were unadorned: no clock, no posters, nothing to suggest her current location.

Five bunk beds lined the room. Ten beds, four more of which were occupied. Celine moved to the closest of the beds and stared down at the young woman lying there on top of the plain sheets, her legs straight with her knees together.

Her arms were pressed to her sides as if a stage hypnotist had just mesmerised her and laid her down. Her face was relaxed and her mouth hung open a fraction of an inch. A soft whistle issued forth each time she took a breath. Her honey-blond hair was loose, and several darkened strands clung to the beads of perspiration on her face.

Celine took a step closer. Her face seemed familiar.

"Where the hell am I?" A sense of unease began to worm its way down Celine's spine. "Where am I? How did I get here?"

The girl in the bed continued to snore softly.

She knew this girl. Her face, her hair. What the hell was her name? Celine shook her head to clear what felt like heavy spiderwebs that muffled her capacity to think clearly. She had suffered her first real hangover on the second morning of the vacation. The various cocktails that she had tried for the first time had been wild, but had left her throwing up most of the night. The next morning had been even worse, her head throbbing with an intensity she had never imagined. She had learned her lesson and eased back on the margaritas and mojitos. But this fog that filled her head was different. It felt like she was deep underwater, the pressure pushing at the back of her eyeballs. It hurt to blink.

Like a page being turned rapidly, a scene flashed into her memory. *Four friends at a roughly-hewn wooden table. The music thumping. Drinks with umbrellas and straws that curled into odd shapes. Four friends…*

The identity of the sleeping woman hit her like a slap in the face. "Gillian!" How could she not have recognised her best friend? What the hell was going on here?

Dropping to her knees at the side of her friend's bed, she

shook her vigorously. Gillian Cole's head lolled from side to side, her eyes flickering open for the briefest of seconds, then she lapsed into unconsciousness once more.

"Gillian, wake up. Wake up!"

Gillian's mouth opened, but only for her tongue to run once over her lower lip.

Celine shook her friend violently but failed to elicit any further response. Looking once more around the room she noticed another three forms huddled in the beds, all as still as Gillian. Moving as quickly as her unsteady legs would allow, Celine tried to wake the next person.

The girl in the bed had mocha-coloured skin and a close-cropped hairstyle. She too was unresponsive to Celine's efforts.

Celine bent at the waist as vomit forced its way from her mouth. Waves of panic swept through her. She stumbled to her knees as foul-smelling liquid splattered onto the floor. Tears streamed down her face as her body was racked with powerful heaves.

"They drugged us. Poisoned us," she whispered as the remnants of her stomach dribbled from her mouth. But who were "they"?

Staggering on unsteady legs, Celine made for the only door in the room. The handle turned a quarter-turn, but the door held fast. A heavy sob escaped from her chest. She had known it would be locked even before she had tried, yet the barrier added a tangible weight to her diaphragm. Gasping for breath, she pushed and pulled at the handle and when that proved fruitless, tried ramming her shoulder against the door.

Pain shot through her upper arm as she rebounded from the unyielding barrier. Celine staggered back, clutching her shoulder. Her legs seemed determined to conspire against her and again she found herself on the floor, her left knee bent painfully beneath her.

A surprised yelp caught in her throat as the door opened suddenly. A man filled the doorway. He was tall and heavily muscled, his hair so blond it looked bleached. He wore an expression of mild amusement.

"You're awake again, huh?"

Celine stared up at the man from the floor. "Where am I?"

The man gave only a sneer in response.

"Who are you? Where are the rest of my friends? What the hell do you want from us?" Each question was delivered with an increasing intensity.

But in answer the big man reached down and clamped Celine's arm in a vice-like grip, yanking her unceremoniously to her feet. His other hand closed around her throat. Dark spots whirled in her vision as the big man lifted her up. The arm that she wrestled with might as well be a steel girder. As she stared back at her captor, a vague sense of recognition flared inside her head. She'd seen this man before... but where? *His hands all over her... inside her?* Bile rose in her throat with the thought. *No.*

Before she could reach any definite recall, the man threw her back onto the floor. The air exploded from her lungs as she hit the ground.

"If you're going be trouble you won't last another day here." He sounded European, the way he flattened his vowels.

Coughing and fighting the urge to vomit again, Celine sat up as best she could. Darts of pain assailed her. The big man took a step forward, looming over her.

"Get back onto your bed and shut up. If you make me come back in here, you'll wish you'd never been born!"

Celine thought for the briefest of moments about trying to run past him but knew she would never make it. The guy just about filled the doorway and despite his size, moved as quick as any one she'd ever seen.

She trembled with fear as she held out a placatory hand. Celine received a glare that chilled her blood. The big man pointed a single finger at her bunk.

"Move!"

She limped back to her bed. As she lowered herself onto the firmness of the mattress she dared another look at the man. He had moved to one of the other girls in the room. With little care of causing injury, he opened her eyelids. *His rough hands*. Seemingly satisfied that she was still unconscious, he again pointed at Celine.

Words were unnecessary for the warning to be clear.

He closed the door behind him and Celine heard the distinctive *click* as a lock was engaged. The sound of despair.

Sitting on the bed, Celine scrutinised the room again. The ceiling was solid, no tiles or vents to be loosened or removed. The only window was a simple rectangle, the glass reinforced with a check-pattern of wire. She remembered seeing similar glass in some of the doors at the dance studio she attended a few years earlier.

Above the locked door, a small inverted dome caught her attention. She knew what it was the moment she saw it.

A camera.

Somebody was watching. *They* were watching.

16

As the Jeep bumped along the uneven road, Danny regarded his brother with an air of amusement. "You know, even I got a fright when you burst through that door, and I knew you were coming. Very nearly put streaks in my breeks. Stripping to the waist was a bit over the top, though."

Clay, now back in his shirt, returned a wry smile. He flexed the muscles of his right arm. "I thought it might add a dramatic flair, get their attention."

"Get their attention? They damn near shat tacos!"

Clay raised both palms along with an eyebrow. "Then I guess it worked."

Danny laughed. "Subtle as a sledgehammer, but yeah, it worked."

"There's a time for the stiletto and there's a time for the wreckin' ball. I didn't think the Pancho Villa fan club would appreciate my subtle side."

Danny made a show of looking behind his brother. "You mean you've got one?"

Glowering at his younger brother, Clay huffed, "Watch

it, doofus, or I'll knock the haggis right out of you."

"Nice, more subtlety. Who said that, Mother Teresa?"

Clay reduced his voice to a rasping whisper. "Steven Seagal. You're playing with the big boys now."

"Should I be concerned?"

"Not if you pass me one of those candies off the back seat."

Danny reached his hand into the grocery bag and retrieved a bar. "Butterfinger okay?"

"I never met a candy bar I didn't like."

"Yeah, I've noticed."

Clay held out his hand like a surgeon waiting for a scalpel. He accepted the candy bar and devoured it in three bites. Running the tip of his tongue across his lips he motioned for another.

As Clay began his second snack, Danny used the time to take in Clay's rugged profile.

"What?" asked Clay, without taking his eyes from the road.

Danny gave him an easy smile. "I know we're down here on serious business but it's good to be on the road with you again, big bro."

Clay nodded once in agreement.

"You know, we need to talk about worst-case scenarios before we happen upon one," said Danny. "I know there's a good chance of Celine and the other kids being alive and well, but we've got to consider the crap hand as well."

Clay's voice was like sleet on a tin roof. "If anyone has hurt a single hair on Celine's head I'll bury them and piss on their grave."

"I know, but we're deep in cartel territory down here. Even if it's not them we're up against, they'll probably want to hunt us down if we start levelling buildings and such. You know how the cartels do business; they kill people for looking at them the wrong way. If they get wind of a couple of white boys raisin' hell in their backyard, they'll definitely want to add our heads to the collection."

Clay flushed red, the lattice of scars on his face standing out in angry contrast. "I can't go home without her."

Danny placed a hand on Clay's shoulder. The muscles below felt like plate armour. "Don't worry, Clay, we'll find her and her friends." He didn't add, "If they're still alive." The unspoken words hung in the air between them.

"Jeez!" Clay slammed his foot hard on the brake pedal. Dust and gravel flew. Danny thrust out his hand against the windscreen to keep from being thrown forward against the glass. A dog had taken up residency in the middle of the road. It didn't seem bothered by the screech of brakes.

"What is it with the dogs around here? They all got a death wish?" asked Clay.

Danny puffed out his cheeks. "I'll move him. It may cost another packet of crisps, though."

"Put your foot in its ass and it'll move quick enough."

Danny ignored Clay's grouching. He knew Clay too was a sucker for a pooch and would never knowingly hurt one.

"No way!"

"What is it?" asked Clay, his head poking from the window.

"The dog. The dog from Chacchoben… I'm sure this is the same one."

"That's crazy. They all probably look the same down here," said Clay.

"Not unless they all have the same bullet holes in their

ears." The mutt gave him a look of recognition. Danny reached out and stroked the dog between the ears. Its skull felt like a coconut beneath his fingers. Looking around, he saw no evidence of the dog hitching a ride on the back of a truck. "How the hell did you get down here?"

The dog nuzzled his hand with a dust-encrusted nose.

"Here!"

Danny caught the packet of chips that Clay cast towards him like a circus knife-thrower. The dog responded to the lure of food, tottering after Danny on legs as thin as saplings.

"Now you stay off the road, little fella. The next car that comes along may just run right over the top of you and then you'd be dead tyred."

As Danny slid back into the passenger seat Clay gave him a sour look. "That's the last animal that gets any of my stash."

"Yeah, 'cos you've only got about fifty packets of crisps left back there. Don't want you starving to death in the next half-hour, that would be a real tragedy."

Danny watched the dust-covered dog in the rear-view mirror as they drove away. It turned a circle and flopped down at the side of the road. Soon it was little more than a dark splotch in the distance. "You get a chance to call home yet?"

Clay wiped sweat from his forehead with the back of his hand. "Yeah, I called Sebastian while you were talking to the folks in the grocery store. They're both terrified that their baby's not coming home. We can't let that happen."

"We won't." Danny looked at the scars on his brother's face. What would this job cost them? Would they add to the scars that they both already carried, or would it take a heavier toll?

17

Shadows played out like a puppet show above her head. The tent was big enough for half a dozen campers but Ghost sat alone, a gauze pad pressed to the seeping wound on her lower back. The pain was a low but annoying sting. The pain wasn't the problem. She knew better than to leave even a minor wound open and untreated. The Yucatán jungle was unforgiving. Once the hotels of the coastal resorts were out of sight, nature took over with a savage vengeance. It pushed ever forward, a legion of thickly leaved branches, creepers and tendrils. In the four weeks since she had set up camp the encroaching green canopy had started to take over. She would have a go at it with her machete tomorrow.

Her lips puckered as she removed the gauze from above her belt-line. A constellation of bloody spots dappled the fabric. The wound was little more than a deep scratch, but it stung like crazy as she dabbed it again with the Bactine-soaked pad. The bugs would find it irresistible if she left it untended. She didn't mean to get sick, unable to continue her path.

"Just a scratch. I've had worse," she told herself. "Must have caught it on the wall when that dickhead body-slammed me."

Outside, an animal emitted a harsh squawk. A spider monkey, maybe? *Don't see many of them anymore.*

Satisfied that the wound on her back had finally stopped seeping, she tore open a square packet and pressed the adhesive sterile pad to her skin.

A quick glance at the clear plastic jerrycan showed it still held about eight of its ten-litre capacity. She twisted the cap open and after plucking several foil packets from her backpack, added the water purification tablets to the tepid liquid. She tightened the cap of the drum and gave the whole thing a vigorous shake.

Now that her first aid and water duties had been taken care of, she lay back on her sleeping bag and thought about the day's events.

"Siddown, chile… tell your mama 'bout today's happenins." She smiled briefly as she heard her mother's sing-song voice. Memories of homemade gumbo and jambalaya made her stomach rumble. Mama had always been a bit heavy with the Tabasco but that was okay. *It gives a tingle on the tongue, not a kick in the pants.*

As she opened a packet of trail mix, Ghost licked her lips in memory of the fat fingers of okra, plump shrimp and rich red bell peppers. The dried mixture of nuts, granola and fruit tasted like flecks of cardboard as she recalled her time at home. That seemed so long ago, almost unreal, like a life she had watched in an old movie.

She turned on her side and gazed at the various deadly

items in her tent. Rope, knife, machete, pistol, Taser, shotgun and rifle all within arm's reach. Dried food, water, wind-up radio, backpack and her boots. All utilitarian items, so different to the things she had treasured in her previous life. She had nothing, now, without a purpose.

"And what's *your* purpose, you broke-ass bitch?" she asked herself. As often happened, the sound of her own voice surprised her.

Closing her right eye, she focused her attention on the small radio, its perforated case and folding handle. Allowing her vision to drift in and out of focus she confirmed what she already knew. She had pronounced blurred spots in her left eye. They weren't going away. They weren't getting any better. Were they getting worse? She wasn't sure. Would she go blind?

"You won't live long enough to go blind. Save your worries for something that matters a damn."

She picked up a compact from a small bag at the foot of her sleeping bag. The clamshell opened to reveal the circular mirror. The ruined features that stared back seemed to mock her in their severity.

"They thought you were dead. But you're not. Not yet." A tear rolled down the raised mesh of scars that was once flawless ebony skin. Discarding the mirror, she lay down and forced the tears back. "Too much left to do, but I won't stop. They'll have to kill me for real next time. Don't worry, Lauren, I'll take as many of them with me as I can."

Another extended squawk sounded through the canopy. "Yeah, spider monkey."

Ghost reached for the shotgun, a pump-action Remington.

She laid the weapon across her chest, hugging the blued barrel as a child would cuddle a soft toy. Sleep crept upon her like a thief in the night.

Outside, the spider monkey gave another vigorous hoot before falling silent.

18

The trees and foliage that encircled the bar loomed around the single-storey structure like a sentient beast from a Lovecraftian tale. Long curving branches pointed accusatory fingers as if in silent and sinister warning. Shades of dark emerald intermingled with dried leaves and fronds the colour of late summer straw. The area in front of the bar was bare earth, hard packed and spotted with chunks of weathered limestone. A pothole deep enough to break an axle in lay like a punji-trap for unwary drivers. No red cow offered a greeting at this bar, but the bass line of rock music that cut through the humid air with a steady *boom-boom-boom* told them this was the place.

Clay avoided the pothole and parked the Jeep to the left of the doorway. The door to the bar was open, wedged by a chunk of limestone that looked like anaemic coral.

"You want to play it the same as the last place?" asked Clay.

Danny stared at the open doorway. A faint tingle ran its way down the length of his spine. It was a feeling he had experienced many times previously, a feeling he knew better than to ignore. The men in this bar would be armed. Armed and more than willing to use their weapons. "I'll go in first, but we need to step lightly here. I think these boys will be bigger fish than the Red Cow brigade."

The scars on Clay's face crinkled as he grimaced. "I could just ram this Jeep through the wall and then we could speak to whoever is left standing."

Danny knew Clay was only half joking. He'd done the very same thing with an earthmover a while back, wrecking a Florida Keys mansion in the process. "Let's give diplomacy a shot. It's worth a try before we explore… other options."

Danny looked around what passed for the parking lot. He counted six vehicles. Four pickup trucks and two battered sedans. Three of the trucks were less than ten years old and looked to be in good condition. That said a lot. Probably meant they were never used as utility vehicles. In contrast, the rear of the fourth truck's tailgate was down and twenty or so fence posts and a loose coil of chicken wire were arranged neatly in the bed. All that remained of one tail light was a rusting hole and a protruding wire. Behind the farm truck stood two battered motorcycles. Both looked as if they had been assembled from junkyard spares.

The bar was twice the size of the Red Cow. A fading layer of whitewash coloured the cinder-block exterior. Above the door, the remains of a single bulb hung below a rusting shade. Blurred shapes moved behind the grimy window.

"Phones on." Danny gave a single nod then left the Jeep. The late-afternoon heat hit him like a slap. Taking a long breath in through his nose, he held it for a four-count then exhaled slowly through his mouth. He stepped inside.

The interior of the bar was bigger and better than the Red Cow. The walls were decorated with a wide assortment of motor memorabilia. Number plates from different countries were hung like pictures at various points on the walls. US, Mexican, British and even a few Japanese plates were displayed. In between the plates stood several recognisable decals. Chrysler, Mercedes, Rolls Royce, Daimler and Fiat on one side, with Suzuki, Triumph, Honda, Kawasaki and Harley-Davidson behind the bar.

The steady bass line filled the room. The rock music was modern, and Danny found himself nodding along to the frenetic rhythm of guitar and drums. Ignoring the undisguised looks of hostility from the dozen or so men, he moved to a free stool at the bar.

The barman stared back at Danny impassively, his pockmarked face giving nothing away.

"*Una Modelo cerveza, por favor,*" said Danny.

After long seconds of consideration, the barman replied in English. "No Modelo here. We got Sol, Dos Equis or Tecate."

"I'll take a Tecate then, please."

"You want a glass?"

"Nah, the bottle's fine."

Danny had barely taken the first gulp of the pale lager when three men surrounded him. The man at Danny's right shoulder poked him with a stiffened finger.

"No, I'm not lost, and no, I'm not a *tourista,*" said Danny as he turned to face them.

The man who had jabbed Danny stood silent for a moment, his mouth open as his opening gambit was stolen.

Danny fixed the man in the centre of the trio with a steady gaze, unblinking. The subtle energy inside the room shifted to one of expectation. He took stock of the other men in the bar: three immediately within arm's reach; four at a table to his left, a geometric pattern of dominoes laid out on their table. Another two sat behind them at a table with an overflowing ashtray as a centrepiece. At the far end of the bar, six men sat around a longer rectangular table.

Fifteen men. Sixteen, if you included the barman. A lot of variables.

Danny smiled and pointed to the table of dominoes. "Hey, I haven't played doms for ages. You guys like to gamble?"

The men exchanged glances.

"You like to gamble?" asked Danny again, this time adding a little more enthusiasm to his voice.

The man in front of Danny raised his chin, his curiosity piqued. "What you got in mind?"

"What's your name?" asked Danny, as he gave another friendly smile. "What do these guys call you?"

The man hesitated for a moment then answered. "Benito."

"Pleased to meet ya, Benito." Danny extended his hand. "John Douglas."

After scrutinising the newcomer for long seconds, Benito shook his hand.

"Who's the fastest guy in here?"

The look of suspicion was still evident on Benito's face. "What you mean, fastest?"

"Like, who's got the fastest reflexes," said Danny.

Benito looked at the men at the domino table but offered no name.

Danny fished a five-peso coin from his pocket. The centre of the distinctive coin was coloured gold while the outer ring was silver. Danny held the coin in the palm of his hand. "I bet I can snatch this coin out of any man's hand in this room."

The neatly trimmed line of black hair on Benito's top lip curled into a misshapen glyph. "I've played this game before... when I was a child."

Ignoring Benito's sarcasm, Danny continued, "I'll bet you fifty dollars that I can do it three times in a row."

"With any man in the bar?"

"With anyone you choose."

Benito nodded to one of the men at the domino table. "Robert."

The men in the bar formed a loose circle with Benito, Danny and Robert in the centre. Several of the men pulled rolls of notes from their pockets, rapidly chattering as they agreed side bets.

"Robert?" asked Danny.

The young man looked Danny up and down, seemingly unimpressed. "We're not all called Miguel, you know."

Danny returned a tight-lipped smile. "Hold out your hand."

Robert stood immobile, hands on his hips. The only things that moved were his eyes as he regarded his challenger with overt suspicion.

"Come on, man, hold out your hand. I bet I can snatch this coin three times in a row before you can close your hand." Danny held out the coin and waited. "Fifty bucks to you if I can't."

A muscle in Robert's jaw twitched once as he looked to

Benito. A curt nod from Benito and the young man slowly extended his right hand. Danny placed the coin in the centre of his upturned palm.

"You look like you work out. Good arms. How old are you? Twenty? Twenty-five?"

As Robert's mouth opened to answer, Danny shot his left hand forward and took the coin. "That's once."

"No fair, man, I wasn't ready." Robert's voice carried an angry edge.

Danny gave a short laugh. "Okay, just checking you were awake."

Robert took back the coin. This time he moved his feet a little wider than the width of his shoulders and lowered his weight as he readied himself. Slowly he extended his hand inch by inch. "Not 'til I say I'm ready."

Bets were made and accepted in haste from the onlookers.

"You call it," Danny looked at Benito. "He looks like Quick Draw McGraw."

"Ready!"

"*Estás listo?*"

"I said I was read—"

Danny took the coin, his left hand a blur.

Robert clenched his fists as a ripple of laughter broke from the spectators. More than one fistful of crumpled notes was exchanged.

"You're too close."

Danny held out the coin, which Robert reached for. "That's two."

"Do it from further back," said Robert through clenched teeth. A single bead of sweat trickled down the side of his face.

Benito looked between the two men then flicked his fingers as if shooing Danny away. "Take a step back."

"Hey, man, that wasn't the deal," said Danny. Three of Benito's friends edged towards him.

"Do it," said Benito. "It wasn't a request."

Danny took a step back on his left heel.

Robert raised his outstretched hand, coin in the centre of his palm.

Danny inhaled slowly, the fingers of his left hand wiggling like seagrass.

Robert scrutinised his face with a new intensity.

Danny's left hand twitched but it was his right that struck out like a cobra, snatching the coin free.

"*Mierda!*" spat Robert.

Danny flicked the coin high into the air with the tip of his thumb then caught it in a single fluid motion. "Wanna go again, double or nothing?"

Benito spat a gobbet of saliva at Danny's feet. "I have a different game for you. It's called 'give me all of your money or I shoot you in the face'."

Danny allowed a curious smile to creep onto his face. "Shoot me? With what?"

As Benito reached behind his back with his right hand, Danny performed three actions almost simultaneously.

One: He cupped Benito's left elbow and pulled him forward, causing him to stagger.

Two: He slipped behind Benito and snatched the weapon from his waistband.

Three: He looped an arm around the Mexican's throat and pressed the revolver against the side of his head.

As the other men went for their guns, Danny yanked Benito backwards so no one in the room had a clear line of sight.

"Easy, guys!" said Danny. "I didn't come in here looking for trouble."

"Well, you sure as shit found it, *pendejo*," said Robert.

"Put your weapons on the floor and kick them towards the door."

None of the men moved to comply. A bottle tumbled to the floor. Danny glanced at the weapon that he held pressed against the side of Benito's skull. "This is a nice piece. Ruger revolver, six shots, single action."

He rapped the barrel against the side of Benito's head, just hard enough for effect. The sound was loud and ominous in the sudden silence of the bar. "Put your weapons down nice and easy and kick them over there. Do it or Mr Mussolini here gets the first one in the brain pan."

Benito spewed a series of curses and commands in Spanish. After a couple of seconds, the two men with the pistols placed them on the floor. Both looked like standard Glocks.

"Kick them over to the door."

The men glared at Danny with undisguised venom but did as ordered.

"And now the knives," said Danny. The barrel of the Ruger never wavered from Benito's head. "Come on, get on with it."

A collection of hunting knives and a couple of switchblades joined the surrendered pistols.

Danny twisted Benito to the left and stared at the barman. "Knock the music off."

The barman complied, the bar falling into silence. "You

got anything tucked away under the counter I should know about?"

The barman's face contorted as he replied in the negative.

"You sure? If I come over there and find a weapon, you'll be getting the second bullet."

The barman shuffled from foot to foot momentarily then reached slowly beneath the bar.

"Go easy!" warned Danny. The barrel of the Ruger stretched the skin at Benito's temple.

The baseball bat the barman retrieved was an old-fashioned Louisville Slugger. The dark stains on the business end told of more than one head-bashing. He tossed it over the bar, where it clattered against the floor.

"Alrighty, then," said Danny. "Now that I have your attention, we're gonna sit down like grown-ups and I'm gonna ask a few questions. If you play nice you'll all still make it home for your five o'clock burritos. Now, sit your arses down. You too, Babe Ruth."

The barman skulked around the end of the counter and joined the rest of the men. Danny pushed Benito into a seat of his own, placing him with his back to the rest of his gang. Only when he was satisfied that he could see all the men in the bar did Danny sit down opposite the leader.

"I'm looking for a girl that went missing down here a week or so ago. Her name is Celine Chavez. She would have been travelling with three other kids. Two more women and a young man. All from the States."

Danny held up the picture of Celine.

"Never seen her before," said Benito with a voice devoid of emotion.

"Take a closer look!"

Benito stared at Danny for long seconds, his gaze alternating between the Scotsman's weathered face and the Ruger that was now pointed at his chest. "They didn't come in here."

"Okay, so they didn't come in here. Did any of you see them at all? Any of you?"

Benito ran his hand across the side of his face. The men behind him all remained silent. "We have nothing to do with the kids going missing."

Danny gave the smallest of nods. "I believe you, but I also believe that a bunch of rough arses like you must know what's going on in your own backyard."

Benito fidgeted in his seat. He again ran his hand across his face. "We hear the stories like everyone else. Nothing to do with us, though."

"Who takes them?" asked Danny.

The shrug given by Benito sent sparks of anger through the Scotsman.

"You shrug again and I'll shoot one of those idiots behind you in the kneecap!" Danny aimed the Ruger at Robert's leg. "Who takes the people that disappear?"

Benito closed his eyes for long seconds. A loud rumbling outside interrupted his answer. A large motorcycle was approaching.

"You expecting anyone else?" asked Danny.

"Guys come and go. I don't keep a leash on all of them." Benito began another shrug but stopped himself.

"Keep sitting as you are with your hands on the tables." Danny's tone held no room for negotiation.

The engine idled for a moment then fell silent. Seconds later, a loud cracking sound followed. Danny smiled briefly. He knew what had occurred.

Clay entered the bar with an unconscious body tucked under his left arm. A large purple bruise had already begun to swell on the left side of the man's face. "Ding dong, Avon calling."

Danny smiled as Benito looked up at the new arrival, his mouth agape. "Chollo…"

Chollo's unconscious body was dumped without ceremony onto the floor next to Danny's seat.

"Gatecrasher," said Clay. The big Texan dropped to one knee and scooped up the two pistols. "Finders keepers."

Danny tapped the butt of the Ruger twice against the tabletop. "Now, you were about to tell me what happens to the kids."

Benito made fists then visibly relaxed as he began to talk again. "It doesn't happen very often. The ones who disappear are usually in ones or twos. It's rare that a group of four goes missing."

"So, who takes them and where do they go?"

"I only know what I've heard. Not saying it's the truth," said Benito.

"Just tell me what you know."

"There's a place south of here, deep in the jungle, some kind of compound. I've heard that it is these men that take the kids."

"Compound? Like a military base?" asked Danny.

"No, not military and not cartel."

"If you say '*el Diablo*', I'll kick your arse."

Benito smiled bitterly. "No, not *el Diablo*. Some kind of cult. I've heard that they take the kids and convert them into believers."

Danny exchanged a brief look with Clay. "Believers in what?"

Despite the earlier warning, Benito gave another impassioned shrug. "I dunno, man, cult shit."

Danny gritted his teeth. "Do you know where this compound is?"

"No. Again, only stories."

"And what do the stories say?"

"That about fifty miles from here is a camp, the compound. The kids go into this compound and are never seen again. There is a small town nearby called Chios. Men from the compound sometimes show up in the town. Bad men. Gringos."

"Chios?" Danny pulled his cell phone from his pocket and loaded the map app. "Show me where."

"I don't think Chios is on any map. It's more of a... shanty town. It hasn't been there for very long, maybe only ten years or so."

"So how will I find it?" asked Danny.

"There is a Mayan site a few miles away. It has half a mile of white road. An ancient Mayan road has been found there with its surface still intact. I think it is around there somewhere. The town takes its name from the site."

"So, it's not Chacchoben?"

"No. Chacchoben is only a few miles that way." Benito hooked a thumb over his shoulder.

"I was told that Celine and her friends may have been

heading to the Chacchoben ruins. Could they have been taken from there?"

"*Sí*. There are a lot of quiet roads down here. Lots of opportunities to make someone disappear."

"How about I make *you* disappear?" asked Clay.

Benito flinched as the menace in Clay's voice carried across the bar.

"Show me on my phone where you think Chios might be," said Danny.

The rest of the bar remained still, the men unmoving as Benito nervously scrolled his way through the map. Finally, he looked up at Danny, pointing to the screen. "Around there somewhere, I think."

Danny tapped the screen and a small flag marked the indicated point. He regarded Benito with intensity. "Do you have anything else to tell me? Anything else that may be useful?"

"I don't think so."

"Okay, then." Danny lifted the Ruger level with Benito's forehead. "I'll be taking this."

Benito dipped his chin once but said nothing.

"Let's keep this little afternoon chit-chat between us. If I hear otherwise, I'll come back and put holes in all your precious parts. Understand?"

"*Sí*, I understand."

Danny clicked the hammer of the Ruger back to its resting position. "It would be in your best interests to sit quiet and not move for at least five minutes after we've gone."

19

Celine sat on the edge of the bed she had been told was hers. The other women in the room were stirring. How many hours had passed since the big guy with the hair had roughed her up? She wasn't sure.

On the adjacent bed, Gillian Cole opened her eyes.

Celine scooted over to the side of her friend's bed. "Gillian. Thank God you're awake."

Gillian blinked rapidly and began rubbing her face with both hands. She lurched drunkenly upright, then immediately flopped back onto the bed. "Uh, I think I'm going to be sick."

"Here, sit up," said Celine as she supported her friend's shoulders. "Take deep breaths if you can."

Gillian coughed and retched several times but brought up little more than a thin stream of saliva. "Can I have some water?"

"There isn't any in here."

Gillian looked at her friend then looked around the room, her eyes still glassy and unfocused. "Where the hell are we?"

A fearful tremor ran through Celine. Her voice was

little more than a whisper. "I think we've been abducted. Kidnapped."

"What?" A brief unbelieving smile crossed Gillian's face, but quickly abated. "What in hell? Who the hell has kidnapped us?"

"I don't know who they are. I've only seen one man, a big white-haired freak, he nearly choked me to death when I tried to get out of the door."

"Are Marco and Laura here as well?"

Celine shook her head as tears began again to run down her face. "I don't know. I haven't seen them. I've only been awake a little while... I don't know how long. My head is all mixed up. Everything is a blur. I think they must have drugged us. I don't even know how long we've been here."

Gillian pointed to the other two women who had begun to stir. "Who are they?"

Feeling helpless, Celine could do little more than shrug apologetically. "I don't know, but I think they're in the same crappy boat as we are."

"They drugged us," said Gillian, as her friend's words finally registered with her. "How did we end up here? What's the last thing you remember?"

"I've been trying to figure that out myself. My memories are jumbled. I remember being at the hotel and I remember the four of us setting off for the pyramids in the rental, but after that it's all mixed up. Just odd flashes really."

"Yeah. Marco wanted to see some ruins that hadn't been properly explored..." Gillian's brow furrowed.

Celine nodded. "Yeah, that's right. Marco. Marco and...?"

"Laura!"

"Marco and Laura. Gillian and Celine. Just the four of us. Right?"

"Yeah, just the four of us. Do you remember getting to the ruins? I think I remember looking down into a giant sinkhole," said Gillian.

"A cenote." Celine nodded again as her friend's words caused her own memories to surface slowly like bubbles in warm tar. "That's right. We stopped near the ruins, couldn't get any further with the car."

"We met someone on the path?" Gillian looked for confirmation.

"Yes." Both young women stared at each other as they tried to recall more details. Celine looked at the two other women on the adjacent beds, but they failed to spark any fresh recollections.

Gillian clenched her hands into fists. "It was a couple. Remember? The guy was tall and skinny, looked kind of goofy. His girlfriend was a lot shorter than him."

"She had her hair in cornrows. Coloured beads in the ends," added Celine. "A white girl with cornrows, I remember that now. We talked to them for quite a while. It was the guy who told us about the cenote."

"Yeah and we all drank water from the cenote. The goofy guy went down and filled his canteen, remember. He told us it was the purest water on earth."

"The canteen!" exclaimed Celine as logic filled another small part of the puzzle.

"Oh crap, the canteen must have been spiked," said Gillian. She cupped her face in her hands. "Did he even get the water from the pool?"

"I can't remember. I think we were too busy talking to Little Miss Cornrows. How could we be so stupid?"

"What the hell do they want with us?"

"They'll probably try to ransom us back to our parents."

"Kidnapped. Holy shit."

"I don't know how long we were out of it. Could have been hours," said Celine. "I read about date rape drugs a few months back. The bastards probably doped us with Rohypnol or GHB... I can't remember how long the drugs last. Shit, I suppose it depends on how much you were given."

Gillian clasped both of Celine's hands and pulled her close. A deep sob escaped her chest as she hugged her tight.

"I know, I'm scared too," said Celine.

"It's not just that."

"What then?" asked Celine.

"I think we've been here longer than a few hours."

"What do you mean?"

Gillian pointed to her legs. "I shaved my legs on the morning we set off for the ruins. Now look at them. That's about a week's growth."

Celine recoiled as if she'd been slapped. "A week? No way! We would be sick as dogs without any food or water."

"Well, I feel like death warmed up and you look like crap as well," said Gillian. "I could have eaten and not remember."

"I know, but a week?"

"Hey, maybe you're right. I'm so mixed up. My head feels like I'm deep underwater. Even when you're talking to me your voice sounds funny, kind of echoey, like you're talking down a tube or something. My eyes hurt too."

"That's the drugs; they must still be in our systems,

messing us up." Celine held up her hand and touched her thumb to each of her fingers in turn. "I feel kinda numb. Same in my feet. Like pins and needles."

"I feel like I've just come off a rollercoaster. My stomach is doing loop-the-loops. My head's not much better."

"Yeah," agreed Celine. "I felt like that when I first woke up. Thankfully it passes."

On the bed opposite Celine's, the girl with the mocha skin rolled onto her side. Her eyes opened but remained unfocused. Both women, Gillian clinging to Celine for support, moved to the side of the black woman's bed.

Celine squatted down, moving close enough to whisper in the stranger's ear. "Hey, do you know where we are?"

She opened her mouth but voiced no answer.

"Hey," Celine shook her by the shoulders, gently at first, then more vigorously. "Hey! Wake up. What's your name? Do you know where we are? Hey! Hey!"

The young woman pushed feebly against Celine's chest. Twisting to one side, she flopped back down onto the bed. Her eyes closed.

"Let her be," said Gillian.

"I want answers," said Celine, her face flushing red.

"I do too, but she's still out of it. We'll try again later." Gillian moved to the window and pressed her palms against the metal frame, inspecting the criss-cross wire. "Shit."

"I tried to open the door as well but some scary freak with white hair stopped me... hurt me. Did I tell you that already?" said Celine.

"I think so." Gillian stepped towards the door. "I'm going to try anyway."

Celine held up a hand in warning. "Wait."

"We have to get out of here; find Marco and Laura."

The short walk between the window and the door was interrupted as the fourth woman began to twitch and buck erratically on her bed. Within seconds, her arms and legs began to thrash back and forth in short and violent jerks.

Taken aback, Gillian stepped back in surprise. "What's wrong with her?"

Celine stared at the convulsing woman in horror. She'd seen people having fits on television but never in real life. "I don't know. Epilepsy?"

She was deathly pale. Thick foamy vomit filled her open mouth and ran down the sides of her face. The veins on the side of her throat bulged.

"Turn her on her side!" yelled Celine as she moved forward to help.

The woman coughed once, one final hollow whoop. Her eyes were instantly devoid of life.

"My God! She's dead."

"She was sound asleep ten seconds ago, and now she's dead. Jesus Christ, what's happening here?" Celine's voice was strained with renewed fear.

"We've got to get the hell out of here!"

"We need to be careful!" Celine pointed to the small inverted dome on the ceiling. "I think they're watching us."

Gillian extended her middle finger to the camera in defiance. "We've got to try. Come on."

Both women jumped in surprise as the door was flung open. The man with the white hair stared at them with undisguised pleasure. "It's time."

20

"Mexico sucks!" declared Clay.

"No, trying to find an unnamed set of ruins that isn't on the map sucks."

"Yeah, well, for now all of Mexico sucks."

"At least we're one step closer to finding Celine and the others, and now we've got some basic kit," said Danny as he examined the procured weapons. The two matt-black pistols were identical: Glock 17s. Older models, but in good condition, and loaded with full magazines. Seventeen rounds in each.

Clay hunched over the steering wheel. "We don't even know if they work properly. Only one clip each, so we can hardly go plinking tin cans now, can we."

"Pull over."

"Why?"

"Just do it, ya big ape," said Danny.

Before the Jeep had fully stopped moving, Danny sprang from the vehicle. With a Glock in each hand he sighted upon the trunk of a tree some twenty feet away. The pistol in his left hand fired. A triangular sliver of tree bark spun into the air. The pistol in his right hand spat a single bullet. Another chunk of bark sprang from the tree an inch from the first.

"There, they both work." Danny climbed back into the vehicle. He gave Clay a double thumbs-up to add to his irritation. "You want me to test the Ruger as well? We're in the middle of nowhere with no one to hear it."

"Not much can go wrong with a revolver. I'll save those six shots for someone who deserves them."

"We just have to find the bastards first."

"Sooner the better. I just hope she's okay. I have to get her home safe."

"I know, big bro. We will. If I was lost, I couldn't hope for anyone better to come looking for me than you. Sebastian and Salma know that, too."

"Oh man, you didn't see their faces. The look in their eyes was horrible. I've never seen anyone look as bad. You know how happy-go-lucky they both are, Salma was like *The*-friggin'-*Exorcist*, she was so upset. And Seb just looked so… ashamed."

Danny nodded. "At least he didn't come charging down here, and then not be able to bring Celine home once he'd found her. He did right waiting for you."

"I'm not sure they were waiting for me. I just happened to turn up at the right time. I think they were just going around in circles trying to get information from the authorities down here."

"Hey, take this next turn on the right. I think this may be the road we need. This should take us towards Chios."

"You call that a road?" asked Clay. The gap in the trees was barely wide enough to steer the Jeep into. Leafy branches scraped along the roof and sides of the vehicle as they entered the dark green portal. The light dimmed almost immediately as the jungle threatened to envelop them.

Clay braked and pointed at the road ahead. "It just keeps getting better and better."

A fallen tree spanned the width of the narrow road.

"I'll go check it out." Clay reached for the Ruger. "You watch my back just in case this is a trap."

Danny nodded and picked one of the Glocks from the side of his seat. It was an old highwayman ruse that had been around since the days of the horse and carriage. The bandits would block the road and when the occupants of the vehicle began to move the obstruction, they would find themselves staring down the business end of a musket.

The trees and foliage formed a thick green curtain on each side of the road, plenty of cover for a would-be highwayman to spring from. The waning daylight cut interspersing daggers through the thick canopy. Danny pressed himself against the side of the Jeep. He scanned the trees, his eyes moving slowly from shadow to shadow, searching for any sign of danger as Clay moved to inspect the tree.

Tucking the revolver into his waistband, the big Texan squatted at the upper branches of the tree. He struggled to find a grip that provided the required leverage, one of the branches snapping off in his hand, but after a few false starts managed to drag the fifteen-foot length of timber to the side of the road.

"I was half expecting a bunch of desperados to come charging out from the treeline," said Clay as he climbed back into the Jeep.

Danny gazed at the surrounding trees for another few seconds, then joined Clay back inside the vehicle. "Nothing would surprise me. But I guess trees do just fall down sometimes."

Clay resumed his usual driving position, hunched over the wheel with his head thrust forward. "You sure we're headin' in the right direction?"

"As far as I can tell. We need to keep following this track until we get to Chios. This is the only road that Benito could point to on the map."

"But Chios ain't on the map," said Clay.

"No, but if a shanty town was out here they would still need a road to get in and out, right?"

Clay frowned, the scars on the side of his face crinkling. "I guess. It's gonna be dark soon. Better get a bit of a tailwind going."

"Just don't crash into any trees on the way."

21

Ghost settled comfortably into the dead leaves. The serpentine roots of a towering kapok tree provided her with a natural camouflage. Dressed in a black jumpsuit with a ghillie camouflage net draped over her head and shoulders, she lay flat on her front, indistinguishable, just another curve of the tree. Only her eyes moved as she surveyed the network of buildings some two hundred feet in front of her.

It had taken over half an hour to cover less than twenty feet. Slowly, ever so slowly, she'd inched into her chosen position, pushing her rifle ahead. She was almost sure that no one was looking up from the supposed safety of the compound below, but one mistake might mean death. The early evening light was beginning to turn to orange as the sun dipped towards the horizon. The elongating shadows would only help her remain unseen.

A high chain-link fence encircled the camp. She had on previous nights worked her way around the entire barrier, seeking a viable point of entry. None had presented itself. The fence was well constructed and kept clear of encroaching plant life. The fence could be easily scaled. There was no barbed wire to deal with, and it wasn't electric. But storming the castle was not an option. One woman against all the men inside? Unacceptable odds.

Studying the layout of the compound, she focused first on the squat two-storey building directly in front of her, a picture of utilitarian blandness; all of it painted a dull green. A single door sat at the centre of the ground floor. Either side of the door, small rectangular windows peered back like the eyes of a disapproving parent. The windows of the upper floor were slightly larger than those below but showed no decoration. A series of smaller structures formed a loose horseshoe around the main building, linked to it by walkways. At the back was a wide shed that housed the pigs. Those God-awful pigs.

Ghost remained motionless, breathing into the ghillie net. She knew it was a waiting game, that it was too risky to attempt to take the fight inside the compound. No, she would continue as she had over the previous weeks. She would wait until a lone target presented itself, then she would follow unseen and strike them down at the most opportune moment.

"You know patience be a virtue, chile." The breath caught in her throat as she realised that she had spoken out loud again. *I need to be more careful!* This time the words stayed firmly inside her head.

The rifle propped on her right shoulder, a battered Marlin 336, was also wrapped in a layer of ghillie cloth. The ultra-lightweight netting was decorated with a scattering of leaves. She had stolen the weapon from the cab of an unlocked truck several weeks earlier.

A door in one of the buildings swung open and a lanky man in faded denim stepped into view. He shaded his eyes as he walked to a panel truck. He slid the side door open and took out a large cardboard box.

Ghost flexed her hands. Shooting him with the rifle would be a short-lived victory. She was saving the rifle for the leader of the group. One shot would do the job. One shot, righteous and true.

She inhaled slowly. The mixed aroma of tree, ground and her own slightly pungent sweat was now very familiar to her senses.

As she had many times previously, she willed her elusive enemy to step out into open view. "Come on, you bastard. Where are you?"

The man made a second trip to the van. He retrieved another box and carried it inside the building as he had the first.

"I can see the trained monkeys, but where's the damned ringmaster?" she whispered. If he would only step out into the light. "Put a bullet right through your heart. Let's see if you still look as smug when it's *your* blood pumping out into the sand."

A harsh squawk like a rusty nail being prised from seasoned wood cut through the canopy. The man at the van looked out into the darkening treeline. He paused, setting another box back into the van.

Ghost's hand crept inch by inch towards the rifle. The man walked to the front of the panel truck. Cupping both hands around his eyes, he stared unmoving at the trees.

Put a hole in him, chile.

"Shhhh." She increased the pressure on her trigger finger, feeling the mechanism. If the man moved to raise the alarm his death would be instant. She could feel the steady rhythm of her heart beating, thumping inside her chest. "Don't make me kill you. Go back to work. Go back to work."

The man moved his right hand inside his jacket. She slowed her breathing again.

Her index finger fluttered, the tension on the trigger at the maximum.

Her target pulled a pack of cigarettes from his pocket and sparked a lighter. The flame served to illuminate his face for a brief second as he puffed the cigarette into life, blowing a cloud of blue smoke into the air.

Ghost relaxed her finger, the trigger moving back a fraction of an inch to its resting position. She watched the man finish his smoke, cast it aside in a small shower of orange sparks and again pick up the box. He closed the sliding door of the van by bumping it with his butt. The door of the building slammed closed behind him.

Ghost settled back into watching the main house. Patience was the key. "Come on, asshole. Show yourself."

22

"Well, that's just great," said Clay. "No more road. What's the point of having a road that just stops in the middle of nowhere without warning?"

Danny shared an exasperated look with his brother. The two faint ruts in the ground that formed the meagre path they had been following terminated in a circular clearing. The heavy foliage reflected the light from the Jeep's headlights in a dozen shades of green. The clearing was barely big enough to allow a mid-sized vehicle like the Jeep to turn around. Gnarled roots and branches pointed accusingly at the brothers.

Danny looked up as he stretched the muscles in his arms and shoulders. The sky was darkening rapidly. "Looks like we're camping here for the night. We'll set out again in the morning, when the light is on our side."

Clay turned off the engine, stepped from the Jeep and glared silently at the trees.

"I can see by your face that you're not happy about this, but if we get lost out here at night we could end up on the wrong side of Crapsville."

"And we're not lost as it is?" asked Clay.

"Not lost, just assessing." Danny dropped to one knee and rubbed some of the red earth between his fingers. The soil in the small clearing looked more like hard-packed terracotta than regular dirt. "Not much chance of getting tent pegs into the ground. I think we need to string a couple of guy lines between these trees."

Clay stood with his arms crossed over the wide expanse of his chest.

"Hey, you just stand there and glower, I'll set up camp. I'm sure there will be a T-rex by for you to wrestle with later."

Danny rummaged through the contents of the trunk.

"You bought pop-up tents? That makes life a lot easier." Danny moved with graceful ease between the trees at the edge of the clearing, carrying two tent bags, each the size of a large trashcan lid. With a couple of shakes, a tent sprang open and assumed its shape with a dull *pop*. Despite his earlier misgivings, he managed to hammer home several pegs into the hard-packed earth at the corners. Danny held up a handful of the pegs and began to shake as if having a seizure.

"What the hell are you up to?" asked Clay in a gruff voice.

"I'm on tent-a-hooks!"

"Dumbass!"

"Hey, be careful, you almost smiled there, big bro."

Clay gave a despondent shrug. "I thought we would have made better progress than this. I feel annoyed with myself. Salma and Sebastian will be sitting at home worrying themselves sick."

"We've been through this. They know that you'll do

anything to bring their little girl home to them."

"I know that but—"

"Clay, we've been here less than a day." Danny's voice took on a firmness he was unaccustomed to using with his brother. "We're making steady progress. We've already done more than the cops have in a week. We'll get some shut-eye and start out fresh at first light. We're in the right neck of the woods, at least."

"I just keep thinking about what could be happening to Celine right now, as we sit down to toast friggin' marshmallows for supper. What may have already happened to her."

"Tell you what, why don't you get a fire going while I finish setting up this other tent? I could murder a cup of coffee about now." Danny raised an eyebrow. "You did buy some coffee, right?"

"Best in the whole damned store," grumbled Clay.

"Well, we're in the middle of a jungle, there's bound to be a lot of dead wood lying around for the picking, can you get busy with that? I'll gather the kindling from the edge of the clearing."

Clay found the large bowie knife in the rear of the Jeep. He unsheathed the blade and left the scabbard lying on the hood of the vehicle. The corners of his mouth curled briefly. "I think I brought enough dead wood with me."

"Just get on with it, ya big ape. Oh, and if you need something to carry the wood in, just use your hat. You should fit about a two-day supply in there."

"Just get on with the tents or I'll stick this up your ass and toast you like a hot dog."

"Wow, prophetic or pathetic... I can't decide." Danny shook the second tent from its circular packaging. He smiled as the tent popped into its preformed shape. "Hey, I went to see the doctor the other day. He asked what was wrong with me. I said, 'One day I feel like a tepee and the next I feel like a wigwam.' 'That's it,' he said, 'you're two tents!'"

Clay shook his head and pointed with his blade. "I'll get the firewood."

"Too tense... get it?"

Clay was already gone. The wall of green foliage shook where he had pushed through.

Danny finished securing the second tent. The surrounding trees provided a natural windbreak so there was little chance of the tents blowing over in the night. Satisfied, he began to unload a selection of foodstuffs and unpacked a mess kit.

As Danny read the labels on the cans, he started to sing. "Beans, beans, the musical fruit. The more you eat, the more you toot."

"Who are you speaking to?"

Danny pivoted into a fighting crouch, his open hands forming blades in front of his face. The grey-haired man that stood before him stared back impassively.

"Where the hell did you come from?" demanded Danny.

"Well, I was born near Chetumal, but I've been over here for quite some time now."

Danny was annoyed at himself at letting the man get so close. He appeared unarmed save for a small knife on his hip. If he had wanted to do harm, he could have been upon Danny with little or no warning.

"You here by yourself?" asked Danny.

The old man held his arms out to his sides then looked around himself in an exaggerated slow circle. "I believe I am alone. Were you expecting someone else?"

"I wasn't expecting anyone at all. We're in the middle of nowhere," said Danny. He let his hands drop, feeling a little self-conscious squaring up to a man in his seventies. "You live out here?"

"I do."

"Nearby?"

"Close enough to walk to on tired legs."

"Chios?"

"Close to Chios, but far enough away so they don't bother me with their noise." The old man looked with interest at the items Danny had unloaded from the Jeep. "Oh, and you're saying it wrong. You should make the 'o' longer. Chi-*oos*."

Danny beckoned him forward. "You must know everything about the people around here... the people in Chios."

He smiled as Danny corrected his pronunciation. His eyes twinkled with a boyish mischief as he answered, tapping a finger to the side of his head. "I know lots more about those people than I care to know, but there's no way to un-know something once it's in there."

"I guess not." Danny extended his hand in greeting. "Danny Gunn. What's your name?"

The old man took another step closer and shook his hand. His fingers were as dry and tough as kindling sticks. "My name is Semeel Jak Shanarani."

"Your name sounds more Asian than Mexican."

"That's because most Mexican names are from Spanish.

Mine is from the old tongue. It means 'Forest Walker' or 'Walker in the Woods'."

"Very apt, I'd say."

"Apt?"

"I mean it suits you."

"Thank you. You can call me Jak. Most do."

Danny pointed at the tinned food at his feet. "You eaten supper yet, Jak?"

"Not so much that I couldn't try whatever you have there."

"Nothing exciting, I'm afraid, just some chilli and beans and stuff. My brother's out there somewhere gathering wood for a fire."

Jak hooked a thumb over his left shoulder. "He's fifty yards that way."

Danny looked in the same direction, but the encroaching trees blocked any hope of spotting his brother.

"You can't hear him huffing and puffing out there? He sounds like he's in a bad mood."

"He's okay. Just to warn you, when he gets back he looks big and scary but he's my brother and won't do you any harm."

Jak's face was the colour of weak coffee, deeply tanned and leathery. When he smiled the lines on his face were so deep you could wedge a penny in them. He flexed the ropey muscles in his arms. "Maybe you should warn *him* about *me*."

Danny smiled, warming to the stranger. "Maybe I will, at that."

Jak folded down into a cross-legged position with a fluidity that belied his years. "So why are you and your big and scary brother so far out at nightfall? You get yourselves lost?"

"Not exactly lost. We're looking for some kids that went missing out here. We think they might have been looking for the Chios ruins, and got themselves into trouble and couldn't get back. Or they may have been taken."

Jak flexed his hands, the knuckles bony and callused. The skin on his hands was a shade darker than the rest of his body. He took a pack of cigarettes from the pocket of his threadbare cotton shirt and offered one to Danny.

"Thanks, but no. They've never been my thing."

Jak shrugged in acceptance as he lit his cigarette with a small disposable lighter. He studied Danny with hooded eyes. "The missing kids are yours?"

"One of the girls is as good as family. Her folks live with my brother in Texas. She came down to Cancún on vacation with three of her friends. They never came home."

"I think I know who took your girl."

23

Clay arrived back at the makeshift camp with an armful of fallen wood and broken branches. He looked first at the ancient Mexican, then his brother. "I leave you for five minutes and already you've taken in a lodger."

Danny finished spooning a second can of beans into the cooking pot before he answered. "This is Jak. He lives close to Chios. He's got some very interesting information. Oh, and he's joining us for supper."

Clay dropped the large bundle of wood in front of the Jeep and clapped his hands together to shake off the worst of the detritus from the branches. He looked Jak up and down then extended his hand. "Clay Gunn."

Jak straightened up from his cross-legged position and accepted Clay's greeting. "Semeel Jak Shanarani, but you can call me Jak. When you say that you are brothers…?"

Clay smiled; they had been through this conversation countless times before. "Yes, we are full brothers. I take after Dad's side; Danny is more like Mom's."

"You speak with very different accents," observed Jak.

"Our parents spent as much time separated as they did together. It wasn't exactly the most straightforward of marriages, that's for sure," Danny explained. "I spent most of my time in Scotland with my mother's family. Clay grew up more with Dad and his family in Texas."

"You up to speed with the potted history of the Clan Gunn now?" asked Clay.

Jak nodded. "Families can be complicated. It is good that you are together as grown men."

"It is," agreed Clay.

"I knew someone like you would come. It was only a matter of time," said Jak. He licked his lips as he gave a none-too-subtle look at the pan full of beans. "Are you going to get that fire going?"

"As we speak," said Danny, arranging the kindling and dried leaves into a small pyramid. He sparked his lighter and touched the flame to the leaves, blowing gently at the base until the fire sprang to life. Danny then began to add slightly larger pieces of wood, building the fire slowly but surely. "Tell Clay what you told me."

Jak took another long look at the pot of food before speaking. "I think I know who took your girl."

"Celine. Her name is Celine Chavez," said Clay. He stared at the old man with impatient eyes. "So, what do you know?"

"There is a place, a camp. The men who live there are bad news. They are like the coyote; they prey on the weak. They don't take too many, not enough to get themselves noticed, not enough to cause any big news."

"They took my Celine and her friends. Believe me,

they've gotten themselves noticed." Clay's voice was like gravel on a tin roof.

Jak looked at Danny. "You're right. He is a *little* scary."

"So where is this camp?" asked Clay.

Jak nodded in the direction of the setting sun. "It's about ten miles that way. You can get there by road, but not this way. You would need to go all the way back to the main road south of Chacchoben and keep following it south, go all the way around on the 307. Then take the 186, then the road to El Progresso back north and look for the road from there. I'm not sure which road leads in, so you would need to work through each one in turn."

"And end up on some back road just like this one?" said Clay, his voice tinged heavily with impatience. "Mexico sucks."

"Maybe." Jak offered a noncommittal shrug. "It'll be an unmarked road like most around here. If you took the wrong one you would be no further forward."

"Have you seen the camp yourself, with your own two eyes?" asked Clay. "I'd be really pissed if we spend a day going round in circles looking for a camp that turns out to be a rumour."

Jak pulled his attention from the pot of food that had begun to simmer gently over the small campfire. "It's real. I've seen it with my own two eyes."

"And you know how to get there on foot from here?" asked Danny as he gently stirred the food.

"I know the way," said Jak.

"Can you lead us there in the morning? Will you help us find Celine?" asked Clay.

Jak studied the brothers for long seconds, his eyes roving in silent appraisal. "I will help you."

Danny spooned a generous helping of the canned chilli and beans onto a tin plate. He passed it to Jak, who accepted it with outstretched hands. "Eat up. You look like you could stand to put on a few pounds."

Jak nodded in agreement. "I love my food. I'll try anything, but it doesn't seem to stick to my ribs."

"For an old guy who lives out in the middle of the big green, you talk a bit like a Brit. Not your accent, but some of the phrases that you use are things we used to say back home in Scotland. Like food sticking to your ribs."

"I'm a man of many layers," replied Jak. "I had a friend from Britain, an entomologist. He came to study the butterflies and bugs of the Yucatán. We were friends for many years. I learned most of my English from him."

Clay topped up the fire with another couple of branches before beginning his own meal. He sat with his legs outstretched. "Tell us some more about the compound. Who runs it? How many men?"

Jak blinked slowly. "I'm sorry, I don't know much about them, no names or numbers. They keep to themselves. They do have a steady stream of visitors to the camp."

"Do the men at the camp look like soldiers or cartel?" asked Clay. "Do they carry a lot of guns?"

Jak frowned in recollection. "I've only seen them a few times but no, they just look like ordinary people. They don't wave guns around like the street gangs. But I know they are bad men. The looks on their faces tell all. They all look like cats watching fish in a bowl."

"What about the camp itself? What does that look like?" asked Danny. "Take your time, try to remember as much as you can."

"I happened across it by accident. I was out looking for wood to carve—I make walking sticks and things to sell—when I came across the camp." Jak traced a circle in the air with his right hand. "It's surrounded by a fence. There's a big double gate at the front, chain-link like the fence. There's a big house at the centre with smaller buildings out the back, a horseshoe shape."

"Are there any watchtowers or sentries posted at the fence or gates?" asked Clay.

Jak shook his head. "No. Last time I was there I only saw a couple of men. They were carrying a young woman on a stretcher from the back of a van into one of the buildings behind the house."

"What about cameras? Did you notice if they had any CCTV?" asked Danny as he finished his food.

"I can't remember seeing any, but I wasn't looking for them, so I can't say either way."

Clay looked at Jak, the scars on his face crinkling. "Did you report the thing with the woman on the stretcher to the cops?"

"You come from America; things are different there. Here, most of the police are only interested if it serves their own agenda. They are all after their *mordidas*, their 'little bites'."

"Bribes," said Danny. "They want paid extra to do their own jobs, or to look the other way. We call them 'bent coppers' in the UK."

"We call them normal cops in Mexico," replied Jak.

24

Celine's heart sank as a second man appeared behind the white-haired thug. He was a foot shorter than his companion and much wider. His arms and shoulders, both in bulk and definition, told of many dedicated hours spent in the gym. The man's tanned skin was decorated profusely with intricate tattoos. Tribal art blended with strange esoteric symbols, visible on his arms, shoulders and upper chest. Celine fought a shiver. Were either of these men responsible for the pain between her legs? What had they done to her while she was unconscious? She forced back the bile that rose again in the back of her throat.

The white-haired freak strode forward and pressed two fingers to the side of the dead woman's throat.

"She gone?" asked the man with the tattoos.

He received a single nod by way of an answer.

"Hogs are eatin' white meat tonight." Tattoo smiled. His accent was distinctive—he was from the States. "What about her?" he asked. He tilted his head at the recumbent woman.

The blond man moved to the side of her bed and checked

her pulse. Using his thumb, he peeled back her eyelid. The woman stirred briefly but remained unresponsive. "She's alive but still well under."

"Who the hell are you?" demanded Gillian, her chin thrust forward. Celine reached for her friend's arm.

Tattoo looked her up and down before answering. "We're your new best friends."

"Come on, it's time for you to move. Time to meet the boss."

Gillian pointed a finger at the white-haired man. "You better let us go right fucking now. We're from the States! My father works for the state attorney in Texas. If you let us go right now, maybe you won't spend the rest of your lives in a cell."

Tattoo stood silent for a moment, legs apart, hands on his hips. Then he emitted a short barking laugh. "Where the hell do you think you are? Beverly Hills? You shut your mouth and do exactly as you're told, or you'll end up with the pigs like that one."

Gillian flinched as if she'd been slapped. The venom in the man's voice suggested this was no idle threat.

The white-haired man glared at the two friends. "Enough of this shit. Time to move. The boss wants to look at you. Oh, and if you try any crap like trying to run, I'll break your legs. You'll spend the rest of your days chained naked to that bed."

Celine and Gillian exchanged a subtle look. Both knew each would be on the lookout for any opportunity of escape.

Celine held up a placatory hand. "Okay, we're coming. Will we be able to see our friends?"

Tattoo frowned momentarily. "Friends?"

"Marco and Laura," said Celine. "Are they here? They were with us... before."

"Enough. I ask the questions. Get moving." The white-haired man stepped into the hallway.

Celine and Gillian were jostled into motion by Tattoo. "Follow him."

There was no chance of fighting the two brutes. Celine hung her head and stepped through the door into a narrow, windowless hallway that smelled of disinfectant. There were several doors, all securely closed. The hallway terminated at a steel door.

The white-haired man glanced up at another dome set into the low ceiling. After a few seconds of waiting, the lock disengaged with a metallic *snick*. As the door opened another stretch of enclosed hallway was visible. The corridor again ran straight, with no visible windows. Another single door lay at the far end of the walkway.

"Where you taking us? Who is your boss?" asked Celine as she was ushered through by her captors. When nobody answered, she began again, "Where you taking—?"

Tattoo reached forward and clamped his fingers tight onto the muscle at the side of her neck. An involuntary squeal of pain escaped her lips.

"Quiet!" Tattoo released the hold and shoved her forward.

The door, steel-plated like the previous one, was equipped with a simple intercom unit. White-Hair pressed the red button at the base of the console. "Open up."

With an identical metallic *snick* to the previous door, it swung open.

"What the hell?" Celine pulled Gillian close. The area beyond provided a sharp contrast to the white utilitarian decor of the holding room and prison-like passageways. The door opened into a wide lobby. Paintings framed in an eclectic mix of gold and chrome decorated the pastel-blue walls. Portraits of unfamiliar historical figures, most with high collars and stern faces, hung next to landscapes, which hung next to abstract cubist works in gaudy splashes of colour. The floor tiles were a mosaic, a spiralling cosmos. Randomly coloured tiles added to the celestial design. In front of a set of double doors at the far side of the room stood a silent sentry.

"Keep moving." Tattoo pushed them into the lobby. The door clicked shut behind them.

The sunburnt sentry scrutinised the party as they approached, his gaze lingering on the two young women. As the party drew close, he opened the nearest of the two doors for them.

Celine looked into the next room with trepidation. A soft red light illuminated it, providing a sinister aspect. "I don't want to go in there."

Gillian's face was stark but she remained silent. She clutched Celine's arm.

Tattoo thrust his knuckles into Gillian's back at a point between her shoulders. The blow was little more than a jab, but it served its purpose. Gillian lurched forward into the room, taking Celine with her.

The walls and floor were coloured red by the light. An intense but unfamiliar aroma filled the air. Wisps of serpentine smoke turned lazily before them.

At the centre of the room sat a solitary figure, chin resting on his knuckles. One leg was thrown carelessly over the side of his plush throne-like seat. The polished leather of his calf-length boots shone scarlet in the light. His dark brown hair was cut short and his goatee was comprised of carefully sculptured pencil-thin lines of hair. He gave a shark-like grin as the women stumbled into the room.

Gillian thrust out her chin. "What is this place? It looks like some cheap-ass vampire movie." She focused on the man at the centre of it. "Who the hell do you think you are? You better let us go right now or you're in a world of trouble, mister!"

The man gave a single contemptuous flick with his finger. Tattoo stepped forward and slapped Gillian hard in the face, so that she fell back.

"Plenty more where that came from if you open your piehole before you're told to."

"Please don't hurt her!" yelled Celine as she huddled over her injured friend. "We just want to go home."

"You want to go home?" The man on the seat flashed another grin. "This is home, now." He beckoned them. Helping Gillian to her feet, Celine tried to support some of her friend's weight as they walked towards the chair.

"Welcome, my pretty little things. Tell me your names." The man sounded almost paternal. "It's alright. You may speak. No one *wants* to hurt you here."

"Where are we?" asked Celine. "Who are you people? Why are we here?"

"My, oh my, three questions. Which should I answer first?"

Celine pulled Gillian close to support her weight more

comfortably. "Why are you keeping us here?"

"Before I answer your questions, your names..."

"I'm Celine Chavez. This is Gillian Cole. We were with another two friends, Marco Kenner and Laura Troutman. Are they here as well?"

The man ignored Celine's question. "You are safe here. Safe from the evils of the world. Safe from all the corruption and dirt and worry. We are a family here. Everyone plays their part. You must now play yours, my pretty little things."

"We don't want to be here. A woman just died in front of us. We just want to go home and be with our families again," said Celine. Tattoo moved within arm's reach with a single stealthy step. Celine gave him a wary glance but continued. "Please! Just let us go home."

"But my little Celine, I've already told you, we are a family here."

"We just want to go home!"

"If I let *you* leave, my little Celine, what will become of your dearest Gillian? Personally, I would like to see no harm come to her, but I can't speak for the rest of the members of our family. Some of the men have been known to lapse into base savagery, not something I condone, but..."

"What do you want from us?" asked Celine, pulling her friend closer. "We have a little money we can give you."

"What money? Show me."

Celine's eyes darted from side to side in realisation. "I don't know where my purse is, but I can get some money. If we could call home, our families would send some to you."

"Your families, they are super-rich, yes?" The man raised his chin in mock expectation. "Is Papa Chavez a CEO with deep pockets? Does Mr Cole have mega-shares in Microsoft?"

Celine struggled to swallow, her words like pebbles in her mouth. "My father is a gardener, my mother a housekeeper."

The man laughed out loud. "Ah, of course they are, modern Mexicans living the American dream right there. How the Chavez family has flourished. Cut the grass, clean the pool, cook the dinner. You must be very proud."

"Just let me call them. Please."

"And what about you, Missy Cole? What delights do the Cole family bank accounts hold? What do your parents do to earn their way in the world?"

Celine squeezed her friend's arm, knowing that Tattoo was in easy striking range. Gillian said, "Dad works at a car dealership."

"So not a power player for the state attorney after all. And Mommy dearest?"

"Mom's a homemaker."

"Homemaker? Ha!"

"Don't you laugh at my mom, you son of a bitch!" Gillian clenched her fists. Celine exerted a steady pressure on her arm.

"Save your energy, pretty thing. You may just find you like it here." The man uncoiled himself from the seat. "Come, walk with me. I'm sure you are curious to see the house?"

"I don't want to see the house. I want to go home." Celine took an involuntary step backwards as her tormentor moved close enough to kiss her.

"Please come with me. That's the last time I ask nicely." Despite showing his perfect white teeth in a grin more befitting a television evangelist, the menace in his voice was unmistakable.

They were ushered into yet another contrasting room. The lighting was provided by a series of utilitarian standing lamps. A young woman with short red hair sat behind a wooden office desk. A collection of debit and credit cards was arranged to one side of the laptop at which she worked. A single folding chair was on the other side of the desk.

The woman looked up, a smile forming instantly as she looked at the leader. After a second or two she turned her gaze to the two women. Using one finger, she moved the closest of the credit cards to the edge of the desk. "Gillian Cole?"

The silence hung in the room like cigarette smoke.

The redhead seemed to be enjoying the moment. "Gillian, sit down and take a breath."

Tattoo shoved Gillian into the seat.

"You need to give me your PIN numbers and your online banking details and passwords. You too, Celine."

Gillian shook her head in disbelief. "You're from the States?"

"You look surprised." The redhead smiled again. "Michelle Getty. Detroit born and bred. Now... PIN numbers and online usernames and passwords."

"You're robbing us?"

Michelle tapped the edge of the credit card against the table. "No, you're helping fund our sanctuary. Think of it as a charitable contribution to a very worthy cause. Please don't make me ask again. PIN numbers and online usernames and passwords."

White-Hair gave a low growl by way of a warning. Celine and Gillian flinched like scolded children. Gillian gave the required details with a tremor in her voice.

Michelle flicked a finger at Celine. "Now you. Same again."

Celine gave up the information without a fight. Michelle tapped at the keyboard with practised ease. After a few meagre seconds, she looked up to the leader and gave a satisfied nod. "I can access both bank accounts."

Running his thumb and forefinger over the neat lines of his goatee, the leader returned the redhead's smile. "Efficient as always, Michelle."

"Thank you, Master Ezeret."

Gillian leaned close to Celine. "So the asshole has a name."

Master Ezeret looked past the two captives and raised his chin in a subtle motion. "Take Celine back to her room."

"What's going on?" asked Celine, her arms snaking around Gillian's waist.

Ezeret smiled. "Nothing to worry about, my pretty little thing. I merely want to introduce Gillian to some of the more established members of our group."

"Why can't we meet them together?"

"I can tell by the fear and suspicion in your voice that you are worried, but why would I attempt to deceive you? If I wished you harm, I would do you harm, right here and now." Ezeret spread his hands and evinced another smile. "It's late and the moon is high. Time for you to rest. She'll be back with you in your quarters in no time."

White-Hair reached out and took hold of Celine by the back of her neck. "Move. Now."

"I'll be alright," said Gillian, her voice barely above a whisper. The look in her eyes told a very different story. The brief words of reassurance did not prevent Celine's heart racing as the two friends were separated.

25

The rising sun burned through the canopy with bright daggers of light. The three men had broken camp before dawn. After a quick breakfast of coffee and granola bars, they'd loaded the tents and camping equipment back into the Jeep. The brothers carried only the most essential kit on their persons. Moving with a steady gait, the old man led the way. Danny followed with Clay a few steps behind. Using a trick they had learned from their father, the brothers spoke in turn of any points of interest as they passed.

"Tree with no leaves," said Danny.

A minute later Clay added, "Rock shaped like a popsicle."

Jak cast more than one curious glance at the brothers as they spoke. After a while, he paused. "You're marking your way back to your vehicle."

Danny nodded. "We may not have you to lead us back again. We've been moving steadily south-west from the Jeep. We just might have to double-time it back again if things go tits-up."

"I like the way you talk," said Jak. "You sound like the

school caretaker from *The Simpsons*."

"That's just great, I meet a random Mexican Indian in the middle of the jungle and he compares me to Grounds-keeper Willie."

Clay nudged Danny with his elbow as he drew level. "Do your Sean Connery, that'll impress him no end."

"I love Sean Connery. He was my favourite James Bond," said Jak as he looked back over his shoulder.

"Well, Jak Shanarani, you're a shite for shore eyes."

Clay barked with laughter. Jak raised one eyebrow but said nothing. After a couple of seconds, he resumed his pathfinder duties. Danny regarded him with growing admiration. The old man never faltered as he picked his way through the thick vegetation. At various points the path transformed from wide and easy flattened ground to natural tangles of roots and branches. Jak navigated around the thicker copses with ease.

"You boys ever seen a cenote before?" asked Jak, pausing at the rim of a wide circular chasm.

"Aye, we both have, but they're still damned impressive to look at," answered Danny. The nearly perfect circle of the sinkhole was bordered on all sides by intrusive emerald shrubs with thick spears of fern-leafed branches. The edge of the weathered limestone was smooth and gave way to a sheer thirty-foot drop. The water within the base of the cenote was of a blue so dark it looked unreal. Long ropey tendrils, erratically dotted with small leaves, stretched from overhanging branches all the way down to the surface of the water.

Jak stared into the natural well for a minute before speaking again. "You know how they are formed?"

"I do," said Danny. "The limestone is worn away over thousands of years from below by underground rivers. Eventually the rock gives way and drops into the chasm, and forms the sinkhole."

Jak rewarded him with a lopsided smile. "Looks like someone paid attention at school."

"Sadly, that's not true. I hated school. Most of what I know is self-taught from books or the TV."

"Or he just makes it up," added Clay.

Jak gave another brief, uneven smile. "No one really knows how far the waterways run but there are hundreds of cenotes spread out in every direction. Cave divers have explored a lot of them now, but there are still hundreds of miles of tunnels down there."

"The subterranean world." Danny picked a small piece of limestone free from the edge of the cenote and tossed it underhand into the water below. The dark blue water swallowed the stone without a sound. "Is it true the ancient Mayans used them for human sacrifice?"

"Well I'm no historian, but I think they have found bones at the bottom of more than a few. Some gold and jewellery too. I suppose they had to put the bodies somewhere after they cut out their hearts on the top of the pyramids. Pretty hard to dig graves when the ground is mostly limestone."

"It would be easy to fall into one of those if you were wandering around out here at night," said Clay.

Jak gave a single slow nod. "Most locals know where they are and are careful around them, but every now and again someone takes the short way down. Sometimes they manage to climb out, sometimes not."

"I was in one years ago. It had stairs carved into the rock and lights strung up on the walls," said Danny. "I think that was over near Chichen Itza."

"Yeah, they have opened a few up and made them safe for the tourists," said Jak, with a tone that suggested disapproval.

Clay gave another glance at the sinkhole, then said, "We're burning daylight here. Time to move."

Without another word, Jak pointed along the narrow path they had been following and then moved on. His pace quickened and the brothers followed his lead.

"Whoa!" Danny stopped suddenly. A set of majestic stone steps towered above him, rising out of the thick vegetation. Tree roots thicker than his leg traced the path of the stone steps like monstrous green veins. A wide crack marred the lower steps. The face of a carved serpent peered out from the foliage.

"There are many pyramids around here that the jungle has taken back," said Jak dismissively.

Danny shared a look with Clay.

For the next few hours they travelled at a steady clip. All three men lapsed into a mutually comfortable silence, only broken by Clay's and Danny's logging of natural reference points. Jak's feet brushed the ground as he walked with slightly bowed legs, hardly bending at the knees as he moved.

Danny glanced at his wristwatch. "We must be getting close to the compound now. We've been on the move for three and a half hours."

"About another fifteen minutes." Jak took another couple of steps then turned slowly, his nose held high as if smelling the air. "That way."

Danny followed the line of Jak's outstretched hand. He could see only more of the same, gnarled tree trunks and invasive branches and sprouting vines. A low stone wall poked out of giant tree roots.

"Can you smell it?" asked Jak.

Danny adjusted his backpack to allow a moment's relief from the heat that had built up between his skin and the fabric. "Smell what?"

"Smoke and people smells."

"People smells?"

Jak nodded. "People smells. Smoke, food, garbage, cars... people smells."

Danny sniffed the air. "I can't smell anything except jungle."

"You have your skills, Mr Gunn. I have mine." Jak gave a dismissive shrug.

Clay caught up, still chewing a strip of beef jerky that had been occupying his jaw for the previous five minutes. "We gettin' close?"

Danny pointed in the direction Jak had indicated. "Fifteen minutes out. We need to go silent from here on."

"Not a problem. The next voice I want to hear is Celine's."

"When we get to the camp we'll scope it out properly. We need to know what we're dealing with," said Danny. "Figure out how best to go at them... *if* Celine and her friends are in there. This may need to be clinical, not hot and heavy with the boomstick."

Clay's voice matched the cold look in his eyes. "We haven't got enough ammo for that anyhow."

"Let's hope we don't need a lot, then."

Jak looked between the two brothers. "This challenge will not be decided with bullets alone. It will be decided by the spirit of the jaguar."

The scars on the left side of Clay's face crinkled as a sullen frown began to form. "Let's keep moving. Every moment we waste means another moment Celine may be in danger."

Jak held up a placatory hand. "Wait a moment, Clay. Take some water. You'll need it once you enter the testing grounds."

"The what?"

Jak sat on a small outcrop of gnarled tree roots and sipped some water from a flask before continuing. "This has all happened before, and in time will happen again."

"Quit speaking in riddles, old man." Clay's voice carried the first tinge of anger.

"You think I just happened upon you two by chance?"

Danny and Clay exchanged a brief glance.

Jak took another sip of water. "I knew you would come. I dreamed about it. I knew where you would be and when you would be there."

"So now you're a psychic Mayan medicine man?" said Clay. "We don't have time for this."

Jak continued to sit as if Clay had not spoken. "There are many stories about two warrior brothers who fought battles against the evils of the world, the hero twins. One brother was a fast and cunning warrior, wily and skilled with many weapons. The other brother was skilled with the blowgun. He was bigger than his brother and bore many battle scars over his face and body." Jak cast a slow but deliberate eye over the lattice of white lines that creased Clay's skin.

"We both have more than our fair share of scars," Danny said.

"The hero twins fought many battles, many trials and challenges. They were both warriors, both skilled ball players too, as many true Mayan heroes were. They fought against the lords of the underworld. The brothers passed through many tests and trials, faced many deadly tasks."

Danny rubbed the back of his hand across his chin. "Kind of like Castor and Pollux from Greek mythology."

"I do not know the Greek myths," said Jak. "In some versions of the story the twins were sometimes helped by an old sage and the spirit of a dead princess."

"And what, you think that we're the hero twins reincarnated?" scoffed Clay. "Horseshit. I've had enough of these campfire stories. Celine may be in a world of hurt and we're shooting the shit about old stories."

Jak regarded Clay with rheumy eyes, then stood up and began to lead the way again. "We will see what we will see."

"You believe any of that hooey he just spouted?" asked Clay, hanging back so that Jak couldn't hear.

Danny gave a shrug. "I've heard stranger stories in my time. You have too."

"If he thinks we are the hero twins reborn, you do realise that he thinks he is the wise old sage, here to guide us?"

"Aye, I kind of got that," said Danny.

"And?"

"Probably hooey, like you said."

"He'll be selling us bottles of snake oil before we know it," said Clay.

Danny smiled at his brother. "Anyway, you can't be the

blowgunner twin reborn. You can't shoot for shit."

"Dumbass."

"Still, we both were warriors—well, soldiers, anyway. And ball players too. You were a so-so quarterback for a while in high school and I was a damned nifty striker back in the army team."

"I don't think soccer and high-school football is what he meant," said Clay as he followed the old man. "And there was nothing so-so about my football sk—"

He stopped talking suddenly as Jak raised a hand. They were approaching the camp.

26

Celine sat on the edge of her bed, her head in her hands. The dead woman was gone, only a foul-coloured stain on her bedsheet to show she'd been there at all.

"I still can't believe this is really happening. It's like a nightmare." Celine looked at the black woman, who was now fully awake and sat perched on the end of her own bed. She'd introduced herself as Rebecca Dale. She was also from the US.

"Did you meet the leader?" asked Rebecca.

Celine nodded. "Master Ezeret. He scared me. The way he looks at you. He smiles, but his eyes are weird, like he's trying to hypnotise you or something."

Rebecca puffed out her cheeks. "That man is like the Devil. He doesn't do much of the dirty work himself, but his little mind-warped minions are always scuttling around, desperate to please him."

Celine wiped away the tears that traced their way down her face. "How long have they kept you here?"

"Truth is, I don't really know. Maybe a year."

"A year?" Celine's voice was high and shrill.

"I'm not sure exactly how long, though." Rebecca glanced from side to side. "Every once in a while, they slip you a dose of the essence and you're gone again. When you wake up you might have lost a few hours or a day or a week. It really screws with your brain. Your memory gets so scrambled, you can't tell what was real or if you just dreamed it."

"How many guards do they have?" asked Celine.

"I'm not sure, I don't think I've seen more than nine or ten, but like I say, they keep spiking us so it's hard to keep track of anything."

"You called it 'the essence'?"

Rebecca sneered. "Oh, that's what they sometimes call it, like it's some kind of joke. I heard one of the men, the big one with the white hair, also call it 'Devil's breath'. I think they're both the same thing."

"Has anyone managed to escape?" asked Celine.

"I don't think so, but I'm not sure. When my head is clearer I sometimes remember different faces that I've seen. Different people come and go. I don't think they get to leave."

"So where do they go?" asked Celine, a knot forming again in her stomach. "What happens to them?"

Rebecca closed her eyes, but not before tears escaped down her face.

"Rebecca, talk to me. What happens to them? What's going to happen to us?"

When she answered, her voice was low and suddenly devoid of emotion. "People come to the camp, mostly older men. They take us under the main house."

"Under the house? Then what? What happens under the house, Rebecca?"

"Bad things, horrible things."

"Tell me!"

"Sometimes it's the guards, Ezeret's followers. Other times it's the visitors. Sometimes it's both. I think men pay to come here to do things…" Rebecca turned her head as if she was going to vomit.

Celine clenched the edge of the bed to stop her hands shaking. "What happens under the house?"

"Bad things. They call them *the games*."

A twinge from between her legs. Celine bit the inside of her mouth, tasting blood. "Sex games?"

"Sometimes. Those aren't the worst."

Grim realisation swept over Celine as her mind considered all the depraved acts that visiting men might pay for. Depraved men who would travel to a place like this. To a place that held kidnapped victims in secure sheds. Her stomach bucked wildly. "What else?"

Rebecca shot up from her bed and began pacing back and forth. "I only remember flashes."

"Tell me."

"I remember… fights."

"What kind of fights?"

"I remember the sound of screaming."

"Jesus."

"I remember blood, lots and lots of blood."

Celine stood and pulled Rebecca close. "We've got to get out of here."

"The worst thing of all is the… audience. The men laugh and cheer like they're at some damned football game or something." Rebecca sank back onto the bed again. "At least when they drug me I don't remember that laughing for a while. It's the cruellest sound I've ever heard."

"Jesus Christ, that's horrible. Like something out of a horror movie."

"Then after the fights, it's our turn. Even with all the drugs, I remember what happens after the fights." The haunted look on Rebecca's face said enough.

Celine's head snapped towards the door. "Oh no. They took Gillian. What if they took her under the house?"

Rebecca said nothing, her head lowered.

27

Ghost awoke in the same prone sniper position she had fallen asleep in. Her cheek rested upon the stock of the Marlin rifle. The hunter's ghillie net clung momentarily to her face like a second skin. She blinked several times, trying to make sense of her surroundings. Then she remembered. The leader of the compound had failed to present himself as a target again.

"Another day gone. Another day I failed you, Lauren." Ghost scowled, disappointed in herself as she had been many times before.

Mayhap today be the day, chile?

"Be quiet. No noise. You know the rules."

Mayhap today be the day when you catch a bullet in the head?

"Shut up," whispered Ghost.

Mayhap today be the day when they catch you like a rat in a trap and take you back in there.

"No! I won't let that happen."

Mayhap today be the day that they gang rape your worthless black ass and leave you dead for real this time?

Ghost pressed her forehead into the roots of the tree. Unchecked tears ran down her face. "No."

Who's goin' to save you, huh?

"I'll save myself."

You didn't save Lauren…

A deep sob racked her body. "No, I didn't save Lauren."

She lay motionless, for how long she had no recollection. Then she blinked and her mind came back. The compound was as quiet as a graveyard. She propped the Marlin against a tree root, the barrel of the rifle still pointing at the main house. Moving at a snail's pace, she pulled a narrow plastic bottle from a pocket on her right leg. The water it contained was tepid but welcome as she slaked her waking thirst. She chewed on a granola bar, her gaze never straying far from the house. She ate a second bar. Then, with a soft curse, she began to inch backwards. It took five minutes, but finally she was satisfied that she was fully out of view of the compound. She took care of her insistent bladder.

She had her trousers half-zipped when she felt eyes on her. Her hand flew to her pistol, but when she looked around all she saw was a dog. Her voice was a whisper. "Damn it, dog, you just nearly got a bullet between the eyes. Where in hell did you come from?"

The dog stared back at her.

"Jeez, you look like you've been in the wars, too."

The mangy canine had little fur left on its body. A long, ragged scar decorated one side of its body, and what looked like an old gunshot wound had left a neat hole punched through one of its ears.

"Go on, now. Get along. Scat."

The dog stared back without moving an inch. Ghost flicked her fingers several times. "Scat!"

She cast a wary glance over her shoulder. The compound remained quiet. Squatting, she picked up a small stone. The dog stared back as she feigned a throwing action. "Get along."

The bedraggled canine turned its head, looking away from her.

With a huff of annoyance, she pelted the dog on the rump with the pebble. "Beat it, you've no business here."

Despite the blow, the dog stared directly at her again. Then, slowly, it turned on bony legs and lifted its muzzle as if sniffing the air.

She tightened her jaw. There, a hundred yards or so away, at least three men were moving through the trees. Moving slow and silent. Moving like hunters, like killers. Her hand moved to her pistol again as she crouched at the side of the tree. Her eyes flicked from the approaching men to the mutt.

The dog was gone.

28

Danny moved diagonally, not fully crouching but stepping with care, scanning the ground ahead for twigs or branches that might snap underfoot and betray their approach. Clay followed in Danny's footprints.

Ahead of them, Jak pointed twice at a cluster of rocks. He sat down as Danny drew level. Jak's voice was barely above a whisper. "The camp is straight ahead. You can't miss it."

"You waitin' here?" asked Clay, looming over him.

Jak gave a little smile. "I have guided the warriors to the gateway. It is up to the brothers themselves whether they enter the underworld and are victorious in the challenges ahead."

"So, you're waitin' here, then?"

Danny leaned on the rock next to Jak. "We owe you one. You saved us a lot of time yomping around the jungle. We need to get close to the camp now, decide the best way to go in."

"Good luck. I hope you find the kids you're looking for. The underworld can be a treacherous place. Nothing is as it seems. Trust your hearts and be true to your cause."

"We're hardly gonna stop off for ice cream on the way," grunted Clay.

"The hero twins of old faced trials of fire, water, combat and cunning. You must be ready for anything if you are both to succeed."

Danny patted Jak on the shoulder. "Fire-water, combat and cunning. You just described a Gunn family wedding. Sleep easy, Jak, it's the yahoos in that camp that are in for a rude awakening. Clay and I will be taking Celine and her friends home. That's what we came to do, and we're not leaving without her."

Jak gave a single nod. "I will find you both again before you leave."

Danny returned the nod then began silently picking his way towards the camp. Clay followed close behind.

After ten seconds, Danny glanced back over his shoulder. Jak was already gone.

Moving with practised stealth, both brothers dropped to a crouch at the side of a wide tangle of tree roots. Ahead, the terrain sloped downward to reveal the camp. As Jak had told them, a chain-link fence formed the perimeter, and beyond that they could see the buildings that made up the complex.

Danny shifted his weight to one side as Clay slowly pointed his blade to the left of the house. Clay's voice was a whisper. "Looks like a goddamned prison yard. My money's on those buildings on the left. You see how those blocks are linked to each other? You could walk a prisoner from one end to the other without them seeing the light of day."

"I see them," replied Danny.

"So whaddya think?"

"We've no way of knowing how many men are keeping them captive, how many we'd be up against. I think we go in on stealth mode, then bring the boom hard and fast if we need to."

"If they've hurt Celine…"

"Don't worry, big bro, there'll be time for payback later. Let's focus on finding out if she's there. Then get her and her friends out in one piece. That's our primary objective."

Clay nodded.

"You hunker down here while I circle the camp. I just want to see if there's an easy way in. No good kicking in the front door if the back door's been left open."

"Roger that." Clay reached for his walkie-talkie. "Comms on. Give me two minutes to scan, see if I pick up any chatter."

Danny remained motionless as Clay worked his way through the full twenty-two channels on the handset. All remained silent.

"Go. We're back on channel three."

Danny left his backpack propped against the tree next to Clay. Adopting an almost simian crouch, he moved from tree to tree using the tangled roots and foliage as natural cover. It took a full seventy minutes before he again dropped to one knee next to Clay.

"No anti-personnel measures at the fence, no spikes, razor wire or electrics. At the rear of the house there's a full-size generator, so we can take out their power easy enough. Also, there's a big open pen back there too. They've got about a dozen pigs, big ones. Ugly bastards."

"What about breaching? I'd be happy to kick down the front door if there's no risk to Celine."

"I'd give good odds that if she's here, she's locked inside one of those huts. I'm sure you're right: that's a prison block. That needs to be our first target. We break in as quiet as we can, find Celine and her friends, and get them out alive. Depending on how things go, we can boost one of those vehicles to the side of the house and burn some rubber back to the real world."

"Well, I'm ready to go," said Clay through clenched teeth.

"Clay…"

"She's in there. I can feel it. If the goddamned cops in this backwater country had done their jobs, they could have found this place as quick as we did."

Danny hoped that they would indeed find Celine alive inside. His right hand touched the Glock 17 tucked into his waistband, snug at the small of his back. The second pistol weighed heavy in his thigh cargo pocket. Shooting even a single round would rouse the whole camp. He drew his knife from his hip pocket, pushing on the small thumb stud so that the blade opened silently.

He'd taken only a couple of steps towards the camp when three men emerged from the front of the house. Danny dropped to one knee again and knew Clay had done the same without looking back. Two of the men carried crossbows, while another hefted a hunting rifle fitted with a scope. None of them looked Mexican. The tallest had stark white hair. The other two were smaller, one with a shaved head, the other thickset and covered in tattoos. The man with the white hair said something into a radio handset and moments later the door to the "prison huts" opened. Another two men stepped into the sunlight, a young woman held between them.

Danny heard the grunt of anguish from Clay. The woman was petite with shoulder-length black hair. Celine?

The men thrust her towards White-Hair. For a moment, her face turned towards the treeline.

Not Celine.

She was dressed only in a bloodstained T-shirt and panties. Her movements were erratic, her limbs jerking in random directions, her head bobbing like a hungry seabird. White-Hair stepped close to her, handed his crossbow to the tattooed man, then pulled a syringe from one of the utility pouches on his belt. Without warning, he jabbed the needle into the young woman's shoulder. The effect was almost instantaneous. She sprang away with a howl.

One of the men jogged over to the main gates and pulled them open.

White-Hair made a show of looking at his watch. He spoke just loud enough for the brothers to hear. "You have two minutes."

The woman looked back at the huts, then at the open gate. She took a few faltering steps before breaking into a headlong sprint.

She was lost from Danny's sight in seconds.

The five men shared a brief laugh, then started after her.

Danny shot a look over his shoulder. The pale scars on Clay's face stood out in stark contrast against his flushed skin. He moved inches in the direction of the fleeing woman. He clenched his fists, his knuckles turning white. "Damn it, we came for Celine!"

Danny held his icy gaze for a moment longer. The single word Clay spat was one he would never repeat in church.

29

The white-haired man, Ulrich Weiss, smiled as he jogged after the girl, listening to her crashing through the undergrowth. She had only two more uses.

First: *The hunt*.

Second: *Pig feed*.

The guest had paid extra to play the game. Master Ezeret had granted the man's desire, for a price. Everything had its price. Inside the compound, anything was made possible. Master Ezeret was correct in his teachings: enlightened men would pay almost any tithe to indulge in those darkest, forbidden desires.

Civilisation was a gossamer veil, a fragile illusion. He had seen such things many times. In the wars he had fought in, women and children had been raped and disfigured by men in the most brutal forms. *Why?* Because it could be done. He knew what truly lay in the savage hearts of men. Murder, lust, unbridled cruelty to those who dared oppose. Yet the darkness did not repulse him. No, he had embraced the crimson path. Master Ezeret had shown him the way.

The guest's shaven head glistened with perspiration, a smile spreading across his rubbery features. "Are you enjoying yourself, Mr Hull?"

Hull nodded vigorously. "But what if we lose her?" gasped Hull. "What if she gets away?"

"She won't. She's thirty metres to our left. She's hiding behind one of those trees."

Hull's eyes followed the direction of Ulrich's index finger. "I don't see her."

"You don't need to. I know where she is. I can hear her every step, her every whimper."

"But I will get to shoot her, right? That's what I paid for."

Ulrich gave a single curt nod. "Yes, of course."

Hull's grin stretched his jowls like a rubber mask.

"Better if you nock so you're ready," said Ulrich.

"Nock?"

Ulrich ran a hand through his white hair. "Arm your crossbow. Pull back the string and nock a bolt to the latch point."

"Oh, like you showed me earlier," said Hull with another grin. Like they were two buddies about to shoot tin cans from a wall rather than commit cold-blooded murder.

"Like I showed you earlier," agreed Ulrich. "Let's move."

The group paused. Hull, sucking in a great lungful of air, placed his foot in the cocking stirrup and pulled back on the string until it clicked into place. He fitted a twenty-inch bolt, which, Ulrich knew, had an expanding broad-head tip. "Ready!"

Ulrich pointed to the tree to his left. "Let's shoot some pink meat."

With Weiss leading the way, all five men set off at a run. His heavily tattooed second-in-command, Ramon, and the other men from the compound fanned out into a loose skirmish line as they kept pace with Ulrich. Hull stayed close.

A flash of arms and legs darted between two trees directly ahead of their path.

"There she is!" yelled Hull, the excitement in his voice unmistakable. He lifted the Excalibur crossbow to his shoulder but the woman was already gone.

The men fanned out in a wider formation, their eyes scouring the trees ahead. Another flash of motion. The back of a sweat-stained T-shirt. Matted hair swinging wildly as she ran. The crossbow discharged with a *snap* and the bolt cut through the air. "Shit! I missed her."

The young woman gave a startled yelp as she looked back at her pursuers, her eyes white and stark against her dirt-smeared features. She dodged away at an angle from her previous path.

Ulrich looked at Hull. "You want me to clip her wings, slow her down a little so you can take the trophy shot?"

Hull was trying to reload his weapon faster than he was capable, his hands fumbling with the next bolt. "Yes, slow her down, goddamnit. That little cow is fast on her feet for someone who looked almost dead half an hour ago."

Ulrich gave a brief smile. "That's the juice I gave her at the gate. Liquid barbies. It'll be starting to wear off now."

As if on cue, the young woman lurched back into view, vomit flying from her mouth in a wild spray.

"And the comedown is a bitch!" Ulrich shouldered his weapon with practised ease, unhurried. Snugging the stock with the side of his clean-shaven chin, he squeezed the trigger and his bolt flew free. The carbon arrow shaft caught the woman just below the right buttock, the point springing out six inches from the front of her thigh. She went down with a scream of surprised agony. Thick tree roots gouged their way into the ground to her right, a wide cenote to her left. Gasping, she rolled onto her side, away from the precipitous edge of the cenote.

The men closed on her like a pack of ravenous wolves. Hull aimed his weapon at the fallen woman.

"Please!" she cried. "Don't!"

Taking a step closer, Hull looked at Ulrich as if unsure what to do next. His mouth worked but the words didn't come out.

Ulrich smiled and tilted his head in encouragement. "Go on, then."

"I… I don't want her to die straight away."

"Shoot her in the arms or legs, then; she'll last longer that way," replied Ulrich. Beside him, Ramon nodded in agreement.

Hull adjusted his aim, tracking the young woman as she pulled herself backwards, the bloodied bolt still protruding from the ruined muscle of her leg. He ran the tip of his tongue across his lips, then pulled the trigger. The bolt cut through her raised right hand as if it were made of nothing more solid than paper. The bolt continued its path, sinking into the base of the tree behind her. The woman emitted a harsh series of gasps, her eyes wide, fixed on her ruined hand.

"Whoa!" Hull exclaimed with apparent joy. "Did you see that? Oh, shit. Look at the hole right through her hand."

"Nice shot," laughed Ulrich.

Hull was nocking another bolt when something large and primeval burst from the trees behind him.

Ulrich staggered back in shock as Hull's head sprang from his shoulders with an abrupt spray of blood. The headless corpse dropped to the ground, landing on top of the fallen crossbow. Within a second, the curved tip of a huge knife burst through Ramon's chest, its bloody tip pointing to the sky. Ramon emitted a single simian grunt as he arched up onto his toes.

The stock of the crossbow flew to Ulrich's shoulder as the monster behind Ramon stood up to his full height. The left side of his face carried deep scars, which stood out in bold contrast against his tanned skin. His bared teeth and ferocious stare sent a chill scuttling down Ulrich's spine.

The man with the rifle, Jason, turned, his mouth opened in a silent grimace, his weapon raised. Then a smaller man combat-rolled into the small clearing, and whipped out his hands so fast they were a blur. Ulrich stared in disbelief as three mortal wounds began to pump bright red blood. The second man had slashed a deep cut into Jason's inner thigh, thrust several times into his ribs and finished by ramming his blade through his throat. Jason staggered a few steps, then dropped to his knees, a Rorschach of blood on the ground below him.

Ulrich swung his crossbow to the new target, but the smaller man was already on the move even as Jason was bleeding out. His aim faltered as the scar-faced man slung a huge arm around Ramon's waist and, growling, stepped him bodily forward, using him as a shield. The blade still protruded from Ramon's chest.

"*Scheisse!*" Ulrich had only one chance with the crossbow. The big guy would be on him in seconds.

A brief gurgling rattle pulled his attention back. The smaller man had slashed his blade across the throat of the last man from the compound. He clutched his neck, unable to halt the crimson waterfall. The smaller man darted behind the body too, shielding himself.

His men had been disappearing for a while, usually without trace—though sometimes a body part would be found on the road to the compound. These must be the killers.

Ulrich sensed he was moments away from death, and smiled. He would take as many scalps as possible before he fell. He turned his crossbow back to the injured woman and pulled the trigger. The bolt struck home deep into the centre of her chest. She slumped to the ground. A single red bubble formed at her lips, then popped without a sound.

The monster with the scars let out a cry of rage.

Ulrich dropped his crossbow and drew his pistol instead, a P7. He raised the compact Heckler & Koch and snapped off four rapid shots, two at the monster and two at the wiry little bastard.

He would not go down without a fight.

Clay felt two rounds slam into the body of the man he was holding up as a shield, but nothing lethal burrowed into his own flesh.

White-Hair continued to walk backwards, pistol raised. He held his pistol like someone who had practised for many hours on a range, popping neat holes through paper targets.

He returned Clay's baleful stare. "Who are you?"

"The man that's gonna end it for you." Clay stalked forward, glaring over the dead man's shoulder.

"You think so?"

"This ain't my first rodeo."

"Nor mine!"

White-Hair tossed something underhand onto the ground at Clay's feet.

Danny shouted a warning. "Grenade!"

Then the world turned inside out.

A mind-numbing flash.

Can't breathe.

Pain.

Can't breathe.

The brief sensation of falling... then darkness.

30

Ghost had watched the three men approach the camp, moving like jungle cats. The old man, a local if his looks were anything to go by, exchanged a few words then moved off into the jungle like a disembodied shadow.

She had lain as still as a corpse, barely ten feet from where the two men observed the compound below. Listening to the guarded whispers of the two men, she decided the big guy was a fellow American, a southerner too, by his accent. The other she wasn't sure of, Irish maybe? His accent sounded funny, his words like splinters of glass to her ears.

Her rifle was hidden on the other side of the trees, closer to the men, so she couldn't risk going for it. Through one barely open eye she watched them. Hoping that they would not see her hiding place.

When the smaller man moved away, leaving the big guy alone, her fingers brushed the butt of her holstered pistol. If she so wished, she could steal upon him and put two in the back of his head. But they were watching the same men she hated. The men inside the compound. The two arrivals were not her enemies. But why were they spying on the camp?

Watch an' learn, chile.

The big guy's back seemed as wide as a bear's. A sleeping beast… yet she knew he didn't sleep. He was watching the compound with a discipline that she had never seen before. And suddenly the smaller man was there again, next to the big one. No sound, no warning, just there.

Who were these men? Certainly, men of skill. A half-remembered passage from her mother's beloved Bible sprang to her mind: *There were giants on the Earth in those days. Men of old, men of renown.*

Something about the two men had struck a chord with her, that was for sure. Were these men of renown? The big guy nearly qualified as a giant; he looked like a wrestler.

The two men broke from their position and set off at a run. What had they seen? Were the men from the compound approaching?

She unfolded her body from the V-shaped tree root in which she had ensconced herself. The men were moving at a good clip, fading into the emerald foliage. She bolted after them, grabbing her rifle as she passed it.

They flitted stealthily from tree to tree. Somewhere ahead she could hear other voices. She knew that these voices would belong to the men from the camp. They would be out to play one of their sick games, games that always left an innocent body on the ground.

Would these two men have the power to stop it? Is that why they were here?

Her feet made no sound as she skirted the path taken by her quarry. She kept the rifle close to her body, afraid that one of them would glance back and see her black-clad figure in pursuit. A pained scream sounded through the trees. The men increased their speed.

Ahead, they split up, knives drawn, the big one going left while the smaller, faster man cut right. Ghost pressed herself against the side of a tree, its smooth bark warm against her shoulder. She could see three men through a gap in the trees. She knew there would be more. She recognised only one of them. The guy with the tattoos. That cruel bastard. She remembered how hard his hands were.

For a fleeting moment, she wondered how this would play out.

Then the carnage began.

The big man raced into the clearing. The breath caught in her throat as he took off the bald man's head with one swipe. For the next few seconds her mouth hung open behind her lightweight mask. The two men tore into the group, blood spraying in every direction.

Damn it, who were these slayers? Professionals, certainly. No one could deal death so efficiently in such a short space of time.

Ghost scooted sideways. The natural cover was sparse so she took a few backward paces, taking care to remain unseen by the combatants.

A series of pistol shots rang out in rapid succession.

A brief glimpse of blond hair. No, not just blond. White hair. Him!

A nightmare memory invaded her mind with a suddenness that caused her to stumble. The white-haired man, his hands tight around her throat as he rammed inside her with bestial aggression. Behind him men had cheered.

Gritting her teeth so tight she could taste blood, Ghost rounded the wide tree trunk. Dodging the edge of the cenote, she sought her target. She was only steps away from the big man with the knife. He had impaled the tattooed bastard. She brought her rifle to her shoulder, the shock of white hair in her sights.

Then the world exploded.

She tumbled backward, the rifle slipping from her grasp. She went down ass-first, dimly aware of her legs folding over her head. Then she was falling. Something unbelievably hard slammed into her back. Then water, an unexpected cold, engulfed her. She tumbled, unable to breathe, vision dimming.

Is this how it was to end? Dead in a damned sinkhole?

You ready to lay down an' die?

Water rushed into her mouth.

You had enough chile. Just give it up…

Purple spots swam across her vision. She didn't know where the surface was. There was something huge in the dark water next to her.

You failed. Just like you failed Lauren.

No!

She kicked out with a new-found determination. Then her face broke the surface and she sucked in a desperately needed breath. Some twenty feet above her the circular rim of the cenote channelled and intensified the daylight, causing her to wince.

Beside her a man bobbed to the surface. Scars cut a lattice on the upper left side of his face. This was the big man she had followed.

Coughing the last dregs of water from her throat, she swam towards a raised outcrop of limestone. The big man with the scars slowly dipped lower in the water. His head went under.

Without conscious consideration, she turned and powered back to him, catching him around his wide neck. Damn it, he felt like a sack of rocks. With effort, she hoisted him onto her chest and again kicked out with her legs. After what seemed like an eternity of struggle, she reached the outcrop. Dragging him by his left arm, she managed to pull him far enough that his head and chest were clear of the water.

His chest rose regularly. He was alive but unconscious.

The opening of the cenote above gave way to a much wider, bowl-shaped cavern below. Her rifle was nowhere to be seen. Her hand went to her hip. The Glock was still secure in its holster.

The big man stirred, his eyes opening briefly then sliding shut again.

Ghost drew her pistol. The Glock 19 was an efficient weapon at up to fifty yards, give or take. At this range, she could kill him with a popgun.

You save him just to kill him now?

No.

Then stop being a damn fool an' put away that shooter.

31

The percussive blast from the grenade slammed into Danny, knocking him clean off his feet. The bastard with the white hair had thrown it into the clearing at their feet along with the crossbow. The rapid shots from the pistol had kept him busy, the bullets thudding into the dying human shield. Then came the double blast. Danny had been close to grenades before, but never this close. Only the body he used as a bullet-catcher had saved him from being ripped apart. A high-pitched squeal sent pained shocks reverberating through his skull. Darkness extended over him, warm and comforting. *Just lie down for a little while, take a rest. Get back up when your head is clear.* No! If he stayed down, he was dead.

Get up!

Casting aside the man whose throat he had just opened, Danny used the tree against which he had been slammed as a leverage point. Hand over hand, he climbed to his feet. The ground beneath him felt as unsteady as a ship on rough seas. Something was stinging his eyes. He rubbed the back of his hand across them; it came away stained red. He wasn't sure who the blood belonged to.

Bodies lay strewn around the small clearing. The woman they had failed to save, impaled by the crossbow bolt. The two men Danny had taken down with his knife lay like crimson-coloured marionettes.

"Clay?" called Danny, his voice little more than a croak. "Clay?"

A spike of furious concern powered Danny to his feet. Where the hell was Clay?

"Don't move!"

Danny pivoted towards the unfamiliar voice, his hands snapping up into a fighter's guard. He listed to one side. Something painful tugged at the joint of his left knee.

"Get on your knees. Hands on top of your head. Do it!"

Danny stared at the white-haired man with an angry indignation. A tricky bastard, and dangerous, to be sure. Danny regarded the pistol that was aimed at him with the same indignation. The man knew enough to stay well out of arm's reach.

"If I have to tell you again, I'll gut-shoot you and leave you out here to die slowly."

Danny held his position.

"I know you're fast. I saw what you did to my men. But you're not faster than a bullet, and that's what you will get if you don't get on your knees."

Danny continued his baleful stare but dropped first to one knee, then the other. He placed his hands on the top of his head, lightly interlacing his fingers. "Where's my brother?"

"Brother?" White-Hair smiled, his pistol never wavering from Danny's chest. "The big guy was your brother? Huh."

"Where is he?" Danny's voice was like a winter wind.

The white-haired man made an arcing motion with his free hand, with an accompanying whistle. "He went into the hole. Sank like a stone. No great loss, I think."

An ice-cold fist twisted the contents of Danny's stomach. White-Hair skirted towards him in a loose circle, the pistol always trained on him.

"Keep facing forward."

Danny grudgingly acquiesced. If the man planned on shooting him, he could have done it easily from across the clearing. He obviously had something else in mind. At least he was still breathing.

Clay.

He refused to believe his brother could be gone. Clay was one tough son of a bitch.

The blow to the nape of Danny's neck was not totally unexpected, but it hurt like a bastard anyway. His head was still reverberating from the grenade explosion. The new assault sent Danny tipping forward onto his hands, darkness again pushing in at the corners of his vision. Through sheer force of will, Danny levered himself back up onto his knees. He raised his hands but was a fraction too slow. The heel of White-Hair's boot crashed into the side of his face with brutal effect.

Darkness swept over him like a blanket.

The throbbing in the side of his face was the first thing he became aware of, even before he opened his eyes. A thick glob of congealed blood filled the cavity between his teeth and his left cheek. Sitting slowly upright, he pursed his lips and spat out the bloody lump. Danny worked his jaw, first opening it wide then squeezing his teeth shut. No broken jaw, no dislodged teeth, just good old-fashioned pain. *Alrighty, then…*

He was surprised to find he wasn't bound or handcuffed. As he stood, he took in the room: a simple rectangle, maybe six by fifteen, no windows, no furniture, a single inset bulb, cinder-block walls, one door. They must have brought him inside the compound. "Well," he said to himself, "you wanted a closer look."

Knowing it was futile, Danny checked his pockets and belt for weapons. Nothing. His phone, watch and wallet were gone too. He still had his belt, with the hidden set of lock picks, but the door had no keyhole. Danny's eye twitched as he silently berated himself. The skin on the side of his face was tender to the touch. The white-haired bastard had caught him a good one.

He had plenty of time to berate himself. Getting blown on his arse by a grenade was something that should never have happened. He would have been killed if it weren't for the man he'd been using as a shield. And where was his brother? Was he still alive?

After what seemed like an hour or so, he heard the voices. Men's voices, maybe four. The words were muffled but Danny guessed their intent. They were coming for him.

32

Celine Chavez pressed her ear to the door, but could hear nothing but her own pulse. She and Rebecca had been brought back to the main house and locked in a room she hadn't seen before.

Rebecca's head drooped forward as she paced in front of Celine.

"What's happening?" whispered Celine. "Where are they taking us?"

Rebecca looked over her shoulder only long enough to hook a single finger and point downwards.

Feeling like her mouth had suddenly been sucked dry of all moisture, Celine wondered again what had befallen Gillian.

The room in which they had been placed was little more than a closet. The men had ushered them inside without any explanation. Celine again pressed her ear to the door, but jumped back as the handle turned, followed by the *click* of a lock disengaging. The door opened and the same two men who had locked them in beckoned them out. Celine thought briefly again about making a break for it. But where would she run to?

With one man leading the way and the second one tailing, they were hustled through another door and down a steep staircase cut into the natural bedrock.

Celine gasped as she stepped from the stairway. Rebecca's comments had not prepared her for this. The massive room looked like it had originally been a cavern but had been excavated and extended. The walls were cut smooth in places; elsewhere they were rippled and contoured like a riverbed. A row of electric bulbs was connected to a single thick cable that had been strung above head height and pegged to the wall in loose loops. The cable stretched the full circumference of the cavern. The centre of the room was a wide circular pit, about seven feet deep. Several dark red smears stained the walls of the pit. Seven rows of bleacher-style seats had been fashioned in the manner of an amphitheatre. A dozen or so men sat in a group, all at the far side of the pit. Several of the men looked up from their conversations, their eyes roving over Celine and Rebecca with interest.

A new knot of apprehension tightened in Celine's stomach as she was shoved forward. The man behind her bent close. Celine flinched as his lips brushed her ear.

"Sit down here and don't move."

Celine sat, feeling the heat from Rebecca's leg against the outer edge of her own thigh. Another dozen or so young men and women were escorted into the cavern. Many shared the same unfocused look in their features. *The essence.*

One of the young men stared directly at her. His head tilted to one side as he scrutinised her.

"Marco!" Celine stood up as she recognised her friend. Marco Kenner quickly raised his hand to his chest, his palm angled towards her. He gave a slight pushing motion with his hand. Celine sat down, her attention flicking from Marco to the guards, then back to her friend. She mouthed the words, "Have you seen Laura?"

Marco gave a noncommittal shrug. He rubbed a hand through his thick brown hair, usually pristine but now hanging in unruly strands over his forehead.

Celine pointed to the empty seat next to her, and Marco edged over and sat down. The guards were preoccupied with bringing another four young women into the cavern chamber, and the others who had come in with Marco were also sitting down now. Nobody seemed to be paying attention to Celine and Marco.

Celine hugged him. "I was so worried about you. Are you sure you haven't seen Laura?"

Marco leaned forward and cupped his face in both hands. Talking through his fingers, he said, "I'm not sure when I saw her last. My head is so messed up, I can't think straight. I think they separated us when they first brought us here."

"I was in a room with Gillian, but they took her away this morning. I haven't seen her since either." Celine realised she was still hugging Marco, but didn't let go. He had always been like a big brother to her, watching out for her at school, keeping the asshole jocks from bothering her too much.

His brown eyes looked like pools of warm chocolate as he leaned a little closer. A single tear rolled down his face. "A man came into my room… He… He strangled me with a towel, rolled up like a rope."

"Oh Jesus, Marco."

He continued, his voice wavering a little. "He kept doing it over and over. I tried to fight back but I couldn't stop him. He'd choke me until I blacked out, then I'd wake up and he'd attack me again. Over and over. I thought I was going to die."

Rebecca leaned in, too. "That's just one of the many sicko games they like to play."

Celine was about to ask another question when an imposing voice cut across the chamber.

"If I tell, will you listen?" Master Ezeret had entered the chamber and now stood at the far side of the pit, his arms outstretched.

The men closest to Ezeret clapped their hands. "We will listen," came the collective response.

"If I show you, will you see?"

"We will see."

"If I challenge, will you rise?"

"We will rise."

"Who here is ready to be challenged?"

One of the men sprang to his feet. "I am ready."

"Will you face death yet not turn your face away?" asked Ezeret, pointing at the volunteer.

"I will not turn away."

Ezeret smiled broadly, his fingers teasing his sculpted facial hair. He beckoned the man forward. "Then enter the pit if you dare."

Ezeret turned his gaze to the captives. With what looked like no more than a second's thought, he flicked out a finger. The guards moved to either side of the young man that he had chosen and propelled him to the edge of the pit.

Celine's breath caught in her throat as the young man was pushed over the edge. He landed in an untidy heap. He was so slim he looked almost feminine, his short blond hair matted to the back of his head by dried blood. His left eye socket was ringed by a livid purple bruise.

Celine found herself gripping Rebecca's and Marco's hands as Ezeret lifted a polished wooden box. He slowly opened the lid, pivoting to display the contents to all. Two knives, their blades long and straight, sat on a silken interior.

"Are you ready to face the trials?" Ezeret asked his follower.

"I am ready." The man plucked one of the knives from the box. He moved to the edge of the pit and dropped inside.

Ezeret turned to the younger man, who was using the wall of the pit to pull himself upright. "Are you ready to face the trials?"

The young man looked around the chamber. Celine gripped the hands of her companions tighter as she recognised the look of utter hopelessness on his face. Ezeret repeated his question but, after again receiving no response, tossed the second knife into the pit.

"Please! I just want to go home." The young man's voice was one of the saddest sounds Celine had ever heard.

Ezeret clapped his hands together three times, the retort as sharp as pistol shots. "Let the trial begin."

The man with the knife strode forward and swung his weapon in a wide slash. A line of crimson appeared across the top of the young man's chest. Clutching at his ripped skin with one hand while the other formed an ineffective barrier, the young man tried to back away. A second slash with the knife opened a gash across the palm of his outstretched hand. A rumbling patter of applause came from the men at the far side of the pit.

The young man, now streaked with lines of red, fell against the pit wall, mewling. Celine willed him to pick up the knife. To fight back. Crying out, the young man stared down at his own flowing blood.

Ezeret pointed to the knifeman, his motions exaggerated like a stage performer. "Will you seize the prize?"

"I will."

"Then take it and be reborn."

The knifeman gripped the young man by the ear, now cowering like a beaten child, yanking his head to one side. The knife stabbed deep into the soft tissue of his throat, flesh proving no match for steel, once, twice, three times. The third blow left the blade embedded deep behind the dying man's collarbone. The attacker wrenched the knife from side to side like a workman prying a stubborn nail from wood.

Celine screwed her eyes shut as a crimson spray jettisoned from his ruined flesh in rhythmic, violent spurts. The sound of the audience cheering on their murderous companion assaulted her ears. When she finally found enough strength to look once more, the knifeman had smeared every inch of his face with the dead man's blood. The young man lay twitching against the wall of the pit. The blood-soaked victor was helped from the hole by his companions.

Master Ezeret closed his eyes as if in prayer as the acolyte stood before him. He traced a pattern with his left hand. "Rise, my brother. You are renewed and reborn. Now take your fill, enjoy your prize."

Another cheer went up from the spectators.

A few of the captives were selected seemingly at random to stay behind. The guards moved among them with hungry eyes. Celine prayed that she would not be chosen. She could not bring herself to look at the selected prisoners. That's how she now thought of them. *They are the guards; we are the prisoners, the captives, held against our will.*

33

Clay awoke with a start, his clothes sticking to him like a second skin. A black-clad figure sat nearby on a low outcrop of rock, a mask obscuring their face.

Rolling onto his hands and knees, Clay levered himself upright. Water dripped from his fingers. His bowie knife dangled from his wrist, secured to him by a narrow nylon lanyard. With a practised pump of his elbow, his hand closed around the hilt of the oversized knife.

"Where's Danny?" Clay took an aggressive step forward.

"Easy now, big fella. I damn near put my back out haulin' your half-ton carcass out of the water. If you mean the smaller guy you were with, I think he's still up there."

"Where the hell are we?" asked Clay.

"We got our fool selves blown into a damned sinkhole. You were going down like the *Titanic*, so I saved your sorry ass. Wasn't sure you were gonna wake up for a little while there. You're welcome, by the way."

"That white-haired son of a bitch suckered us with a grenade."

"I think it was two. Boom, boom, and then we're free-fallin' into this cenote."

"So—" Clay sheathed the bowie, slipping the noose of the lanyard from his wrist "—who are you and why were you pointing a rifle at that asshole?"

"My name… does it matter?"

"Does to me. Clay Gunn, at your service."

"Clay Gunn, huh? Suits you. Guessin' by your accent you're a southern boy, Clay?"

"Texas born and bred. You?"

"Pearl River, N'Orleans." She stood up. "My real name's Rosa, but you can call me Ghost."

"What's with the mask and the ninja act, Rosa?" asked Clay.

"Ghost."

"Ghost."

"I've been waiting for a shot at the white-haired freak—Ulrich Weiss, his name is—as well as his boss for quite a spell. Figured this would be as good a chance as any. Lost my damn rifle when we went into the water."

"Does he live at the compound, this Weiss?"

"Yeah. He lives there. Sick son of a bitch. Can't believe I missed him again."

Clay pointed at her head. "You can take the mask off now."

Ghost paused, her hand hovering near the side of her face. "It's probably better if I keep it on. I'm not so pretty under here. Scars."

Clay shrugged and pointed to the lattice of white lines on his own face. "See yours and raise you."

Ghost slowly pulled on the fabric and the mask dropped in a loose fold to her collar. Clay stared at her face without any discomfort. Like his own, the left side of her face was battle-scarred. But where Clay sported an assortment of narrow white lines, Ghost's were thick fingers of ruined skin, nubby and irregular, stark and raw against her mocha-coloured skin.

"Not so pretty, huh?"

Clay tilted his head to one side and half smiled. "Join the club."

Ghost gave a little laugh, almost childlike.

"Seriously, leave the mask off. Scars don't bother me none."

"I'm pissed about losing my rifle," she said. "Took it from one of the assholes from the compound. Got most of my stuff from them."

Clay's hand went to his waistband, but came away empty. His Ruger was gone, too. He swore under his breath. He hoped Danny had managed to hold onto the Glocks. He plucked his Motorola radio from his pocket. He keyed the mike three times in succession. The unit was dead and dripping water. He tucked it back into his pocket. "That what you call the camp back there? The compound?"

Ghost gave a single nod. "That's what some of the assholes in there call it, like it's some damn country club or somethin'."

"How did you end up out here in the big green, anyhow?" asked Clay.

"Kind of a long story."

"Good, you can tell me while we figure out how to get

out of this sinkhole and back to the surface."

Ghost puffed out her cheeks before she spoke. "We were on vacation. Me and my younger sister, Lauren. She'd just turned twenty-one, so I thought a week or two backpacking around the Mayan sites and a party night or two in Cancún would be just the thing."

Clay could feel water squelching in his boots as he walked. The air in the cavernous cenote was still and cool. "Go on."

"We were having a great time. We buddied up with another couple of girls, said they were from Nebraska. They had an old VW bus, the kind you see in sixties movies. They said we could bunk with them for the night, save on money for a room. The last thing I remember is drinking a beer one of them gave me. When I woke up I was inside that goddamned compound, locked in a cell. Lauren too."

"They drug you?"

"Guessin' so. I hate those bitches, taking other women to a hellhole like that."

Clay clenched his teeth. *Is that what happened to Celine and her friends?*

"They kept us there. Abused us for weeks and weeks."

"Abused you? Who did?" growled Clay.

"The men. A couple of the women too. The men changed, new faces arrived every few weeks then they would leave again. But some of them were always there. Weiss. The tattooed one, a few others. You ended the one with tattoos, stuck him like a pig." Ghost nodded at Clay. "And the leader, of course. He calls himself Master Ezeret. He's an evil, self-righteous prick. He's the one I want most."

"Master Ezeret?" Clay flicked a few drops of water from his fingers. "What do you know about him?"

Ghost traced a hand across her ruined features before offering more. "I don't know much, only what I've been able to get out of his men before I kill them."

Clay raised his eyebrows but said nothing in judgement. He didn't blame her for taking lethal revenge. "You kill many of them?"

"Only a half-dozen or so. I got two this week. They're getting careless, arrogant assholes. I watch and I wait and when I get the chance I end it for them."

"You bagged two men from the compound on your own this week?"

"Damned if I didn't. A day apart, I think. I lose track of time; my head gets all messed up with that junk they doped me with. One man was a town over. I stole a truck and followed him, took him after he left a cantina."

"And the other?" asked Clay, his admiration for Ghost increasing as they walked.

A tight smile crept across her face like a winter sunrise. "Fed him his own drugs in a bathroom stall. Shot the guy he was dealing to as well."

"So, about Ezeret?"

"He showed up here with a van full of money and a dozen or so followers. They say he used to be some kind of motivational speaker or therapist, some bullshit like that. I'm pretty sure if I can put a bullet through his brainpan, then this'll all be over."

"That his real name? Ezeret? Sounds kinda phony."

"None of the men I killed knew if that was his real name

or not. A lot of them just call him Master. He's a sleek son of a bitch, as evil as they come. He starts talking in the ear of one of his lackeys, smiling like that cat who's got the cream, suggesting ways that they can torture you, but making it like he's liberating them or something."

"How many men has he got guarding the prisoners?" asked Clay. As he walked, he stooped occasionally to peer into a crevice, seeking egress from the cenote cavern. The water directly below the cenote opening was illuminated by the bright daylight, but as they moved further away the cavern began to dim, the rocks casting indistinct shadows.

"I'm not sure. Best guess, about ten or twelve left. There's a few women too, but they just fawn around after Ezeret most of the time. Sad little bitches."

"A dozen men, huh? Less the ones that we've taken out?"

"Nah, I reckon still at least ten left, maybe more. But I'm just guessing."

"We have to get out of here and help Danny."

"We'll get out. These places are like Swiss cheese, full of holes and tunnels. Might take a while, though."

"We gotta pick up the pace. Danny and Celine could be in a world of hurt. We gotta get back up there and pitch in. A-sap!"

"Celine? She your girl?"

"She's the closest thing I've got to a daughter. Her family lives with me."

"Okay." Ghost bobbed her chin. "A-sap? You a soldier boy, Clay?"

"Was. A long time ago. I was a Ranger."

"Figures. You're as big as a bear but move like a tiger.

Military trained. Makes sense, now."

Clay gave a short bark of a laugh. "Danny says I'm as graceful as a gorilla in wet Levi's."

"I like the sound of Danny, but no—you're no gorilla."

Clay tipped the brim of an imaginary hat. "What about you? You serve?"

"The only thing I ever served was ice cream in the mall."

"Yet you've managed to kill all those guys from the compound."

Ghost paused mid-step. "It's not the killing that I find hard; it's the not dying alongside them. I wait for my chance, every single day. I watch them. I wait and when one of them is exposed, I take him. No mercy, no second chances."

"You want to kill 'em all?" asked Clay.

"Yes, I do."

"Good! Hold that thought."

34

No matter how tightly she screwed her eyes shut, Celine Chavez could not erase the image of the young man's ruptured throat. The blood cascading down his chest, the look of absolute desperation as his life drained rapidly from him. Her breath caught in her chest, her heart still pounding a staccato rhythm that echoed in her ears.

The guards, two nondescript men with faces that conveyed the same level of compassion as granite, ushered her and a few others back to what she now thought of as her cell. The door clattered shut behind them.

Celine reached out and grasped Rebecca's and Marco's hands. Marco had kept his head down and followed Celine into the room. The guards had shown no interest, simply herding him in with the young women.

"Gillian!" Celine rushed over to her friend, who now lay curled on her bed. "Are you alright? What happened to you? Did they hurt you?"

Gillian had her knees tucked high, her arms wrapped around her shins. She did not answer.

"Gillian?" Celine tenderly brushed back her friend's lank hair. She recognised the same defeated look that the dying man had worn. "What did those bastards do to you?"

Only Gillian's eyes moved, slowly coming to focus upon Celine. "He walked me around the house, showed me every goddamned closet and room in the place. We ended up in his bedroom, his chambers, as he called it. I don't know how, but the next thing I remember I was naked and that bastard was on top of me. It was so unreal, like I was watching it happen to someone else."

"Oh, Gillian! I'm so sorry for leaving you with him. We need to find a way to get the hell out of here. All of us."

Rebecca exhaled slowly as she shook her head. "They're always watching, even when you think they're not. A few have tried to break out since I've been here. They tend to end up in the pit like the guy we just watched die, or they take them outside and we never see them again. God only knows what happens to those ones."

Gillian stared up at the small inverted dome on the ceiling. She extended her middle finger and held the defiant gesture for long seconds. "So what do we do? Lie around here and wait for them to rape me again, whenever they want?"

A chill ran down Celine's spine. *What if we can't escape? What then?*

Marco slowly raised his head. "I think we're all going to die here. They're never going to let us leave, way too risky. We're all going to end up in the pit. Dead."

"No, Marco," Celine snapped. "We're going to get out of here because we're going to work together, all of us. We'll find a way out. Our families must be looking for us by now, right?"

"I don't even know how long we've been here. My head is so messed up I can hardly remember my own name," said Marco.

Celine sat on the edge of Gillian's bed. "Let's get our brains in gear. We're not stupid; we can figure out a plan between us, right?"

She received no answer.

"Rebecca, tell us everything you know about this place."

"I don't know much. I don't know what I can tell you that'll be any use."

Celine's voice dropped to a conspiratorial whisper. "Tell us anyway. Let's start at the beginning. How many men guard this place?"

"I don't know exactly, maybe a dozen or so. The faces change, but I told you already, the essence they spike us with screws up your memory."

"Okay. The leader, we know he calls himself Ezeret. What about the others, do you know their names?"

"The big guy with the white hair, I think he's German. Not sure of his real name. Vice or something like that, maybe? He seems to be in charge of the guards. You see him a lot more than Ezeret. But Ezeret is at all the games. He loves being centre stage. Asshole."

Celine glanced back at Gillian, who had curled up into a foetal position.

"We know that these rooms lead directly to the main house and down to that chamber below, but what about outside? Have they let you out there at all?"

"I've only been out a couple of times. There are some other buildings as well. I think the guards live in those. And there's a great big pig pen at the back of the house. They had a few of us mucking it out while some of the men fixed up the fence posts." Rebecca rubbed a hand across her face. "I found a foot."

"What do you mean?" asked Celine.

"When we were shovelling out the pig shit. I found a foot."

"A human foot?"

Rebecca nodded. "It was a woman's foot, small. It still had nail polish on the toenails."

Celine chewed her bottom lip in a moment of grim realisation. "That's how they get rid of the bodies. Like the guy they just murdered. They'll feed him to the pigs. Pigs eat everything, don't they? Even bones. Nothing left, gone without a trace."

Marco sniffed. "That's what's going to happen to us."

"Shut up, Marco. That's not going to happen. We need to keep our wits about us. That's the only way we're getting out of here. What if we could steal the keys from one of the guards?" asked Celine, as much to herself as the others. "What else is outside?"

"The whole place is surrounded by a fence," replied Rebecca.

"Could we climb it if we got outside?"

"Yeah, I think so."

"No spikes on top or barbed wire or anything like that?" asked Celine, a small kernel of hope beginning to grow.

"I don't remember seeing any, but..." Rebecca swirled her hands at the side of her head.

"What about cars? Did you see any vehicles out there?

Anything we could steal and use to escape?"

Marco sat up for the first time. "Yeah, if we could get to a car or something... I can drive anything. Car, van, truck. I could get us out of here."

"Next time any of the guards come, we all need to watch for where they keep their keys. If any of us gets the chance, we steal them and break out the first chance we get."

Celine hugged Gillian close. "We're going to get out of here."

"As plans go, it's pretty damn thin," said Gillian.

"Friggin' anorexic," said Marco, managing the barest hint of a smile.

35

Danny slowed his breathing as the voices drew closer to his door. At least four men. They made no effort to lower their voices or conceal their intentions. All spoke in English.

"The boss wants him questioned. We need to know where he's from and if there're any more with him."

Danny rolled his neck and shoulders then bounced lightly on the balls of his feet, rapidly shaking his hands as he moved.

"Don't worry, I'll have him spilling his guts in less than five minutes."

A smile devoid of humour crept across Danny Gunn's face. He snapped out four piston-like punches then raised each of his knees in turn. His left knee ached, but still gave full range of motion.

"The Master will have his answers before it's time for today's lesson."

A buzzer sounded, then the door began to open.

Now!

Danny launched himself forward, his right heel stamping

hard just below the handle. The door catapulted open like an oversized mousetrap. One man, red-haired and freckled, was already falling, clutching at the gash down the side of his face. The baton he had been holding in his left hand clattered to the floor.

Three more men stared at Danny, momentarily frozen by the unexpected outburst. One was blond with circular John Lennon glasses, one black-haired in a leather waistcoat, his paunch pushing through the gap. The last man sported a buzz cut and a handlebar moustache; a united nation of assholes. All three carried identical batons, plain black wooden staves, twenty-four inches long. Nothing fancy, but still lethal in the hands of someone who knew how to use one.

Continuing his forward motion, Danny dropped low, his right knee almost on the floor, and snapped a punch into the solar plexus of Buzz Cut. As the guard reeled backward to avoid the blow, Danny achieved his real aim, snatching up the fallen baton.

The hardwood shaft felt cool and familiar in his grasp. Although no master of its finer intricacies, Danny had studied the brutal martial style of *escrima* some years earlier. Born on the blood-soaked battlefields of the Philippines, *escrima* was based on the deadly movements of sword and dagger combat. Its flowing patterns could be deceptively beautiful when performed in a stylised martial display. Stripped to its essence, it was horrifically effective.

Danny ripped into the four men without mercy. A backhand blow sent the closest man staggering a few steps on unsteady feet, his baton held high in defence. Danny pivoted and struck out with his right foot, planting the toe of his boot into the groin of the guy with the Lennon glasses. Lennon doubled over, a high-pitched squeal escaping from his lips. The baton Danny wielded slammed into the base of the man's skull. The impact had the retort of a pistol shot. Lennon dropped onto his face.

Swearing as he came, Buzz Cut brought his own weapon down at Danny's head in a vicious swipe. But Danny wasn't there. He shifted his weight and angled away from the skull-cracker; his own baton deflected the strike and caused Buzz Cut to overextend his reach. In a continuous figure-eight, Danny snapped his weapon into the man's elbow, ribs and kneecaps. Buzz Cut froze momentarily, his face aghast at the multiple explosions of pain. Danny finished him with a forehand strike that sent three of his front teeth rattling across the floor.

With blood trickling down his face, the guy with red hair clambered to his feet and rushed at Danny, arms extended as if to bear hug him. With a grunt of contempt, Danny snapped out his left hand in a lightning-fast jab. Red was halted mid-motion. Danny hit him again. "Aye, everybody's got a plan till they get punched in the face!"

The pudgy guy in the waistcoat closed in and cocked his baton back like a javelin thrower. With a roar that belonged in a samurai movie, he swung his weapon at Danny's face in a wide circle. Danny stepped inside its deadly arc. Lifting his own baton with both hands, Danny watched Waistcoat's wrist snap into an unnatural angle; an angle that his bones were never designed to withstand. Waistcoat's weapon spun away like a detached helicopter blade. A low keening moan now replaced the roar of a second earlier. As the potbellied warrior clutched his broken arm to his chest, Danny thrust the tip of the nightstick deep into the hollow of his throat, crushing the fragile cartilage within. Waistcoat went down onto his back, eyes bulging, gasping for breath.

Danny turned back to Red. "You've got one chance to talk, or I leave you here bleeding out or braindead."

The man's already pale face turned ashen as he looked at his fallen comrades, battered and bleeding but still breathing.

Danny stared into his eyes for the briefest of moments before deciding. He set on the three downed men with unbridled fury. Blood splattered the walls as he scythed into their faces with the nightstick. His voice was cold when he turned back to Red. "Four kids were brought in here a week or so ago. Three wee girls and a boy. Celine Chavez, Laura Troutman, Gillian Cole and Marco Kenner. Where are they?"

"Please... I don't know any of their names."

"But you know they're here." Danny raised his baton in warning. "Get on your feet. You're taking me to where they're being held, and you'd better hope they're all still okay. If any one of them is hurt, I'll snap your neck." He grabbed Red by the hair and hauled him to his feet. "Which way?"

Red pointed.

"Move!"

Danny frog-marched Red along the unadorned corridor. Overhead, a fluorescent tube buzzed and guttered. None of the men had carried radios or any other visible weapons. Danny had seen their type many times before in war-torn corners of the world. Opportunists with a chance to vent their cruelty, unchecked by civilised rationale. "Any funny business and I'll leave you lyin' here deader than a dodo!"

Red hunched forward as Danny continued to muscle him on.

"I'm not sure which rooms your friends are in."

Danny rammed the tip of the baton into the small of Red's back. "Then we'll open every room 'til I find them. You got keys?"

Red nodded frantically, his eyes wide as he looked over his shoulder at the scowling Scotsman.

"Get them out and ready. If I meet any of your buddy boys or I hear an alarm, you're the first to get it."

"Okay, man, take it easy."

Danny rammed the baton into Red's back again. "Look here, you piece of shit, just be thankful my brother isn't here just yet. He would have pulled your head off your little pencil neck already."

Danny readied himself as Red inserted a key with a red fob into the simple lock and turned the handle. No armed men swarmed through the doorway; there was only an empty passageway identical to the one in which they stood. Several doors dotted the length of the corridor.

Danny moved his captive forward at a trot, keeping him slightly off balance, ready for any attempted violence by Red. He knew better than to ever underestimate even a skinny perverted waste of skin like Red. It didn't take an athlete to stick a knife in your guts if you were caught napping.

"Open it!" growled Danny, pointing at the first of the doors. The door was comprised of a single piece and looked to have a steel plate riveted into the wood.

Red changed keys, this time selecting one with a yellow fob.

Danny glanced down. "Do all these doors take the same yellow key?"

"Yes."

"And the red key opens all of the junction doors?"

Red nodded again, his fingers trembling as he held the keys.

"And the green key?" asked Danny.

"That gets you into the main house."

"Are all the doors in the house locked as well?"

"No. Just these ones. No one goes into the house unless we take them anyway."

"So, these three are all the keys you need?"

Red nodded again, turning to face Danny, his Adam's apple bobbing up and down.

"You ever been made redundant?" asked Danny, a slight smile curling the corners of his mouth.

Red stared back at him, his own mouth slightly open. "Huh?"

"Let me put it another way: your services are no longer required." Danny brought the baton down across the side of Red's face. Red bounced once off the door, then landed face down, silent and unmoving. A pool of crimson slowly began to form a bloody halo on the floor around his head.

Danny kicked him to one side and picked up the fallen keys. He used the yellow key to open the door. Wasting no time, he stepped inside, holding the door open with his foot.

"Celine!" his voice was low but urgent. "Celine Chavez!"

Three faces stared back at him. Celine wasn't there.

36

"Celine!" Danny Gunn's voice was like gravel down a drainpipe. "Celine Chavez!"

None of the three young women that stared back at him was Celine. All three wore the same harrowed expression. The room had a distinctive smell, a smell Danny was very familiar with. The room smelled of fear.

One of the women stood up. Her hair hung in strands, dark circles under her eyes. "Celine is my friend. What the hell have you done with her?"

Danny took a quick step into the room. It looked like an old-style army barracks: camp beds and plain walls. Utilitarian and drab. "I've come to take her home. Who are you?"

"Laura Troutman. We came down here on vacation together," she replied.

"Laura?" Danny looked at the young woman again. She was almost unrecognisable from the picture Clay had shown him in Cancún. "Do you know where Celine is? Have you seen her?"

"No. I haven't seen her. I was in here with Marco for a few days, but he was so out of it, I don't know... I don't know what happened to him."

"Okay, you need to come with me, right now. We're gonna find Celine and the others, then we're gettin' out of here. Stay a few steps behind me. If any guards come at me just get out of the way so you don't get hurt."

Laura stared back at him, unmoving.

"Move your arse! We don't have much time."

The mistrust in her face was evident. "Who are you?"

"You know Clay Gunn? Celine's family lives with him. I'm his brother, Danny. Now, come on."

Laura took a single tentative step then hustled forward. "I haven't seen Clay for a few years, but Celine talks about him all the time. He's really big—"

"And I'm not, I know. But I am his brother."

"Okay..."

"Stay close," said Danny. He looked at the other two women in the room. There was a look of absolute defeat and hopelessness in their faces. "Can you run? Come with me if you want out of here."

Laura shook her head. "I think they've just been dosed again. They'll be like the walking dead for a few days yet."

"Shite," swore Danny. "Come on, then. I'll make sure someone comes back for them later."

Danny moved back into the corridor, with Laura close behind. He unlocked the next door and opened it with no wasted motion. The room was empty of occupants. A row of beds, arranged asymmetrically along either side, seemed to mock him. "Come on. We need to keep moving."

Keeping the baton readied in his right hand he moved to the next door, using his left to unlock it.

As the key began to unlatch the tumblers within, a voice cut in from behind. "I knew you were a slippery bastard. Dropped four of my boys already."

Danny pivoted, bringing his cudgel into an overhead guard position.

"You can drop that."

It was the same white-haired man who had bested him earlier. His pistol was aimed at his head. Danny placed the baton by his feet.

"Kick that away, slowly."

"You want your dildo back? Here, have it." Danny sent it across the length of the corridor.

"I can't leave you alone for two minutes, can I?"

Danny fixed him with a look that could curdle milk, but said nothing. He was too far from the gunman to do anything other than die if he moved.

"What's your name, little man?"

"Why? You adding me to your Christmas card list?"

"I like to know the names of the men I kill, gives me a sense of… completion."

Danny scowled. "Cross the T's, dot the I's, right?"

"Exactly. I'll go first. Ulrich Weiss. The last man you'll ever see."

"Danny Gunn. Right backatcha, ya fucknut."

"British?"

"Scottish."

"Huh." Weiss shrugged dismissively. "Finish opening that door, then. You, girl, get inside."

Danny glanced at Laura then gave her a small nod. "Go on. I'll be alright."

As the door opened he glanced inside. Four faces looked back at him. The one in the centre drew his attention like a beacon. Celine.

Laura scooted into the room.

"Close it again," ordered Weiss.

Danny pulled the door shut. The lock snapped shut with a click that seemed to mock him.

Weiss held the pistol steady, aimed at Danny's chest as his left hand moved to his hip. He drew a second weapon. The guy liked his kit. Danny recognised this one too.

"Shite!" He barely had time to utter the curse before the wired electrodes from Weiss's Taser made contact. Raw electricity ripped through his body, shutting off his ability to breathe, sending his muscles into forced hypertension as his nervous system short-circuited. He went down onto his knees.

Danny looked up to see Weiss giving him a shit-eating grin. When Weiss hit him with an extended second charge, Danny slid into darkness. He registered Weiss raising his boot but was in no position to stop it.

37

"Hey, I think I see daylight." Clay pointed to a patch of rocks high up to his right. They cast a faint, jagged shadow like a child's painting of a mountain range. "I'll give you a boost up. See if we can squeeze through."

Ghost moved over to the smooth limestone wall. A narrow outcrop jutted out enticingly about six feet above her head. "Ready when you are, cowboy."

Clay squatted, his back to the wall, then cupped his hands together. Ghost placed her left foot in his grip. "On three. One, two, and three."

Ghost was cast up into the air. Clay smiled as he watched her catch the ledge and haul herself over. "Any good?"

"Give me a minute. It goes back aways."

As he waited for Ghost to return, his thoughts strayed back to Danny. He was sure that his younger sibling would be okay. Danny was as wily as a bobcat. But surviving was only part of the plan. They'd come to find Celine. The hilt of his bowie knife felt like an old friend. For a moment, he relived the grisly sensation of driving the blade through the tattooed man's body. He would gladly impale every man in the camp if it meant Celine's safe return.

"Any luck up there?" Clay's voice echoed in the cavern.

There was no response. Clay's head jerked up as a dark thought hit him like a slap. What if Ghost escaped but left him down here to fend for himself?

"Ghost?" Then louder. "Ghost! You find anything?"

Clay frowned at the outcrop above his head, then backed up a few steps. He was mid-action of rocking back on his heels in preparation for a running leap when the familiar face stared down at him.

"It's going to be tighter than a new pair o' dancin' shoes up here, but I think we'll get through."

"Watch out, I'm coming up." Clay leapt, catching the edge of the ledge easily, and hauled his bulk onto it. The top of his head brushed the overhanging rock. He rested his hand on his upper thighs, taking a deep breath. A slow pounding took up residence behind his eyes. Damned grenade.

"You okay?" asked Ghost. "You look kinda hinky."

"I'm fine. It's just every minute I spend down here is a minute Celine could be in real danger."

"So, let's get ramblin'." Ghost hooked a thumb over her shoulder. "We'll head back to my camp and grab some new kit, then go and get this party started."

"You've got spare weapons?"

"I've got a few toys that may come in handy," she answered. "Come on. This way."

Clay watched her move ahead at a brisk pace. Within thirty seconds she dropped onto all fours, scuttling along with ease. Clay followed, his back scraping against the rock, spurred on by the light ahead. Daylight. Freedom. Celine. Danny.

The passage narrowed so that Ghost's figure blocked out the light as she crawled ahead of him. The brightness of the daylight caused a brief halo effect around her.

"Sunshine dead ahead," she called in a sing-song tone.

Despite struggling to keep moving forward without tearing skin, Clay gave a brief smile. Ghost had a voice that wouldn't be out of place in a choir. Memories stirred, of sitting Celine on his lap when she was fresh out of kindergarten, him singing Johnny Cash songs, his deep monotone suited for little else. Celine had applauded with unbridled enthusiasm as only an innocent child could. His thoughts were interrupted by a dazzling light. Ghost had made the end of the narrow tunnel. He traversed the remaining stretch of ground by shrugging his body like an oversized caterpillar. Then his unspoken fears took form. It was as if the tunnel had suddenly contracted, tightening around his chest. He tried wiggling side to side but found no purchase with his feet. The tunnel was too narrow for him to fit through. Anger flashed though him as he strained against the narrow, unyielding aperture of rock. A low growl built in his chest. The seams of his shirt began to pull and separate, but he was held fast.

"You okay there, big fella?" asked Ghost.

"Damn it. I'm stuck."

"Relax, Clay. If my ass fit through, which isn't exactly the smallest, you can fit through too."

"I'm stuck," Clay repeated.

"Take a deep breath, then relax. Breathe it all the way

out. I want you to relax every muscle like you're having a massage. Okay?"

"Okay."

"Now, stay relaxed, but gently stretch out your arms to me."

Clay forced himself to relax, following Ghost's instructions. Her hands were cool as they closed around his wrists. She placed her feet either side of the tunnel mouth. Clay slid forward on his stomach as she gave a slow and steady pull. The pressure around his chest slipped away. He gripped the outer lip of the tunnel and dragged himself free with a grunt of undisguised relief. Ghost offered a hand, but Clay lurched to his feet under his own steam.

"I was never built to be a tunnel rat. Thanks, Ghost, that's another one I owe you."

"Hey, we're out of there, that's the main thing, right?" she said. After looking up into the sky for a few seconds, she pointed at a narrow gap through nearby trees. "We need to head back that way."

"You sure?"

"Pretty sure. I followed you west from the compound and my camp is just short of three miles north of it."

"Smart. Far enough away to stay unnoticed, but close enough to keep tabs on them each day," said Clay. He was liking Ghost more and more. "We need to hustle. I've been underground and out of the game way too long. I've got to get back to the compound."

"Come on then, let's get moving." Ghost moved silently, barely disturbing the overhanging branches of the encroaching trees.

Clay tilted momentarily to one side, an angry buzzing in his ears. He'd felt this way before. The grenade blast that had sent him tumbling into the cenote had left him with a bitch of a concussion. Slapping face-first into water from twenty feet up probably hadn't helped him much either. He'd pushed through worse in the past, but knew the toll.

With a determined grunt, he started after Ghost. Time enough for recuperation after he knew Celine was safe.

38

Celine rushed from the bed as she recognised her missing friend. "Laura, are you okay? We were so worried about you."

Laura opened her arms as Celine moved to embrace her. Seconds later she was joined by Marco. "Celine! Marco! Gillian!"

Tears ran down Celine's face as the friends huddled together. "I was worried we'd never see each other again."

Laura, now crying too, kissed each of her friends in turn. "I love you guys."

Rebecca stood outside of the huddle. "You four all came down here together?"

Celine, still clinging to her reunited group, answered in the affirmative. She turned her attention back to Laura. "That man at the door—not the white-haired freak, the other one—who was he?"

"He's here to save us. He said he was Clay's brother."

"Clay?" Hope surged in her chest. "Did you see Clay too?"

"No, only… I think he said his name was Danny?"

"Yeah. That's Clay's brother. I've seen him a few times over the years, but he looked quite different back then. His hair was always very short. He always looked kinda angry. Clay talks about him all the time." Celine closed her eyes, saying a silent prayer of thanks. If Danny was here to rescue them, then Clay was here too. "Danny and Clay are here for us. When they come, we've got to be ready to move."

Marco nodded. "You think they can get us out?"

"It's what they do. They used to be soldiers." Celine recalled a few of the wilder stories that she'd heard about the Gunn brothers over the years. A small but emotion-filled sob escaped her chest. "Uncle Clay will kill every last one of them!"

The corners of Laura's mouth turned down before she spoke. "I hope you're right, but the white-haired dick just pulled a gun on Danny, got the drop on him good. That's how I ended up in here with you."

"Don't worry. Even if they've managed to corner Danny, Clay is still out there. He'll get us out."

Marco shook his head, his hands scrubbing at his hair. "So, we're down to one man already? This just gets better and better."

A flash of anger ripped through Celine, taking unexpected voice. "And what fucking good have you been, Marco? You hardly knew your name a moment ago, so shut your mouth. Clay *is* coming for us."

Marco reeled as if he'd received a physical blow.

"I… I didn't mean…" He reached out to Celine, his hand hovering awkwardly in the gap between them.

Taking a deep breath, Celine forced herself to calm down.

She knew Marco was as scared as the rest of them, and he was a soft-hearted goof at the best of times. The pain showing on his face and the waxy sheen of perspiration that coated his features made her soften as quickly as she had angered. She squeezed his hand. "It's okay, Marco. I know you're as scared as the rest of us."

Rebecca gestured to the locked door. "What the hell do we do while we're waiting for the rescue party to arrive?"

Celine visualised Clay's hulking frame bursting through the door, guards lying motionless at his feet. "We think, talk, prepare. And when they come, we move our asses as fast as possible."

Rebecca lifted her chin. "What about me? They'll be coming for you and your friends. Will they take me with them too?"

Celine stared back at her with bold intensity. "We're all going home. Clay won't leave you here. I promise you that."

Celine looked at the faces surrounding her, all now looking to her for leadership. A brief sensation of nausea rolled through her stomach. She was unsure if it was the remnants of the mystery concoction of drugs or a nervous reaction to the thought of Clay and Danny being so close. Her initial excitement wavered slightly, now turning into an octopus of doubt, each tentacle that now writhed in her torso carrying a different fear. Was this the drugs? Were they making her paranoid? She still didn't know what the hell was in the concoction they'd been doped with. What had Rebecca called it again? The essence? Damned mind-scrambling Devil's breath. Her memories were jumbled. An image: *a muscular arm around her throat, a rough hand down her pants, invading.*

"You okay?" asked Laura, reaching for her friend.

"I'm fine. We just need to stay ready."

Laura glanced up at the camera dome near the door. "You really think Clay and Danny will be able to get us out of here?"

"I do."

"But there's all those men out there and you've just seen what they're capable of." A single bead of sweat rolled down the side of Laura's face.

"Clay has always been so big and gentle around us—my family, I mean—but I've heard a few stories from my dad. I know he's really tough. He worked as a doorman in some of the worst bars in Texas and he didn't do it because he needed the money."

Marco glanced warily at Celine. "Knocking a few drunks around is one thing, but these guys are another kind of threat altogether."

The muscles in Celine's jaw bunched with tension. "I'm telling you, Clay and Danny will get us out. They managed to save a British journalist a while back against a squad of trained soldiers."

"But how are they—"

"Shut up, Marco!" Gillian's voice caused him to jerk his head back. "Listen to what she's saying. We've got to be ready to run like hell when the cavalry gets here."

Celine balled her hands into fists. "Not just run. We may have to fight as well. We've all seen the faces of the men here. You've all seen enough movies to know that once you've seen the face of the killer, you're as good as dead."

39

For the second time that day, Danny Gunn awoke in a strange room. This time his hands were secured behind his back. Yet at least he knew Celine was alive.

He pursed his lips in annoyance. The Taser shock had knocked him on his arse, but it was the boot to the side of his head that had put him out. That was the second time that white-haired bastard had done him over. Ulrich Weiss. That was a name that needed scratching off his hit list before this was done. Weiss was no fool, if his two previous encounters were anything to go by. Danny was determined not to lose to him a third time.

Rolling to his knees, Danny Gunn tapped his wrists together. A metallic tone answered him. Handcuffs, not rope.

"Alrighty, then." Danny sat up and pushed his hands as low as possible. It was the work of moments to slip cuffed wrists around his legs so that he could see his hands. Looking down at the cuffs, he allowed himself a little smile. They were standard-issue police cuffs: two ratchet bracelets connected by a short chain.

As a younger man, Danny had been a Houdini buff, tinkering with padlocks and knots to emulate the escape artist. He could open most locks without trouble. Handcuffs were sometimes a different ballgame, depending on their make and model. These cuffs didn't worry him.

"Easy money," said Danny. He plucked the compact shim set from the inside lining of his belt. Moving with practised ease, he selected a small strip of metal and rotated it in the keyhole with the lightest of pressure. The cuff popped open with a barely audible *click*. Repeating the deft motions with his left hand took a few seconds longer. *Damned left hand, needs more practice*. He tucked the pin back into the lining of his belt, then turned his attention to the door.

There was no keyhole accessible from the inside, just a flat plate below the stubby handle. There was nothing to be gained by attacking a secure door. With nothing else to do but wait, Danny leaned his back on the wall opposite the door, and silently began to count. Ninety-four minutes later, he heard the sounds of men approaching. While measuring the time in the cell he had also loosely refitted the cuffs around his wrists. Loose enough that he could pull his hands free in an instant, but to a casual observer he would still appear shackled.

"I am going to open the door now," Weiss called in his usual flat tone. "If you attack I will shoot you, and this time it will not be a stun gun."

The key slipped into the lock. Despite the warning, Danny considered an aggressive rush. But being shot dead in a cell was not part of his plan. Taking a half-step back, he readied himself to receive pain if it was dealt out. Celine was here, alive if not well, but she was still breathing. That was the priority for now.

The door opened and a guard that Danny had not seen before crouched in the opening, a Taser pistol aimed at Danny. Behind him stood Weiss, his P7 trained on Danny's chest.

"Step out. Do it slowly," commanded Weiss.

Danny lowered his head, feigning capitulation, and did as requested. "Where are you taking me?"

Weiss took measured steps backward as Danny advanced. Weiss tilted his head. "That way. The Master wants to see you for himself, ask you the questions I sent my men to ask earlier."

"I'm flattered," said Danny. "The man behind the curtain wants to speak to little old me."

"You may not be so cavalier when he's done with you."

"You never know. We may become BFFs."

"Move it, or I will put a bullet in you." Weiss's gaze flicked briefly to the guard. "And don't even think about grabbing him. I'll shoot him dead just to get to you." The guard didn't seem fazed by Weiss's declaration.

Danny tensed his arms as he was escorted into the main house, adding to the illusion that he was still handcuffed. The guard kept the Taser pistol close to his hip as they negotiated the two locked doors that formed the path to the house. As the second door closed behind him, Danny found himself in what he was sure was the main lobby of the house. A solitary guard was posted in front of a set of double doors.

Danny glanced at the spiral mosaic on the floor, then at the seemingly random assortment of art on the walls. "Who did your interior design, Coco the clown?"

"Shut your mouth and keep moving," said Weiss.

Danny slowed his pace slightly, hoping that Weiss would close the distance between them.

"I won't warn you again. Keep moving or I'll put one through your kneecap."

"I'm moving. I'm still a bit shaken after you suckered me with that Taser."

Weiss showed Danny something that loosely resembled a smile.

"Will there be tea and scones at this meeting with the boss?" asked Danny. "Or will it be the blood of virgins from a crystal chalice?"

Weiss thrust his pistol forward. "I will enjoy watching you die, funny man."

Danny paused mid-step and looked Weiss up and down. "If I had a pound for every time some arsehole with a gun told me that, I'd have more money in the bank than the Rockefellers."

"Move!"

Danny followed the guard into a room illuminated by a scarlet light overhead. At the centre of the room sat a solitary figure. He slouched upon an oversized chair, his booted feet crossed at the ankles.

"You do know Halloween isn't for months yet, don't you?" asked Danny as he approached the seated man.

"So, you are the one proving somewhat troublesome to my men. I thought you'd be bigger."

Danny gave a single shrug. "My girlfriends all tell me size doesn't matter, it's how you play the game."

"Weiss informs me that your name is Danny Gunn. Interesting name."

The corner of Danny's right eye twitched as he silently berated himself. He had told Weiss his name in a rare moment of macho bullshit. He knew better than to give away even the smallest advantage.

"Seeing as we're getting all cosy together, what do I call you?"

"You may call me 'Master'."

"Never gonna happen, slick."

"Too proud to bow to your superiors?"

"Old enough to know that a superior mind would never expect anyone to bow to them," replied Danny. "So, you can forget that 'Master' shite."

The man leaned forward, as if to get a better look at his challenger. His chin jutted as he spoke. "My name is Sean Ezeret-Dunn. My people here call me Master Ezeret."

"Your people?" Danny cast a glance at Weiss. "Is that just your little Red Hand Gang, or does that also include all of the kids you abduct, abuse and kill?"

40

"You okay there, big guy?"

Clay leaned against a gnarled tree. "Give me a second and I'll be good to go."

"What is it?" asked Ghost.

"My ears are buzzin' like a hornet's nest," replied Clay. "My balance is still skewed as well. I feel as pitiful as a three-legged dog."

"Getting blown outta your footprints by a grenade will scramble your eggs, sure enough."

Clay forced himself away from the support of the tree. "You seem to be doing just fine."

"I've been through worse." Ghost waved at her scarred face. "Besides, you were right on top of that thing when it went off. I think I threw myself back out of surprise and followed you tail over titty-bag into the sinkhole."

Clay emitted a guttural sound as he straightened up again.

"Even tough guys like you get concussion, y'know," said Ghost.

"I haven't got the time or the inclination to be concussed. It's like you just said, I've had worse, too."

"Come on then, we're nearly at my camp. A quick re-up and we'll go find your girl."

"Celine."

"Yeah, Celine."

"And Danny," added Clay.

Ghost tilted her head to one side but said nothing.

"He's still alive," said Clay. "Danny's faster than double-struck lightning. He'll be raisin' hell without me and that just doesn't sit right."

"Then let's keep moving so we can go join the party."

Clay took a deep breath and, after holding it for a six-count, moved after his black-clad guide. "I'll owe you big time after we get done with this shit-kicking contest."

Ghost offered him a wan smile. "Mama used to say that the best friends are often met under the worst conditions. You get me close enough so I can put a bullet through Ezeret's heart, and we'll be square as square is."

"You want to tell me a bit more about how you got those scars?" asked Clay, as he followed Ghost's lead toward her camp. "Sometimes talking things through lets them sit a bit easier in your mind."

Ghost didn't turn to look at him. "After they brought us to the compound they kept us drugged for days on end, weeks maybe. I didn't know my own name, I was so messed up. I remember the men taking us down under the main house, down with the others, me and my sister."

"Lauren."

"Lauren, yeah, sweet Lauren. She was only a kid, just

turned twenty-one. They had some twisted gladiator shit going on down there—they have a pit and everything. I remember one poor guy getting his head hacked off with a machete. So much blood."

Clay's balance tilted again, but he forced himself to keep moving. "They make people fight?"

"Yeah, usually one of their own against one of the captives; at least that's how I think it was most of the time."

"I know it hurts, but what happened to Lauren? Where is she now?"

"Those bastards killed her." Ghost's voice carried the slightest tremor, but she continued. "One night after the men had finished with us they dragged us both into the yard. We were already beaten to a pulp. I was so messed up I couldn't walk. They tied Lauren to the fence by one hand. Then Weiss brought out two crossbows."

He knew the next part before he heard it.

"They stood around laughing as if it were all a big game, some kind of joke, all while my little sister begged and cried for her life. Every time I tried to help, one of them would kick me back down. They kept her like that for what seemed like hours. Then those bastards began to fire arrows at her. The first shot went through her foot. I'll never forget the sound of Lauren screaming. More men came out of their cabins to watch like it was big game night or something. They shot her seven times before she stopped screaming. The silence was worse. My beautiful little sister was gone, stolen from me by those sadistic pieces of filth."

"I'm sorry about your sister." The words tasted sour in his mouth.

"Every time I tried to get to her, they knocked me back down. Then Ezeret came out. I pleaded with him, but he just gave me a shit-eatin' grin and whispered to Weiss. They brought one of the other men forward, a little skinny bastard with jam-jar glasses. They gave him a knife and let him loose on me."

"Was he the one that cut your face?" asked Clay.

Ghost gave a single nod. "I think he was one of the visitors. I blacked out, thought I was dead. I guess they did too."

"But you didn't die."

"Part of me did," said Ghost. "I woke up when the pigs started to eat me."

"Jesus!"

Ghost turned to face Clay. Her voice was barely above a whisper. "They ate Lauren, my sweet, beautiful little sister Lauren. There was almost nothing left of her. I managed to crawl out the pig pen by squeezin' between the bars of the fence."

Clay reached for the support of a nearby tree as his vision blurred. Bile rose to the back of his throat. "Why did you stay after you escaped? After all the ordeals they put you through, why didn't you try to make it home to your family… to the outside world for help?"

Ghost brushed a miniscule insect from the side of her mouth. "I had no one to go back to. It was just me and Lauren."

"Your ma?"

"We lost Mama back in Katrina. My father left us when I was six, just headed on up the road one day and never came back. Lauren was just a little girl when Katrina hit so then it was just the two of us. I tried to do the best I could for her."

Clay placed his hand on Ghost's shoulder. "I can tell how much you loved her."

"So, I stayed here. I crawled out of the compound through a waste pipe covered in blood and shit and vomit and out into the jungle. I should have died, but I didn't. Something kept me going."

"And when you became strong again you started killing those fuckers?"

"I don't know how long I was out there in the jungle. I must have wandered in circles for weeks and weeks. Eating bugs and iguanas to survive. Can't remember much of it, my head was so messed up with the crap they used to dose us up with. I started to steal things. My tent and some other kit. Stole them from the backs of cars when I could. I should have died. But here I am, right?"

"Here *we* are," added Clay. "You're not alone anymore."

41

"What's the deal here?" Danny Gunn took another calculated step closer to Ezeret. "I thought it may be linked to the illegal trade in human organs or some sinister shite like that, but after watching your dick-squad here chase down and murder that young woman, I dropped that idea. I think you're just a bunch of sicko bastards that have found a corner of the world away from prying eyes. A corner where you can act out your vile psycho fantasies and not get chased down by the law. Am I getting warm?"

Ezeret clapped his hands together, then shifted his weight so he sat on the edge of his ornate seat. "When I look at you, you know what I see?"

"Handsome bastard, hung like a cart horse?"

"I see a man that denies his own darker, deep-seated passions. When I look into your eyes, I can see them bubbling away just below the surface. Violence, anger, a man sick of being constrained, sick of being held down by the hypocritical ideals of modern liberal apologists."

"I'll stick with 'handsome bastard'," said Danny as he

glanced at his captors. Weiss now stood with his P7 pistol clasped near his hip, the muzzle pointing at Danny's chest.

"A man tired of living by the sugar-coated rules imposed upon the world by the self-important hypocrites in office. Who are *they* to say what is right or wrong? Who are *they* to dictate what you can or can't do? In ages past, when a conquering army took a city, unfettered raping and pillaging followed; not only was it allowed by the generals, but it was encouraged. The enlightened men of yesteryear understood those primal needs and let their armies quench those most essential desires to the full."

Danny rolled his shoulders, fixing each of the three men with a baleful stare. "Just because shit happened in the past, doesn't make any of it right. And you're hardly a conquering army, more like a bunch of rabid dogs that have banded together. Abducting tourists and God knows who else then using them for your sicko fantasy games is just plain old evil. You can try to dress it up as much as you want, but it's for twisted arseholes and that's that."

Ezeret shook his head slowly. "I am unrestrained, and I show others how to become so in turn. It is only when we are free of false morality that we truly discover ourselves. We find out what truly lies behind the facade imposed upon us by this world of banality. 'Do what thou wilt shall be the whole of the law.'"

"Do you really believe the shite you're spouting, or is this for their benefit?" Danny asked.

Ezeret stood up from his seat. "Every man has the right to live by his own law, to live in the way he wills, to pursue his own chosen path. Here I have created my own path and others have chosen to follow that same red road as I."

"Go fuck yourself, Ezeret," spat Danny. "And you can save your half-arsed Aleister Crowley quotes for someone who hasn't read a book for themselves. The kids you've abducted and murdered didn't choose your damned red road."

Ezeret placed his palms together as if offering a prayer. "I look at you and see a man who has stepped beyond the bounds of the law when it suited you to do so, perhaps in acts of revenge or retribution. I can see it in your eyes right now. The delicious promise of violence like a lion in a cage. Only let the lion out once and he will kill his keeper to be sure."

"When the time comes, I'll kill every last one of you."

"There it is!" said Ezeret. "The violent undercurrent that confounds so many of the world today. Join us and you can let the beast loose, let the lion out from the cage forever. Weiss tells me you put down a handful of my men on your own, armed with nothing more than a billy club, and you killed two armed men with a knife outside. Impressive. Join us and you can live proud and unfettered like a warrior of old."

"Do you practise this bullshit in front of a mirror?"

"I learned many years ago, one of the greatest pleasures in life is holding another man's life in the palm of my hand. It's intoxicating." Ezeret's eyes flashed as he perched on the edge of his seat. "Each man that wins a victory in the trials is reborn, set free from the chains of bland social conformity. Give me rape, give me murder, anything but the ordinary."

"Trials?"

"Some of the men enjoy the thrill of combat."

Danny shook his head. "There's no victory in killing one of your captives. That's not something I'll ever do, but

I will happily end it for any of your grunts that you put against me."

Ezeret clapped his hands together, sharp and loud. "Oh, I think I can find a challenger or two more than able to test your abilities. If you will not join us, you will serve to set another seeker free."

"If he's one of your arsehole brigade, bring it on. I'll knock a hole in his head you can see through."

"That's the spirit, Mr Gunn. But I warn you, two men may enter the trials, but only one may ever leave."

"I can live with that risk," said Danny.

"Weiss, take Mr Gunn to see Michelle, then see to it that he is properly fed and watered. Tonight shall be a special night."

Weiss brought his P7 pistol up and gave Danny what he took to be a dismissive sneer. "Move. The last door on the left."

Danny remained motionless, hoping that Weiss would take a step into arm's reach. "Who's Michelle?"

"Move. I won't ask again," said Weiss.

"You still gonna shoot me, Weiss? But if you shoot me I won't be able to appear on tonight's fight card."

"I can live with that risk," said Weiss with a cold smile. "Move!"

"I'll move when I'm good and ready," said Danny, drawing out each word. He turned his gaze back to Ezeret. "But only after you promise me that this Billy Idol reject is the one I get to fight first."

Ezeret gave a brief laugh. "Resourceful you may be, but you're no match for Weiss."

"We'll see when he's the one in front of me, won't we?" Danny remained stationary. "So, who's Michelle?"

"Just let me shoot him. He's more trouble than he's worth," said Weiss.

Ezeret wagged a finger. "Mr Gunn, if you please."

Neither Weiss nor the other guard had succumbed to frustration and stepped within range. Danny allowed himself the briefest of smiles. *Can't fool them all the time.* "Okay, let's go meet Michelle. I hope she's better company than you three fuckwits. You make the Stooges look like geniuses."

Ezeret sat back in his seat. He failed to respond as Danny gave him a finger wave. "Kill you later, alligator," said Danny.

The corners of Ezeret's mouth curled for the briefest of moments. "In a while, crocodile."

Danny walked to the door as directed. He wondered where the hell Clay had gotten to. He could only stall them for so long.

42

As Clay followed Ghost into the small clearing he grabbed at another tree to prevent himself from falling. A constant hissing tinnitus had taken up residence in his ears, a dull ache behind his eyes. Despite his assurances to Ghost, he knew he was in trouble. He had been rattled before, once quite seriously on the rodeo circuit after taking a kick to the side of the head. But this was different. Clay had never been knocked off his feet by a grenade explosion but had been around many others that had. He knew the signs. Loss of balance, nausea, ringing in the ears and waves of unexpected fatigue.

Ghost stopped suddenly, spreading her arms wide. "Welcome to chez Ghost. It's not much, but it's home."

Clay pushed himself off the tree and followed her closer to a tent at the opposite side of the clearing. The surrounding tree branches seemed to point at him with accusatory fingers. "We can't stay long. We need to arm up and get back to the compound."

Ghost pursed her lips. "Not before you drink a whole lotta water and get some painkillers down your gullet."

The offer of water sounded like a fine idea. Clay's mouth was dry and tinged with the taste of copper.

Ghost ducked inside the tent, returning moments later holding an aluminium water bottle. "Take small sips at first."

Clay accepted the bottle. "This ain't my first rodeo."

"And I don't want it to be your last, so hush up, sit your big butt down and start sippin' on that water. I'll get you something to take the edge off."

Clay dropped to one knee. If he sat down, he wasn't sure that he'd be able to regain his feet. Ghost emerged again from the tent and handed him three lozenge-shaped pills. "Here, these will help with you getting your bell rung."

"What are they?" asked Clay.

"Just paracetamol, nothing exotic. They won't slow you down, but they'll help with that wasp buzzin' in your ear."

Clay swallowed the pills with a long pull on the water bottle. "You got that too?"

"Like a son of a bitch." Ghost swallowed her own pills.

"You said you have some more weapons tucked away?"

"I have," replied Ghost. "Not enough to wage a war, but enough to set one going."

Clay emptied the water bottle in one long pull. "I'll take some more water if you have it."

"Sure. You want Evian or Perrier?" Ghost took the bottle from him with a sly smile.

"I'm quite fond of San Pellegrino if you have it," replied Clay.

"I'll check my stockroom for you." Ghost dipped back inside the tent again. "Sorry, we seem to be out of that brand. Will lukewarm river water suffice?"

"I guess it'll have to." Clay drank half the bottle down. "You know, I was once so thirsty I actually tried a Bud Light."

Ghost smiled, the scars on her face bunching into thick ribbons. "Man, you must have been desperate."

"I think they must distil piss from old folks' homes then boil all the flavour out."

Ghost laughed out loud. "Are you a beer snob, Mr Gunn?"

Clay finished the water bottle. "I guess I am. All the best people are. Have you got anything that we can eat on the move?"

"Your belly rumblin'?"

"Always," replied Clay.

"I've got some jerky strips and granola bars. Hardly the best—"

"I'll take them," said Clay. "We can eat as we load up, if that's okay with you?"

"Sounds like a plan. I'll pass my spare weapons out first."

A minute later, Clay looked down at the meagre assortment of kit. A machete, a basic single-edged hunting knife, a coil of climber's rope, a Taser and a semi-automatic shotgun. "Is this all you have?"

"Apart from my pistol and my knife." Ghost pursed her lips. "If I knew you were coming I'd have stocked up, but yeah, this is it."

"How many shells have you got for the shotgun?" said Clay, picking up the weapon. "Remington 1100. I used to have one like this back home."

"I haven't got many, but it's fully loaded already. Let me get the others out." Within seconds Ghost produced a clear ziploc bag that looked more suited to holding a school lunch. Inside the bag, Clay counted seven shells.

"You sure it's fully loaded already? Eight inside?"

"Damn sure. Loaded it myself."

"Okay then." Clay shouldered the shotgun, pointing it away from Ghost. "This is a workhorse gun, tactical model too. Nice."

Ghost gave a brief snort. "Stolen, like almost everything else I have here. Never had chance to use it yet."

"You any spares for your pistol?" he asked.

"Two spare clips. Never leave home without them." Ghost tapped her right thigh pocket. "And I've got my hook knife."

"Huh?"

Ghost drew a curved blade from her waist in an inverted grip. A small ring covered her index finger, locking the knife in her hand. "Stole this too."

"Ah, a karambit blade, nice. I've seen Danny use one of those." Clay drummed his fingers on the side of his own knife. "I prefer a full-size bowie myself, always gets the job done."

"A Texan with a bowie fetish, that's original."

"Hey, if it ain't broke… You mind if I hang on to the shotgun?"

"It's yours, Clay. Here's the spare ammo too. Make every shot count."

"Damn right I will. You ready to go?"

"I…"

"What is it?" asked Clay. Ghost stood motionless, eyes cast to her feet. "Hey, you don't need to come with me. I'd understand if you didn't."

Ghost held out a strip of silver metal some nine inches long. The sun flashed, reflected for a moment.

"What is that?" said Clay.

"When I woke up half past dead in that pig pen, I said there was nothing left of sweet Lauren, but that wasn't true. This was left. When she was a teenager she came off her bike and broke her leg in two. I was always telling her to slow down, but she wouldn't listen. I sat in the hospital all night as the docs patched her up. She hobbled around on crutches for weeks with her leg stuck out to one side. She looked so damn goofy and cute at the same time. This is the pin from her leg. This is all that's left of my dear, sweet sister, a damn titanium pin."

"We'll get payback for Lauren, I'll make sure of that."

Ghost slipped the slender rod into her right thigh pocket.

"You ready?" asked Clay.

"As I'll ever be."

"Then let's go get Celine and Danny."

"How's your head?" asked Ghost, as she picked up the Taser and rope. She tucked the machete into her belt at the small of her back.

"I'll live."

"Hey, wait up a minute, I've got something else to take those asswipes in the compound." Ghost ducked behind the tent and retrieved a black refuse sack tied into a ball-shaped bundle.

"What's that?" asked Clay.

"One of their men. We had a disagreement and he lost his head." Ghost opened the bag.

Clay looked inside. "Damn!"

43

"I was wondering where I'd put my card." Danny looked down at the meagre contents of his wallet spread on the table before the red-haired woman. "You want my money, huh? If you're hoping to retire on my dime you're gonna be sorely disappointed."

"Regardless, I still need your password," said Michelle.

"You know, I try not to swear in front of ladies, but you're no lady, so stick it up your arse!"

Michelle gave a small smile. "There's two ways of doing this, Mr Gunn."

"I'll take the hard way and save you the speech. You're not getting my money. I'll need it myself after I've killed all you maggots."

Michelle tapped the edge of the credit card on her desk. She looked first at Danny, her head slightly tilting to one side, then her focus shifted to Weiss. Her tongue pushed out her top lip. "Mr Weiss?"

"Give her the account details or I will put a bullet in your knee."

Danny turned slow and easy, folding his arms over his chest. "See, here's the thing, you've threatened that a few times now, but Master Bater through there wants me to fight tonight in his little shits and giggles show, so I don't think you will shoot me unless I come at you."

The guard holding the Taser raised his weapon an inch and took a step closer. With the smallest of movements, Danny slipped his cuffs and threw both hands out as if to grab the stun gun. The guard flinched, his finger squeezing tight on the trigger. Danny snapped his upper body aside. The Taser discharged first with a pop then a rapid series of clicks. Michelle squealed as the twin electrodes caught her in the chest, the raw electricity knocking her from her seat. She landed in an untidy heap at the side of the desk.

Danny skipped away from Weiss. "Well, that was a shock to her system." He wagged a finger at the guard. "Premature electrocution? Don't worry, lad, you can get little blue pills for that now."

Weiss pulled a radio handset from his belt. "Medic to the office, immediately."

Danny crossed his arms. "If we're finished here, I wouldn't mind a bite to eat and a bottle of your finest ale."

"You think this is the Marriott or something?" Weiss's face was white with strain.

On the floor, Michelle turned onto her side, her face slack, her eyes bewildered. Saliva dripped slowly from the side of her mouth as she struggled to form a word.

"You want a hand back up there, jelly legs?" asked Danny.

"Stay away from her!"

Danny looked Weiss up and down. "I'm beginning to

think you're all bark and no bite. Oh aye, you caught me with a couple of cheap shots and shame on me for letting you, but when it comes down to it I will end you. You won't be able to do a thing to stop it."

"Enough of your crap," said Weiss. "You're going back to your cell. Tonight I will watch you spill your blood in the pit, and I will laugh as you fade away like the little man you are."

Danny reached down and hauled Michelle into a sitting position. She flopped against the desk. Glancing at the computer screen, he was surprised to see how late it was. He'd been unconscious twice. Damn it, where the hell was Clay?

"Okay, back to my room it is." Holding out both hands in feigned submission, Danny moved away from the groaning woman. "Do you have Netflix in any of the rooms? I wouldn't mind catching up on an episode or two of *Jessica Jones* while I'm waiting around for your goon squad to get their shit together. I figure it may take a while."

The guard with the Taser looked first at Danny, then at Weiss.

"If the rest of your team is as sharp as this one, I'll be back in my room in five minutes or less. A bit of binge watching will help pass the time."

"Enough!" said Weiss. "And put those cuffs back on right now."

Danny looked down at the restraint dangling from his left wrist. He slipped it free and sent it spinning across the room. "Nah, I never liked jewellery anyhow."

44

Ezeret inhaled deeply, enjoying the many distinctive flavours contained within the cigar. He studied the results of his internet search. He did this regularly, searching for any giveaway clues from his previous life to his present incarnation. He had told the troublesome Scotsman that his name was Sean Ezeret-Dunn, but that was a lie.

As with many lies, there was a kernel of truth hidden within. He had been born Sean Bolivar Swan, a native of Panama City, his parents both respected professors. He had a natural aptitude as a scholar, excelling in languages and philosophy. But it was the more esoteric subjects that piqued his interest. The human mind or, more specifically, the manipulation of the mind proved fascinating to the young man. He made a study of neurolinguistic programming. After becoming adept at reading and controlling the non-verbal response patterns of his subjects, he moved on to the deeper study of hypnosis and mind control. First, he mastered the techniques of stage hypnotism, the basic but essential skills to access the subconscious mind. As he gained success, he discovered the darker applications of his craft.

Was it possible to shape a mind, turn it into the instrument of his own will and desire? With a little experimentation Ezeret had found not only that it was possible, but that it was relatively simple. In the months after his graduation he had attracted a core group of followers. As his skill in hypnosis grew, so did the level of influence he could exert upon his subjects. He quickly realised that although some of this was due to the power of suggestion, much was simply capitulation. His followers wanted to please him. Like many before him, he seized upon this attraction with zeal. He began to study the lives and methods of cult leaders who had come before, especially Charles Manson and Aleister Crowley. Different men in different times, yet both attracted willing followers to their dubious cause. Ezeret selected words and teachings from both, and combined them with his ever-expanding knowledge of mind control to fashion his own flavour of dark philosophy.

The Scotsman had surprised him by recognising Crowley's words. They were hardly a secret, yet Ezeret found that most educated adults had not heard of him.

Ezeret entered the words "Daniel Gunn" into the search bar of his laptop. A dentist in Minnesota, an ice hockey player, a tennis pro... He scanned the other results on the first page. None of them matched the roughneck he had in his cells. Ezeret clicked on the "images" option and scrolled down the page. There he was! Ezeret recognised the look in his eyes. The photograph showed a much younger version of Gunn, but those same intense eyes were unmistakable.

"Found you," said Ezeret. The photo showed Gunn

dressed in an army uniform, a rifle held across his chest. Ezeret clicked on the "view page" button below the image. The page loaded to show a collection of snapshots of different soldiers. All of them were Royal Green Jackets. Ezeret read the brief block of text below the pictures, explaining that the Green Jackets were one on the highest-regarded regiments of the British Army. Ezeret smiled, then took another long draw on his cigar. "How is it every soldier in the world thinks their unit is the toughest and best?"

Ezeret cared little for military men. So many lived in the glory of their past, even when their service was uneventful. Yet he acknowledged that many of them were mentally tough, men to be reckoned with. If they could be turned to his way of thinking they could be useful. Weiss exemplified that to the full. He had served with the German KSK, an elite special forces unit. He was ruthless and cruel and Ezeret loved him for it.

Pausing to remove a tiny fleck of tobacco from his lip, Ezeret heard the distinctive *ping* from his cell phone. He opened the text message. There were no words, only a smiley face emoji. The delivery would arrive tonight, as expected.

He had first encountered Devil's breath on a visit to Colombia. The seeds of the borrecherro tree, powdered down and ingested, turned the user into a zombified puppet, with little or no memory of what had taken place while they were under its influence. His followers, and more recently his clients, required a continual supply of victims to satisfy their desires. The Devil's breath allowed them to apprehend targets without violence and reduced the chance of failure almost to zero. Once the victim had ingested the drug, they were powerless to resist. They were brought back to the compound and interned while still completely docile and compliant.

Ezeret thought again of Danny Gunn. Should he simply dose his food and drink and control the unruly Scotsman that way? No. That would be too easy. Besides, he wanted to see what he could do in the trials tonight.

The Scot would no doubt add to the spectacle his followers loved. Of course, he would never be allowed to prevail unless he joined the ranks, and Ezeret knew the chances of that conversion were almost non-existent. He had met men like Gunn before, men of principle, men of renown. But his death in the trials would allow the guards who'd suffered at his hands to celebrate. Ezeret glanced at the clock. Late afternoon. The cartel would be here soon.

The couriers from Los Espadas delivered a package of the white powder once every six weeks. As a goodwill gesture, Ezeret encouraged them to stay the night at the compound, free to enjoy any vice their hearts desired. He was sure they, too, would enjoy watching the Scotsman spill his guts into the sand.

45

Clay cradled the shotgun loosely across his chest. The buzzing in his ears had subsided, but the ache behind his eyes was proving more stubborn. Ghost moved before him, always in a semi-crouch, never making a sound.

She scooted to one side, drawing her pistol in a fluid motion. Clay dodged against a tree. Something had moved on the path ahead. He exhaled slowly as he raised the shotgun into a firing position.

Ghost held her left arm out to her side, palm down. Then, as slow as melting ice, she extended one finger and pointed to a position to the left of the meagre path. The foliage shuddered.

Clay sighted on the bush, his finger tightening on the trigger, then stopped as he saw what it was.

"You again!" said Ghost.

"You gotta be kidding me," added Clay. "That damn dog is like a bad debt."

The mangy canine looked back at Clay and Ghost in turn.

"You seen him before too?"

"More than once. Something ain't right with this picture."

Ghost raised one eyebrow.

"Danny and me nearly ran over it in a town miles and miles from here, then he turned up large as life a couple of hours later. There's no way he could have run after us and kept up."

"You sure it's the same dog?"

"Yep. See those scars on its flank and that hole through its ear? Same each time."

"I spotted him just before you and your brother arrived at the compound. Nearly plugged him then, too."

"It wouldn't do to shoot the messenger."

Clay snapped the Remington in the direction of the new voice. "Damn it, Jak! You nearly got a gut full of buckshot."

"Please don't do that," Jak said. "I like my internal organs right where they are."

Clay moved his weapon away from the old Mayan. "What the hell are you doing here? I thought you were heading for the hills."

"You thought wrong," Jak said, smiling like an aged Mona Lisa. "I came back to see the next part of the story unfold."

Ghost looked at Jak, her eyes narrowing, then to Clay. "You know him, then?"

"We ran into each other last night. Jak led us to the compound," explained Clay.

"I was waiting for the brothers to arrive," said Jak.

"You knew they were coming down here?" asked Ghost.

Clay gave out a low grunt. "Jak thinks Danny and I are some kinda heroes reborn and he's our spirit guide or something. A load of hooey, if you ask me."

"The hero twins were sent by the gods to face the trials of the underworld," said Jak.

"And you think Clay and his brother are what, reincarnations of these twins?" Ghost's eyebrows curved into high arches.

"Maybe," said Jak. "The twins were helped on some of their trials by a princess who had returned from the realm of the dead. She was, like the brothers, scarred by her many adventures. Her skin was the colour of the darkest night and the brothers considered her an equal."

Ghost ran her fingers across the deep channels in her face as Jak continued. "The princess came from a faraway land and her heart had been cut from her chest by the dark lords of the underworld. The princess was clever and used trickery and guile to take on the dark lords."

"Thanks for the history lesson. So why are you here?" asked Ghost.

"We all have a part to play in the game."

Clay exchanged an impatient look with Ghost. "Just stay well out of the way when the bullets start flying."

Jak brushed a speck of dirt from his left hand. "I trust the great blowgunner not to shoot me."

"Is the mutt yours?" asked Clay. "He keeps turning up like an ugly cousin."

"Well, let's just say that Chaac and I are friends. At times, he is my eyes and ears."

Clay grunted something unintelligible.

"Chaac and Jak?" asked Ghost. "Sounds like a bad rap duo."

"I'll be near when you need me," said Jak.

"Stay safe, dude," said Clay before turning back to Ghost. "Daylight's a-burnin'."

Clay followed close behind Ghost, their voices barely above a whisper as they drew closer to the compound.

"Is he for real?" asked Ghost.

Clay gave her the flat-eye. "Just because he believes, it doesn't make it real."

"Hmmn." Ghost slowed her pace. "The compound is just through the next line of trees. How do you want to do this?"

"I'm going through the front door. The time for subtlety is past. If I'd just shot those assholes that were chasing down the girl, I wouldn't have got my ass blown up by a grenade. This time it's shock and awe."

"Shock and awe. I like that sound of that. How can I help?"

"When he scouted the perimeter, Danny said there was a power generator at the back of the main house. Could you knock it out?"

Ghost's eyes flashed as she answered. "Consider it done."

"When we get to the camp you go wide, and when you get my signal, cut the power."

"What signal?"

The lattice of scars on the left of Clay's face crinkled as a cold smile spread across his face. "You'll know it when you hear it."

"And then what?" asked Ghost.

"Then feel free to kill any asshole that crosses your path. This is all or nothing. I'm not leaving without Celine and Danny."

"Shock and awe."

"Shock and awe," said Clay.

46

There were other people being led past the door as it opened. Looking over the guard's shoulder, Celine recognised a couple of faces from the chamber under the main house. Some had the now familiar vacant expression, a few gave fearful glances as they were ushered past by more guards.

Sometime after they had returned from the chamber, food and drink had arrived via a stainless-steel trolley. The man who brought the food pointed to the meagre offerings, then at Celine and her friends. The sandwiches were bland, sliced ham on white bread, cans of soda. That had been how long ago? Celine wasn't sure.

The new guard at the door beckoned them to follow him. Celine was sure that it would lead to nothing good. "What's happening?"

He looked Celine up and down, his gaze scathing. "Follow the others. Shut your mouth."

We need to be ready...

Gillian walked alongside her as they moved along the enclosed passageway. Celine wrinkled her nose at the pungent smell. Body odour and fear. Feeling suddenly self-conscious, she lowered her nose and inhaled. Ugh.

"Keep moving," said the voice from behind.

Keeping her chin lowered, Celine inspected every part of the corridor, desperate for something that could be used to their advantage. There was nothing. No fire extinguishers to be sprayed in the faces of the guards or used as bludgeons, no window latches that could be snapped off and used as impromptu daggers. Nothing.

The group huddled together as they passed through the doorways. The temptation to sprint for what she thought was the front of the main house was hard to resist. But it stood to reason that if the guards were this diligent at keeping the corridors securely locked, the front door would be too.

Her heart was hammering against the inside of her chest as they again descended the stairs to the underground chamber. As they entered the amphitheatre for the second time that day, she noticed that there were faces she had not seen before. More captives sat in rows on the bleacher-style seats. Celine counted the others. Eighteen. Eighteen more captives in addition to Celine's immediate group. That made twenty-three captives in the room. There could be more elsewhere. How the hell did they manage to get away with the continual abductions? Yet they did. Rebecca had told her as much. New faces appeared, familiar ones vanished. She was afraid to imagine their fate.

On the opposite side of the pit, guards had begun to assemble. The door by which they had entered slammed shut, the sound echoing ominously around the chamber.

Several more guards entered at the other side of the pit.

But not just guards. One of the burlier men propelled another captive in front of him. The burly guard held a long pole, the kind used by dog catchers to secure dangerous animals. The long silver pole ended in a noose, which was pulled tight around the man's neck.

"That's Danny!" Celine clutched at Gillian's leg. "That's Danny. What are they going to do to him?"

"How is he going to help us?" asked Marco in a whisper.

Celine ignored him. "Where the hell is Clay?"

Danny was forced to the edge of the pit. Only then was the noose loosened and two men armed with pistols drew down on him. One of the men dipped his pistol to the pit. Danny levered himself into the space below. Spotlights shone into the pit, throwing the bleachers into shadow.

Danny's Scottish accent echoed around the chamber. "Well come on then, what are you waiting for? Let's get the show on the road. Which one of you tools is going to fight me, eh?"

Celine stared at Danny with hope welling in her heart. Clay told stories of how Danny was the meanest streetfighter he'd ever seen. She hoped that wasn't just one brother bigging up the other. She'd already watched one man die in the pit.

Ezeret stepped into the chamber on the opposite side. He held his arms out level with the floor. The chatter in the room fell silent. Next to her, Gillian stared at her feet.

"If I tell, will you listen?"

The men closest to Ezeret clapped their hands as they had before. "We will listen."

"If I show you, will you see?"

"We will see."

"If I challenge, will you rise?"

"We will rise."

"Who here is ready to be challenged?"

One of the men separated from the group. He sported a series of facial piercings. "I am ready."

"Will you risk death yet not turn your face away?" asked Ezeret, pointing at the volunteer.

"I will not turn away."

Ezeret gave a single nod then beckoned the man forward. "Then enter the pit, if you dare."

"Is that the best you could muster?" asked Danny. He shook his head. "Come on down you little skid mark, it's your funeral."

Celine smiled despite the promise of impending violence. "Get him, Danny," she whispered, "smash him up."

Ezeret spoke again, his words echoing around the chamber. "Are you ready to face the trials?"

"I am ready."

Ezeret pointed to Danny, who was now leaning against the wall of the pit with his arms crossed, as if he didn't have a care in the world. "Are you ready to face the trials?"

"Enough of your shite, get your man down here," replied Danny.

Ezeret produced a rectangular case as he had at the previous trial. He slowly opened the lid. "You may choose your weapon."

The guard reached out and took hold of a long-bladed machete.

Ezeret turned to look down at Danny. He tossed a small black object into the pit. "You had that on you when Weiss brought you here. I hope that will suffice?"

Danny stooped and picked up the object. A blade a few inches long sprang from his fist. "You found my Fox. I thought I'd lost that for good."

Celine's earlier smile seemed like a distant memory as she watched the guard drop into the pit. His machete looked massive compared to the stubby little blade that Danny held along the side of his leg.

"Let the trials begin," shouted Ezeret.

The guard cut the air with the machete as he advanced. Danny remained motionless. His opponent's blade glinted wickedly. *Why wasn't Danny moving?*

The machete streaked through the air.

Danny burst into action. His left hand plucked the machete from the man's grip seemingly without effort. Then Danny walked to the other side of the pit.

What the hell?

The guard took one faltering step then dropped to the ground. A stubby black handle jutted from the side of his neck. Celine inched to the edge of her seat. She hadn't even seen Danny stick him. *Jesus, he was fast.*

Danny rested the machete across the back of his shoulders in what looked like another careless pose. "I guess he couldn't cut it. Now, who's next?"

47

Clay rested on one knee, taking deep breaths as Ghost silently flitted from tree to tree. He had no doubts about her now. Ghost had already proven herself to be both capable and resourceful.

He turned his attention to the front door of the main house. That was the way he was going in. Then he would clear the house room by room until he found Celine and her friends. He was counting on Danny being in there, too. He looked at his meagre supply of weapons again. He wished dearly for a tricked-out M4 and a saddlebag full of ammo. The shotgun and blade would have to suffice.

A vehicle was approaching. Its rumbling engine sounded alien in the jungle. A high-end pickup truck swung into view, the flatbed covered by an all-weather tarp. The tinted windows made it difficult to see how many passengers it carried.

Clay scuttled along the fence as the pickup reached the gates. A man in faded denim and a backwards baseball cap stepped out of the house into the late-afternoon sun to open the gates. Once the truck had stopped by the front door, all four doors opened simultaneously and the occupants of the vehicle climbed out. Five men, all trim and athletic. Their dark suit jackets and crisp white shirts provided a sharp contrast to the light blue denim of their host.

One of the visitors carried a sports bag. The driver of the pickup truck stepped forward and clapped his host on the shoulder.

The man from the compound seemed in a hurry to get them inside. Clay allowed a bitter smile to creep across his face. The gates had been left open. A rookie mistake that would cost them dearly. Running at a steady gait, he entered the compound. The enclosed row of buildings swept off to his right; he was sure that was where Celine would be. Celine and her friends and God knows who else. Pressing himself against the wall, Clay paused, half expecting a shout of alarm to give away his presence, but none came. He looked again at the row of buildings, each one connected to the next by an enclosed walkway. The windows of the squat buildings were of frosted glass. No movement or lights showed from within. The front-door handle was hot to the touch, and opened without a sound. These guys were way too complacent. Clay had seen it all before. Men who thought they were untouchable often became careless, full of their own sense of menace.

Clay stepped inside the house, pulling the door closed behind him. He swept the room with the shotgun, ready to put a ragged hole in whoever was there, but it was empty. The suited visitors were nowhere to be seen. One of the doors to the right must lead to the outbuildings. He moved directly to the first one. The room it led to was empty of occupants. A pair of low couches separated by an ornate table and a wall full of books made the room look like a library. He moved to the next door. It held fast. He noticed a small white switch to the side of the door and pressed it. A short buzz sounded, and he heard the lock disengage. Reaching into a pocket, he pulled out a strip of beef jerky that Ghost had given him back at her camp. Biting off a length, he pushed the remaining strip into the cavity of the lock. He stepped through into a corridor lined with prison-like doors, and let the door swing closed behind him—the dried beef prevented the lock re-engaging. Moving at a steady pace, Clay wedged each door open with a small bite of dried meat.

Every room was lined with bunk beds and showed signs of recent occupation: scraps of food, an open bottle of water, a discarded sweatshirt. But no Celine. No one at all.

His lip curled as he retraced his steps to the main building. She must be somewhere in the main house. "Damn it!" He'd been so fixated on the jailhouse-style outbuildings that he'd forgotten what Ghost had told him: the captives were taken *under* the house. Ghost hadn't told him how to get below ground, and he hadn't thought to ask. Clay pushed the door open and stepped back inside the main house.

There he found the same man who had greeted the suited visitors. "Are you new?"

"And improved," growled Clay. "Where are the kids?"

"Huh?"

"The captives, the prisoners."

The guard jabbed a finger behind him. "They're all down below. Master Ezeret has got some extra trials going on tonight. Some tough guy they brought in from the jungle. Some kind of troublemaker."

Clay almost smiled. *Danny!* "How do I get down there?"

The man turned and pointed to a door behind him. "Through that way. The stairs lead all the way down."

"How many of our men are down there?"

The man gave a slight shrug. "All of them, I think. Well, apart from me, that is."

"One last question. Who were the suits that you just let in?"

"The suits?" The guard looked around as if the men in question were somewhere in the room. "Oh, those are the bad men, but Master Ezeret says that even the bad men of the world can serve a good purpose."

Clay spoke through clenched teeth. "Who are they?"

"Cartel. Los Espadas. They bring in the Devil's breath. Master Ezeret says—"

"What are the cartel boys packing?"

"Huh?"

"What kind of weapons?"

"Huh?"

Clay's finger tightened on the trigger. "You ever sleep with any of the kids they bring in here?"

The guard laughed. "So many I can't even remember their faces. Give me rape, give me murder, give me anything but the mundane."

Clay raised his shotgun and pulled the trigger. The guard went down in a spray of crimson, his chest a bloody ruin. The sound of the shotgun echoed like a burst of thunder in the lobby. "Was that mundane enough for you?"

Seconds later, the lights went out.

48

Danny looked down at the body at his feet. The guy had come in swinging, his arm extended like a child in a slapping match. He'd paid dearly. It was a simple act to step straight into the eye of the storm, one hand taking his weapon, the other delivering a backhand stab to the soft spot just below his ear. The man was dead before he realised his mistake. Danny wrenched the blade free.

As he made a show of looking around the chamber, Danny counted the men staring down at him. There was a chance he could get through them all with the machete and knife, but it would take a while. If even one of them was carrying a pistol he would undoubtedly be shot dead.

"So, who's next?" shouted Danny, adding as much cockiness to his voice as he could muster. "Come on, Ezeret, I thought you said you were going to find me someone worthwhile to fight. What kind of half-arsed trial is this?"

Ezeret clapped his hands twice. All eyes in the room turned to him. His voice cut across the room with undeniable authority. "If I challenge, will you rise?"

"We will rise."

"Who here is ready to be challenged?"

A thickset man stepped up on his seat, his barrel chest straining the wifebeater vest he wore. His dark brown hair was slicked straight back, with sideburns that tapered into points. "I am ready, Master."

"Will you risk death yet not turn your face away?"

"I will not turn away," replied the man.

"Fuck me, Eddie Munster really let himself go," said Danny. He looked up at Ezeret. "Really? This Oompa Loompa on steroids is the best you could manage from the faithful horde? You really need to recruit some better henchmen."

Ezeret raised one eyebrow. "Why, Mr Gunn, you are quite right. Let's make this a little more interesting, shall we?"

"Anything would be better than the guff you're peddling."

One of the guards scuttled to Ezeret upon command. Moments later, the man produced a set of manacles. Danny watched Eddie Munster reach out with his left hand. One end of the manacles was fastened securely. With his free hand, he accepted another machete from Ezeret. He lowered himself over the edge of the pit, his legs dangling free, then dropped to the floor. With his machete cocked over his right shoulder, he extended the manacle.

"The challenge has been set, Mr Gunn. Will you rise?" asked Ezeret.

Danny stepped closer, ready to move if Eddie Munster tried to sucker him. As he clicked the manacle around his own left wrist he wondered again where the hell Clay had got to.

"Are you ready to face the trials?" demanded Ezeret.

Munster held his blade aloft. "I am ready!"

The guards applauded.

Ezeret pointed at Danny. "Are you ready to face the trials?"

"As I'll ever be."

One of the guards gave a loud whistle and shouted, "Split him open, Damien. The hogs are eating meat tonight!"

The laugh died in Danny's throat as he saw Weiss enter the room with five new men in stylish suits, clearly distinguished guests. Only when the new arrivals had been seated on the front row did Ezeret turn his attention back to the pit. "Let the trials begin."

There was a muffled boom from above the chamber, then the lights went out. The spotlights dimmed to a faint orange, the meagre illumination lasting for only a few seconds, then utter darkness.

Danny breathed a sigh of relief.

Clay had arrived. About friggin' time too.

The most common attack with a machete is a forehand swing on a downward diagonal plane. The head is the usual target. Danny did not use the most common attack. Instead, he yanked Damien's manacled arm up into the air, pulling him off balance. In one continuous motion, Danny ducked under the man's arm and sent his own blade deep into his opponent's waist. Damien gave out a sharp cough as Danny straightened up behind him, wrenching his captured arm up his back. In the pitch-black chamber, Danny continued to move. The machete bit deep into the soft flesh of Damien's locked elbow. Damien screamed. Other voices cried out in the darkness. Danny slashed again with his blade and felt Damien's arm detach from his body. Danny let him fall, still screaming, at his feet.

Ezeret shouted, "Weiss! Get the lights back on!"

The beam of a flashlight cut into the pit a second later, lancing left and right. Even as Damien writhed on the floor, blood spurting from his severed limb, Danny vaulted the edge of the pit and dragged himself free.

"Celine Chavez!" roared Danny. "Celine, it's Danny Gunn, Clay's brother! I'm here to get you home."

"Danny!"

The beam from the flashlight lanced left and right. Angry confused voices echoed around the chamber. Someone crashed into Danny; a young woman cried out in surprise.

"Celine, where are you?"

"I'm over here." Celine's voice came from somewhere on his right.

More lights bounced around the chamber as several of Ezeret's men activated cell phones. The shadows danced wildly. Danny raced to where he'd heard Celine's voice, calling out again as he moved.

"Danny!"

Then suddenly Celine Chavez was clinging to him, her arms tight around his chest.

Lights bobbed and turned, first one way then the other. Angry voices rang out, dire violence promised. Ezeret raised his voice above the rest. "Weiss! Kill Gunn now!"

Danny spoke directly into Celine's ear. "Stay behind me. Keep your head down and be ready to run. We're going back through the main house. I'm sure Clay's up there."

"Okay!" Celine nodded her head furiously as she watched several lights bob closer.

An urgent voice called out from behind an approaching light. "I've got him!"

Danny slashed down with the machete, aiming behind the light. The blade struck something hard and the man went down, a strangled scream following the light as it fell. Something warm and wet spattered Danny's face.

Celine grabbed the cell phone. She shone the light towards the door above the amphitheatre seats. "That's the way out."

"Move," said Danny. Shots rang out across the chamber and sparks flew from the seats just in front of Danny's legs. Someone close by folded at the waist and silently toppled to the ground.

Celine turned and shouted to the shadow-streaked faces behind her. "Follow Danny!"

49

Ghost leapt high and hauled herself over the fence. The bag tied to her belt bounced heavily against her hip. She drew her pistol and took a deep breath. Moving directly to the large generator at the rear of the house, she glanced over to the large animal pens. The smell. She remembered the horror inside. Those hulking pigs, relentless and ferocious.

Forcing the beasts from her mind, Ghost dropped to one knee at the side of the generator. A green fuel tank towered above her head. A thin metal casing protected the inner workings of the attached engine. Ghost pulled open a door on the side of the casing. The generator rumbled quietly. A small LCD screen glowed with a muted green light. Below the screen sat a series of buttons, each with a corresponding green light. She looked at the two large buttons, one green and one red. The red button had the legend "Emergency Shut Off" printed below. *Maybe it is that easy,* thought Ghost.

Now all she had to do was wait for Clay's signal.

Yeah, you just sit around on your butt while he does all the real work, chile.

Ghost twitched her head to one side. When she'd been alone, Mama's chiding hadn't bothered her so much. She had lost sweet Lauren… how long ago? Now she had Clay, a new friend, someone real to talk to—she'd thought till now that maybe Mama would quieten down for a spell.

You gonna let him down the way you did your sister?

"No!" Ghost's voice was a harsh whisper. She focused on the red button on the generator panel. How long would it take for Clay to get inside the house?

Boom!

The sound came from inside the main building. Clay!

Ghost smacked the protruding red button hard with the palm of her hand. The generator cut out within two seconds. After moving to one side, Ghost fired two shots into the control panel. The first left a neat hole through the LCD screen, the second obliterated the red shut-off button.

Ghost ran for the house, checking the huts as she passed. The first four proved empty. The ordinary furnishings and possessions inside sickened her. Books and magazines, a CD player, throw pillows. Were these the trappings of the same men and women who were capable of horrific levels of abject cruelty?

As she threw open the fifth door, closest to the main house, a man dressed only in a pair of boxer shorts stepped into her path, rubbing his face.

"What happened to the lights?" He took a step back as Ghost raised her pistol.

The eagle tattoo that covered the man's chest brought back a searing memory. A sweating body on top of hers, hands wound tight in her hair holding her down, him thrusting into her, other men laughing. The eagle tattoo right in front of her eyes.

Ghost slammed the butt of her pistol into his face, knocking him to the ground. "You rapist piece of shit!"

"No, wait…"

"What's wrong, tough guy?" She lowered her pistol. "Haven't got the balls for it anymore?"

"Wait!"

The suppressor on Ghost's Glock 19 reduced the sound of the two shots to that of a door slamming shut. The first left a red ragged hole in the front of his shorts, the second caught his scream as it drilled through his throat. The man fell back, silent, blood spilling from both ends.

Ghost ran for the house. She reached a simple wooden door, no windows, and turned the handle. It held fast. Staying close to the brickwork, she sprinted along the side of the house until she reached a second door. The upper half of this door was decorated with six small windows. She tried the handle; again, she found it locked. Flipping the pistol, she hammered out the window closest to the handle with a few sharp taps. Reaching in through the hole, she turned the rotary lock. The door swung open.

She found herself in a kitchen. It was dark and smelled of old food and cleaning chemicals. On the counter was a half-eaten sandwich—but all her attention was taken by the kitchen knife that lay alongside it. The blade was long and thick. Ghost snatched up the knife and held it just below her pistol, wrists crossed. A muffled sound deeper in the house set her moving again, but before she could investigate she heard the harsh crack of a pistol shot, then the boom of the shotgun. She dodged to one side, back against the wall, and trained her pistol on the door. The door crashed and a man ran into her. Her head hit the wall. The man on top of her was easily twice her weight, his face rough with stubble. Ghost squeezed the trigger. The Glock 19 bucked in her hand.

The man yelped and grabbed at her weapon. Needles of pain jabbed her spine as they fought. Her left arm was pressed tight to the side of her hip, the knife digging into her flesh. He was way too strong. The bones in her wrist were ready to snap. Then the pistol slipped from her grasp. The big man reared up and slammed the weapon at her head. She avoided the brunt of the force, but sparks still spread in a sudden cascade behind her eyes. Her left arm sprang free. The knife! She brought the weapon into his right side, feeling the blade grate against bone. The second attempt scored a deeper hit. As his bulk shifted off her, Ghost slashed higher. The blade caught him across the bridge of the nose, splitting the cartilage and adding to the warm spatter on her hands.

The big man stumbled back, the pistol falling from his grip, a low monosyllabic chant issuing between his cupped fingers. "Ah, ah, ah."

Ghost used the wall to lever herself upright. She leapt at him, her arm outstretched like a fencer. The point of the blade went in deep beneath his chin. He dropped to his knees then onto his back, heels scraping the floor as he gurgled wetly.

You stuck him good, chile.

Ghost sought her fallen pistol, only breathing again when her hand closed around it.

50

Ulrich Weiss snorted a short breath filled with resignation. He had advised Ezeret not to give any opportunity to Daniel Gunn. The man was trouble, rattlesnake trouble. Maybe he should have just given him a third eye back at the sinkhole. Yet, despite the sudden darkness and the screams that followed, Weiss felt a surge of adrenalin. Gunn was at least worthy of a fight, someone to prove a challenge.

As his flashlight beam cut into the confines of the pit it revealed Damien, his arm missing from the elbow down, mewling like a beast on the butcher's block. Gunn was no longer in the pit. Shit, the wiry Scotsman was fast.

Weiss's light caught the cartel men, their faces grim, pistols raised. He drew his own pistol as he cast the flashlight over the confused crowd of captives at the far side of the pit. Some milled and surged into each other while others sat unmoving at the change of events. Weiss knew that some of the captives would still have the essence in their bloodstreams. The smallest dose of the Devil's breath kept them docile and virtually zombified. They should have dosed Gunn. Damn Ezeret and his sense of grandeur. There was a time for entertainment, sure, but poking a rabid dog with a stick was never a good idea.

There!

The P7 pistol spat four times in rapid succession. A body crashed to the floor, but not Gunn's. The beam from the flashlight caused the surrounding darkness of the chamber to appear an even deeper black. Shadows flitted and merged as bodies moved en masse, pushing, jostling, voices cried out in confusion. Weiss glimpsed Gunn for the briefest of moments and snapped off another shot. Sparks lanced through the darkness.

Weiss shouldered one of the guards aside. The man tumbled back, the cell phone in his hand causing new shadows to play around the chamber like a deranged puppet show. Weiss emptied his pistol then changed the magazine. There was a huddled group of shadows at the doorway. More captives? Once through the door they would have free access to the main house. If the generator was down, then the magnetic door seals would be out. With no power supply, the doors would push open easily. Only the holding rooms and the first interior door required keys to open them.

Weiss shouted over the rising clamour, "The door! Take them down! Now!"

Several of the guards responded to his command and raced up the seating, grabbing onto the closest of the shambling crowd. Bodies tumbled, cries of alarm echoing through the chamber as several of the captives were wrestled to the ground.

Weiss again tried to draw a bead on Gunn. Where the

hell was he? He paced the edge of the pit, hoping for one clean shot at the interloper. One of Ezeret's guards tumbled sideways from the lowest of the benches. As the man tried to catch himself, his elbow caught Weiss full in the face. A moment of weightlessness and then Weiss's back slammed into the floor of the pit, both flashlight and pistol flying from his hands. Something warm and sticky coated the right side of his face. Groaning, he reached for the flashlight, its beam illuminating the two ruined bodies next to him. Damien was still moving, but barely, his mouth opening and closing like a floundered fish. Weiss found his fallen handgun and clambered as quickly as he could out of the pit.

The guards had managed to subdue several of the more docile captives, who now regarded Weiss with vacant stares.

Ezeret's voice cut through the confused babble. "Who will rise to the challenge? Who will quell this impetuous uprising?"

Several of the guards responded to Ezeret's challenge.

Gunn was no longer in the chamber, he was sure. Weiss cast another glance in Ezeret's direction. He was still talking. Weiss had heard it all a hundred times. The cartel men were at the top of the short stairway at the far side of the pit, the second doorway that led back into the main house. Ezeret would make sure the Los Espadas soldiers were ushered to safety. He couldn't afford to make an enemy of them.

Weiss moved up the seats as rapidly as he could, his breathing ragged and uneven, knocking guards and captives out of his path. He *had* to put a bullet in Gunn's head.

51

"Drop the shotgun!"

Clay's jaw clenched.

"Do it or they'll be scraping your brains off the wall."

Then the lights went out.

In one motion Clay pivoted, dropping to one knee, and squeezed the trigger of the Remington. The flash from the barrel of the shotgun was bright in the sudden darkness. A man-shaped shadow dove back through the doorway, his pistol spitting a brief tongue of flame.

Clay followed at a rush. The room was full of angular shadows. A rounded shadow of deeper black moved at the far side of the room and Clay squeezed the trigger. Glass exploded, and a flash from the opposite side of the room told of Clay's error. The mirror lay in a thousand shards. How many years of bad luck would that be?

A bullet smacked into the stock of his shotgun, nipping into the skin between his thumb and forefinger, branding his flesh. His hand opened involuntarily. A second shot cracked into the door frame inches from his head. As Clay crashed to the floor his left shin cracked against something hard and unyielding. The shotgun slipped from his grasp. His face slammed into something wooden. Several more shots cut through the darkness, striking the wall behind. Surging to his feet and fighting against the encroaching dizziness, Clay grabbed the wide desk he had just fallen against and hoisted it into the air. A lamp clattered to the floor. Shots slammed into the desktop as Clay raced forward, then the shooter yelled out as he was knocked back into the wall.

Clay slammed the desk, slick with his own blood, into the man like a battering ram. Then his adversary surged back against him and the desk crashed to the floor. Clay's eyes had adjusted to the darkness enough to see the guard was clutching his chest. As Clay closed on him, the man leapt away and brought his pistol back into play. Clay dipped his shoulder and rammed the guard back into the wall. The pistol barked once more then fell silent, despite the man's repeated pulls on the trigger.

Clay grabbed his throat and squeezed, crushing the cartilage in the guard's neck in one violent second. Leaving the man to choke, Clay retrieved the Remington and made his way back into the dark lobby.

Moving back to the door first indicated by the denim-clad guard, Clay swept the lobby with the business end of the shotgun, turning in a slow circle. "Fool me once," he said, his voice like gravel on a tin sheet.

His attention snapped to a door at the far side of the lobby. Harsh sounds were coming from the other side. A pistol shot, muffled but still recognisable to his ear. A series of curses and yells, the sounds of combat. Clay stalked towards the source of the noise, ready to obliterate anybody that wasn't a friend.

Ghost stepped into the lobby, pistol in hand, a dark spectral silhouette. "Don't shoot. It's me."

"You meet a welcome party in there?"

Ghost moved closer to Clay, silent as ever. "An asshole the size of a bear, ran straight into me. Knocked me on my ass. I guess he was high-tailing it away from you."

"You put him down?"

Ghost slapped Clay lightly on the shoulder with the back of her hand. "You think I'd be yakkin' in here with you if I hadn't?"

"Good on ya, girl. Come on. We're going down below the house. That's where Celine and the others are."

"How can you be sure?"

"That guy there spilled the beans before I spilled the rest of him."

Ghost looked down at the splayed figure on the floor. "Okay then, Ranger Gunn, lead the way."

"It's probably gonna be darker than a lawyer's heart down there," said Clay. "Be careful."

Clay was one step towards the door when it was flung open and a rabble surged out, cell-phone lights spilling over their faces.

"Danny!"

Clay grinned at his brother. Celine sprang forward and wrap her arms around his waist.

"Clay! I knew you'd be here too."

"Are you okay? Did they hurt you?"

Celine shuddered as she clung to him bodily. "I thought we were going to die."

"Not if I have anything to do with it," said Clay, returning her embrace. Then he gently released her. "Come on. We've got to get you out of here."

He looked over her shoulder at the others. There were a dozen or so freed captives with Celine and Danny.

"Aye, it's time to make like a shepherd and get the flock out of here. There's trouble two steps behind us. Ezeret's guards will be coming this way."

Clay spat words through clenched teeth. "Good, I'm fixin' to kill every last one of them before I'm done."

"We've got to get Celine and the others out of here first." Danny spoke fast as he moved to let another captive step into the lobby. "We need to get to the vehicles outside."

Clay looked down and for the first time noticed the severed limb dangling at the end of Danny's manacle. The corner of his mouth twitched into the smallest of smiles. He would get the details later. "Danny, you take point and I'll bring up the rear."

That was the moment that the white-haired man stepped through the door. With a guttural curse, he sent three rapid shots into the crowd. His hand streaked to his torso and a moment later a cylindrical object flew across the room.

"Grenade!" Danny shouted.

The explosive rolled across the tiled floor like a rattle of phantom bones. In the open, a grenade was a very dangerous weapon; in a confined area, it was utterly devastating. Anyone within five metres of the detonation was hamburger.

Weiss ducked back into the doorway, loosing off another pistol shot.

Clay took a rapid step and kicked out with his right boot.

The grenade followed the white-haired killer back into the darkened doorway. A second later, a brain-numbing explosion turned the stairwell into a scene from Dante's *Inferno*.

52

Celine heard Marco Kenner emit a harsh cough as the pistol shot sounded across the lobby. Her friend doubled over as if he'd been punched in the stomach. As Danny shouted a warning of "Grenade!" she closed her eyes, waiting for the pain to rip her apart.

An explosion did come, but instead of shredding her flesh it boomed from the subterranean chamber below the house. She opened her eyes. Marco gave a protracted groan as she knelt next to him. Holding the cell phone over his torso, she could see his hands were a dark crimson.

"I've been shot," said Marco. Sobs racked his body. "I don't want to die. Celine, please, I don't want to die."

"You're not going to die. We're going to get out of here. We're going to get you help." Celine looked at Clay as he dropped to one knee next to her. The look in his eyes was dire.

"We need to move." Clay pulled off his shirt. "Sit him up. Marco, I need to tie this around you. It's gonna hurt but it'll help slow the bleeding."

Marco yelled in pain as Clay pulled the arms of the dark shirt into a tight makeshift bandage.

"Keep pressure on the wound as much as you can," Clay told Celine. "Someone help her. We've gotta move."

Gillian slung Marco's left arm over her shoulder and between them they hauled their injured friend to his feet. The noise he made was ungodly. Another young woman Celine didn't know was on her knees, her hands at her blood-covered shoulder. Laura helped her up.

Danny's voice cut through the clamour. "Clay, we need to move."

"Stay together, people. Danny, you and me on point. Ghost, you cover our back?" Clay sounded strong and fearless. Celine felt a surge of pride. The Gunn brothers would get them home.

"Covered." The black-clad figure Clay had referred to as Ghost held a pistol in one hand. As she angled the cell phone, Celine could see the deep rutted scars on her face, thick ribbons of raw pink etched into her ebony skin. *What had this woman been through?*

Clay opened the front door. He took a quick glance then ducked his head back inside. No bullet storm followed him.

"Move!" ordered Clay.

The day was fading, but the humidity hit her like a slap in the face. The early evening sky was rapidly darkening, the setting sun an angry orange ball. The trees surrounding the compound were reduced to misshapen silhouettes. Celine blinked several times as she took in her surroundings. An expensive-looking pickup truck was parked at an angle just outside the door, but there were too many in the group to fit in one vehicle. As if reading her mind, Danny pointed to the pickup.

"Clay, you see if you can get that started. I'm going for one of the vans round the side of the house."

Clay nodded in agreement. "Ghost, watch the door while I get this jalopy running."

Ghost pivoted and aimed her pistol back at the house.

Danny took off running as Clay opened the driver's door. Seconds later the engine of the pickup sprang to life. Clay beckoned to her. "Celine, you're in here with me."

As Celine and Gillian steered Marco to the back seat of the pickup, Clay ripped the tarp covering from the flatbed. Laura helped the woman who had been shot in the shoulder into the back seat with Marco. The smell of blood and fear was thick in the confined space.

Celine beckoned to Rebecca, who stared back but didn't move. Celine couldn't make sense of her expression. "Rebecca, come on. Get in the front here with me."

Rebecca climbed into the front of the pickup before Celine had finished, hugging her close.

"I keep expecting someone to grab me and drag me back into that hellhole," gasped Rebecca.

"Let them try," said Clay. "As many in the back as you can. Don't worry, Danny will be back with another vehicle in a minute."

The truck rocked as half a dozen of the other captives clambered into the flatbed. The pickup settled lower as its suspension creaked.

Celine looked at Clay, the scars on his face, the cold look in his eyes, a look she hadn't really seen before. Clay was a great gentle bear of a man, yet she knew he was a warrior. His scars bore testimony to that.

The group that had followed them from the subterranean chamber were mostly women. Apart from Marco, she could only count another two men. Several had not made it out of the chamber. The pickup was full and there were still another eight milling nervously between the house and the vehicle.

Celine watched Ghost move into a semi-crouch. A man appeared in the doorway holding a pistol of his own, his arm outstretched. A brief flash from Ghost's weapon and the man pitched onto the ground, clutching his chest. The breath caught in Celine's throat as Ghost put another shot into the back of the man's head.

As Ghost moved back into her guard position, pistol aiming once more into the doorway, Celine dialled 911 on the cell phone. The screen showed a "no service" message.

"Keep trying," said Clay.

Marco let out a wail from the back seat. "Jesus, it hurts so bad."

Celine twisted in her seat to look at her friend. Even with Clay's shirt tied around his middle, she could see that Marco's torso and hands were stained a dark crimson. His face was deathly pale in the waning light.

Clay's voice snapped her attention back to the front seat. "At least something is going our way. Those numbnuts left the keys in the ignition and the gates are open."

"I guess they didn't expect the Gunn brothers to arrive and spring us out of that nightmare factory," said Celine.

"I'm more than happy to crash the party. I'm just pissed that I didn't get here sooner."

"You're here now," said Celine. "I can't tell you how glad I am to see you. I was so scared in there. They spiked us with some sort of mind-control drug."

"Devil's breath," added Rebecca.

"Yeah, Devil's breath. It really screws you up. I can't hardly remember anything after they brought us here. It's all just scrambled fragments. They could have done anything to me and I wouldn't remember." Celine forced away the thought of the pain between her legs.

Clay's knuckles turned white as he gripped the steering wheel. "We're gonna get you somewhere safe. Then I'm gonna come back here and kill 'em all."

53

"Follow me," said Ezeret, using his cell phone to cast a meagre light down the passageway. There was almost no signal this far out in the jungle, but he kept the phone fully charged and ready to use. The first reliable coverage was miles away. "This way."

The men in suits followed with raised pistols. Los Espadas were no small-time dealers; they were bringers of death. He had previously witnessed how they dealt with threats. There was nothing they would not do to survive and protect the reputation of their organisation.

Moments later, they heard a grenade detonate. That was bound to be Weiss's handiwork. He was the only one of his men who carried such weapons. Some of the others owned pistols but rarely carried them; as a rule, batons usually sufficed.

"Who are these sons of whores?" the leader of the group growled in Ezeret's ear. "If this is some kind of trick, I will rip out your heart and feed it to those pigs of yours."

Ezeret turned, almost nose-to-nose with his accuser. "It's

no trick, Angel. I think these men are family to one of my latest acquisitions."

"They're tearing your place apart. This is not good for either of us. But it will be worse for you if they have brought the law here. I am leaving now, but if one of these bastards gets in my way they will die a thousand deaths."

Angel Velasquez was not making idle threats. If he said he was going to kill someone, that person was as good as dead. "Come this way. This passageway leads to my private room. From there you can leave by the side of the house."

Angel snorted through his nose. "You need some proper men around this place, not these pencil-dicked assholes you have as guards."

"What if I paid your men double what I just paid for your last shipment of Devil's breath? That's a lot of cash for killing these upstarts and giving me back my... *followers*."

"Is that what you call them? Followers? Ha." Angel tapped his pistol on the side of his head. "It will cost you five times what you paid for the delivery, and my men will skin these bastards alive in front of you."

Ezeret's throat tightened. Five times? That was a *hell of a lot of money*, but he knew that the cartel soldiers were more than capable of ending this situation. "I will have to owe you, but you know my credit is good."

"Yes, you will owe me!"

He'd just made a deal with the Devil. Angel Velasquez was a dangerous man with serious aspirations, but also a man with carnal appetites that he willingly slaked beneath Ezeret's own house. Ezeret smiled in the darkness. It was a deal he felt sure he could manipulate to his eventual benefit.

"I want the men dead and as many of my followers back in their cells as possible."

"We will kill the men, then your little minions can round up a few drugged-up prisoners. Or is that too much for them as well?"

"This way," said Ezeret. Moving as quickly as the darkness permitted, he led the cartel soldiers into his bedroom, which smelled strongly of burning incense. This was the place he brought the choice picks from the captives. He didn't bring every one, just those with a spark of defiance in their eye. There was nothing like watching that glimmer of hope, that fire that made them fight, extinguish. The tiniest amount of Devil's breath transformed the most defiant subject into a subjugated toy, a toy that he was free to play with in whichever way he pleased.

"If they are trying to free your people, they will have vehicles waiting outside. We need to get out there right now. We will hit them before they leave the compound," said Angel.

"This way." Ezeret crossed the room and unlocked a set of double doors. As the doors swung open, the sound of an engine swept in on the evening air.

Angel pushed past Ezeret, the rest of his men following close behind. Ezeret, unwilling to be needlessly amid real danger, held back, watching the cartel soldiers run to the fight. Something his father used to say sprang to mind: *You don't buy a dog and bark yourself.* No, he would let Angel's men do the barking and the biting. He hoped that Weiss would prove his worth and hamper Daniel Gunn's escape attempt. Between the two, Weiss and the cartel, the transgressors would be crushed.

It would be very bad for business if Gunn did escape with any of the captives. The last thing he needed was a police investigation. He already paid a hefty subsidy to several government officials to prevent such an occurrence, but the price would increase exponentially if he wanted to make an investigation go away. The local police and the men in the official offices all expected and received their monthly *mordidas*, their "little bites". Those little bites were sure to grow to veritable banquets, banquets he had no desire to provide.

As he stood in the failing light, he pinched the bridge of his nose. Maybe he should have listened to Weiss and given Gunn a healthy dose of Devil's breath; that would have allowed for an easy execution.

The sound of more gunfire snapped his thoughts back into focus. Angel's men must have closed in on Gunn and his little band of escapees.

54

Danny sprinted along a paved walkway that traced a path parallel to the side of the house. He ignored the first vehicle he saw, a compact Mazda, and moved to a larger panel truck. It was a basic model Ford Transit, big and boxy but very functional.

Kneeling at the side of the vehicle, he stretched out the severed arm, which was still attached to his via the manacle chain. Two deft chops with the machete cut through the limb at the wrist. Danny knew better than to try and cut through the chain with a machete blade. He wound the length of chain around his wrist. It would be a simple matter to pick the lock once they were free and clear of the compound. The door of the van opened without resistance. The interior smelled of cigarettes and body odour. Danny climbed into the driver's seat. A quick check showed that the keys were not in the ignition. He reached up to the sun visor—nothing.

"That would have been too easy." Danny moved from the van to the closest door of the Quonset huts. It stood to reason that the van would be parked as close to the owner's room as possible. Danny held the machete close to his right side as he opened the door. The day's failing light cast dark shadows.

"If I was a key, where would I be?" Danny hunted through the dark room, passing over a vase empty of flowers, a statuette of a rearing horse. Then his hand closed on a small wooden bowl. Inside was a small bunch of keys.

Back at the van, the longest key on the set slipped into the ignition. The engine sprang to life, the deep bass of the diesel engine sending vibrations through the whole van. He turned on the headlights and drove back to where Clay and the others were waiting.

A young woman slid open the side door. "It's full of boxes."

Danny sprang from the seat and moved to the side of the van. "Then friggin' throw them out!" Not waiting for assistance, he lobbed the boxes out. One split and emptied what looked like blank DVD cases onto the ground. Another spilled out an assortment of plastic ponchos.

"What are you waiting for?" Danny's voice was thick with impatience. "Get yer arses in here! Now!"

He ushered the rescued captives into the cargo space, reminding himself that they were all in a state of shock, probably still under the influence of the drugs Celine had told him about. He was glad to see that the rest of the group were spurred into motion by his action, and clambered inside of their own accord.

"Try to stay low and hang on to each other." He pulled the sliding door shut. "Ghost, was it? You're with me in the front."

"You go on without me." The black-clad woman kept her pistol trained on the door of the house.

Danny got back into the driver's seat. Ghost pulled what looked like a refuse sack from her belt and lifted out a grisly trophy. She set it on top of one of the discarded boxes, angling it so it faced the door.

Ghost looked around and saw he hadn't driven away. She leaned in through the open passenger door.

Danny stared at the disembodied skull. "Heads you win?"

"And tails, they lose!" replied Ghost. "You're Danny, Clay's brother?"

Danny shifted the van into drive. "Aye, that's me."

"You go on without me," she repeated. "I'm staying here. I'm going after Ezeret, the leader. I don't think I'll get a better chance than this. I need to put that asshole in the ground."

"There's still too many to kill on your own," said Danny. "You'll die."

"I never planned on walking away from this. So long as I take that evil son of a bitch with me, I'll go happy."

"We need to get these people to safety," said Danny.

"That's yours and Clay's job. Mine is finishing things here."

"Ghost—"

The back window shattered as a series of gunshots cut through the air. The suited men he had seen earlier rounded the corner of the house, pistols blazing. Ghost turned and snapped off a rapid series of shots. Leaning across the seats, Danny grabbed her collar and hauled her into the van as he stamped down on the gas.

Clay's shotgun boomed and the men in suits scattered like bowling pins. Danny wrenched on the steering wheel, angling the van so it faced the gates. The scream that Ghost gave carried unmistakable fury as she emptied her pistol at the men.

Several faces peered from the back of Clay's stolen pickup as it raced through the open gate. Danny followed his brother into the darkness of the Mexican jungle.

55

Clay drove the pickup as fast as safely possible. The road was little more than twin ruts worn into the hard-packed earth. Branches scraped at either side of the vehicle like the claws of some monster from a dark fable. The pickup truck bumped and shuddered as it cut along the narrow path. There was no space for another vehicle to pass.

"You okay?" asked Clay.

Celine nodded. "I'm worried about Marco. He looks terrible."

Clay glanced over his shoulder. Marco's head bobbed and rolled from side to side. "It's a very bad way to get shot but it can take a long time to die. If we get him to a hospital there's a good chance they'll save him."

Celine nodded again, the smallest of smiles showing what Clay took to be hope. Her face was tinged blue by the dashboard lights. He took no pleasure in lying to her. Without immediate surgery, most victims died of a gunshot wound to the abdomen, hydrostatic shock, infection and loss of blood all taking their toll. The force from a bullet spread through the surrounding tissue like a miniature tsunami. Nature never designed the human body to be shot.

Danny's van was right behind, its headlights burning bright. Clay reached over and squeezed Celine's shoulder. He could feel the tension in her muscles. She was safe, she was alive; that's what mattered. Yet something in her face had changed. Clay had seen it many times before, usually in the eyes of young soldiers: their first encounter with the reality of war altered them forever.

"I saw men die today." Celine's voice carried a slight tremor. "One of the captives died, before Danny showed up. They put him in the pit and one of the guards just cut him open. I've never seen so much blood. It was horrible. The man rubbed his blood all over his face after he'd watched him die."

"Don't worry, they can't harm you now. I'll die before I let that happen," said Clay.

Celine took another fretful look at Marco. "Not everyone made it out of there. I saw a couple of women go down when Danny was trying to get us out. That white-haired asshole shot them. We just left them there. I don't know if they were dead or alive. Oh, Clay, we left them behind."

Clay exhaled long and slow. "It doesn't sit well with me either, not one bit, but I came here for you. You're my primary concern. Once I know you're safe I will come back. I'll get as many home as I can."

The pickup lurched as the wheels hit a deep rut. A branch whacked solidly against the passenger door. Celine flinched.

"Danny," said Celine.

"What about him?" asked Clay. He glanced in the rear-view mirror. The van's headlights were close behind.

"He killed two of Ezeret's men in the pit like they were nothing."

"They *were* nothing. Scum that deserved whatever he served up for them."

"He moves really fast."

"That he does. He's an ornery little shit at times, but there's no one better in an honest-to-God, balls-to-the-wall street fight."

The pickup bounced again, the suspension bumping loudly, and Marco cried out from the back seat.

"Damn it, just what we don't need. A fork in the road." Clay made an instant decision and swung the pickup to the left. The next five hundred yards tested the suspension even more. Marco cried out each time the vehicle bounced on its springs.

"Do you know where you're going?" asked Celine.

Clay answered from the corner of his mouth. "Away from that damned compound."

A large outcrop of rocks standing much higher than the roof of the pickup caused a V-shaped deviation in the road. As Clay guided the pickup around the tight curve, he cursed and slammed on the brakes. "Well, that's a shit-stuffed chimichanga."

The road ahead was bisected by a deep channel, like a giant had dragged an almighty furrow with a clawed hand. There was a bridge of sorts, fashioned from two horizontal girders placed parallel across the crevice. Four upright spars of metal had been welded to the girders. A thick tangle of barbed wire encircled both posts and girders at either end. Without heavy-duty wirecutters and time they didn't have, there was no way to continue any further.

Danny's van rolled to a stop behind them. Danny was alongside Clay's window within a few seconds. "And it was all going so well."

A worried murmur arose from the flatbed. Clay gritted his teeth. "There's no room to turn around. Gonna have to back up to that fork and take the other road."

"Ghost tried to tell me this was a choke point, but you were motoring some. I couldn't stop you in time."

"At least we've put some distance between us and the camp. We need to get these injured kids to a hospital before we lose any of them." Clay did not have to elaborate on the dangers of untreated gunshot wounds.

Danny pivoted, looking back along the path they had followed. "You hear that?"

"Engines!"

"They're coming after us and we're stuck in this bottleneck. We'd better back-pedal sharpish or we'll be sitting ducks."

"Go!"

Danny sprinted back to his van. The vehicle began to reverse almost immediately. The sound of screeching metal cut through the darkening jungle as the van sideswiped the outcrop of rock. Despite the loss of a fender, it continued to reverse at a steady clip. Clay negotiated the obstacle without collision.

Danny's van had almost made it back to the fork when the first bullets cut the night air. Two new sets of headlights burned bright behind the van. Clay hefted the shotgun from his lap as he braked.

Ezeret's men had found them.

56

Danny hunched in his seat as an angry lead-bodied wasp punched through the side window of the van just above his head. The window disintegrated into a thousand tiny shards. "Get down. Lie as flat as you can!"

The passengers pitched to the floor of the van. With only a baleful stare as forewarning, Ghost flung open the passenger door and was swallowed by the thick foliage almost instantly.

Several more bullets punched into the van, in one side and out the other. Nervous yelps at different pitches issued from the floor. Danny pressed down on the gas pedal as far as it would go. Staring into the wing mirror, he could see two vehicles blocking the road: a pickup, not unlike the one Clay had stolen, and a boxy sedan. Men in suits were spread out in a skirmish line, weapons raised, peppering the van with bullets as it sped towards them. The rear of the van slewed from side to side as Danny struggled to keep to the narrow track. A scream rang out from the floor of the van as a bullet found flesh.

"Hang on to something! We're going to hit them hard!"

The shooters leapt in different directions to avoid being crushed. Danny grimaced as he rammed the parked sedan. The deafening sound of protesting metal echoed through the inside of the van, adding to the shrill cacophony. The sedan bucked to one side, its hood crumpled and windscreen spiderwebbed.

One of the women in the back of the van began to repeat the same prayer over and over like a mantra. "Please God, don't let me die. *Please God, don't let me die.*"

"Shite!" The boxy sedan, although shunted to one side, still blocked the road. Danny shifted into drive and the van lurched forward. "Hang on, I'm hitting them again."

The van had only gained twenty feet when one of the shooters sprang up, his pistol level with Danny's face. With an angry yell, Danny wrenched the steering wheel in the man's direction. The bullet smacked into the padded headrest with a disconcerting *whump*. The shooter leapt away from the van again, this time tumbling into the dirt.

"That was too close for comfort," Danny said as the tyres of the van lost traction. The other shooters were up and back in the fight. Bullets cut through the van. The vehicle was never designed for the jungle track and Danny cursed under his breath as one of the rear tyres blew out. The van dipped to the rear right corner, instantly becoming even less responsive.

Clay stared at him through the open window of the pickup, his face a glowering mask. The pickup was angled just behind the rocky outcrop that Danny had pranged. The barrel of the shotgun extended from the window. The gun boomed twice in rapid succession and the shooter closest to Danny pinwheeled to the ground.

Danny gritted his teeth. They didn't have the firepower to engage the four remaining shooters. The risk to the rescued captives was just too high. Danny stabbed a finger towards a gap in the trees. A blocked bridge in front and a roadblock behind. "I'll make my own bloody road."

Clay's shotgun roared again. Several of the pistols answered. The shooters had retreated, using the wedged vehicles as cover.

Danny hit the gas. It felt like gravity had found extra purchase on the van's frame, each second longer than the last. He was sure a bullet would find its mark any moment and he would end his days bleeding out in an unnamed pocket of the big green. He grinned in defiance as the tyres finally gained traction and the bullet-riddled panel truck shot off the narrow road and into the dense jungle.

The shotgun boomed again, and then the lights from Clay's pickup were bright behind him.

"Stay close, big brother," yelled Danny.

Danny steered the van down an uneven slope. The gaps between the trees were haphazard and he sideswiped more than one obstacle. The sounds of impact inside the van were deafening. The passengers in the back yelped intermittently, as Danny fought to keep it moving. The gradient of the slope increased. A branch thicker than Danny's upper arm whipped across the windscreen with a loud *thud*, and the glass fractured. Another tree branch shattered it. The surrounding canopy was dark and oppressive as the van's headlights illuminated only the foliage directly in its path.

Danny only managed a brief bark of surprise as he tried to steer away from the shard of rock that jutted from the ground like the dorsal fin of a colossal shark. The passenger side of the van slammed into the unyielding rock with a howl of screeching metal. The van lurched into the air as the side door ripped open, buckling at an unnatural angle. Despite the damage, the van continued to move, listing and shuddering like a dying beast.

Danny glanced over his shoulder. Flashes of light from the damaged door caused a strobe effect on the stricken faces that stared back at him. One of the younger woman gave a heart-rending sob. They all looked so young.

The steering wheel was slack in his hands. The dashboard lit up in orange and red.

Time seemed to dilate to an agonising slowness again as Danny focused on the massive tree trunk standing directly in their path. It was nearly as wide as the van itself. He wrenched the wheel to one side and stamped down on the brake pedal. The van hardly deviated from its path.

"Hang on!"

Too little, too late!

Then the world folded around him. The right front corner of the van smashed inward with terrible ferocity. With no seat belt to hold him in position, he was thrown bodily through the windshield. Missing the tree by mere inches, Danny tumbled in a desperate cartwheel. Keeping his head tucked and covered with his arms, Danny landed first on his chest, the breath exploding from his lungs, then his legs continued his uncoordinated gymnastic tumble. A tree branch knocked him into a thick bush.

Danny came to his senses hanging upside down, only the palms of his hands on the ground. Emitting an elongated moan, he set about gaining his feet. The thick leaves of the shrub seemed determined to continue their hold on him. Letting his arms bend, he tucked his head tight and pedalled with both legs in turn. Then he was falling again, rolling onto his back.

"Danny!"

Danny was lifted to his feet as if he weighed no more than a child.

"Holy hell, brother! Are you okay?"

"Marks out of ten for a shitty landing?" groaned Danny.

"*Nil points!*" said Clay. "And you take the piss out of my driving."

A pained shriek from the ruined van set Danny stumbling to the source of the sound. Clay followed close behind. Hardly an inch of the van seemed undamaged. Countless spots of light shone through the bullet holes in the mangled body. "Looks like a damned mirrorball."

Danny shielded his eyes as he stepped into the full glare of the pickup's lights. One of the rescued women lay at the side of the van, her right leg twisted at an angle that made Danny wince.

Danny exchanged a look with Clay, who retrieved the shotgun from the pickup and took up position to watch for their pursuers.

57

Cuchillo watched the bullet-riddled van veer off the narrow path and allowed himself a humourless smile. The driver was audacious, but they would kill him anyway. All challengers to Los Espadas suffered the same fate: an agonisingly brutal death.

"Everybody still breathing?" Angel asked.

The man who had taken a hit from the big man's shotgun ripped off his suit jacket. Several dots of crimson showed on the sleeves of his shirt, but his armoured vest had taken the worst of it. The vests were lightweight and comfortable to wear even in the oppressive heat of a Mexican day, the best money could buy.

"You're bleeding," said Angel. "You going to be okay, Mako?"

Mako gave a sullen nod. "I've had worse."

Cuchillo listened to the sound of branches snapping and shale being cast into the air as the fleeing vehicles drove away. They wouldn't get far. Too many trees, too many holes in the ground. As if to acknowledge his thoughts, the unmistakable sound of rending metal echoed up the slope.

Mako tapped the barrel of his pistol on the side of his head. "I'm good to go."

"You all carrying spare clips?"

"Of course," said Cuchillo. "Never leave home without them."

"We go on foot from here. These sons of whores will not see another sunrise. If you can, you take them alive. If not, dead works for me too." Angel pulled Mako close. "You stay close to me, my friend."

Mako gave another nod as sullen-eyed as the first. A malicious grin showed his neat white teeth.

"When we bring back these sons of bitches, Ezeret will be deep in our debt. That means the price of the delivery will be going up and that means more of a take for all of you," said Angel.

The cartel soldiers had no need of sophisticated tracking skills. Twin lights illuminated the trees a quarter-mile down the slope. They set off at a controlled jog towards the lights.

At the rear of the group, Cuchillo paused and looked back the way they had come. He squinted into the darkness for any sign of danger. He dropped into a crouch as the rest of the group continued their path.

Something there?

Cuchillo moved into deeper shadows, straining to identify the threat he sensed behind him.

Crouching next to the moss-covered tree trunk, he scrutinised everything within sight. The sun was just a narrow sliver of orange peeking above the horizon. It was almost impossible to tell where one tree ended and the next began.

Had a shadow moved over there? He couldn't be sure. He raised his pistol, aiming into the darkness, ready to drop anything that moved. It was neither a sight nor a sound that saved Cuchillo's life in that moment but his sense of smell. The faintest whiff of something that did not belong among the trees—blood and sweat. As he threw himself bodily from his resting position, three sharp discharges sounded only yards behind him. Sighting on the brief flashes, he squeezed his own trigger. The retort from his weapon was loud and aggressive, the five shots following each other within a split second. Cuchillo raced for cover, putting another tree between him and his quarry. Had he hit his target? Another two muffled shots from his left told him no. A bolt of red-hot pain seared across his back as one of the bullets found flesh. An involuntary yell escaped his throat. Moving at a sprint, he ducked behind another tree trunk.

Cuchillo glanced down the slope. The rest of the team were out of sight. His nose wrinkled as he took a deep breath, trying to smell again the scent that had warned him moments earlier. The wound across his upper back was burning. Biting down against the searing pain, he forced himself to relax. One mistake might prove to be a fatal error. He still hadn't got a good look at his assailant. Only a dark shadow. Yet shadows didn't carry pistols and suppressors.

58

Only Ghost's dark eyes showed from behind her mask. There was a burning pain in her left side where a bullet had cut, but at least a yelp from the mark suggested one of her own shots had found its target.

She dodged around another tree. She closed her left eye, the vision blurred there already.

He be close by, chile, better step careful.

As she sprang from her cover, Ghost squeezed the trigger three times in rapid succession. The suited man, too, discharged his weapon. The space between them strobed as both pistols lit up the darkness. The other shooter skipped to one side. Another furious exchange and both pistols fell silent.

"Ay! Mi mano!"

Ghost darted first left then right as she closed on the shooter. He was fumbling with his gun. Close enough to smell his breath, she slammed down with her pistol. A satisfying *crack* told her she had struck home. The man's weapon was knocked from his grasp. Ghost pulled the trigger on her Glock, but it remained silent. Then the suited man was on top of her, one of his hands grabbing at her throat. As his fingers dug into the soft skin of her neck, Ghost twisted her whole body and brought the spent pistol into the side of his face. He lost his hold. Moving into a crouch, Ghost switched the pistol to her left hand and drew her blade with her right.

The karambit knife fitted her hand perfectly, her index finger snug in the retention ring, the hooked blade arcing three inches out from the base of her fist. Ghost hissed through gritted teeth as she sprang at the man. She slashed up with the karambit, hearing cloth rip.

He punched her in reply, almost knocking her to the ground. Ghost caught the hiss of steel as he drew his blade.

You've never fought a real fighter, chile. Always took them by surprise. This one's a live wire. He may be the death o' you.

The ground beneath her feet seemed to tilt, become less solid as she shook her head. The knifeman had caught her a good one in the face. Not the first shock to her system that day, but that was okay. She would take a hundred punches for the chance to avenge sweet Lauren.

He leapt directly at her, a blurring black mass, only the white of his shirt and the silver of his blade clearly visible. The cold steel scored her ribs as she twisted out of his path. Her slash missed his throat by a good twelve inches as he faded away from her counter.

One of the great advantages of the karambit is that it is easy to hold onto; the ring around the index finger allows a relaxed grip, even to open your hand without dropping the knife. The disadvantage of the hooked blade is that it is best employed as a very close-quarters weapon. The knife her enemy wielded was long and straight, giving him the undeniable luxury of reach.

They closed again, his blade ripping up towards her abdomen. She gasped as the tip of his blade punched into her stomach. Bracing her left arm, she raked his neck with the karambit. He lurched away, clutching his face, emitting a stream of guttural curses.

Ghost vaulted a fallen tree. Dipping low, she forced herself to ignore the pain in her stomach, busying herself with other things.

Her opponent rounded the tree, knife at the ready. Ghost's legs folded beneath her. The tree behind her spine felt as immovable as a mountain.

"Stay back," she shouted.

"English, huh?" The man held his blade in front of his face. "Here's some advice: if you're going to play with knives, get yourself a proper blade, not a bitch-assed toy."

Ghost laughed. "And here's some advice for you, big shot: never bring a knife to a gunfight."

The four shots sounded like a drum roll. The man sat straight down with a loud cough, his knife dropping from his grip.

Ghost struggled to her feet. "See, when you lie in your bed at night you're probably pullin' on yer pecker for all it's worth. When I go, I practise slippin' spare magazines in and out of my pistol 'til I fall asleep."

"*Pinche puta!*"

Ghost used the tree for support, leaning hard against it with her shoulders. "Goodnight, sweet prince!"

The next bullet snapped his head back. He toppled over and didn't move again.

59

Clay pointed the shotgun up the slope. Celine could just make out the men starting to climb down. Despite the headlights that lit the scene, the men above still hadn't seen the group yet, thanks to the heavy undergrowth. It wouldn't be long before they did.

"Great, just what we need, Los Hooligans hound-doggin' us every step of the way home," spat Clay.

Danny looked up. "You know I didn't invite them, right?"

"We gotta move," said Clay.

"They're going to catch us without trying." Danny motioned at the woman who lay twisted on the ground.

"Damn it, there's half a dozen of those butt monkeys coming. I'd give my back teeth for a fully loaded M4 and a bag of ammo right now."

"My van's totalled," Danny said. "We can't go back that way and we can't run with the wounded."

"Please, don't leave us!" Celine rested a hand on the injured woman's forehead. A mixture of pride and fear swept over her as Danny replied, "We're not leaving anyone behind."

"Everybody, get down!" Clay bared his teeth in the glance he exchanged with Danny. "They're on us in twenty seconds."

Celine said a silent prayer, crossing herself as she did so. Rebecca joined Celine and Danny by the side of the maimed woman. Her words came loud and fast. "We've got to create a diversion. Get their attention. Give Danny and Clay a chance to come at them sideways. Let them get away from us, then everybody scream as goddamn loud as you can!"

"That might just work." Clay traced a rapid arc in the air with one finger. Danny gave a single nod then reached into the cab of the ruined van. The blade of the machete glinted.

The Gunn brothers sprinted away from the group. The shadows swallowed the brothers within seconds.

As soon as they vanished, Rebecca and Celine let loose with bestial screams, long and furious. Gillian and Laura dropped next to them, giving voice. Like a pack of primal creatures, the others joined in the fearful cacophony.

The four men were nearly upon them, bringing the promise of death or further captivity with them. The men moved in pairs, the white material of their shirts looking like V-shaped wraiths in the darkness of the jungle.

Celine continued to scream. Each throat-rending shriek was a sliver of glass scraping the length of her vocal cords. Desperate faces surrounded her. Some crouched at the side of the ruined van, a few still peering from the back of the pickup. All looked as terrified as Celine felt. Yet in the fear was a rising defiance. Clay and his brother were risking their lives to save them. Celine took a deep breath and continued to scream.

The scream faltered in her throat as a loud *boom* split the night. The two cartel soldiers, seconds from running into the midst of Celine's group, spun on their heels. One of the gunmen pitched onto his face in a cloud of red.

Now the cartel men were screaming. Flashes from their handguns accompanied the frenzied burst of fire. To Celine, the three pistols sounded like a firework display, each staccato *crack* immediately followed by another.

Boom!

Clay's shotgun roared again, thirty feet from his first position. A second cartel man went down onto his knees. The man raised his weapon with a string of foul language.

Boom. The injured man was punched into the ground by Clay's follow-up shot.

The closest shooters sent a volley at Clay's position.

The shooter without the jacket turned and fired a shot that missed Celine by mere inches. "Stop that damned screaming!"

Celine fell silent, not because of the threat from the cartel, but from the sight of Danny Gunn emerging like a demon from the darkness. The machete he wielded moved faster than her eyes could follow. The man's severed hand, still clutching his pistol, sprang from his extended arm. The man staggered into the light, blood spraying onto the white fabric of his shirt. Another slash caught him across the side of the neck. The man dropped to his knees. As fast as Danny had appeared, he blended back into the darkness.

60

Clay sheltered behind a tree. The man he'd dropped back up on the road had not stayed down. Barring superpowers, Clay figured the team were sporting ballistic vests.

Every asshole is wearing Kevlar these days, thought Clay.

The remaining gunman pointed his weapon first one way, then another. His face contorted as he shouted, "You will all die at the hands of my brothers. I have more men coming to find you. Your only chance is to throw down your weapons and surrender to me."

"That's not gonna happen." Clay leaned out, aiming the Remington for a head shot. He watched the gunman turn his pistol to the group huddled at the side of the ruined van. Clay's finger tightened on the trigger as he weighed the scenario. He could take the man's head off at this range, but his pistol was aimed almost directly at Celine. One pull of the trigger was all it would take. "Is this what they call a Mexican stand-off?"

The voice of the gunman carried a confident tone despite his team being reduced to the dead and dismembered. "You think I am dumb enough to follow a bear into a cave and not call for backup? Even if you kill me, my men will be here in minutes. You will not leave this place alive. The crows will eat your eyes."

Clay glanced back up the slope. He had no way of knowing if more cartel men were on the way or not.

"I am Angel Velasquez of Los Espadas. I command enough men to hunt you to the ends of the Earth. I will—"

Then Danny was on him.

A swipe from his machete opened a long crimson gash down his arm. Angel's pistol clattered against the side of the bullet-riddled van as it flew from his grasp. Clay broke cover as Danny slammed the hilt of the machete into Angel's open mouth.

Clay trained the shotgun on Angel as he fell to one knee. The noise from the survivors abated to a few nervous gasps.

"Nicely done, wee one," said Clay.

"Backatcha, cowboy. Just taking hands and influencing people." Danny moved behind Angel. After a few seconds, he retrieved the fallen pistol. "Finders keepers."

"Well now, Mr Velasquez of Los Espadas, I'm betting a dollar or two this isn't how you pictured your day when you woke up this morning."

Angel cradled his right arm against his chest. Both his hand and the white of his shirt had turned a dark crimson. "You think this is the first time I have spilled some of my own blood for the job?"

"No, I can see by the look in your eyes this ain't your first rodeo, but it may well be your last." Clay cast another glance up the slope. Nothing moved. He took a step closer to

Angel. "I don't have to explain what a shotgun blast at this range will do to you, even with a vest on. I'm gonna ask a few questions and if you want to see another sunrise, you'll answer quick and true."

Angel spat a gobbet of blood-streaked saliva before he spoke again. "You think I'm dumb enough to believe you'd let me live?"

Danny patted Angel down, pressing his own pistol to the back of his head. Clay gave the smallest of nods as Danny held out the items he had found. A spare mag for the pistol, a billfold and a cell phone.

"You said you called for backup? How'd you do that when cell phones don't work out here?"

Angel struggled to his feet.

"Easy now, or I'll put a hole in you big enough to drive through," warned Clay. Behind Angel, Danny pressed a button on the cell phone. The screen illuminated as a sequence of three musical notes chimed.

"You get what you pay for. Satellite works better out here." Velasquez turned slowly to look at the group huddled next to the crashed van. "You think saving them will make any difference to our operation? There's a million more where they came from. Los Espadas is growing every year."

Clay wedged the barrel of the Remington under Angel's chin. "We didn't come here to cause trouble for Los Espadas. We came to bring my family home."

Angel pressed back against the shotgun. "Ezeret is a client of mine. You bring trouble to him, you bring trouble to me. You see the difficult situation you have placed me in? How will it look for Los Espadas if I let you and your people leave?"

"One pull on this trigger and it won't be your problem to worry about."

"You said you came here to take your family home. The men you just killed were like *my* family, but they were young and inexperienced. The men that are on their way here are full-blood enforcers." Angel stared back at Clay, his face blood-streaked but unwavering. "Do you know what Los Espadas means?"

Danny answered. "It means 'the sword'."

"The swords, plural. There are many of us. We are *guerreros del juramento de sangre*: warriors of the blood oath. Each life we take strengthens the sword, strengthens the bond of the blood oath."

"So how many men are on the way?" asked Clay. He tightened his finger on the trigger of the Remington.

"More than enough!"

"I think me and you are about done here," said Clay.

Danny quickly raised the cell phone. "What's the PIN for this phone?"

"Figure it out for yourself, tough guy."

Clay jammed the shotgun deeper into Angel's neck. "Tell him the number or I'll leave you lyin' here colder than a witch's tit."

Angel Velasquez opened his mouth as a shadow emerged from the trees behind Clay.

Whump!

Angel's head snapped back, a dark hole appearing above his right eye. Clay pivoted in a crouch. "Damn it, Ghost! I almost shot you."

"He had that coming. Him and those other assholes were

all regulars at the compound. You've no idea what these animals are capable of."

"Clay, we'd best get moving. We've no idea how close his men are, or their numbers or capability." Danny moved closer to his brother. "We're on the road to Crapsville here, Clay. We need to get back up the slope to their pickup and car. We can load any injured into your truck, the rest of them can trot along behind. It's going to be slow going."

"It's the closest thing to a plan we've got, so let's do it," said Clay.

"You look after them." Danny pointed at the freed captives. "I'll go and see what I can lift from Los Muertos Espadas."

61

Ezeret wrinkled his nose at the smell in the lobby. He had learned long ago that the dead and dying often emptied their bowels, but the knowledge did little to lessen the stench. It was a stench that had filled the chamber many times. The man that lay before him was spread out like a mutilated starfish. Ezeret recognized the denim-clad man as the light from his phone played over his corpse. He had been a loyal follower. Ezeret turned his head away. "This place is going to take a bit of cleaning up."

"Master Ezeret?"

"Who's there?" *A woman's voice?*

"It's me, Michelle. Michelle Getty."

"Ah yes, Michelle. Are you alright? I heard what happened earlier with the Taser. Rest assured, Gunn will pay. Have you seen anyone else?"

"I heard voices coming from down there."

Ezeret didn't have to move his light to see where she was pointing. He too could hear sounds echoing up the stairwell. "There are flashlights in the kitchen, on the wall next to the big pantry. Go and get them."

It took Michelle less than a minute to return with the lights. She held three under her arm, with one already illuminated in her right hand. "Big Peter is in the kitchen. His throat is cut."

"Never mind Big Peter." He took a flashlight from Michelle. "Follow me."

He heard the gasp from Michelle as the light played over Dennis's body. "Come on, we need to see who else is still alive."

"Ugh, the smell."

"That's the smell of chaos made manifest," said Ezeret. He returned her smile.

As Ezeret moved to the doorway, a new aroma greeted him: burned flesh and ammonia. He descended gingerly, moving the beam from the flashlight over the stone steps. Several bodies lay spread-eagled at the bottom. Two women, captives, stared back at him with dead eyes. The smallest of smiles crossed his face as he stepped over them. Weiss had probably dropped them when he was trying to prevent Gunn escaping the chamber. Another body lay to one side of the steps, a bloody ruin.

A figure lurched into view, eyes wide and angry, his white hair unmistakable.

"What happened to him?" asked Ezeret, pointing to the shredded corpse.

"He caught the worst of the blast from the grenade."

"One of your grenades?"

Weiss grimaced. "Unfortunately, yes. That big American asshole kicked it back at me. I nearly broke my neck jumping down these steps to get away from it. Shoomey wasn't so lucky. I think it went off between his feet."

"Which one was Shoomey?" asked Ezeret.

"He was our mechanic, had all those freckles on his face."

"Ah yeah, Shoomey." Ezeret played the flashlight over Weiss. The right side of his face was swollen, his white hair matted with blood. His right arm was decorated with cuts. "You look like a lion used you for a scratching post."

"I was out of it for a while. What's the state of play now? Where are Gunn and the captives?"

"They got away." Ezeret shrugged. "I sent Los Espadas after them. That should be the end of it."

"If you had listened to me none of this would have happened. You could still have asked your questions and Gunn wouldn't be running around like a damned chop-o-matic leaving a trail of dead bodies behind him."

"He wasn't alone, though, was he? There was a big one with scars all over him, too, with a goddammed shotgun. I caught sight of him just before they all drove away in the vehicles they pilfered. I thought you said you'd killed the man he came with?"

Weiss ran a hand across his mouth. "I thought I had. I couldn't see him after he went into the water in the sinkhole. I figured he sank like a stone."

"Unless his name is Lazarus, he didn't."

"He won't be alive much longer. The other men have taken the captives they managed to grab back to their rooms. There weren't that many—only five, I think. The others followed Gunn out."

Ezeret stepped close and rested his forehead against

Weiss's, with no aggression. "Doesn't the danger make you feel alive?"

Weiss grunted something unintelligible, then said, "I'll chase these hero wannabes down and fill them full of holes. I don't need Los Espadas to do my work for me. I'll take our men and finish them myself."

Ezeret huffed. "Have at it, my warrior. Just don't get in the way of the cartel. I still have to work with them after this is all done."

Weiss stepped back from Ezeret and looked at Michelle. "You, give me one of those flashlights, then go and tell the men to meet me at the front doors in five minutes. Tell them to gather every weapon they can lay their hands on."

"Ah, give me murder, give me rape," said Ezeret, "give me anything but the mundane."

62

Danny picked the manacle off his wrist as he spoke to Clay in a low voice. "Getting all these kids home is gonna be tough. Every time I look at them they seem to get younger and more terrified. One of them is gonna have to drive as well. We'll need all three vehicles, especially with the ones already injured."

"Celine stays with me," said Clay. "We drive one each and Ghost can drive the third."

"What I mean is, I don't want their blood on my hands if they get caught in the crossfire."

"I hear that, little brother, but right now we are the *only* chance they have of getting back to the world. It's a risk we'll have to take."

"Hey, I'm not having second thoughts. I just don't want to see any of these kids breathe their last on our watch."

"So, let's keep moving and do our damnedest to stop that happening."

"At least we've got a bit of kit now. Those cartel boys spent their money wisely. These pistols are top-notch kit.

They're all Coonan .357s. These have been customised by a craftsman, man-killers, no doubt. And they say crime doesn't pay. I managed to rustle up some spare ammo from the dead desperados as well." Danny handed one of the pistols to Clay. "They were wearing armoured vests; I've got those too."

"Good. You put one on. Celine gets one too. Give the other two to whoever you think best."

"You should try one. It'll be a tight fit but better than nothing."

Clay scowled. "They were made to fit guys your size, not mine."

Ghost joined the hurried conversation. "I ended another of the team back up near the top of the hill. He had a pistol, but it's somewhere in the undergrowth now."

Danny looked at Ghost. "You okay?"

"I can't tell where one hurt stops and the next one begins, but I'm still on my feet."

"I hear that. I just got my arse thrown through the van window. Lucky for me, it was already smashed out. The landing nearly broke my back." Danny twisted at the waist. "We need a third driver. You up for that?"

Ghost pressed her palm against her stomach. Her hand came away stained red. She clicked her tongue against her teeth. "I'll do what needs to be done."

"I didn't find any car keys when I searched the men, so I'm hoping the keys are still in the ignition."

Ghost bent at the waist.

"You sure you're okay?"

"Hurts like crazy, but I don't think it's too deep."

"You want me to take a proper look?"

"I'm fine. As a wise man once said, 'I ain't got time to bleed.'"

"We need to get the worst injured into the pickup and on the move, pronto." Danny pushed two of the Coonan pistols into his waistband. He passed the remaining pistol to Ghost. "Keep an eye out while I get them ready to move."

He knelt down by the injured woman. "What's your name?"

"Frances."

"Frances, I'm going to have to move your leg, put it back into place. It'll hurt like a son of a bitch, but I need to do it, understand?"

She gave something that loosely resembled a nod.

"Celine, try to hold her body straight. You too." Danny pointed to the black woman at Celine's side.

"Rebecca," said Celine by way of introduction.

Danny gripped Frances's ankle and pulled. The scream she emitted was enough to score glass. She struggled against him, her screams intensifying. A dull popping sensation reverberated through his hands as her hip clicked back into place. A quick inspection of her left arm told Danny that it was broken. "Celine, keep her arm cradled against her chest as best you can."

Wide eyes stared back at him as he raised his voice. "Anybody that can walk on their own two feet, start walking back up the hill. The injured are going up in the truck. Move it!"

Several of the group climbed from the flatbed of the pickup, where they had been cowering. "Come on, we need to get moving. There are more gunmen on their way and I don't know how long we've got before they get here."

"Celine's staying with me," stated Clay.

"No problem. Get her in the pickup and you can drive it back to the road." Danny cast another glance into the darkened treeline. The landscape was now an abstract picture marked with varying depths of black. Despite her vocal protestations, Frances was hoisted into the back of the pickup next to Marco.

Danny leaned in through the window, close to Frances and the young woman who had been shot in the shoulder. "Frances, I know you're hurting really bad, but I need your help. You need to keep Marco here awake, you understand? If he goes under he may not wake up again. Can you do that for me?"

"Yes."

"Good. I owe you one." Danny turned his attention back to the rest of the group. Several sported cuts and scrapes but they were already starting to walk up the hill. "We need to keep the pickup as light as we can to get back up to the road," he said as he caught up with them. "If it gets stuck we'll need to push it. Once we get back up there we'll take the other wheels and hightail it out of here as fast as possible."

He looked back. Clay was starting the engine, Celine in the passenger seat. The bulletproof vest made her look like a kid playing dress-up.

Danny drew one of the Coonans, then gave Clay the thumbs-up. "Go. We'll be right behind you."

63

Clay steered the pickup back up the path they had cut. The truck moved at a steady pace despite the incline and obstacles scattered in its way.

"I knew you'd get us out," said Celine.

"We're not home and free just yet, but at least we're movin'."

The truck bounced on its suspension as Clay manoeuvred around a rock. A loud moan from the back seat interrupted the conversation. Turning in his seat, Clay felt a lump in his throat. The back seat was awash with Marco's blood. Both the shirt tied around his middle and his hands that clutched at it were stained dark. The dashboard display provided only meagre light, but still enough to see his failing condition.

"There's so much blood." Celine seemed to shrink a little in her seat.

"Wounds can often seem worse than they really are. When you wash them down they can look a lot different."

"Is Marco going to die?"

"We need to get him to a hospital as soon as we can."

"I've never seen anyone turn that colour before." Celine dropped her voice to a whisper. "He looks like a wax dummy."

Clay glanced again into the back seat. Marco lay barely conscious and blood-soaked. Frances was awake, her limbs swollen and dappled with livid bruises. The woman with the injured shoulder sat wedged against the door, her head lolling from side to side.

Clay leaned out of his window as Danny kept pace alongside. "I'm gonna have to take a good run at this last bit, build up enough speed to get over the crest."

"Go for it," answered Danny. "We're right behind you."

Clay spoke to the whole vehicle. "Hang on."

The pickup lurched forward, creaking and shuddering. The engine bellowed as Clay forced it up the slope. There was a second of weightlessness as the vehicle ramped over the crest of the hill. Clay yanked hard to his right on the steering wheel, then they were back on the road. He slowed to a crawl. Ahead, the two vehicles that Los Espadas had used as a roadblock were still in place.

Clay slipped the pickup into park, its engine still idling. "Stay inside."

"I will," said Celine.

Cradling the shotgun, Clay moved warily back to the edge of the road. Within seconds Danny appeared. He began to usher the rest of the group onto the twin track road. One woman vomited into the undergrowth.

"Where's Ghost?" asked Clay.

"She was here a second ago." Danny looked around. "Ah, I see her."

Clay followed Danny's gaze. Ghost was already at the

two vehicles. Her pistol swept left and right as she circled the pickup and the car.

"You mind the flock and I'll get Ghost," said Danny. Clay offered no argument. He didn't intend letting Celine leave his sight, even for a moment.

"Listen up," Clay said to the ragtag group, stark-faced and sweating. "Danny and Ghost are gonna get those two jalopies pointed in the right direction, then we're puttin' this place in the rear-view. With good luck an' a tailwind we won't stop 'til we see city lights. If we run into any more trouble, I need you all to keep your heads down and stay quiet. Can you do that for me?"

Three now familiar faces moved closer. Gillian, Laura and Rebecca—Celine's friends.

"There's space up front for one more in the pickup."

The three exchanged a few words, then Gillian trotted to the front of the vehicle.

"The rest of you can split between the three. It's gonna be another bumpy ride but it's a lot better than walkin'."

Two engines roared to life, one deeper than the other. Clay watched Danny reverse the second pickup, its tail end butting hard up against a tree, then turn it to face the direction they needed to go. Ghost performed a jerky four-point turn in the sedan. Danny held out his thumb in readiness.

"Time to get your butts in a seat. Don't be too particular." Clay made a shooing gesture with his arms. No one needed to be told twice. Laura and Rebecca joined Danny at the head of the line, the rest of the freed captives divided themselves up between the vehicles.

As soon as the vehicles were loaded, they moved off as a

single unit, Danny's pickup at the head of the short convoy, Ghost's sedan in the middle. The road proved narrower than Clay remembered it as they picked their way back to the fork. The V-turn forced all three vehicles to slow to a crawl. For a dread-filled second, Clay was sure that Ghost's sedan was going to become wedged between two trees, but with only the loss of a layer of paint she made the sharp turn.

"Look in the glovebox, see if there's anything of worth in there."

Celine did as he asked. "Nothing in here but a bunch of old papers. A packet of gum. Ah… and this."

Clay glanced at the small package in Celine's hand. The bright wrapping paper was decorated with cartoon characters.

"There's a card taped to it," said Celine. She moved the box closer to the dashboard lights. "It's in Spanish. 'To my darling baby girl Gloria, happy birthday. Love, Papa.'"

Celine placed the present back in the glovebox. "That belonged to one of those men. I don't understand. How could men like that do such God-awful things but still buy a cute gift for their kid? How could they even visit a place like that camp when they have a family back home?"

Clay stared at Ghost's tail lights as he answered. "What sickens me is that not only do they think they are not doing anything wrong, but they actually seek to justify it. One of the men in the house implied that this was an enlightened cure for boredom. Killin' and torture and whatnot. Smiled as he said it."

Celine moved a little closer to Clay. He could feel her unasked question hanging in the air. "We agreed to disagree," said Clay.

"Good."

64

The overhanging branches were now reduced to darkened tentacles, each seeking a hold on the small convoy. Danny glowered at the road ahead, each moment expecting the arrival of more cartel soldiers to be announced by a hail of bullets. There was nowhere to go, no avenue of escape if another squad of brutes did arrive, at least until they found a proper road. The single track they picked their way along wasn't much wider than the vehicles, no room even to turn around if needed. Any threat would have to be faced head-on.

Danny tilted the rear-view mirror, the lights from Ghost's sedan dazzling him from behind.

"I wasn't sure you'd get away from those men again, but Celine was," Laura said. "You and Clay, I can't believe you came all the way down here to save us. Just the two of you. When I saw you go into that fighting pit, I'll admit, I thought you were a goner, but man, I'm so glad I was wrong." Laura shook her head, her words coming in a flurry. "Celine said you and Clay were both soldiers."

"Aye, a long time ago," replied Danny.

"Were you in special forces or something?"

Danny kept his eyes on the road. "No, just regular soldiers."

"She said you were a green beret or something."

"Green Jacket. Quite a different beast."

"But where did you learn to fight like that?"

"I've learned enough to get by. There're men a lot more skilled than me out there."

"But they aren't down here risking their lives to save a few college kids," said Laura.

"I know plenty who would do the same in a heartbeat."

"My grandfather was a colonel in special forces. He was a bit like you: he didn't like to talk about Vietnam or the years after. One of his soldiers got into a lot of trouble."

"Most of us are just thankful if we come home with all of our limbs attached," said Danny.

"Thank you."

Danny glanced across at Laura. He gave her the smallest of nods. A second later he braked. "Aw, come on." On the road ahead, the headlights had picked up the dog he'd become almost used to seeing. Soon, another familiar figure appeared alongside it.

"What is it?" asked Laura, an audible tinge of fear creeping into her voice.

"Jak and Chaac."

"Huh?"

"Long story, but don't worry, he's a friend." Danny buzzed down the window as Jak approached the pickup.

"You went the wrong way."

"Aye, we figured that bit out for ourselves," replied Danny.

"At least you're on the right path now. You need to keep following this road for about five or six miles straight on. You'll come to a crossroads. When you do, take the road south. It's a long trek around but at least you'll be on a proper route. You can pick up the main highway from there and head back north." Jak leaned against the side of the pickup door. Chaac stood silently, his tail tracing a slow crescent in the air. The ear with the hole in it twitched, perhaps tickled by some unseen insect.

"Thanks, Jak. You gonna be okay?"

Jak lowered his voice. "I will be fine. The men that are coming are not coming for me."

"Men? The cartel, Los Espadas?"

"Men are men. There are still more challenges left for you to face. The men that come this way are worse than all you have met so far."

"Have you seen them?" asked Danny.

"I've seen many like them. When I was a very young man, there was a gang that fought for Pancho Villa. It was said they skinned their enemies alive to strike terror into the hearts of men. I think the men that are coming share the same blood as Villa's men."

"Get somewhere safe. If you hear gunshots, head in the opposite direction," said Danny. "We gotta go."

Jak stabbed the air with his finger. "Go fast, but careful. Be ready for danger. You are not home and free yet."

Danny gave a parting nod then accelerated away. Two sets of lights followed behind.

Laura looked at Danny, her mouth twisted to one side. "You know, I took modern history in school. Pancho Villa died nearly a century ago."

"Aye, he's a strange one, right enough," said Danny. "Don't worry about it."

The three-vehicle convoy powered through the dense jungle, an occasional set of unblinking yellow eyes observing their progress. Danny's pickup bumped and jostled as he fought to leverage all available speed from the vehicle without crashing again. The occupants of both the rear seats and the flatbed hunkered down in silence. Danny could smell the nervous tension inside the cab.

"We seem to have been going for hours," said Laura.

Danny glanced at the clock on the dashboard display. "It's only been twenty minutes. The damn dark and this sad excuse for a road has made for slow going. Once we hit the main road we can floor it and put some miles on the meter."

65

Weiss looked at the five men, playing the beam of the flashlight over each in turn. Each brandished a weapon. Three held crossbows, one a rifle and the last man had a long-bladed machete.

Weiss had recovered his P7 pistol from the chamber floor. In addition, he now sported a range of other killing tools. The harness of his webbing vest contained three spare mags for the P7, the last two grenades from his stash and a combat knife. On his belt, he carried a tool that he had not used for some time. The SOG-issue tomahawk was brutal, both in close-quarters combat and as a throwing weapon.

"They have quite a lead on us, so we're going to have to go flat out to catch them, but catch them we will. I want Gunn and the other one dead. No talk, no second chances—*dead!* Pick your shots and make sure they stay down."

"What about the others? The girls?"

"We bring back as many as we can," Weiss said. "If you think there's a chance of them escaping, they die too. No one can make it out or we're all finished here."

"What about the Espadas guys?" asked Thomas, the man with the rifle. His brown hair was scraped back into a tight ponytail.

"If we cross paths, keep out of their line of fire. They are as likely to put you down as the main targets. There is a chance that they have killed Gunn already, in which case I'll be very angry. I want him for myself," said Weiss. "Come on, we need to move."

Weiss moved into the night at a brisk run. The five guards followed close on his heels. Skirting the main house, Weiss made his way to his own private vehicle. The Toyota FJ cruiser was a beast of a machine, the 260 HP engine perfect for the rugged demands of the Yucatán peninsula. Weiss vaulted into the driving seat. The engine sprang to life on the first turn of the ignition. The other five men clambered into the cruiser. Weiss gunned the Toyota before the last man was fully inside. The man gave a short whoop, but managed to haul himself into a sitting position.

"There's only one road out of here, so Los Espadas will be between us and the ones we need to kill. As soon as I can, I will overtake the cartel men and we will take them for ourselves." Weiss yelled to make himself heard above the racing engine as it picked up speed.

Thomas wedged the stock of his rifle between his feet to hold it steady. Within seconds the Toyota was powering down the narrow road. A steady rattle of branches impacting the outer skin of the vehicle provided frenetic timpani as they sped into the stygian darkness. Weiss flipped a switch on the dash. The set of roof-mounted halogens lit up the path ahead, the many shades of green lending a hypnotic effect as the

Toyota continued to accelerate. He grinned at the passengers with cruel amusement as they were jolted around the cruiser. The German forced the vehicle ever faster, missing trees by mere inches, trees wide enough to kill everyone inside if he collided with even one. The jungle was reduced to a darkened blur as he coaxed every bit of available speed from the cruiser.

Weiss leaned into the steering wheel, scouring the road ahead for any signs of his quarry. Something solid impacted the driver's side window and door, causing Weiss to jerk the steering hard to the right. "*Scheisse!*"

The wing mirror on the passenger side was ripped free in a brief explosion of glass and plastic. Weiss swore again.

"Jesus, you're going to kill us before we get near the other guys," said a voice from the back seat.

"Shut up or I will definitely kill you!" Weiss allowed the cruiser to slow momentarily as he brought it back under his control. There were no further comments from the passenger.

"*Ja*," said Weiss as he steered around a curve. "There they are!"

Multiple lights were now visible less than a quarter-mile ahead.

"Is that them?" asked Thomas.

Weiss considered punching the rifleman in the face. "It could be Domino's pizza."

Thomas pulled his chin into his chest. "I was just asking."

"Of course it is them, and it won't take me long to catch them."

"What are you going to do?" asked someone from the back seat. "How will you stop them?"

"Let me worry about that. Just be ready to shoot when

I do," said Weiss. "There! Look, there's three vehicles. Los Espadas are right on their tail."

As the road widened, giving a foot or so more safe space on either side of the Toyota, Weiss coaxed the last ounce of extra speed from the vehicle.

Thomas pointed at the pickup now framed in their headlights. "There's women in the flatbed of that truck."

Weiss gritted his teeth. "And?"

"If that truck is the cartel truck, why is it filled with our women?"

Weiss growled. It made no sense. *If the cartel had already got the women back, that meant they had already killed the Gunn brothers. But if that was so, why were they still racing through the jungle at top speed in the pitch dark?*

As the road bent into a sharp right curve, Weiss got his answer. The man driving the pickup at the rear of the speeding convoy was the big man he had blown into the sinkhole. A boxy sedan car in the middle and another pickup in front completed the running order. If the big guy was bringing up the rear, it made sense that all three vehicles were filled with the escapees.

After giving only a moment of thought to the real whereabouts of the cartel shooters, he turned to Thomas. "Use that rifle! Try to hit the driver if you can, or the tyres if that's too tricky."

Thomas leaned out of the window, hugging the rifle tight against his shoulder. Despite the jostling of the Toyota, his first shot exploded through the rear window of the pickup. Weiss thought he could hear screaming.

"*Ja! Ja!* Again! Shoot them again!"

66

"There's lights coming up fast," said Laura. She had twisted all the way around and now stared out past the other two friendly vehicles.

"Shite! That'll be the other cartel boys. I was hoping we'd be back on the main road before those buggers showed up. We'll just have to keep moving. Clay will have seen them too. I wish we still had walkie-talkies." Danny alternated his focus between the road ahead and the fast-approaching lights in the rear-view, lights that could only mean more danger.

Rebecca Dale shook her head. Her voice was an equal mix of fear and anger. "Are they ever gonna quit?"

"Not 'til we make them," said Danny. The road curved to the right and he focused on not repeating his earlier head-on collision with any rocks. As if in warning, a sharp pain lanced through his neck and shoulder muscles. The earlier crash was beginning to take its toll. Biting down against the discomfort, Danny forced himself to inhale slow and deep. The too-familiar sound of gunfire stopped the breath in his throat. As he glanced into the rear-view mirror, he recognised a telltale muzzle flash. Someone in the vehicle tailing Clay had opened fire. Danny cursed under his breath. His only real choice was to keep moving at full speed, allowing the others to do the same. If he stopped, Ghost and Clay would be forced to stop too. The muscles in his jaw bunched as he registered another muzzle flash. Damn it! Clay and Celine were back there.

With his attention snapping between the road and the rear-view, Danny kept his foot heavy on the gas. Travelling as fast as he could manage, he didn't see the fallen tree lying across the road until it was too late. The bough was as thick as his thigh with several thinner branches reaching out like a dead man's fingers. The pickup truck hit the tree hard. The front wheels bucked up and over the obstacle. Then the rear axle ramped up and over too, in a buckaroo motion. The vehicle returned to earth with a heavy thump. A high-pitched wail sounded from the flatbed.

"They all still in there?" asked Danny.

Laura craned her neck to see through the rear window. "I think so. I'm not sure how many got in the back of this truck."

Ghost's sedan made an ungodly sound as it too crashed over the fallen tree. The front fender angled to one side then disappeared under the car. A second later, Clay's pickup and the pursuit vehicle also crowned the tree.

Another gunshot rang out, loud against the night.

"These bloody goat-track roads are hellish!" Moments later, Danny's mouth twitched into the smallest of smiles as the road widened out to nearly twice its previous width. "Maybe somebody up there likes me after all. We must be getting closer to the main road."

A quick glance in the mirror showed that both Ghost and Clay were still close behind. So too was the vehicle with the shooter in. As if in confirmation, another shot rang out.

"Shite! I knew our three seconds of luck was too good to be true!" Danny narrowed his eyes at the new set of lights racing directly toward him. He knew this was bad. There was a small chance that the approaching vehicle wasn't an enemy, but he knew better than to hope.

Laura gripped his shoulder as if he had failed to see the lights speeding their way. "Danny?"

"Hang on tight, 'cos I'm not stopping!"

"We're going to die playing chicken," said Laura, her voice small and empty.

"Only if we lose." Danny floored the gas. He thumped his palm down on the horn and kept it there. The sound brought new wails from the rear seats and flatbed of the truck. Danny relaxed. A head-on collision was less than five seconds away.

I'm not swerving.

Four.

I'm not stopping.

Three.

Chrissie Haims back in Miami was mighty fine.

Two.

Shite! We're dead.

One...

67

The sound from the rear of the pickup was horrendous. The few in the flatbed of the truck huddled low but their screams were loud and shrill. The back window had been blown in, scattering glass through the cab. The windscreen was spiderwebbed too, severely reducing visibility. Another bullet cut through the cab and punched into the console inches from Clay's torso. Lights began to blink on the dashboard.

"What's happening?" asked Celine.

"I think the ramp over that log has done some damage."

Crack!

Celine ducked her head low.

"Celine!" Clay's face burned red as he reached out to her.

After patting her hand to her head several times, she puffed out her cheeks. "No blood."

"Hunker down as low as you can," said Clay. He cast a baleful look at the vehicle behind. He considered slamming on the brakes, but that would prove fatal for the people in the flatbed. He repeated his words, this time to everyone within hearing range. "Hunker down as low as you can!"

Clay guided the pickup through a dense green arch. Leaf-laden branches slapped against the truck, then the road widened noticeably.

Crack! Another bullet cut through the air near Clay's head.

A woman shouted through the smashed rear window. "Pass me that shotgun!"

Clay glanced back at her. Her black hair clung to her face in long unruly strands. "Can you shoot?"

Her eyes flashed. "Born and raised in Wyoming."

"Okay, then." Clay nodded to Celine. She leaned to one side and gripped the Remington in both hands. Turning the weapon in her hands, she passed it back stock-first.

"What's your name?" shouted Clay.

"Kelly. Kelly Jones."

"Give 'em hell, Kelly."

Almost before he had finished talking, the boom of the shotgun split the night. The vehicle that had dogged them relentlessly veered to one side. The shotgun fired another three times in succession. The rapid rate of fire gave a brief strobe effect in the rear-view mirror.

The twin headlights behind tilted to an impossible angle. The scars on the left side of his face crinkled as he watched the vehicle slam first into an outcrop of rock, then, in a shower of sparks, ramp high into the air. As the vehicle piled back into the road one of the headlights exploded and the hood flew open like the jaws of a feeding shark. The vehicle swung across the width of the road before rolling to a stop. A man leapt from the driver's door. The shock of white hair identified him.

"That asshole's still alive?" In the seconds that the crash had held his attention, Clay had not registered the scene unfolding directly ahead: a new set of lights speeding down the road, on a direct collision course with Danny's truck.

Time seemed to slow as the lights grew brighter. In both the sedan and the pickup, Clay could see heads cast into silhouette. Danny, Ghost, Celine's friends and the others they'd rescued. Powerless to change the outcome, Clay gritted his teeth. A single word formed in his mind: *Danny!*

68

Danny's knuckles turned white as he gripped the steering wheel. The approaching lights had grown impossibly bright. They weren't stopping. A furious roar escaped his throat. If this was the end, he would go in defiance.

The sound of screeching metal filled the truck as the other vehicle veered off at the last possible second. As the pickup took the brunt of the sideswipe, Danny strained to keep his vehicle on the road. The vehicle shuddered as sparks formed a brief flashing aurora around the truck.

"They're real bright sparks," shouted Danny. Both Laura and Rebecca stared at him with wide eyes.

The vehicle was a blur as it flashed past Ghost's and Clay's vehicles, skidding into a tight revolution. Another loud rending of metal filled the air as it rammed into the vehicle that had been hounding his older brother. A quick check confirmed that both Clay and Ghost were still following close behind. Danny puffed air through his nose. Hopefully the cartel men were all dead, or at least too injured to continue.

"You're one crazy-assed looney tune, you know that?" Rebecca gave a nervous giggle.

"You're not the first person to tell me that."

"How did you know they would swerve out of the way?"

Danny answered while keeping the vehicle as close to top speed as he could. "Because nobody wants to die, certainly not in a head-on collision. Even the most determined fighter will veer away from certain death. Something deep in our souls won't let us snuff out the light."

"What about the kamikaze mentality? What if they'd been as mad as you, what would have happened then?"

"We all would have died," said Danny. "I've met a few bona fide psychopaths in my time, but even most of them don't want to die when it comes down to the wire. As for the kamikazes, the suicide bombers and such, the only option is to drop them before they take out their target. That's never a good situation to be in, there's almost always collateral damage."

"*Collateral damage?*"

Danny gave a single nod. "But we're still alive and moving, so all is well."

Laura lurched close to the window, her hands scrabbling at the door. She wound down the window with a frantic motion. The sound of retching came next. Danny kept his eyes on the road as Rebecca reached over to Laura. When she finally pulled her head back inside the truck, her face was bereft of colour.

"I'm sorry," said Laura, dragging her hand across her mouth. "My hands won't stop shaking."

"Don't worry about it," said Danny. "It happens to the best of us."

Rebecca reached out and squeezed Danny's right arm. She smiled. Danny gave her a nod. Sometimes words were not required.

"I'm so dry," said Laura. "I wish I had some water."

Danny looked at the centre console. Two empty cup holders. No water. "Check in the back?"

One of the rescued women leaned forward. Danny could feel her head pressing against the back of his seat as she felt around in the gap below. "Nothing back here."

"We'll get some soon," promised Danny. The passengers lapsed back into a nervous silence. Outside, the darkness seemed to press against the outer shell of the truck.

The road beneath the pickup changed from hard-packed dirt to asphalt. The truck's vibration changed accordingly too, from a constant bumping jostle to a low, continuous hum.

"We must be getting closer to the main road. Tarmac is good," said Danny. As Danny glanced in the rear-view, his upper lip curled to one side. Way behind Ghost and Clay, two sets of lights were again in pursuit. "Hang on to your hosiery, we're not out of this yet."

69

Ulrich Weiss sprang from the vehicle before it had stopped moving. The Toyota FJ cruiser was his own SUV, bought and paid for with his own money. Some bitch in the back of the pickup had opened fire with a damned shotgun. She'd put one load through the centre of his windshield. Ducking low, Weiss hadn't seen the rock at the side of the road and had slammed straight into it. The Toyota was a rugged machine, but it had landed nose first in the dirt. The front and side airbags had deployed in response to the impact. The hood was now gaping open and steam hissed from the stalled engine.

Squeezing on the built-in cocking lever located at the front of the grip, Weiss snapped off three shots, aiming his P7 at the rear window of the pickup. The bitch with the shotgun let loose with another shot of her own. He winced as pellets peppered the raised hood of his listing vehicle.

Spreading his legs into a more stable Weaver shooting stance, Weiss registered a new danger. Twin orbs of light that could only be more headlights, rocketing straight at him. A shower of sparks akin to an angle grinder buzzed into the air as it sideswiped one of the fleeing trucks.

"Watch out!" Weiss yelled to the men still inside the damaged Toyota, as he sprinted out of danger. The speeding vehicle turned tight on its axis and slammed into the front of the stationary SUV. Weiss squinted against the glare of the headlights. The vehicle was impressive. This had to be more enforcers from Los Espadas. As if to prove him correct, an angry face peered from the driver's window.

"I know you. You're the German. Where's Velasquez? He wanted us to help run down some targets." The man's gold tooth caught the light as he spoke.

"I don't know where the others are. I thought I was following them until I realised that their truck was full of our runaways," answered Weiss. He kept his pistol close to his right side, ready if needed.

"You remember me?" asked Golden Tooth.

Weiss gave a curt nod. "I do. You're Verdugo." The executioner.

Verdugo pointed to the receding tail lights. "I take it those are the *pendejos* we are here to find."

"They are," said Weiss as he approached the vehicle. The savage machine, the narco truck, was certainly a thing to behold. He rested the P7 at the side of his hip. He shot a look at his own damaged Toyota. It looked like a toy next to the cartel battlewagon. "You got room for one more?"

Verdugo's smile was little more than a tightening of skin. "Call a fuckin' Uber!"

Weiss opened his mouth to reason with him, but Verdugo revved his engine and with a screech of heavy rubber raced off in the wake of the three escaping vehicles. Holstering his pistol, Weiss reached up and grabbed the buckled hood of the Toyota. With one sharp tug, he slammed the metal lid shut. The hood bounced back open. A heat separate from the Mexican humidity flushed over his face. He touched the side of his face with his fingertips. The skin there felt like plastic. He slammed the hood again. A wide bevel marred the centre of the lid. "Piece of crap!"

Weiss climbed back into the Toyota. Thomas looked up from where he'd been repacking the airbags. The men in the vehicle were all badly bruised, but none of them were out of action. "Are we going after them?"

Weiss glowered at him. "Ask one more stupid question and I will shoot you in the face!"

As he turned the ignition key, Weiss feared the Toyota would not restart. It took three attempts. The engine stuttered, then roared to life. He slammed the cruiser into drive and floored the gas. The Toyota lurched forward a few feet then the engine fell silent again. "*Scheisse!*"

Again, he turned the key. This time the engine fired up and held. Weiss forced himself to take his time. He had no desire to be left with no other option but a humiliating walk back to the compound. There was an unhealthy scraping of metal on metal as he urged the Toyota forward. Pushing down gently at first on the gas pedal, he felt the cruiser begin to pick up speed. The metallic rasping did not lessen as he steered after the Espadas.

"We'll never catch up with them now. The cartel have us outgunned and have a way better truck. We might as well head back home." Thomas pursed his lips as he pushed the barrel of his rifle against the dashboard. "Some night this turned out to be."

The three men in the back of the Toyota yelled out in a single note of surprise as Weiss pulled the trigger of his P7. They hadn't seen him draw his weapon. The single shot was deafening in the boxy interior. The bullet entered just below Thomas's jaw. He shuddered violently, then slumped against his door, bright arterial blood spurting over the window.

"Are any of you three handy with a rifle?"

The man in the middle seat answered. "I am."

"Good," said Weiss. "It's Taylor, right? You've just been promoted."

The Toyota continued to gain speed.

"Climb through and get rid of this cretin."

Taylor did as Weiss requested, opening the door and shoving Thomas's body out into the night.

70

The scars on Clay's face crinkled as he smiled at the woman with the shotgun. He shouted so she could hear him. "Kelly Jones from Wyoming, you've just made it onto my Christmas card list. Shootin' like that will win you a coconut."

"I'm not sure if I got any of them inside, but I'm pretty sure I ventilated their ride for them."

"You hang on to the Remington and do the same if anything else unexpected shows up on our tail," said Clay. "Here's a few spare shells to keep you going. That's the last of them, so pick your shots."

"A packing crate full of these would make me feel much better," said Kelly.

As she stretched her arm into the cab for the extra cartridges, Clay could not help but notice the deep rope burns on her wrist. "A-men to that. Be sure to make each one count." He glanced at Celine. "You hangin' in there?"

Celine responded with a weak smile then looked over into the back of the vehicle. She reached in between the two seats. When she retracted her hand, it was stained crimson. "Marco?"

Clay could offer no words of false comfort. He knew the chances of Marco Kenner surviving his grievous wound lessened every minute that he was denied professional medical attention. The complications caused by leaking stomach acid and bile mixing with blood and other tissue were horrendous, *if he lived*.

Celine cupped her face in her hands. Her body took on a slow shudder.

A confusion of emotions rolled over him. The cold thrill of the fight was now tempered with a sense of grim responsibility for each of these young lives. Celine remained his prime focus, but the unfolding situation had grown into something else, something more complicated. "We have to keep going. I can't do much more for him. I'm sorry."

Two bright spots of light appeared again in the rear-view mirror. With a little more clearance space on either side of the vehicle, Clay continued to test the capability of the pickup. The rumbling vibration changed to a more even tone as the wheels found asphalt. The pursuing lights seemed to enlarge. He knew they were drawing closer. "Kelly!"

"I see them, cowboy."

Clay gave a tight-lipped smile as Kelly wedged herself low against the tailgate. "I'd rather be back there shootin' with you."

"I'm sorry, Clay. We should never have come down here."

"None of this is your fault, Celine." The glow of the lights seemed to fill the mirror. "It's just that when I'm on my own or with Danny, I don't worry so much when the bullets start flying, but this is a different ball game altogether."

"Did you never worry when you were in the army?"

"Hey, nobody wants to get shot, but you go in knowing that's the hazard of the job."

"But out here you've got me and a school-bus-worth of extra bodies to worry about."

"Different time, different hazards," said Clay, again glancing in the mirror. The pursuing vehicle was almost upon them, maybe only five or six car lengths behind. Kelly was still hunkered low. These *kids* continued to surprise him. She knew enough to pick her shots. Only they weren't kids. He had to stop thinking of them in that way. Most seemed to be between eighteen and twenty-five. At their age, Clay had been a serving soldier in the Rangers. That had been his choice. It had been a hard life but a good choice. These were not Rangers, however, these were college kids, caught in a nightmare, traumatised by the horrors they had endured in the compound. Years of therapy probably lay ahead for many of them, yet that wasn't Clay's worry. Ranger training had taught crisis priority, to deal with clear and present danger first. The approaching vehicle full of cartel shooters was as dangerous as could be imagined.

Kelly, still using the tailgate for cover, unloaded on the vehicle. *Boom-boom-boom!* Three shots in rapid succession. Clay watched as the vehicle dropped back momentarily then swung to one side, so it followed at his offside tail. Ahead, Danny and Ghost slowed as they took a full left turn. They were back on the main road.

71

You never could drive worth a damn, chile.

"We're still putting miles on the clock," said Ghost.

A face streaked with dirt turned from the passenger seat. "Huh?"

Ghost offered no explanation. The woman looked stricken already, all furrowed brow and bunched fists. She doubted that explaining that she was talking to the disembodied voice of her dead mother would offer any comfort.

The knife wound in her stomach burned with a strange numbness. The front of her black jumpsuit was wet and sticky, but the patch felt no larger than the palm of her hand. Other pains spread through her body as if seeking solidarity. The muscle in the back of her shoulder, the arch of her spine and her aching jaw all vied for attention.

Beginning to look like a dime-store raggy doll there, chile.

Ghost gave a sideways look at the woman in the passenger seat. She seemed transfixed by the tail lights of Danny's truck. Two of the three in the back seats exchanged furtive whispers. The young man, his eyes dark with bruises, stared out into the darkness of the night. Ghost recognised the vacant expression. The Devil's breath had been well named. She could only guess at the deeper and longer-lasting damage that the drug might have wreaked in their minds, her own included. Would any of the rescued passengers ever be fully normal again? Would they ever be able to sleep sound, safe and secure without worry again? Each had endured unspeakable horrors in the compound, no one had been exempt.

Her hands clenched the steering wheel as her thoughts turned to Ezeret. That sly, manipulative bastard had escaped her vengeance again.

Mayhap those Gunn brothers will do your job for you and put him in a hole in the ground, chile.

"Maybe, maybe not," said Ghost. "I didn't have time to compare scorecards."

"What?"

Ghost paid her passenger no heed. The time for talking would come later. She shifted in her seat, the shard of titanium in her cargo pocket digging into her thigh. *Lauren, sweet Lauren.*

She allowed no more than three car lengths between Danny's pickup and her sedan. Stay close, stay sharp. Lights had buzzed close by, Danny seemingly playing chicken with an oncoming vehicle. It had passed in a blur. But something was happening behind them. Clay's truck swerved over to one side then zigzagged back again. A frantic drumroll and a tongue of flame filled her with dread.

The sedan rattled despite the relative smoothness of the road. Sparks of light flashed through the interior, the smell of burnt flesh strong in her nose. Ghost hunched low in her seat as more bullets cut through the sedan's outer skin. The steering wheel vibrated in her grip.

Her lips curled back over her teeth as the feeling of dread flowed into a burning rage. Ghost's voice was raw as the words exploded from her. "No! You can't have them. These are my sisters, my family. You—can't—have—them!"

Above the starkness of the headlights of the newcomers' car, Ghost could see a dark, man-shaped shadow. A ribbon of flame was ejected from the shadow and she knew what she was looking at: the upper body of the shooter perched on the roof of the vehicle. Clay's pickup was closer to the gunmen but had moved out of the direct line of fire, weaving out to one side. The sedan bucked again. Whatever the shooter was armed with was a lot more powerful than her pistol.

The road was now standard two-lane blacktop, with a flattened dirt verge on either side. No side roads. Nowhere to run. A series of neat holes stitched their way through the roof inches above her head.

Do it, chile, do it!

Ghost gave her screaming passengers only a moment of warning before stamping down as hard as she could on the brakes. The damaged car shrieked in protest as the wheels locked. Ghost clenched her teeth tight as Clay's pickup passed by in a flash of light, but there was no impact. The pursuit vehicle slammed on its brakes, grey smoke billowing as rubber burned on the asphalt. A body catapulted from the roof of the vehicle, passing clean over the sedan. The shooter hit the road head first, arms outstretched. He cartwheeled again, high into the air, and on his second landing stayed down.

The pursuing vehicle, rubber burning as it braked, crashed into the rear corner of Ghost's sedan with bone-rattling force. The smaller car whipped in a tight arc, the bodies inside cast against the doors without mercy. Ghost heard a new sound and was startled to realise it was her own scream. The positions had now been reversed. The battered sedan now sat at an angle behind the shooter's vehicle. Shit and Shinola, it was big!

Ghost had heard of the homemade "narco tanks" but had until now never seen one. The tank was a large truck, much bigger than a standard pickup. Large steel plates with protruding bolts had been welded to the outside, lending the vehicle a savage look: a prehistoric beast fashioned from steel. It looked heavy enough to flatten the sedan into sheet metal. The engine of the narco tank belched dark fumes as it revved several times. The sedan remained silent as she turned the key in the ignition.

A desperate rhythm hammered in her chest as another silhouette appeared on the roof of the tank. The weapon that he held was as fearsome as the vehicle he was perched in. Some kind of machine gun, wide and black. Ghost didn't need to be a military expert to know that box was filled with death. *Close your eyes, chile. You're done.*

The man opened fire and Ghost's world turned to a blood-filled nightmare.

72

To stop the pickup was to die. The only chance Clay had was to lose the pursuing vehicles. That was much easier said than done; this was cartel land, the Devil's backyard. To make matters worse, it looked like Los Espadas' backup team was driving an armoured car. Kelly had unloaded the shotgun into it with little effect. Clay manoeuvred the pickup side to side, knowing a moving target was harder to hit. The gunman had appeared from the roof of the armoured truck brandishing something the size of a SAW, a light machine gun. The heavy and distinctive metallic chatter of the gun filled the air.

Clay swung the pickup as far to the right as the road would allow, then, with a curse, far over to the left. The gunman fired upon the sedan. Tiny sparks flew from the car as the bullets ripped through the roof. The sedan juddered as Ghost braked. Clay shot past the sedan like a rocket. Something dark flew through the night air, landing in a heap in the road. Seconds later, another shooter appeared at the top of the armoured truck. The gun rattled again.

"No!" An icy hand gripped Clay's heart as Ghost's sedan

was shredded without mercy. Part of him wanted desperately to leap from his own vehicle and attack, yet he knew that he was outgunned. Swearing under his breath, he kept his foot on the gas. The only option was to run. The tail lights of Danny's pickup were still visible, twin red dots against the darkness. Behind him the armoured truck manoeuvred away from the sedan. Clay could see fingers of flame reaching from beneath the car's hood. *Ghost…*

Marco moaned again. His head lolled on his chest. Gillian cradled his blood-soaked body against hers. Clay forced his focus back to the road. The armoured truck had picked up speed. The chatter of the SAW again cut through the night. The women in the flatbed were staying low, at least. The road was straight with nowhere to hide. The only advantage the two smaller pickups had was greater speed and mobility. Could they outrun the heavier battlewagon? Another rattle of automatic fire spurred him into trying.

"What's that?" asked Celine.

Clay stared into the darkness. Beyond Danny's pickup, a new set of tail lights was visible. Clay willed the pickup to move faster. *Tac-tac-tac-tac.* A staccato rattle of bullets punched holes through the roof of the pickup. Celine tilted to one side, her head almost in Clay's lap.

"Celine!"

"I'm okay. I'm not hit. That was too close for comfort."

Danny's pickup overtook the slower-moving truck in a confident slalom. The truck was huge in comparison to the two fleeing vehicles. *Tac-tac-tac-tac.* The cartel shooter strafed the air with another volley of lead. Clay kept his foot rammed hard on the gas.

The truck was an old-style Kenworth, piled high with scrapped cars. Clay looked across at Danny as he cleared it. Danny stabbed a bladed hand at the front corner of the scrapper truck, then rotated his hand in tight circles. The last signal was a finger pistol tapped twice in succession.

The pickup slowed as he guided it into position. A quick glance in the mirror told him he had one chance. Clay buzzed down the window and drew the Coonan. Danny's pickup took up the same position close to the front wheels on the opposite side of the big truck. Clay aimed the Coonan at the front tyre. Squeezing the trigger in a rapid three-round burst, Clay placed his shots as close to the wheel rim as possible. It took all three shots, but the tyre burst with a ferocious *bang* that was as loud as the Coonan. Clay stamped down once more on the gas, swinging the pickup back in front of the huge truck. Danny gave him the thumbs-up as he too moved back into position. Clay felt a moment of sympathy for the driver as the truck dropped onto its front axle. A double shower of sparks lit up the night sky. The huge scrapper truck shook and tilted, gently at first, then at more and more of an angle. The cab snapped to the left. The huge trailer jackknifed across the full width of the two lanes.

"Let's see them get around that in a hurry," said Clay.

73

Danny raised his eyebrows in response to Laura Troutman's continued scrutiny. "What?"

"You just crashed a semi without blinking."

"Uh-huh," said Danny. The Coonan felt warm against his thigh. "The driver should be okay, but there's no better roadblock than an eighteen-wheeler. Needs must, and all that. Sorry I had to reach past you both to shoot."

Rebecca gave an exaggerated shrug. "Needs must."

"Aye, damn right."

"Danny, do you ever get scared?" asked Laura.

"Huh?"

"I mean, you're like the Terminator or something. The way you took those guys out earlier, I've never seen anything like it. You're so… *efficient*."

Danny exhaled through his nose. "I take no joy in it, but some people need killing and if it's down to him or me, I would never hesitate. I can guarantee every one of those cartel men would have happily put a bullet through my face without blinking, same with those dickheads back at the compound."

"We all owe you our lives," said Rebecca. "Thank you."

"*De nada*. It burns me inside that not everyone is getting to go home."

"None of us would be, without you and Clay," said Laura.

Rebecca cupped her face in her hands, elbows on knees. "I thought I would die in there, so I think you should get a medal for every one of us you managed to get out."

Danny pondered Ghost's fate as he drove. She was tough and resourceful, no doubt, but it would take the luck of the Devil to survive such a vicious assault. *May the next world be better to you than this one was.*

Danny allowed the pickup to slow as Clay drew level. Danny nodded at the hand signal from his brother. Both trucks rolled to a stop side by side. "You guys stay inside. I'll be back in a minute."

Danny met Clay at the front grille, pistol in hand. "Well, that was hairy."

"You think?" said Clay. "Nice work with the truck. That should slow the assholes down a spell. I vote we hightail it back to Cancún. These kids need food, water and a medic."

"I can't believe there are so many of them. Where the hell are the families of all these kids?"

"Not many people are as stubborn as we are. Most people just trust the authorities to get things done." Danny turned a slow circle as they talked. No new vehicles sped to intercept them. He tapped the Coonan against his thigh. "Ghost?"

Clay slowly shook his head.

"Shit."

"She went down swinging. That's the best we can hope for."

74

A smile crept over Weiss's face like a melting glacier. The sedan, one of the three vehicles he had been chasing, looked like a blacksmith's forge. Wide fingers of orange flame flickered from the open windows. A blackened object dangled below the thick black smoke, jutting from the window. The charred object looked like an oversized spider leg. Weiss knew that this was no arachnid; the burned appendage ended in fingers.

"Do you think Los Espadas got them all?" asked Taylor, cradling the rifle.

"Hard to say. Maybe we still have a chance at redemption." Weiss powered the Toyota along the road. "I want to be able to hold my head up at the end of this debacle."

"What if they get away?" asked Taylor.

"We can't let that happen. If they make it back to the world they'll bring a truckload of trouble down on our heads." Weiss squinted into the stygian darkness, praying for a sign of his quarry. The halogen lights of his truck burned into the night, yet the darkness seemed determined to push back. It was one of the things he liked about Mexico. Ten miles away from the bars and clubs and it felt primal, savage. A man could find himself down here, learn his true self-worth.

"What will we tell Master Ezeret if we fail?" asked Taylor.

"Ezeret is smart enough to know this would come one day. He has a plan."

Taylor adjusted the rifle against his chest. "*Master* Ezeret."

Weiss's jaw tightened. His hand crept closer to the butt of his P7.

Wide-eyed, Taylor held up his hand in supplication. "Take it easy, Weiss. It's just that you're the only one that doesn't address him in the manner he deserves. Master Ezeret lifted me up, showed me the way when I was at my lowest. Without him I would be a shadow, a sadness, a forgotten memory."

"We go back a long way, me and him."

There were lights in the distance. As they drew closer he began to make sense of the scene. A large transporter truck filled with scrapped cars was jackknifed across the width of the two-lane blacktop. To one side of the cab, the cartel's armoured truck was stationary, engine rumbling. The rear doors of the narco tank were open and the cartel men were shouting at the truck driver. The cab of the truck tilted low at the front, the fender almost touching the asphalt, the front tyres flat against the rims. Weiss had no doubt who had shredded the wheels of the semi.

The disabled truck shuddered as the driver fought to reverse the heavy load. Slowly but surely, a gap opened between the front of the truck and the thick trees that formed a natural barrier at the side of the road. As the cartel man moved back to the narco tank, Weiss saw his chance. Pushing the engine hard, he sped past them and through the widening gap. A second later he was on the open road.

The night was not yet finished.

75

Danny spotted the chain-link gate set off the road in a single glance. A padlock and chain dangled like a medallion, holding it closed.

Keeping a wary eye on the vehicle behind, he pushed the stolen pickup to its limits. The engine temperature was beginning to rise, the needle inching ever closer to the red. As new bullets tore through the windscreen he barely had time to duck his head. Another brief flash of muzzle fire told him the shooters were dead ahead, their vehicles cloaked in darkness. Danny braked and slewed the truck in a tight circle. Even as he was mid-turn, he could see Clay doing the same.

"Aye, well this is a shite sandwich!" said Danny as he completed the quick half-donut turn. He had feared this would happen. Los Espadas had undoubtedly called in more shooters. They had cut off the only path available. He couldn't see what kind of vehicles lay ahead. The fact they were there and would be armed and ready to kill was enough.

Shooters in both directions and only one safe option open: the gate. He had no way of knowing where it would lead, but it was preferable to being strafed by a bullet storm any way he cut it. The pickup smashed through the flimsy lock and chain with little problem. The twin gates catapulted open with enough force to rip one clean from its hinges. Clay was only a few feet behind him, crushing the second gate beneath his wheels. A wide flat area to the right of the gates was marked with deep ruts, the result of heavy vehicle use. Several piles of what might have been gravel sat like oversized anthills at the far side of empty space. He could not see any escape route via the clearing. A road to the far left with more potholes than surface traced a path up a steep incline. At the top sat a squat building of cinder blocks. Danny powered the truck up the slope. Both Laura and Rebecca gripped the dashboard as the pickup fishtailed into the tight curve.

At the top of the ramp, a graffiti-covered door of corrugated tin sheets faced them. Several tractor units were parked haphazardly to the left of the building. A wide turning area, the gravel compacted into a smooth surface, filled the area to the right. Clay followed Danny up into the works yard.

A collection of oil barrels stacked close to the roadside caught his attention. "Keep your heads down!" Danny leapt from the pickup even as he stamped down on the brakes. The first drum he handled was empty, but he threw it down the slope anyway. The second was empty too. He picked it up and cast it after the first. The third drum was what he was hoping for: the red diamond symbol decorated with a flame. The barrel felt full. Danny heaved the barrel onto its rim then stepped back and let it fall onto its side. Before he could begin to roll it, Clay was beside him.

No words were necessary.

Clay grabbed the ends of the steel drum and with a grunt heaved it onto the slope. The bowie knife flashed twice, and the cap snapped free from the drum. Another series of stabs punched holes in the body of the drum. Clay gave the barrel a kick. The steel drum rolled down the slope, a constant stream of fuel sloshing free as it went.

Danny was on his second canister when Clay began stabbing holes into the next four barrels. Danny tipped his fuel drum and set it rolling.

"Here they come!" warned Danny. The vehicle that raced onto the access road was moving fast. Too fast to avoid the fuel drums that were now halfway down the slope. The boxy SUV sent the first of the empty barrels flying into the air. The second smashed against the fender, then it too was sent bouncing into the darkness.

As the SUV hit the third barrel, this one full, the sound was very different, the pealing of a dull bell.

Time seemed to dilate.

Danny could feel his heart hammering in his chest.

Ba-dum.

Danny raced to the top of the slope.

Ba-dum.

With a roar, Clay cast another fuel drum down the road.

Ba-dum.

Danny snatched the lighter from his pocket, sparking it to life.

Ba-dum.

Cartel gunmen spilled from the SUV.

Ba-dum.

Danny tossed the lighter into the acrid stream.

Whoosh!

The blue flame snaked down the hill faster even than Danny expected. In a second, each of the punctured barrels was blazing, thick black smoke billowing. A second vehicle raced through the gates. Bullets cut through the night as the last two barrels were sent rolling down the slope. As these two rolled through the stream of fire, they burst into flames at the top of the incline. The blazing containers bounced down the slope like missiles from a medieval siege weapon. One of the drums rolled off the road but the outer skin still trailed flames. Danny pumped his fist in the air, then ducked as the men below fired on them. Clay joined him, dropping to one knee behind an old engine block.

"Persistent little shits, aren't they?" said Danny.

"Ain't they just."

Both now gripped the Coonan pistols, ready. Danny risked a glance around the engine block that was providing cover. A second vehicle had veered away from the SUV, its driver springing from the cab. The shock of white hair betrayed his identity. Weiss.

The front of the first SUV was now engulfed in sheets of fire. Los Espadas were too busy putting distance between themselves and the expanding inferno to focus their shots. The men closest to the burning vehicle were knocked flat as the ball of orange flame exploded in all directions. One of the ruptured fuel drums spun end over end, trailing a loop of iridescent fire. It landed with an audible *whoomp* close to Weiss, sending him tumbling in the opposite direction.

The SUV was now engulfed in a blanket of fire. Danny couldn't tell where the fuel drums ended and where the vehicle began. Sporadic shots buzzed through the air from the cartel shooters as they reformed into a skirmish line. A man was framed in silhouette as he raised his weapon to his shoulder, backlit by the flames. Danny sighted on him with the Coonan. Before he could squeeze the trigger, another explosion lit up the night. A ball of fire expanded along the ground, catching the gunman in its folds. One second he was there, then he was gone.

"Bye-bye, Mr Crispy," said Danny.

"Yeah, just another Kentucky fried asshole," added Clay.

Danny peeked around the engine block and gave a short, barking laugh. "You remember that Butch and Sundance movie?"

"Butch and Sundance died," said Clay as he checked the magazine on his Coonan.

"Aye, let's not do that."

"Wasn't planning on it anytime soon."

"Good to know. At least we have the higher ground. Those butt monkeys will have to climb this hill or risk coming up the road through the flames. Either way, they're not getting up easy." The burning road lay to their right. Danny looked to the opposite side of the lower clearing. "They could try to flank us, but the hill looks almost sheer over there. Tough climb."

"Uh-huh. Looks like there's six, maybe seven of them down there. We've been through worse."

Raised voices echoed up the slope. Danny could see Weiss stabbing the air with his hand. Men moved around him. His white hair was a pale smudge in the glow of the flames. It would be a long shot. Danny rested the Coonan against the engine block. He breathed slow and easy. Letting his vision drift slightly out of focus, Danny aimed at the German, well below that white hair, centre mass. The darkness between them became inconsequential. There was only the target. Danny softened his vision. Weiss.

Boom.

The Coonan bucked in Danny's hand.

Weiss folded at the waist and fell headlong into the ground.

"Whoops. It's a dirt nap for the sour Kraut."

76

"That won't keep them down for long, and we don't have enough ammo for much of a shoot-out." Danny watched cartel men and the few others that had arrived with Weiss scoot for cover. Bullets cut through the night air, several finding the engine block. Probably random shots, as there were as many that whined high overhead and strafed the ground to either side of their cover. Danny pressed his hand against the engine. He glanced at the cinder-block building. "Keep an eye on those shite-hawks. I'm going to see if there's something else we can use."

"Whatever you're gonna do, better make it quick. The shooting is slowing down."

Danny gripped Clay's shoulder. The muscle felt like plate steel. "Aye, they'll soon figure out a wide skirmish line up the hill."

"Smaller groups, twos or threes. They'll cover each other as they move."

Danny handed Clay his Coonan. "If they come, make them earn every step."

Danny kept his head low as he sprinted back past the two pickups. Two ancient tractors sat to the left of the building. One was little more than a bare engine block upon a set of wheels: no cab, no seat, just a misshapen steering wheel. The second looked a better bet. Danny hauled open the door and sprang into the cab, the seat squeaking in protest. The smell of diesel filled his nose. No key in the ignition. No problem. A tray sat to the left of the seat. Danny scooped up the contents. Pliers, a rusted screwdriver and a dirt-encrusted notepad with a pen pushed into the spiral binder. Taking the screwdriver, Danny jammed it deep into the key slot. A hard blow with the heel of his hand wedged it securely into the ignition. Danny pumped the gas pedal, moved the gearstick into position and twisted the handle of the screwdriver. The engine roared to life on the first turn. Danny allowed himself a brief smile. "Well, you're nothing to look at but you sing real nice."

The tractor shuddered into motion. Danny drove towards the cinder-block building, straight into the double doors. The door on the right tumbled to the ground. Danny hauled the tractor into reverse. As soon as he had cleared the front of the pickup trucks, he pointed the tractor on a path to the left of Clay's position. It wasn't the first time he had used a vehicle as a weapon. Adjusting the gearstick and stamping down on the gas, Danny leapt from the tractor, staying low as he landed near the edge of the drop-off. The cab seemed to hang momentarily in space, then disappeared over the precipice.

Danny wasted no time watching the tractor fall. He sprinted back to the broken doors. Even as he ran, he could hear the shouts of alarm from below. Having a three-ton machine barrelling down upon you tended to make you run for cover. As he reached the doors, an unmistakable sound of metal crashing into metal filled the night.

The smell inside the cinder-block building was much the same as in the tractor, just more intense: oil, diesel and body odour. The machine that sat in the centre of the building was an industrial wood chipper, not very useful unless he wanted to dispose of a few corpses. Maybe later. The truck that sat in front of the attached chipper held more potential.

Bottles, cans and plastic containers of all shapes and sizes, too many to count, were stacked on the shelves that lined the walls. Given time, Danny knew he could jerry-rig any number of explosive devices from the likely contents of the workshed—he didn't have time. He moved to the utility truck and tried the door. Locked. A sharp tap with the handle of his Fox ERT solved that problem. He reached through the broken window and popped the door handle. No key.

Outside, the harsh sound of the Coonan rang out, answered by a burst of automatic gunfire. Danny moved as swiftly as he could. He wedged the blade of his ERT into the plastic panel at the side of the steering column and levered it free. The panel cracked, then fell at his feet. Danny pulled hard on the tangle of wires inside, stripping two of insulation and sparking the exposed tips together. The truck engine sprang to life.

Clay's Coonan sounded again. A man was screaming over and over. The pitch of the gunfire had changed, the bursts from below becoming more intense. The single shots from Clay's Coonan sounded like a petulant child snapping at furious parents.

Danny raced back to Clay, who had moved from the engine block to a more advantageous position. His back was pressed against the trunk of a tree and he was taking aim through a gap between two large chunks of limestone. With as few words as possible, Danny told Clay what he planned. Clay's response was an outburst of four-letter words.

Danny gritted his teeth and held out his hand. Clay returned the spare pistol. The robust 1911 frame of the pistol felt sturdy in his grip. Another sustained burst of fire erupted from below, sending chips of wood and bark into the air by his shoulder. Clay risked a look around the tree. "They're starting to climb the hill."

Danny sprinted back to the cinder-block shed.

77

Verdugo pointed to the open gate. Flames danced in the darkness, shadows stretching out over the battle scene. The heavy narco tank had struggled to pass the disabled scrapper, becoming wedged between the front fender of the massive vehicle and the trees lining the roadside. The driver of the scrapper, terrified by the cartel men's guns, kept stalling the vehicle in his haste to move it. It had taken valuable minutes to break free from the temporary blockade.

Cradling his own weapon against his chest, Verdugo flicked a finger at the roof of the armoured vehicle. Bruja scooted back to the open port in the roof. The sound of the cocking bolt of his weapon brought a cruel smile to Verdugo's face. The M249 was a beast. The weapon was classed as a light machine gun, but *light* was a misnomer. The box magazine clipped to the bottom of the weapon held enough ammunition to level a small building.

As the driver of the narco tank guided the nose through the gates, flames reflected from his shaven head. Verdugo called to the other men in the vehicle. "I do not know who these men are, but that does not matter. They will die here tonight at the hands of Los Espadas!"

"Los Espadas!" came the shouted response from all five men.

His pistol bounced against his body in its chest rig. All the men carried the custom Coonan .45. The crossed-swords artwork on the grips was a badge of honour. But the weapon he cradled across his chest was his primary choice. The AA12 shotgun was a monster of a gun. He unholstered it now and ejected the eight-shell box magazine from the fully automatic shotgun and replaced it with a drum magazine. The drum held thirty-two cartridges, loaded with a mixture of buckshot and slugs. The other men, as well as their insignia Coonans, carried MAC-10s. All were deadly.

With a yell, Bruja began firing the M249. The heavy *chak-chak-chak-chak* of the weapon filled the air. The sound inside the narco tank was deafening, the steel walls reverberating.

The men on the ground were all crouching, scuttling side to side as they advanced. A large SUV ahead, that Verdugo vaguely recognised as one of theirs, was now enveloped in flames. A tractor lay at the bottom of the hill, capsized. The upper body of a man lay crushed beneath the machine, one of his legs twisted like putty. The road to the top of the hill was sheathed in fire. What the hell had happened here? The other vehicles had only been a couple of minutes ahead of him.

With a startled yell, the men who had begun to climb the hill parted, darting to each side. A truck, towing some kind of farm machine, burst over the crest of the hill. Dirt and shale flew into the air as the vehicle bounced down the side of the steep slope.

Verdugo glanced at the tractor, the burning barrels and now the rampaging truck, and understood. The targets at the top of the hill were, in effect, throwing rocks. If they were doing that, it meant they had no real weapons to use.

A pistol barked. A single shot from the top of the hill. Verdugo pushed open the door of the tank, its steel plate offering more protection than he needed for a damned pistol. He scowled at the descending truck. It separated from its coupling and tumbled end over end, bending out of shape as it slammed into the hard-packed earth. Verdugo tracked the oncoming vehicle with his AA12. The shotgun remained silent. The truck was unoccupied and rolled at speed between the narco tank and the German's damaged truck. The truck hit the treeline with a loud crunch of metal. The other shooters spilled from the narco tank, their MAC-10s unleashing tight volleys aimed at the top of the hill.

One of the Espadas broke cover and sprinted halfway up the hill. Verdugo knew what he was going for. A shallow culvert etched its way most of the way up the hill. It looked like a sluice for rainwater, just deep enough to conceal a man if he crawled on his hands and knees. From the culvert, he could gain access to the top of the hill and the position needed for a clear shot. He was almost at the culvert. Verdugo willed him on. A brief tongue of flame spat from the high ground and the cartel man pitched onto his face, clutching at his neck as he rolled into the culvert. He lay still, almost invisible in the narrow channel.

Shouldering the AA12, Verdugo sent four rapid shots at the top of the hill. Bruja again opened fire with the M249. Chips of tree bark and dirt sprayed into the air. Another two men made it to the culvert, clambering over their fallen comrade. With a defiant roar, Verdugo climbed on the fender of the narco tank then up onto the reinforced hood. The angle of the tank allowed Bruja a clear field of fire. The M249 would tear the shit out of anything up there. *Chak-chak-chak-chak!*

Bruja's weapon fell silent. Verdugo shouldered his shotgun, the AA12 sleek and deadly. A blur of movement from the top of the hill, moving fast, left to right. Verdugo quickly aimed further to the right of the motion. Two rapid shots thundered. "I am Verdugo—the executioner! You will die here this night!"

His ears ringing from the booming shotgun, Verdugo turned to see why Bruja had ceased fire. The sight that greeted him turned his blood to ice water.

78

Danny wedged himself low under the dashboard of the truck as it careened down the hillside, the gas pedal beneath his shoulder. The protestations of the suspension sounded like nails being pulled from old wooden planks. The wood chipper being towed behind only added to the din, the metal casing ringing like an out-of-tune bell. Lights flashed at the windows as the truck continued the kamikaze path he had set it upon. The Coonan was angled across his chest, ready. If a face appeared at the window, it would receive the harshest of welcomes. The assortment of loose hand tools in the flatbed were scattered as the truck ramped into the air at an oblique angle. Something clattered painfully against his shins. The toolbox that had been under the passenger seat now took a layer of skin from his legs.

Danny tensed, despite his best intentions, as the impact sent a shock wave through his spine. A sharp exhalation helped suppress the roar that threatened to escape from his throat. The rear end of the truck lifted then came crashing down again. The sound of splintering glass caused him to tuck his chin tight to his chest. He lay motionless, counting to ten, forcing himself to wait, pistol at the ready. No face peered at him through the broken windows, no hands pulled at the doors.

Sporadic gunfire rattled on as the cartel shooters harried Clay's position. Danny levered himself up. Drawing and opening his Fox ERT in one motion, he held the rugged blade in his left hand, the Coonan in his right. He took a quick look through the back window. Dark shapes moved almost invisibly in the pockets of blackness. No one was looking at the ruined truck.

Now!

Danny threw open the door and swept the immediate area with the Coonan. Weiss's truck sat to his far right, while the bulky armoured car was just to his left. The silhouette of the armoured truck looked like a machine conjured from the mind of a maniac. Danny kind of liked it, despite himself. A man on the roof of the vehicle was working the light machine gun. A second man stood on the hood of the truck, feet spread wide, a shotgun spitting fire and death.

Danny ran headlong to the truck, vaulting onto the rear fender and from there onto the roof. He sucked in a lungful of acrid smoke. The heavy chatter of the SAW fell silent as the shooter pulled the box magazine from the bottom of the weapon. The man turned, the orange glow from the surrounding flames dancing across his features as he slammed home a new magazine. The grin froze on his face as he saw Danny, who punched the rugged blade deep into the man's throat. Hot blood sprayed on his hand as he rotated his blade then ripped back, severing the windpipe in one severe motion. The man clutched at his neck with both hands then dropped.

Danny immediately took the man's place, his feet braced upon the internal platform. Grabbing the SAW, his fingers closed around the handgrip, index finger curling around the stubby trigger. The machine gun felt like an old friend as he pressed his shoulder into the stock. The barrel was mounted into a swivel mechanism. Danny swung the SAW round so that it was aimed at the man on the hood.

"I am Verdugo—the executioner! You will die here this night!" The man turned, the surrounding flames glinting from a golden tooth. The shotgun he brandished was still aimed at Clay's location.

"Execute this, fuck-nuts!" Danny pulled the trigger.

Chak-chak-chak-chak!

Verdugo shuddered as countless bullets ripped through his chest. As the executioner toppled from the hood of the armoured truck, a fine red mist filled the space he vacated. Danny pivoted, bringing the machine gun to bear on the men scaling the hill. The men closest to the lower ground dropped in a cloud of dirt and blood and shale as the bullets tore them apart. One tumbled into the range of the headlights, his left arm a bloody stump at the elbow. Another hail of bullets found the base of his skull.

Danny sensed rather than saw motion to his right, and turned the machine gun to the new threat. Something thrummed through the air, smacking into the plate steel of the truck. Crossbow! Danny pulled the trigger and Weiss's truck took the full brunt of the assault. Bullets punched through the bodywork. The tyres exploded, dropping the truck onto the rims of its wheels. A bullet, incredibly hot, nipped at Danny's shoulder. Cursing, he spun the SAW round again and shot at the cartel man who'd hit him. The shooter's face was ripped away as he stepped into Danny's line of fire.

Another crossbow bolt cut through the night, so close to Danny's chest that it ripped the fabric of his shirt. *Chak-chak-chak-chak!* The man with the crossbow caught the stream of lead as Danny swung his weapon back to the truck. A brief yelp, a spray of red and the man disappeared. Smoke from the burning barrels plumed into the air, the beams from the headlights casting an ever-changing vista.

Time to move. With a grunt, Danny levered himself from the turret, heaving the SAW free from its mount. Seeking new targets as he moved, he climbed down onto the hood, then slid butt-first down to the fender. From there it was a short jump to the ground.

PAIN! Something exploded into his spine, knocking the breath from his lungs. Danny went to one knee.

Bam-bam-bam. Another three impacts sent him flying. The SAW clattered to the ground. His chest constricted, the pain almost unbearable. His vision narrowed, fading in and out. He could see a hand. It was stained red. It made a fist. His own hand.

Then a new agony assaulted his senses as he was yanked to his feet. The hand around his throat felt like a steel trap. The muzzle of a pistol burned the skin of his cheek.

Weiss's voice was a harsh whisper. "I'm going to kill you now."

79

Clay changed the Coonan's magazine, slapping a fresh one home. "There's never enough bullets."

The barrage of firepower that Danny had unleashed had shredded the enemy, yet there were still enough of them left to prove a challenge. Clay was all too aware that it took only one bullet and one determined man. From his position, he couldn't see the enemy. To do so, he would need to stand upright, perhaps even atop the rock he was using as cover. Not even the greenest of soldiers would risk exposing himself. Death was the sure result.

The mounted gun Danny had hijacked fell silent. Danny had some bat-shit crazy plans, and this surely ranked among them. The plan of rolling down right through the enemy ranks and coming up behind them was as risky as any he had attempted, but the wiry little bastard had pulled it off.

The sound of metal on stone, brief but distinctive, caused Clay to ease away from the protective cover of the tree and rocks. He glanced at the pickup behind him. Celine was in there. The bad men were still coming. If they got past Clay, then her life, and every other they had rescued, would be forfeit.

As he looked back towards the battle, he saw two men emerge from the darkness, one clutching a small boxy weapon, the other a hunting rifle. Clay decided in an instant. The first man went down clutching his throat. The second dropped his rifle and his hands went to his face. A high-pitched wailing filled the air.

"That's what happens when you pick a fight with a pissed-off Texan." The man crumpled to his knees as Clay spat his words through clenched teeth. "Two assholes for the price of one."

"Please…"

Before he could squeeze the trigger again, a fuel drum exploded, a ribbon of orange fire trailing behind. He watched with dread as the flaming canister soared high, then began to fall. The damn thing looked like it was going to land right on top of them. "Celine!"

Then pain exploded in his chest. Clay looked down. The crossbow bolt had entered just below his left clavicle.

The fuel drum slammed into the ground somewhere behind him, a ball of fire radiating out like a bomb blast. Clay tried to tuck and roll but the ground rushed up at him with untold ferocity. His pistol flew from his hand as he landed heavily on his side, the breath knocked from his lungs. New screams filled the air. They seemed to come from every direction.

As he forced himself up, the pain arced through his body. The muscles in his left shoulder contracted so severely he feared they would separate from his bones. His voice was barely a croak, his throat dry beyond belief. "Celine?"

As he managed to gather his legs beneath him, Clay realised he was on fire. Flames had taken hold of his shirt. He ripped it from his back, the agony in his shoulder intensifying. The fabric coiled around the bolt, each tug sending new shards of pain through his chest.

As soon as he'd freed himself from the burning clothing, he gripped the bolt with his right hand. Even the lightest pressure was almost too much to bear. Clay roared despite his best attempts at silence. The bolt remained secure in his flesh. It had passed through his shoulder joint. As he readied himself for another attempt, the rifleman lurched up from his supplicant position. A wide gash had opened his cheek from jaw to ear. The man snatched up his rifle. Clay knew they were too far apart to take him hand to hand. He went for his knife regardless.

Boom! A shotgun roared and the ground around the rifleman erupted in a cloud of dust. Spinning, the man went back to his knees, his rifle barking out a single shot.

Boom! The shotgun roared again, and this time the man was punched into the darkness, his head all but exploding.

Kelly leaned against the side of the truck. Clay puffed his cheeks out and held up a hand in thanks. His moment of gratitude was snatched away as Kelly slumped to the ground. A dark stain spread across her chest. A roar of primeval fury tore free from Clay's throat. He turned to see Celine's face framed in the window of the truck. Sour liquid rose to the back of his throat, the pain in his chest worsening. Other eyes peered at him from the trucks, but hers were all he could see. *Celine.* Her eyes and mouth were both open wide. Her finger stabbed at the glass of the window.

Clay turned as another man lunged out of the darkness, almost on top of him. The man's machine pistol stuttered loud and angry as Clay's bowie knife batted his hand away, sending the weapon spinning from his grip. Then the man, another Los Espadas by his suit jacket, leapt at Clay, his hand closing on the crossbow bolt, driving it even deeper into Clay's flesh. The other hand he brought down in a vicious chopping motion, disarming Clay in turn.

80

Weiss pulled Danny to his feet by his throat.

"I'm going to kill you now." The German wedged the pistol under his cheekbone.

"With a gun? Like a pussy?"

Weiss cocked his head to one side, baring his teeth. It was all Danny needed. Rolling his head away from the pistol, he gripped Weiss's wrist with both hands, wrenching the joint as he turned. The German's arm was locked straight as Danny looped his elbow over the top, his grip tightening. Dropping his weight and twisting, Danny drove the German up and over in a combat throw. Weiss slipped to one side, remaining on his feet, and rammed his knee into Danny's ribs. The pistol barked, the bullet sparking from the side of the armoured truck. Danny wrenched Weiss's wrist again, slamming it into the plate steel of the truck over and over. The pistol fell from his hand. Danny tensed his neck, tucking his chin low as the German strained at the choke hold. Forcing himself to ignore the pain in his torso, Danny slammed the heel of his open hand into the German's face and stamped down on his shin.

The two men circled each other. Flames cast ever-changing shadows, smoke filling the air with a pungent sting. A wide patch of red stained the German's ribs. Danny knew now where his earlier bullet had struck. Weiss cursed in his native tongue.

"Aye, it's a different story when the guy you're fighting isn't filled to the brim with drugs, isn't it?" spat Danny. A spasm of pain shot across his midriff. The ballistic vest he had taken from the dead cartel man had stopped the bullets from Weiss's pistol drilling through him, but the shock from the multiple impacts was proving hard to shake off.

"I'm still going to kill you." Weiss drew a tomahawk and a knife.

Danny snatched his ERT from his pocket, snapping open the blade. Weiss moved into a crouch, his right hand cocking the deadly tomahawk back to his shoulder. The knife he held in his left was nearly a foot long, the straight blade tapering to a needle point.

Danny dodged a thrust aimed at his stomach, ready for the swing that he knew would follow. The triangular blade of the tomahawk cut the air inches from his face. Weiss immediately thrust with the knife again, his movements fluid and confident. The knife blade raked along Danny's forearm, leaving a stinging furrow. Moving away from the tomahawk, Danny launched a backhand slice at Weiss's hands. As the German dodged the cut, Danny ripped up with the ERT. The blade caught Weiss just below his hairline. Danny ducked under the long knife that was aimed at his throat. A crimson sheet streamed over Weiss's face, the wound in his forehead serving its purpose. Danny snap-kicked the hand holding the tomahawk, but Weiss angled away from the force, slashing out again with his knife.

The German roared like a beast as he cut the air with a vicious backslash. Danny caught Weiss's attack on his raised left elbow. Something cracked in the German's wrist and the knife flew from his hand, spinning like a helicopter blade.

Both men moved as a single unit. Weiss raised his tomahawk. Danny slammed his left fist into the German's nose. Droplets of blood flew as Weiss's head snapped back from the blow. The tomahawk cut down at Danny's skull.

But Danny wasn't there. Using a two-step motion, Danny pivoted and was behind Weiss in a split second. The ERT punched deep into his exposed back. Even in mortal agony, the German proved dangerous. Weiss turned to face his would-be killer, jamming his elbow into Danny's face. Danny reeled, his legs suddenly heavy. The ERT slipped from his hand, the blade still wedged deep in Weiss's body. As he stepped back, Danny tripped over one of the dead bodies sprawled in the darkness. The tomahawk skimmed through his hair, mere inches from lobotomising him.

Weiss loomed over him, his blood-covered face that of a monster. The whiteness of his hair, eyes and teeth was stark in the flickering flames. Danny moved to rise from the ground when his right hand closed upon a welcome object. Flopping back onto the ground, he wedged the stock of the shotgun to his hip.

Weiss raised the tomahawk to his shoulder.

The three rapid shots ripped the German apart. Weiss jerked spasmodically, a hole punched clean through his chest. He dropped as if gravity had collected an outstanding debt.

"The way to a man's heart is through his chest," said Danny, cradling the AA12 shotgun. "I'm keeping this bad boy!"

81

Clay screwed his eyes shut as the cartel soldier viciously ground a thumb into his eye socket. The crossbow bolt grated against the bones deep inside his shoulder. Pain forked like lightning through his body.

The man was a foot shorter than Clay but nearly as wide. The strength in his arms was commensurate to the massive muscles that filled his bulky frame. His jet-black hair was cropped into a raised strip, Mohawk style. An S-shaped tattoo decorated the left side of his face.

Clay's balance tilted as if he were on a storm-tossed ship. He shook his head, dislodging the man's thumb. Fighting to remain on his feet, he crashed a massive right hook into the side of the teeth that now sought to latch onto his face. The cartel man wrenched on the bolt as he absorbed the force of the punch and answered with one of his own. Clay tucked his chin and took the punch just below his hairline. The two that followed caught him on the jaw. Lights sparked in his vision.

The blows only added to his fury. In one motion, Clay

caught the man's head between both hands, his grip closing around his ears, and pulled him close. Clay could feel the convulsions of the marauder's body as he held his grip tight. The crossbow bolt had transfixed his right eye, the rigid shaft spearing deep inside his skull. The agony in his shoulder was like nothing he had suffered before, yet he pulled the cartel shooter even closer. As the man slumped, Clay thrust him away with a derisive snort.

Silence descended, the lull disturbed only by the crackle of flames and a quiet groaning. Clay turned a slow circle before he moved to the pickup truck. He placed the flat of his hand against the glass, leaving a red smear behind. Celine nodded as he motioned for her to stay inside.

"Kelly?" Clay dropped to one knee, his fingers moving to the side of her neck. He could feel no pulse.

Boom! The sound of a shotgun snapped him back to full focus. Pushing back his dismay, he scooped up a weapon from the ground, a MAC-10. Dropping to one knee, he frowned into the darkness.

Boom! The shotgun sounded again.

"Clay! It's me. I'm coming up!" The thick Scottish burr of his brother's voice was unmistakable.

"Come on up."

Moments later, Danny's wiry silhouette appeared over the crest of the hill. The weapon he carried resembled a carved two-by-four.

"They all finished down there?"

Danny gave a single nod. "All now honorary members of the dodo club."

"You sure?"

"Aye, a couple were still frisky on my way up. They're not now."

That explained the two shotgun blasts. Clay managed a strained smile.

"What the hell?" Danny reached out, his fingers hovering inches from the crossbow bolt. "Jesus, Clay."

"It hurts a lot worse than it looks," said Clay.

"The last guy I shot had a crossbow."

"Pity you didn't shoot him sooner."

Danny reached out a hand. "You're still walking and talking, so it can't be that bad."

Clay gripped his brother's shoulder. "I can see the worry in your face, wee one. No need, I'm sure I'll live."

"You might not if you call me 'wee one' again." Danny cradled the AA12, the business end pointed away from Clay and the trucks. "What the hell is that?"

Clay looked down at the eyeball wedged midway along the crossbow bolt. "It belongs to one of those desperados. I'll keep an eye out for him later."

Grimacing, Clay straightened his back as Celine climbed from the confines of the truck. He slid the remnants of the eyeball from the arrow, casting it away.

"Are we safe?" asked Celine.

"Not 'til we touch down in Texas," said Clay.

"I mean, are all the ones chasing us… dead?"

"Deader than disco-dancin' dodos, my lass," answered Danny. "But Clay's right. We've got to keep moving. With good luck and a tailwind, we'll make the city by morning light."

Danny ushered the survivors back into the vehicles, then lifted Kelly into the flatbed of his truck, laying her out carefully. One of the women, sobbing, covered her face with her shirt.

Clay looked down again at the bolt jutting from his chest.

"I'll drive from here," said Celine.

Danny cut Clay's protest short. "I think that's best. Give me a few minutes to gather up some weapons and then we're out of here."

Clay slid his bulk into the passenger seat of the pickup. The few minutes it took for Danny to return felt like an eternity. His brother trotted up the slope, his arms full of weaponry. In addition to his chunky shotgun, which he had fashioned a sling for, he held half a dozen more MAC-10s.

"I thought about jacking the armoured truck down there, but one of the tyres is shot out. Got these, though."

Clay nodded to the access road. "At least the fire is dying down. Is the path clear?"

"Aye, we'll need to swing around the drums and the burnt-out jalopy, but we'll manage."

Clay gave a slow blink in acquiescence. He could taste blood in his mouth.

82

Celine's stomach lurched each time a new set of headlights appeared. Clay had lapsed into a brooding silence as the two trucks sped towards the city. The arrow that jutted from his chest was painful even to look at. Celine could only imagine the pain he was fighting against, pushing back. The only indication of his suffering was the fine sheen of sweat that covered his face and the occasional twitch of his scarred face.

Danny had taken the lead and they had rejoined the main road once again. The gunfire, screams and flames were now just another layer of nightmare memories that she felt sure would haunt her dreams for many years to come.

The scars on Clay's face, pale against the tan of his skin, caught her attention as she glanced his way. She now understood all too well what each of those scars may have cost him. A lump grew in her throat as she was filled with a new appreciation.

Her nose twitched as she inhaled the air inside the cab. Sweat, fear, smoke and blood were now smells she feared would never leave her senses. A glance to the back seat sent a renewed worry for Marco's life rippling through her. Her friend looked dead. His face was devoid of colour and covered with a waxy sheen. Gillian had tried to wake him, but nothing was working. A real hospital was his only chance of survival. That meant going all the way back to Cancún, where the closest emergency hospitals were. Danny had insisted on this. Yes, they would pass through a few smaller towns on the way, but he had reasoned that they would be vulnerable to the wrath of Los Espadas if they were still being pursued. The cartel would think little about opening fire in a small rural town or village. Gillian had taken the cell phone from Celine and kept trying to call the police. After twenty or so attempts, she held up the handset.

"The battery is nearly dead on this."

Celine pursed her lips. "Try once every ten minutes. Power down in between. We'll get lucky sooner or later."

Gillian nodded in agreement.

For many miles, the only sound in the vehicle was the constant hum of the engine and rubber on asphalt. The light of a new day began to push against the darkness. They had survived to see a new dawn, something she had doubted many times in the previous night. Sporadic signs of life passed in a blur. Occasional buildings at the side of the road. A gas station, a roadside diner, all in darkness.

"You okay?"

The road widened into a regular highway with a narrow strip of plants separating the lanes.

"Celine? You okay?" asked the voice again. Gillian's voice.

She shook her head to relieve the encroaching reverie.

"Okay. Yeah. I'm okay."

"You were starting to drift."

"I was?"

Gillian reached between the seats and placed her hand on her shoulder. Celine gave her hand a gentle squeeze. The sky had lightened, the sun now cresting well above the horizon. *When had that happened? How many miles had passed without her knowing?* A sign at the roadside told her they were on Highway 307. The clusters of buildings began to grow in both size and frequency.

As they began to pass more familiar landmarks and recognisable place names on the road signs, Celine's heart was filled with hope. They were nearly there. Civilisation meant safety. It meant they could go home.

The indicator on Danny's truck flashed and she followed him to the side of the road. She gently shook Clay awake as Danny approached. Celine managed a wan smile as he rested his forearms on her open window.

"We need to ditch the hardware before we hit the checkpoint up ahead. There are soldiers up there and I don't want to be stuck explaining shit to armed grunts."

Celine looked at Clay. His voice carried none of his usual vitality. "I suppose it makes sense. I don't like the thought of being unarmed, though."

"We can stash a couple of pistols under the seats, but two trucks full of raggedy-arsed gringos with MAC-10s isn't going to go down too well."

"Have at it, little brother."

Celine watched Danny collect the weapons from the trucks and throw each one into the waterway that ran alongside the road. He kept one pistol and handed one to Celine. She tucked it under her seat, making sure it was secure. Clay's eyes closed again.

The two trucks resumed their journey. Pressure built behind her eyes as they approached the checkpoint. To her surprise, the checkpoint was manned by a single uniform, who looked half asleep. He gave little more than a cursory glance at the two trucks rumbling past him.

Danny pulled over at the outskirts of the city. Celine could hear snippets of the conversation he was having with four construction workers. They pointed the way to the nearest hospital. In the new light of the Mexican morning, she looked again at her companions. Clay dozed, the arrow in his chest looking like a dreadful dime-store gag. Marco was too painful to look at. Frances, too, had slipped into a stupor, her limbs swollen into mottled sausages.

Danny swerved into the parking area of the hospital. Celine followed.

83

Spears of bright sunlight chased away the darkness as dawn came. Ghost could hear voices approaching, one male, the other female. The man's voice carried an air of sophistication, every syllable pronounced with deliberation. She knew the voice; she knew the man. The woman sounded like she was from the States. Both the tone and her words indicated that she was not a captive, that she was there of her own volition. Their conversation became clearer as they drew closer, still oblivious to her presence. That suited her fine. She knew she would only get one chance at this last act.

"We leave in ten minutes. Are you ready to do what needs to be done, Michelle?"

"I am. I will not let you down, Master."

"You will be well rewarded. It pains me to leave this house. It holds a special place in my heart, as do you. Yet none of my faithful have returned; they have fallen. They were called but failed the challenge, failed the ultimate trial. You are the only one who has proved worthy to continue at my side, to forge a new path."

"Thank you, Master."

The man's tone changed. "And you are absolutely sure there is nothing left here that the authorities could trace back to me?"

"There's nothing. The laptops are in your car, as are your ledgers and cash. My things are in there too."

"Then you know what must be done. Dispatch the witnesses, then burn the buildings. Set everything on fire. I do not want anyone's lack of caution coming back to haunt us."

"Consider it done, Master Ezeret."

The door opened fully to Ezeret's red-hued room and the two stepped inside. They were three steps inside before they saw the woman sitting in his high-backed chair.

One last job to do, chile, so do it good.

Ghost raised the pistol slowly. Her hand seemed to float in front of her body. Though her enemy could not see it because of the red light of the room and her black jumpsuit, her entire body was blood-soaked. Four bullet holes in her torso. Her breath came in ragged gasps.

Michelle raised her hands in surrender.

Do it!

The Glock barked once, still loud in the room despite the suppressor. Michelle took a faltering step, then a crimson teardrop traced a path down her face. Her mouth opened and closed without sound. She reached a hand as if to hold Ezeret, then fell in an untidy heap.

Do it again, chile. Lauren is watching you. Don't fail her again!

"Wait." Ezeret raised his hands in supplication, a non-threatening gesture. "Please wait. I think you have been sorely treated and I wish to right those wrongs perpetrated in my name."

Ghost coughed, blood running from her mouth. She didn't move to wipe it from her face. "I know you. I have waited for you. You killed my sister, my sweet Lauren. Your men took her out there and shot her to death with arrows. You made me watch."

"And now you have come to kill me?"

"Yes."

"You would kill the very man who gave your life meaning?" Ezeret's voice was warm honey. "You would kill me, your spiritual father?"

The pistol was heavy. The suppressor dipped an inch.

"Look inside yourself. What were you before you were set on this path? Hmmm? What meaning did your life hold? Can you not see that I set you free, liberated you from the banal, the mundane?"

The suppressor dipped another inch. His voice resonated deep within her. His eyes looked... *beautiful*, so big and brown and kind. *How could that be?*

"I can see you have been reborn in the fires of adversity, yet you have not fallen, have not been consumed. Who gave you that strength, who gave you that purpose, if not I? You have been freed from the constraints of this so-called civilised life, reborn as a warrior, a woman to be reckoned with. Put down the gun and come with me. Together we can begin again, free and uninhibited."

The pistol dipped another inch.

"That's it, let go of the gun. You will not need it now." Ezeret's words caressed her, warm and soft.

She did not resist as he gently slipped the pistol from her hand. Her eyes closed... so tired... His words wrapped her like a mother's embrace.

Mama...

Lauren, sweet Lauren.

Her hand closed upon the metal rod in her pocket. When she opened her eyes, the pistol was inches from her face. Ezeret's words were now broken glass to her ears. "You stupid whore! Who are you to challenge me? You are a piece of worthless shit. And you want to know the truth? I have no idea who you are. You said we killed your sister? I don't remember her either. You are maggots, not worthy of remembering."

Come home, chile, come home.

"I'm coming, Mama." Ghost surged from the seat as Ezeret pulled the trigger.

The bullet punched into her chest. Dead centre.

Ghost slumped back into the ornate chair, its legs scraping on the tiled floor. She couldn't feel her arms or legs anymore.

Ezeret staggered back. The pistol clattered to the ground, the sound hollow. The titanium rod that had once held Lauren's broken leg together now protruded from both sides of his neck. He wrenched the improvised stiletto free. Two streams of blood pumped in a frantic rhythm from his ruptured throat.

You did him good, chile. You did him good.

Ezeret turned, gagging, and ran, blood spraying as he went. He managed to reach the doorway before he crashed, face down. A dark pool grew around his head.

Ghost felt no fear as she relaxed into the chair, her breath fading to nothing, the smallest of smiles on her mouth. "I'm coming, Mama."

84

Clay raised his head. The crossbow bolt was gone, a large gauze pad now in its place. A wall-mounted widescreen TV sat opposite his bed. The sound was muted. Clay smiled as Danny rose from his seat and perched on the edge of the bed.

"You're awake. I was starting to wonder if you had paid one of those nurses to slip you some extra sedatives or something. How're you feeling?"

Clay lied. "I feel fine."

"Yeah, right," said Danny. "The doctor had to open you up from both sides just to get the bolt out. He said you may experience some numbness but should make a full recovery with a lot of physio. I told him you were pretty numb before you got shot."

"Dumbass."

"At your service," said Danny.

"Where's Celine?"

"Don't worry, Clay, she's just a few doors away. All the kids are in observation. They're all on hydration drips.

I think there will be a lot of stressed-out but very relieved parents here soon."

"You sure she's okay? I want to see her as soon as I can."

"I'll get her in a minute. The cops are here as well. They've had a run at me already. I was a wee bit selective when it came to bodies hitting the floor. I jumped up and down a fair bit and they're sending a team back to the compound. They should find anyone that didn't make it out with us."

"Good."

"I called Jacob Silverstein, like you asked. He's flying down today with a legal team and some guy called Rainer Brown from the FBI. He a friend of yours?"

"Friend of a friend. He'll help getting everyone back home to their families."

"I don't like the way the local cops were looking at me," said Danny. "They seem very pissed at us. Silverstein will have his work cut out when he gets here."

"Jacob will have them jumping through hoops in ten minutes. Don't say anything else to the cops until he gets here."

Danny stood at the side of the bed and slowly twisted at the waist. The groan he gave said far more than words.

"You okay under the hood?"

Danny wobbled his hand. "I'd be full of holes if it wasn't for the vest I took from the first lot of Espadas. That arsehole with the white hair shot me from behind. My arse end looks like a domino."

"But you set him straight, right?"

"Kinda. I put a hole in him big enough to drive a scooter through."

"Good. That was the same asshole that knocked me into the sinkhole with a grenade."

A tap on the door caught their attention. Clay's face lit up, the scars on his face crinkling. "Celine! Come on in, little darlin'."

Celine trotted into the private ward and hugged Clay.

"Did you manage to call your parents yet?" asked Clay.

Celine nodded, tears running down her face. "Mom was kinda hysterical."

Clay stroked Celine's hair. "We'll be home soon."

Celine climbed on the bed, her arms around Clay. She was asleep in seconds.

Danny kept his voice quiet. "I'll head back to the hotel and pick up our passports. We may need them pretty soon."

Clay nodded, his eyes closing.

85

Clay and Celine were both still asleep when the door to their room opened. Danny looked up from the magazine he was half reading, thoughts of marlin fishing forgotten. "Jak?"

"You look surprised to see me."

"Actually, I'm not." Danny rose from his seat and shook the old man's hand. "Where's Chaac?"

"He's outside. He didn't care for being left out there, I can tell you that." Jak smiled and nodded at Clay's sleeping form. "I see the hero twins prevailed."

"Aye, aye, the hero twins made it back from the underworld."

"I knew you would." Jak took Danny's chair without asking. He leaned forward, his elbows resting on his knees. "Ghost, too, walked the path of the righteous warrior. I pulled her from her car. It was shot full of holes and was on fire. There were others in the car, but I could do nothing for them. She should have died there but she would not give up. We went back to the compound."

"Jesus, I thought she died in the car."

"Ghost fell at the compound, but she took the leader down before she went into the forever night."

"She got Ezeret? That's good. She was a hell of a woman. May the next world be better to her than this one was." Danny slowly rubbed his face. "And you're sure she got Ezeret?"

Jak gave a single nod. "I'm sure."

Danny lowered his head in tribute. He hadn't even known her real name. She had given everything. Jak twisted in his seat. Danny looked down at him, his head cocked to one side. "How did you get here? How did you know where we were?"

"I went back to the clearing where I first met you both. I drove your Jeep back here. I may have eaten some of the food that was left in there... well, Chaac ate some of it too."

Danny smiled. "But how did you know where to find us?"

"I am Jak. I know things."

"Like that explains everything?"

"It does for me," replied Jak.

"Are you staying a while? I know Clay will want to see you when he wakes up."

"I'll be here until you head home."

"That's great. We owe you so much, Jak."

He waved a hand dismissively. "*De nada.*"

"At least let us take you out for a steak dinner. It's going to be a day or so before we can fly home. You up for that?"

Jak gave him a sly look. "I'm not really dressed for a dinner date."

"If we bought you some new duds, would you eat with us then?"

"If you insist. I would need new boots as well."

"No problem."

"Maybe a hat?"

"Anything you want, you old chancer."

The smile dropped from Jak's face. He leaned closer to Danny. "You both still have many challenges to endure. The path you walk is not a path of peace."

Danny shrugged. "The Gunn family motto is 'either peace or war'. I'm easy with both."

Jak reached out and took Danny's hand. "You have walked through fire before, but this is *nothing* compared to what lies ahead for you and Clay. Dark clouds are gathering, and you know what they bring."

There was no humour in his voice.

86

The taxi ride from Miami International Airport to Coral Gables was an easy run. Danny settled back in the cab, still bruised and sore. Chrissie Haims didn't start work until six in the evening on a Sunday. Plenty of time for the reunion he had planned.

As expected, Jacob Silverstein and his team had secured their release from the Mexican authorities and had helped the survivors reunite with their families. The story had made international news. The DEA had offered their services to the Mexican government to help scour the compound for evidence of the perpetrators. Several more women had been rescued by the joint task force, and were even now being reunited with their families.

Marco had undergone emergency surgery in Cancún and was expected to make a slow recovery. The bullet had torn up his stomach, but miraculously missed his other major organs.

Danny, Celine and Clay had flown back to Texas together, along with her school friends. After spending a couple of days relaxing with Clay and his surrogate family, Danny had decided to leave them to their own devices and had hopped on a plane back to Miami.

The street was quiet as he climbed from the taxi. He slung his backpack over his shoulder and headed for the front door, a bouquet of flowers in his hand.

There was a line of yellow tape sealing the closed door. An icy hand gripped his heart.

As Danny reached the door, a voice from behind caused him to spin.

"Hey, what's your business here?"

Danny glowered at the man. "And who might you be?"

"Bob Spengler. I live two doors down."

"I'm a friend of Chrissie's. What happened here?"

The man walked up the path. "You haven't heard? I'm so sorry, man. Chrissie was murdered two days ago. The cops think it was a home invasion gone wrong."

The flowers landed at Danny's feet. "Have the cops arrested anyone for it?" His words felt like broken glass in his throat.

"Not according to the morning news. I'm sorry, man. Were you good friends?"

Danny didn't answer. He pulled out his phone, casting a look at the fallen flowers. Chrissie's favourites.

Thick raindrops began to cast dark spots on the sidewalk.

"I'm sorry, man," said Bob, pointing to the sky, "I gotta go. There's a storm coming."

Danny picked the first name on his contact list. The call was answered on the fifth ring.

"Clay, it's Danny. I'm so sorry, but I need you."

ACKNOWLEDGEMENTS

A novel is a many-faceted creation. The story is just the beginning. I would like to thank the following people for their help, support, guidance and services:

Wendy Hilton, for indulging me.

Miranda, Sam, Lydia and Philippa from Titan Books.

My brother, Matt Hilton.

ABOUT THE AUTHOR

James Hilton is the author of *Search and Destroy* and *Fight or Die*, the first two novels in the Gunn Brothers series. He is a 4th Dan Blackbelt in Shotokan Karate, and has worked as a martial arts instructor, which has been invaluable in crafting his fight scenes. He is currently planning a YA series. He lives in Carlisle. His brother is bestselling thriller author Matt Hilton.